⫟ **W9-BUV-527**

# THE CRITICS LOVE MEAGAN McKINNEY!

"In the manner of Nora Roberts, McKinney makes a
successful transition from romance to mystery/suspense.
Well-paced, with strong characters, this novel works as
both a thriller and a romance."
—*Publishers Weekly*

"Meagan McKinney certainly knows how to hold readers
on tenterhooks."
—*Rendezvous*

"Faultless . . . wonderful . . . this ambitious, sweeping
romance has everything."
—*The Times-Picayune* on *Till Dawn Tames the Night*

"Strong characterization . . . distinguished by its colorful
setting, gothic sensibility, and the interaction between its
appealing protagonists."
—*Publishers Weekly* on *The Ground She Walks Upon*

"Beautiful, masterful, rich, powerful, and seductive. *Till
Dawn Tames the Night* has all the allure and darkness of
*Wuthering Heights* and the warmth of Judith McNaught's
*Once and Always*. Readers will be held captive by this
eloquent love story."
—*Romantic Times*

PAPERBACK EXCHANGE
640 FEDERAL ROAD
BROOKFIELD, CT. 06804
203-775-0710

Turn the page and see why . . .

# *IT WASN'T EXACTLY THE WAY SHE'D PLANNED TO MEET THE MAN OF HER DREAMS. . . .*

Claire bit into her hot beignet. Powdered sugar sprinkled down, and she cursed the navy silk blouse she wore. Brushing at the stains, she took a sip of coffee and chicory, and savored it as if it were wine from the gods. All the gourmet coffees in the world couldn't compare with a steaming café au lait on the sidewalk of the centuries-old New Orleans French Market.

The throng of tourists before her parted. Through the crowd she watched as a tall, well-built man in his thirties rose from one of the park benches and walked purposefully toward her. He was the kind of man any woman would stare at. He towered over the tourists. His shoulders in the white henley T-shirt he wore were powerfully broad, his hips nicely narrow in faded jeans. He had a legal folder under one arm.

He was her type, all right. She could actually fantasize about a guy like that.

He stepped onto the sidewalk of the café. She averted her gaze, embarrassed that he might catch her staring at him.

The legal folder landed on her table.

She looked up into eyes that were not just blue, but intensely blue—electric and with a dangerous predatory glint. He pulled out a black wallet and flipped it open. It didn't take her long to read the initials next to the I.D. card—FBI.

Ordering coffee, he took the seat opposite Claire and began to untie the folder.

"Sit down, Ms. Green. Let's get acquainted." He looked up from the folder. "That is, unless you want to call your attorney."

# A MAN TO SLAY DRAGONS

## MEAGAN McKINNEY

**ZEBRA BOOKS**
**KENSINGTON PUBLISHING CORP.**

ZEBRA BOOKS are published by

Kensington Publishing Corp.
850 Third Avenue
New York, NY 10022

Copyright © 1996 by Ruth Goodman

All rights reserved. No part of this book may be reproduced in any form or by any means without the prior written consent of the Publisher, excepting brief quotes used in reviews.

If you purchased this book without a cover you should be aware that this book is stolen property. It was reported as "unsold and destroyed" to the Publisher and neither the Author nor the Publisher has received any payment for this "stripped book."

Zebra and the Z logo Reg. U.S. Pat. & TM Off.

First Hardcover Printing: February, 1996
First Zebra Printing: July, 1996

Printed in the United States of America

10  9  8  7  6  5  4  3  2  1

# Author's Note

This book was conceived and written before the tragedy in Oklahoma City. My research into survivalist and militia organizations led me to believe these groups represented serious danger, not only because of their pathological ideologies, but because, due to lack of media attention, they were nearly invisible to the American public. During the critique process of this novel, I was forced time and again to explain these groups which I found so terrifying, and everyone else had never heard of.

Sadly, they are now far too familiar to Americans. I urge all my readers to support Congress in its effort to prevent another terrorist bombing.

—Meagan McKinney
New Orleans

To everyone who made this book possible—to Pamela Ahearn, my wonderful agent, to Denise Little, a great and very patient editor, thanks for your caring, and finally to all the lawyers besides Claire Green. To Donna Green, Rose Marie Falcone, Barbara Bennett, Rick Schroeder, and my husband Tom. You guys prove there are some custodians of justice out there. (And we didn't even need to call in ZOE.)

For Richard John Lafayette Roberson
My little hero.
May you always slay the dragons.

*Anyone who doesn't worry about being a monster . . .*
*Is one.*
—ROBERT RUTHVEN

# Prologue

There were a million ways to relive a childhood. Liam Jameson relived his in dreams. Blessed nighttime dreams that sugar-coated the endings. Revisionist dreams. Aching, bittersweet dreams. Dreams of what had been and what should have been. Never the nightmares of what was.

He was always going back to Oklahoma. In his mind, it was 1969 all over again, that astounding summer when Neil Armstrong took the first step on the moon. Liam dreamed again and again about that lunar landing. Just like all the other boys in America, he'd made the decision then and there to be an astronaut.

Armstrong was a hero. There were no gray areas to mull over. There was nothing to figure out. An astronaut who took the first step on the moon was a brave man. Say what they would about the breathless expense of a moon shot and the irksome pointlessness of it that later dogged NASA, in the annals of history Neil Armstrong was untarnishable. He was what every kid wanted to be. He was a bona fide member of the Good Guys. He was a hero, and nobody, not anyone in the entire world, could say he wasn't.

*"I'm a hero, Liam." Twelve-year-old Joey Ableman circled once on his shiny, spanking-new Stingray bike, then to really*

*show off, he did a small wheelie, leaning way back on the neon-orange banana seat.*

*"Aw, anybody could have saved that baby from drowning. Didn't take much. I coulda if I'd been there." Liam waved away the road dust created by the circling bike. He made a point of giving Joey a "no-big-deal" scowl, but it was just a put-on. Joey was a hero, and he was more than a little awestruck. Yesterday, the townsfolk of Taylorville had gathered for a little ceremony for Joey, and the mayor had even presented the boy with a brand-new bike. Joey's picture was front-page in the* Town Talk *today. The caption beneath it read:* JOEY ABLEMAN, FATHERLESS BOY, NOW THE HERO OF SUNSET TRAILER PARK. *It then went on to announce his heroism when he'd jumped into Catmine Creek and pulled out a two-year-old girl who'd crept from her trailer home while her mother slept.*

*Yep. There was no getting around it. His best friend, Joey Ableman, was a certified hero all right—the paper even said it—and as much as Liam found it hard to admit, he was impressed. Damn impressed. He'd been on this earth almost thirteen years now and had never met a true hero face-to-face.*

*"You gonna ever give me a turn on that?" Liam's voice cracked, the curse of the pubescent boy. He stared at the Stingray as it went around and around with his friend. It sure was a cool bike, but Liam knew he didn't deserve it like Joey did. He hadn't been there to save anyone. He wasn't a hero, he was just friends with a hero. But maybe friendship would be enough for a spin on the bike anyway.*

*"Can you do this?" Joey took off down the long stretch of dusty road that headed toward Tulsa. He stopped in the distance, turned around, then rode back at a ferocious speed, finally gaining enough to bunny-hop the huge pothole that marked the entrance to the Sunset Trailer Park.*

*"I might if you could ever see to giving me a chance—"*

*"Liam! Liam! You get in here now, boy, and help your pa! He's getting ready for his shift."*

*Liam looked toward the direction of his mother's voice. She* stood in her housedress behind the screen door of a rusting, weed-encroached trailer home. She'd been pretty at one time, or so Liam had been told. A real Irish rose, his father had said, probably reminiscing about the old days, before the seven kids and the sixteen-hour days at the meat-processing plant. Now Liam didn't see any of the Irish rose in his mother. Moira Jameson looked like most of the women at the Sunset Trailer Park: dirty housedress, a baby permanently attached to one hip, the frazzled, weary expression.

"I gotta go, Joey. Maybe after dinner, if I can sneak out, we can go to the swimming hole, huh?"

"Sure." Joey stopped the bike and stared almost forlornly at Liam. Liam guessed it wasn't as much fun having a new Stingray when there was no one around to show it off to.

Obediently, Liam went into the trailer. His mother's harangue followed him like the caw of a blackbird. "Liam! I just ironed that shirt for you, boy! Why'd you go and wrinkle it all up now? Never mind. You children'll be the death of me. Now go and help your pa. Fetch the lunch pail and see if we have anymore Spam in the icebox."

The trailer was dark inside in contrast to the sunny day. Briefly, Liam glanced out the screen door. The rectangle of light showed the green fields of corn just beyond the trailer park. A blacktop road bisected the landscape and at the very end of it Joey rode his new Stingray.

The picture through the screen door was like a movie scene viewed from the darkness of a theater. To Liam, it was beautiful. Later, as a man, he would think of it like the cover of the Saturday Evening Post. Green fields, a kid, a new bike. America.

Joey Ableman was a real-life hero, he thought as he headed through the crowded dimness of the house trailer. He'd gotten a brand-new bike for his heroism and his picture in the paper. Liam kind of wished it had happened to him—he knew he would have saved that Johnson baby if he'd been there— then he could have been a hero too. But since it hadn't hap-

*pened to him, he was sure proud of one thing: The hero, the celebrated face around Taylorville, good old Joey Ableman, was his very best friend in the world.*

"*Are you a hero, Pa?*" *he asked while he reached for the Wonder bread and French's.*

*Spitting distance from the kitchenette, shaving in the tiny bathroom, his father stood before a foggy mirror, sleepily scraping his face with a Gillette.*

"*Ain't never been a hero like Joey, son, sorry.*"

*Liam slapped some yellow mustard on two pieces of bread, his brow wrinkled in thought. It didn't make sense, this hero business. Of course Patrick Jameson was a hero. He was his dad. The greatest man he knew. He'd had to have done something heroic at one time in his life.*

"*You ain't never saved no one?*" *Liam closed the two sandwiches, then wrapped them in wax paper and stuffed them in his father's peeling lunch pail.*

"*Nope. Never, son.*" *Jameson wiped his face with a towel and slipped into the shirt still hanging by the ironing board that blocked the kitchen. The inside of the trailer was sweltering, but his father looked cool and crisp in the newly starched shirt. "If you want to be a hero like Joey, you go right ahead, Billy boy. You can be a policeman like your uncle Kenny in Boston and save people all day long.*"

"*Uncle Kenneth was a policeman?*"

"*Yep.*"

"*And a hero?*"

"*Yep.*"

*Liam handed his father his lunch pail. The kids all lined up, as was their habit when Dad was ready for his night shift.*

"*Now, you all be good and help your ma. I love you,*" *Jameson said sternly. He kissed each one on the forehead and saved his wife for last. "I'll be putting in some overtime for that air conditioner, so it'll be around noon before I get back.*"

*Liam's mother nodded, the same old resigned expression blanketing her features.*

*Through the screen door, Liam watched as his father jumped into the old Dodge pickup. Lunch pail next to him on the torn cloth seat, he pulled out of the trailer park and onto the ribbon of road, a billow of dust in his wake. The pickup truck turned left. To the right, Joey rode his Stingray, around and around in the hazy Oklahoma summer eve.*

## Tulsa, present day

Special Agent Liam Jameson awoke with a grunt. Inside the sleeping bag, his entire torso was covered in sweat. His chest stuck to the camouflage flannel lining. He edged upward and sat up, his breath quick and unsteady.

He looked around the shack deep in the isolated woods. Men slept all around him, on cots, in bags, some just curled up with a pillow. With all the fatigues, the place looked like an encampment of Salvation Army rejects, and if not for the tattoos and automatic weapons, it could have been. These guys were just scum, and, God, he was tired of being around scum, acting like scum. It was a good thing the ATF raid was tomorrow. One more survivalist mental case to deal with, and he was sure that this time he would just kill the bastard.

That wouldn't make him anybody's hero. Damn sure not the FBI's.

He leaned against the wall and felt the cracked, cool plaster against his skin. A man moaned in the far corner of the room. Denny. The guy had been shot in the leg, and one thing you didn't do when you decide to re-create white-supremacist Armageddon is take a gunshot wound to the hospital. So Denny rotted in the corner, delirious with fever, too drunk on whiskey to even care about his leg. He was probably going to die, but no one cared. The dirtbags went right on their merry way, holed up in the compound, paranoidly planning their holocaust for anyone black or Latino or Korean. It was ironic that the only one who even cared that the guy died was the one who did him in the first place.

He shouldn't have shot him. Liam still had a hard time remembering the incident. Denny pulled out the .45. He stuck it in Liam's face. The argument had been over where to put the group's children, should there be an assault on the compound. It was just macho bullshit; maybe Denny never meant anything by pulling the gun and sticking it in his face. But with the hole of that .45 staring at him, Liam saw red. He grabbed the gun and pulled it away. Denny lunged, and Liam shot him. He just pulled the trigger and watched the bastard crumple at his feet.

He fit in well at the compound for an undercover agent. He could act like a psycho better than anyone, and sometimes it bothered him that he could find such a level of comfort among these people. He was FBI, he should have been a hero. Instead, he did his best work being a piece of scum.

Heroism was a bitch anyway, he thought, ignoring Denny's drunken moans. It rarely got you anywhere. Nice guys did finish last. His mind went back to his dream and his father. Patrick Jameson had died of a coronary long before his son graduated at the top of his class from the FBI academy in Quantico, but even now Liam remembered the dogged things his father did to keep the family going: how he would come home dead tired after a long shift, wrap his clothes that smelled of raw meat in a special hamper so that his mother could get them to the Laundromat without them collecting maggots; how he always considerately showered before falling into bed. Too, Liam remembered the obligatory lineup of kids at the trailer door when his father was ready to go for another shift, and the way it still hurt to recall Patrick Jameson's cursory but relentless "I love you" to each of his children.

Liam wiped the sweat from his brow with his forearm. He'd had the dream. The one with Joey and the Stingray. Man, he looked forward to getting out of Kineson's dump and having a beer in his old haunts without having to worry about some crazed survivalist with a bad case of angry-white-man syndrome. If they found out he was an infiltrator, they'd take off the back of his head with an M-16.

The situation was absurd. He was stuck undercover at a militia camp, waiting for dawn, when the ATF and the rest of his FBI unit were going to raid, and here he was dreaming about '69 and Joey Ableman's new Stingray.

He took a deep, calming breath and laid his head back against the wall, ignoring the broken, crumbling plaster. He hated that dream. It always ended there, with Joey riding his bike in the distance, the sun setting, and his father taking off in the other direction, heading for the meat-packing plant.

He supposed he should be grateful he never dreamed the rest of that day. Or, rather, night. Of the ambulance screams at midnight, and of Mrs. Porter, the owner of the trailer park, sobbing into her apron. Then of dawn and the slow, methodical procession of black body bags out the front door of the Ableman trailer. Joey was dead, his big sister, and his mother, all because some sociopath drifter had arrived in town just in time to see the hero's picture in the paper. All because the paper made note of where the kid lived. All because there were predators out there who liked to kill.

Liam swallowed a groan. He still had this image of Joey in his mind. Of him circling on his brand-new Stingray until he halted at the rise in the road where a man stood. The guy's legs were spread apart, a smile creased his dirty face, and he leaned on the handle of a woodman's ax as if he were Fred Astaire leaning on a cane.

Of course, it didn't happen that way. Dalton Lee Wayne had used a gun. Joey and his sister probably didn't even wake up. Joey's mother had taken the worst of it.

Liam would never forget that day the summer of '69 when his father had casually confessed to not being a hero and when Joey Ableman had been murdered. It was as clear as the Okie sky in a drought that being a hero was complicated stuff. A true hero was difficult to define, and sometimes downright impossible to even justify—he sure knew that when, as a kid, he'd had to stare at the three closed coffins, and, like the rest of Taylorville, grieve for Joey's heroism.

Liam shut his eyes. There was nothing more to do but wait patiently for sunrise. He was nuts to be in the middle of this ticking bomb, and sometimes he wondered what drove him to take the chances he did. It sure wasn't the need to be a hero. After Joey died, he no longer had the desire to be one. Instead, he became the antihero, the town bad boy, constantly testing his own mortality, and his own morality.

He took one last glance around the room at the pile of sleeping men; Denny had finally fallen into drunken silence.

Liam wondered if he was becoming too much like them. The undercover work had always been a cinch, the milieu was instinctively familiar. Violence, anger, brutality—he understood them. Maybe it had to do with being a man; maybe in the end it really was just testosterone that drove the male race.

But some days he worried he was way too in touch with the dark side of his soul.

Yet maybe a little of Patrick Jameson still lingered within him. His father had been no celebrated man, yet he'd seemed bigger than life to his son, as big and herolike as the Irish cop from Boston, the real hero in the family. Patrick Jameson was no hero, but Liam still thought about him in that way, and still grappled with his shortcomings.

He smirked. Hell, the idea of heroism was best left to philosophers and moviemakers, not to feds that were prone to kamikaze missions. The only thing he knew for sure as he gazed over the room of sleeping men was that sometimes a philosophy could be distilled down into one pure formula. And he'd done that for himself.

Maybe Patrick Jameson had been a hero after all. Because maybe being a hero was as simple as just making sure you were never one of the bad guys.

## ❧ 1 ❧

Special Agent Liam Jameson leaned back in his govern-
ment-issue Naugahyde desk chair and surveyed the mess.
Zip-loc bags were everywhere: on the credenza, spilling off
the file cabinets, heaped on his desk. They were filled with evidence from the Kineson case: spent shotgun shells, guns and
ammunitions magazines, screaming pamphlets from the
Utah Separatists Movement, original enameled swastika pins
from the Third Reich. The mess would have delighted the average old-line KKKer.

· "Hey, Jameson, why does it take thirteen Klansmen to
screw in a light bulb?"

Jameson turned to his partner, McBride, who was sitting
by his desk comically knee-deep in mercenary magazines they
had confiscated from the Okie headquarters house. "All
right. Why does it take thirteen Klansmen to screw in a light-
bulb?"

"Because it takes one Grand Wizard to screw in the bulb
and twelve FBI infiltrators to take notes."

Jameson grimaced. That's all he needed today. Sure it was
becoming a cliché. The FBI had had their thumb on the Klan
for well over a decade now; no one in the Klan made a move
without five feds up their butt watching every move. But it
was still necessary, what these people did. Unfortunately, it
was still necessary. Everyday potential followers of the old-

line KKK fractured into hundreds of other groups: White Aryan Resistance, National Socialist Liberation Front, skinheads, Nazi punks, jack-booted Billy Bobs who were nothing but good old rednecks calling themselves patriots and militiamen. Whatever they were, they were out there, with a thousand names and a thousand different approaches, but all the same philosophy. It didn't matter who they hated. There was now a hate group organized to destroy just about anyone. They hated Democrats, Republicans, the IRS, the ATF, Big Government, tree huggers, blacks, Farrakhan, Jews, women, and people with the name Jones. Their choices came from an à la carte menu. But though the targets sometimes changed, the unifying force was that they all loved guns and hated somebody, and it was an ugly mix.

"Look at this . . . ooohh, man, I want one." Obviously bored, McBride reached down and flipped open one of the magazines to show a bosomy, half-naked woman wrapped around an AK-47. He smiled. "God bless Kineson. I love these rednecks. They have absolutely no desire for subtlety."

"I'm a redneck, remember? If I might remind you, that's why I was given the case to head."

"Oh, yeah. I forgot." Slyly McBride added, "I guess you'd prefer I call Kineson a culturally challenged nonurbanite instead, huh?"

Jameson bit back a smile. "Screw you."

He surveyed the mess in front of him and swore it was multiplying. There were seven bags full of spent casings, three sawed-off shotguns, and a heavy family Bible that had the names of all the black families in town penciled inside the front cover with little burning crosses sketched next to each name.

God, guts, and guns, he thought, and savored the warm glow of a job well done. The old Bible was the pinnacle of three years of hard work. It was the damning evidence. It was so damaging, he could almost understand Kineson's rage when they took it from his house. After all, what on earth was the world coming to? If the family Bible wasn't safe from the FBI, nothing was. Damn. Maybe there was a need for the militia after all.

"Listen to this." McBride scooted his chair closer to Jameson's desk.

Jameson ignored him.

" 'Bob's law-enforcement products. Beat the streets! Protect and equip yourself with body armor, batons, holsters, scopes, knives, camping, and survival gear for your off-duty adventures.' " McBride laughed. "What the hell kind of off-duty adventures require body armor?"

Jameson shrugged. He didn't even look up.

"Get this one. 'Guide to Terrorists is designed to help understand the worldwide terrorist phenomenon. The study includes guide to target audiences.' " McBride lowered the magazine and said, "Target audiences, don't you love it. No pun intended, I'm sure. I swear I am not making this up." He read aloud, " 'This guide covers all potent facts in this complex and dangerous arena.' " McBride looked up. "Now, what do you think they really mean when they use the word 'potent'?"

Jameson threw a Ziploc bag full of casings at him. McBride neatly ducked and continued to scan the ads.

"The hell . . . ?"

Jameson couldn't take it anymore. He rolled his eyes and said, "Quit reading that shit. You're supposed to sort it, not read it."

McBride stared at the magazine. His mouth had dropped open so wide, Jameson couldn't stand it anymore. He rose from his chair and snatched the magazine, curious to see what it was.

"You ought to have Gunnarson read this ad, man," McBride said. "Look at the fifth one down on the left. The one with the bold type. You can't miss it."

Jameson scanned the classifieds. The magazine was called *High Risk*. It was a basic guns and ammo mercenary magazine, a step lower, perhaps, than *Soldier of Fortune.* It made noises about serving the law enforcement community, but most of its readers, when it came right down to it, weren't police officers. They were paramilitaries, uneducated good old boys obsessed with weapons and death. It was a fanzine for police wannabes. It fed upon the militia groups that proclaimed they were protecting the Constitution, and it gave a lot of "inside" information, just the kind to pump up the paranoid. The brotherhood of the paramilitary could be likened only to a group of boys whispering in tree houses about their "secret" club and going through solemn blood-brother ceremonies. But these grown-up boys were a helluva lot more dangerous than those innocents still in their school-days. Mercenary magazines made readers believe they were among an elite law enforcement profession, a group so private and powerful that they were everyone's watchdog, everyone's judge, jury, and executioner. Basically, they sold the Big Lie. It was all a sham to make money, just like the *Playboy* man wasn't really a handsome, go-all-night jet-setter, but a fourteen-year-old boy with sticky sheets.

"Are you getting it, Jameson?" McBride asked.

Jameson didn't respond. His attention was nailed to the classified.

"What do you think? Should we show that one to the section chief? Looks like a gun-for-hire ad if I ever saw one."

Jameson lowered the magazine. A little furrow marked his brow.

"Well, what do you think?"

"I guess we should bring it up." Jameson closed the magazine and flipped it onto the desk. "But right now, let's sort through this junk so Avery can take it to Evidence and lock it up."

"Man, that's a gun-for-hire ad if I ever saw one. Someone had better get on it," McBride said as he shuffled through the rest of the stack of magazines.

Jameson opened to the classified again. He read:

WANTED: A man to slay dragons. Write ZOE, Box 5671, Grand Central Station, NY, NY 10036

A man to slay dragons. Jameson couldn't get the phrase out of his mind. It might be some kind of gay talk, but gays didn't advertise in merc mags; they were pretty much the antithesis of any philosophy those publications spouted. The ad was encoded, he knew that much. It sure sounded like a gun for hire. The section chief would be the one to determine what they should do about it.

Jameson began to sort through the Ziploc bags, and for the moment he put dragons and ZOE out of his mind.

"What do you think it means?" Section Chief Gunnarson treated every agent as if he were a psychologist. He never made broad prejudicial statements, and he was always polite, and he always asked for hunches. Jameson knew that was why Frederick Gunnarson was the best of the best.

"I think like McBride. It's a gun for hire. No doubt about it." Jameson shifted in his chair. He always felt like the damned Okie redneck he was in front of Gunnarson. Compared to the Harvard-educated sixty-year-old, he was nothing but a wet behind-the-ears kid trying to learn at the heels of greatness. It didn't matter that he'd just wrapped up the Kineson case—the pinnacle of his career—he hadn't been the one to solve the Taylorville murders. No, Gunnarson had been the hero in that case. It was Gunnarson who fingered Dalton Lee Wayne, one of the most notorious serial killers of the sixties.

"If it is a gun for hire, the New York authorities should go after this." Gunnarson made a note on a clean pad of paper with a shiny black Mont Blanc.

Jameson looked at his chief at the other side of the desk. As always, he was awestruck. The differences between them glared, and he was again nagged by the self-doubt that had dogged him at the FBI academy. Here he was, in this elite circle, with Gunnarson the sun and all the rest of them planets, but though Gunnarson was more than twenty years his senior, it wasn't age that made Liam acutely aware of their differences.

Now, as Liam watched the chief make notes with the Mont Blanc, he suddenly realized how he felt in this elite unit of the FBI. Chief Gunnarson and his group of Ivy League–educated FBI special agents were all expensive fountain pens, and Liam Jameson, the kid from the trailer park near Tulsa, hell, he was afraid to admit it, but he was just a fifty-nine-cent Bic.

There should have been resentment mixed with that thought, but there wasn't any. He was too overwhelmed by respect for the man in front of him. Jameson had joined the FBI because of Gunnarson. Three of the Dalton Lee Wayne killings had happened in his hometown; it was his best friend Joey Abelman who'd been murdered. And sitting in front of Liam now was the man who'd made him decide to go to the academy. He wanted to be just like Gunnarson because Gunnarson was the man who caught Joey's murderer.

The White Knight from Quantico—that was what insiders called Gunnarson—had found the slime that had killed Joey Abelman, his family, and twenty-five others in a serial killing that shocked the nation. Gunnarson's achievement had cinched it for Jameson. Liam, the blue-collar kid from south of Tulsa, wanted to become just like him.

Now he actually worked for him, but all Jameson could ever think of was how he would never be able to live up to his chief's image. No matter how many cases he cracked, no matter how many scumbags he put behind bars, he was never going to be this white knight. Deep down, he didn't look at himself as anybody's hero. There was too much darkness inside him, too much violence he didn't understand. Shooting Denny Freeman in the shack while he was infiltrating the Ki-

neson compound proved it. He grappled with right and
wrong, never quite able to get a firm grip on them, but Gunnarson was so sure. That was why he still looked at the man
like a wide-eyed little boy would. Even Gunnarson's choice
of clothes said confidence. The man wore Hickey-Freeman
suits and silk rep ties. His gray hair was short and always perfectly clipped.

Then there was Jameson. When he'd been in Quantico, he
did his best to look slick, but all he could afford were cheap
suits, and his ties never seemed quite compatible with his
jacket. In the Tulsa unit he worked mostly undercover, so he
knew what to wear to look like a lowlife. At the office he
pulled his dark hair into a ponytail; other times, he just let it
run wild. Ironically he had one special talent for FBI work
that Gunnarson would never have: Liam Jameson could look
just the redneck he still feared he was.

"Well, about that ad, I'll let the proper authorities take it,
sir. I just thought I should bring it to someone's attention."
Jameson stood.

Gunnarson waved him back down with the Mont Blanc.
"Fax the ad to New York and let me know what they say.
I'm going to let you take this one."

"I'll do it right now." Jameson took the magazine off
Gunnarson's desk.

"So when's this wedding we've been hearing about all
these years?"

The question caught Jameson off guard. He felt a tightness in his chest. Again he shifted in his chair. "We called it
off, sir. Mary Elizabeth didn't like Tulsa. I guess three years
was too long to wait for a wedding."

Gunnarson looked at him as if he were looking at his own
son. Behind all the polish and professionalism there was still
a human being there inside. Jameson's admiration only in-
creased. "I'm sorry about that. You could use a wife. At least
to help match your goddamned ties."

Jameson looked down at his tie and grinned. "Yes, sir."

"We could have had you transferred, you know."

"I know, sir. But I'd have to leave the unit, and it was clear she wanted back inside the Washington Beltway more than she wanted me. She wasn't my type anyway. All those uppity Georgetown manners. Damned Yankee is what she was. Good riddance."

Gunnarson laughed.

"I'll send that fax to New York right now, sir."

"Take care of yourself, Agent Jameson. I understand you've got a commendation coming to you."

"Yes, sir."

"You deserved it. They tell me you almost got killed in the raid. Kineson's gun was aimed right at you."

"Yes, sir. 'Almost' is definitely the word, or I wouldn't be here talking to you now. It's good to be back."

"Get a haircut, Jameson."

Jameson nodded. He took the magazine and left Gunnarson's office.


The fax reached Jameson's desk a little before six P.M. He was ready to call it a day, when the head of the typing pool slipped the folder into his in box.

Jameson gave it a cursory once-over. The fax said nothing he didn't expect. The Manhattan police had never heard of anyone or anything named ZOE. They saw no crime. If there was one under way, the only involvement they could muster was to find a policeman to answer the ad.

Liam slipped the fax back into the file and tossed it on his desk. It was the end of a long day, and he looked forward to a beer and maybe a steak dinner to celebrate the conclusion of his latest case. Grabbing his jacket, he shrugged into it, cursing. He hated the whole deal—a formality he was no longer used to. In the heat of a late Indian summer, he barely made it to his car, where he could take the damned thing off again.

McBride had left the building an hour before. The smart aleck had gone to meet his girlfriend. The place was nearly deserted. Nothing was hopping now that the Kineson case was concluded. Jameson did notice that Gunnarson's light was still on. He poked his head through the door and said, "Good night, sir."

Gunnarson looked up from a paper he was reading on his perfectly neat desk. The Mont Blanc lay idle by his hand. "Did you ever hear from New York?"

"Yes, sir. Not much they can do except maybe answer the ad and look into it that way."

"I see."

"Well . . . have a good evening, sir."

"Jameson?"

"Yes, sir?"

"You answer the ad. Check it out. Whoever's behind the thing will believe an inquiry from Tulsa is less suspicious than one from Manhattan."

Jameson almost dropped his jaw. "I don't know that I'm qualified. This isn't really my area, sir. I'm a militia specialist. Hate crimes. You know that's my area, not gun for hire."

"You've proven your expertise ten times over with that last case, but it's time to move on. You know my philosophy. I don't want my agents to be specialists. I want them all to be the Leonardo DaVincis of crime fighting. Broaden your horizons, Jameson."

*A man to slay dragons.* Jameson still couldn't get the phrase out of his head. He wasn't a man to slay anything but perhaps a deer or two when he'd been younger, and even then, ever since Joey Ableman was murdered, Jameson hadn't been able to justify hunting anymore.

Besides, he wasn't the hero, or, rather, the antihero these people were searching for. He was no assassin. Still, the question of what this strange group, this ZOE, searched for burned into his subconscious.

"Answer the ad, Jameson. Tell me what you find."

Jameson looked at his hero, his god, his nemesis. He nodded.

## ❧ 2 ❧

Claire Green closed the polished walnut door to her law office and went to her desk. With trembling hands she retrieved a photocopy from an envelope she had stuffed into her slim Mark Cross briefcase. Opening it, she shook her head as if in disbelief and picked up the phone.

"Phyllis, this is Claire. What do I have in my hands here? What is this ad?"

She was silent for a moment, waiting for the person to speak at the other end. The receiver remained silent.

"It came anonymously here to Fassbinder Hamilton, but you know my secretary often opens my mail," Claire whispered into the phone, into the listening silence at the other end. "And what is the meaning of this thing? Why wasn't I informed of this? You purposely left me out, and I have to tell you, I think I know why. You're doing something illegal, aren't you?"

There was another pause, then Claire gasped, "I demand an answer!"

The woman's voice on the other line was deathly calm, as if she'd prepared every word in advance. "We were protecting you, Claire. We don't want you involved in this, so hang up the phone, throw away the paper in your hand, and forget about it."

"You were protecting me? For God sake's, Phyllis, I'm

ZOE's attorney. I'm supposed to handle the group's legal representation, but how can I do that when you aren't even informing me of what's going on?"

Claire grabbed a notepad. It was out of paper. In frustration, she snatched a piece of law-firm stationery. "Look. Tell me where to meet you and when, and I'll be there. I want to hear everything. You've got a lot of explaining to do, Phyllis. A lot."

She listened and scribbled down the name of a restaurant. After a quick good-bye, she replaced the receiver.

Deep in thought, Claire folded the stationery with *Fassbinder Hamilton* engraved across the top. In tiny little letters to the left of it, along with one hundred and ten other names, was the name Claire Green. One little worker bee in the prestigious Wall Street hive of Fassbinder.

The intercom nearly sent her to the ceiling. She took a deep breath, then pressed the button. "Yes?"

"The deposition, Ms. Green. They called and said they're waiting for you in the conference room."

Claire ran a hand over her crown as if by smoothing her hair she could smooth her frazzled nerves. "Okay. Thank you, Karen. I'll be right out."

She took a deep breath, stood, and gathered several thick folders that were on her desk. It would take all her concentration to follow the deposition, because all she could think about was ZOE.

ZOE.

The Café des Artistes was crowded for a lazy autumn evening in Manhattan. Claire left the traffic of Columbus Avenue and consoled herself with the upbeat atmosphere of the restaurant. Just the sound of laughter and ice tinkling in Friday-night highballs unwound her.

The maître d' escorted her to the table. Phyllis sat there,

her back to one of the paintings of nude nymphs for which the café was famous.

"Darling." Phyllis stood, leaning on her ever-present cane, and gave Claire a hug. "We really should do this more often. How long has it been since either of us girls had a night out?"

"A long time," Claire said as she helped Phyllis regain her seat.

"But we shouldn't have picked this place." Phyllis glanced around at the numerous life-sized paintings. "I mean, who can eat with all this young, taut flesh mocking you?"

Claire smiled. One painting was like an Alma-Tadema Roman bath scene. It could have been entitled "The Bathing of the Numerous Pubescent Virgins."

"Oh, cottage-cheese thighs, how I hate you now," Phyllis lamented.

The waiter came for their drink orders. Phyllis ordered a martini, Claire a spritzer. When the man left, there was a moment of silence. Seconds of pure tension.

"Tell me about the ad, Phyllis." Claire could hardly look at her. She loved Phyllis. She felt betrayed when she saw the ad from ZOE. Something was going on and they had left her out. On purpose. It boded ill. And it was on the verge of destroying a valued friendship. The sixtyish, red-haired woman sitting across from her at the table had been like a mother. Phyllis had held her when she had cried, Phyllis had talked to her on the phone deep into the night when Claire had felt alone and afraid. In the ZOE meetings, they'd shared their most anguished moments, such as the time Phyllis recalled losing her leg. It had happened with terrifying speed. The mugger was in front of her, demanding her purse, then she was sprawled on the bike path of Central Park in broad daylight, her right leg destroyed below the knee by a shotgun blast, her last memory of the event that of the back of a man running away.

It wasn't easy being a victim, Claire thought defiantly, but it was worse being a criminal. It had to be, or nothing in life would make sense anymore. And she couldn't stand by and watch the women she loved turn into criminals.

"You haven't been to the meetings in a long time," Phyllis began after the waiter brought their drinks. "We're doing a lot these days. The thing has really grown."

"What do you mean? There are new members?"

"Well, what we used to be was just a victims' rights group. A place where you could come and share your grief with other women, who would understand and support you. Now we're so much more." Cryptically, Phyllis added, "So much stronger."

"I haven't been attending the rapport sessions much because I've been busy, but I'm still ZOE's legal council, Phyllis." Claire hated to chastise, but something needed reining in and she needed to find out what the beast was. "I must be kept up-to-date if I'm to remain ZOE's attorney. I just can't see this ad and close my eyes—"

"We're really making great strides. A psychotherapist joined us, you know. She was a rape." Phyllis twirled the skewered olive in her martini. The woman appeared so casual, Claire would have thought they were discussing whether to buy that expensive Jaguar Phyllis had her eye on and not whether the group ZOE was somehow dipping its toe into the filthy waters of vigilantism. "We've added almost twenty members in just four months. Remember when Alice Whitney died? She left us everything. Her entire estate. Our bank account looks like it belongs to the NRA. We've hit well into seven figures."

Claire stared at her. Phyllis was definitely acting strange, as if the woman were somehow detached from what she was saying. As if somehow she'd so convinced herself of a lie, reality was the thing that didn't seem real anymore.

Claire took a deep sip of her wine, then wondered why she hadn't ordered anything stronger. She feared she might need it. "Tell me what's going on. I demand to know. I must know or—or—I resign as ZOE's attorney."

Phyllis glanced up at her as if in surprise. "You founded ZOE, Claire. You're going to abandon us? Just when we're going somewhere? Just when we're starting to accomplish something?"

"Phyllis, I'm not going to represent an organization that isn't telling me what they're doing. My intuition says something illegal might be going on here, and I took an oath when I passed the New York bar. Besides, I need to sleep at night. I can't look the other way."

Phyllis's smile was warm and genuine. The old Phyllis. "You're just not that kind of attorney, are you, dear? You never were. Ethics just means so much to you, Claire, and we all know that. That's why we love you. Respect you."

"Tell me about the ad, Phyllis."

The woman took another sip of her martini and looked away. "Maybe you should quit the group. You're the only attorney in New York City with a conscience, so why waste all that altruism on a group of helpless victims who are standing up and taking some of their power back."

Claire tapped her knuckles on the table. It was a nervous habit, something she did when she was wrestling with a problem. "Why are you playing these mind games with me, Phyl? I thought we were friends. Best friends."

The older woman took another deep drink of her cocktail, then neatly placed it back on the napkin. She paused and said, "If I tell you, you'll be involved. So either walk right out of here and resign forever from ZOE, or prepare yourself to be involved."

"Tell me, and then I'll decide."

"I tell you, and the decision will be made for you."

Claire released a frustrated sigh. But she didn't leave.

Phyllis began. "All right. I'll tell you, Claire. You've seen the ad. Somewhere in our midst is the snitch who sent it to you, and you can be sure that I will find out who that snitch is."

"Just tell me," Claire insisted.

"Of course, you will go to the police with this information. The books are clear on attorney-client privilege. The privilege stops when the law is broken, and, I confess, we're breaking the law." Phyllis locked stares with her. She smiled, but the woman smiling now was someone Claire didn't know at all.

"The group has labored over what to do with the funds." Phyllis stirred her drink. Her steady nerves were something to behold. "The consensus in ZOE was that we all wanted to do something good with it, but we couldn't see donating to some charity that would spend three-quarters of the money on a society fund-raiser and the rest on a high-tech phone system that would E-mail pleas to a message machine and call it a victim hotline."

"I can understand—"

"We wanted to control our money and what we did with it. You understand. It's hard not having control over things. Loss of control is what we fear most. It's the definition of victim." Phyllis gave her that stare again. The stare of a stranger. "Are you following what I'm saying, Claire?"

Claire shook her head. "I don't know what you're saying, Phyllis. What, are you really trying to turn ZOE into a vigilante group?"

"Turned."

"Because as your legal council, I'm obliged—" All at once Claire shut her mouth. She pinned Phyllis with a stare of her own. "Did you say turned? *Turned?*"

"We really didn't want you to get involved in this. You haven't been coming to the meetings, and since you're a member of the bar, we were afraid you would try to stop us. It's your group, Claire, but—"

"It is my group. I started it. ZOE's named after my sister, for Christ sake." Claire's nerves felt like they were on fire.

"I know that. But you're a lawyer. We knew you'd have a dilemma."

"You're damn right I have a dilemma."

Phyllis looked around the restaurant. Several people had glanced over when Claire raised her voice. She turned back to Claire and said, "We voted to keep you out of this. I'm violating the group's ethics by telling you." Phyllis downed her martini. "Damn Caroline. I know she's the one who sent you the ad. She was the only dissenter."

"Well, thank God someone has some sense." Claire grasped her wineglass with a shaking hand. "I just can't believe this. I can't believe it. So tell me everything. What's the ad for? How long has it been running? Tell me. Confess. What have you done?"

Phyllis shook her head. "This isn't fair. We didn't want you to know—we didn't want to put you in this position." She paused. "Before I tell you anything, Claire, I think I can speak for everyone in ZOE in that we wouldn't blame you if you wanted to cut your ties to the group. Here's your chance, darling, so take it. You don't know that much yet. If you want out, leave right now. Because when I tell you what's going on, you will then become a charter member of the new ZOE."

"But it was my organization," Claire said in a whisper. "I named it after Zoe. My own twin. I don't want to abandon it. I just want to know what you're doing. How long has the ad been running?"

Phyllis released a long sigh. "Four months." She reached out in supplication. "Oh, Claire. We don't want to hurt you. All any of us ever wanted was justice. But justice is so terribly costly, so brutally elusive."

"Tell me what's been going on," Claire urged. "Tell me or Caroline will tell me, I know it."

"All right. I'll tell you . . . but remember my warning. You'll be tainted just like the rest of us. And you won't be able to run, Claire."

"Tell me, Phyllis. Let me be the judge of that."

"ZOE decided to have a lottery."

"A lottery?"

"Yes, but not the fun kind of lottery. This isn't a church bingo. It's more like a Shirley Jackson kind of lottery. If your name gets picked, you don't win money. You win vengeance."

Claire stared at her unblinking for so long, her eyeballs grew dry. "Are you saying what I think you're saying? That you win some kind of a murder?"

"No, dear. An execution."

The impact of Phyllis's words knocked the breath out of her.

Phyllis waved to the waiter. In the silence, she ordered another martini. Neither of them said anything until the drink was delivered. Claire noticed that Phyllis's hands continued to be rock still. She looked into the other woman's eyes and wondered if she was seeing insanity.

"Explain," Claire finally whispered.

Phyllis took a long, leisurely sip. "It's like this: We didn't know what to do with the enormous bank account, we knew only that we wanted to keep it within the members, to directly have it help the members. So we decided to have a lottery. To each winner we assign a set percentage of our resources, including but not limited to our bank account, and we set a period of time in which those resources can be spent. If we can help, we do all we can during that time. If we can't, we move on to the next winner."

"When you say 'help,' what exactly do you mean?"

"If we know who the guy is, well, then, that makes it easy and certainly cost effective. If we don't, we do everything we can during the allotted period of time to find him. We search him out. You know, Claire, it's true what Malcolm X said. When there's no justice for you in the law, then the law does not apply to you. I believe that now. We found that without the law, we could do what the police could not and would not do. It's shocking how much is known on the streets about a crime that's never passed on to the cops."

Claire stared into the face she thought she knew so well,

and suddenly she could see that the old Phyllis was indeed gone. The rational and kind older woman who had always held strong was gone. In her place was this woman fractured into madness. "I can't believe this," Claire mumbled. "I can't believe what I'm hearing." The entire room was spinning. The nymphs, so pretty when she came into the restaurant, now looked almost malevolent, as if they were there only to lure young men to their deaths.

"Are you ready to order?" An energetic, smooth-skinned waiter stood over the table, a pleasant smile on his face.

Claire looked up at him. She almost wanted to shout at him and ask if he knew he was in the company of murderers.

"I don't think we're quite ready yet," she heard Phyllis say brightly, "but do bring us some of the baby zucchini appetizer. I absolutely adore it."

"Very good." The young waiter smiled and waved to the busboy to refresh the ice in their water glasses.

When the busboy had gone, Claire just stared dumbly at Phyllis. She was at a loss. Something was up, she'd known that from the ad, but the truth came as a vicious shock. "Malcolm X recanted," she whispered. "And so did Nathan Bedford Forrest. They all came to see that vigilantism wasn't the answer. You've got to see that too."

"They were men. They had more justice in their lifetime than we could ever have in ours."

Phyllis's cynicism was an old familiar to Claire, but she never thought her friend would begin to live it. Cautiously, Claire tried to reason with her. "Malcolm X was black. He was a minority. He knew all about injustice."

Phyllis put down her drink. This woman that Claire didn't know let anger ride over her pretty face until it was almost hideous. "Are you telling me, dear, that Malcolm X knew more pain, injustice, and abuse in his lifetime during the Jim Crow era than today's average black woman raising five fatherless kids up on Lenox Avenue? A woman who scrubs public toilets just to have a job? Are you telling me that? It's absurd. I ask you, in fact I demand it, where is her justice? Where is her right to accountability? And where is her God-given right to have the means to pull herself up by her boot-straps? It's in the toilet that she scrubs every day, that's where, because how can she do anything to help herself when she's the only thing holding six lives together? And still, though burdened with the problems of the whole world, by every statistic she's holding those lives together making less than a man of her same background and race. Don't give me any examples of men, Claire. *Men* have it good."

Claire released an inward grimace. She'd learned a lot from her friendships with older women, and mostly it was an appreciation of her moment in time. Older women were either still trapped in the sexist la-la land of the fifties, or they were bitter from the gift of a cutting-edge mind and the glaring lack of opportunity. Phyllis was of the latter group. She made Claire wonder what her own granddaughter's potential would be like, and she made Claire envious of it. Claire Green's granddaughter wouldn't have the trials that her grandmother had.

"ZOE wasn't created to be a man-haters club," Claire said finally, choosing her words with caution. "It was meant to be a victims' rights organization. Just a forum where we could share our pain. You guys have done more for me than anyone else. I had no one, and you all kept me from being alone with my grief. I'll always be grateful for that. I thought it would be good to get together and air our common tragedies. I thought it would be cathartic." Her voice started cracking with frightened tears. "I didn't think it would turn into this."

"But you haven't been coming, Claire. You haven't stayed informed and kept up. I know—I know—you've been busy, but people do what they want to do. You've been staying home because ZOE was frustrating you. There's only so much rehashing of an event any person can do. What's therapeutic is action. We came to realize that, and now we've decided to give that."

Claire shook her head. She didn't want to admit it, but Phyllis was pretty close in her analysis. "No, I really can't believe this—"

"Are we ready, ladies?" The perky waiter had returned.

Woodenly, Claire opened the menu and ordered the first thing she saw. Phyllis took a bit more time. When they were alone again, Claire knew she wouldn't be able to eat what she'd ordered, especially after she asked the next question.

"So have you caught anybody?"

"I can't tell you that. That's controlled by three people. We call it the trinity: the ZOE member who wins the lottery, the executioner, and the judge."

"I see now how you pick the ZOE member." Claire paused. Her voice shook. "And I think I know how you pick the executioner. It's through this ad, isn't it?"

Phyllis didn't answer.

"Okay," Claire continued. "I have those things figured out. But who acts as the judge?"

Phyllis just stared at the nymphs. "You were the top person in our organization, Claire. You founded it, you were our attorney of record. But you didn't come to the meetings anymore. We couldn't pick you. You weren't on the inside anymore."

"The next person in line, then, would be you. Are you the judge, Phyl?"

"If we were to do this, we decided we couldn't have fifty women knowing all the details. It would be too messy. Surely one of them would feel guilty and maybe go to the police. The only way we could act was through anonymity and silence. That's why we picked the trinity. That's why only the ZOE victim, the assassin, and the judge ever know what happened during any particular win of the lottery. That's the only way to keep control."

Claire could hardly believe what she was hearing. The day had started out so normally—a bagel for breakfast, the number three train to work—but now the bottom had dropped out of her life. She'd been invited to look over the precipice of evil and she had begun to slip. "Caroline sent me the ad. What are you going to do about dissenters?"

"Caroline can't tell you anything more than what this ad says. Out of the trinity, only the judge knows all the details. I pick the assassin, Claire. All the ZOE victim knows and will ever know is that her turn came up at the lottery and there was a successful or unsuccessful extermination. So let Caroline go to the police. You can go to the police too, but they would never be able to make a case. They have three people to find and hook together and they'll never be able to make all the connections because only I know who all three of them are. Only I am privileged to have all the details. And you know, Claire"—Phyllis looked deep into Claire's eyes, so deep Claire could see the insanity there gleaming like a hard, intractable diamond—"I'll never tell the police anything. They were of no help to me when I lost my leg. They were no help at all."

Despair settled on Claire like wet sand. The crime that left Phyllis with half a leg had finally sent the woman over the edge. Phyllis couldn't take being the victim anymore, and now this terrible balm was the only thing that soothed her.

"I'm afraid, Phyl. I'm afraid," Claire gasped, unable to even think how to convince this madwoman to come back from the edge.

Phyllis reached over and touched her hand. "I was afraid to go to kindergarten even though I knew it was good for me. If you think about it, this is that same kind of fear."

Phyllis could be so wise, so strong. Claire already felt the hurt of her absence. She couldn't understand how such a towering person could topple so far. "You know I have to stop this. Absolutely, I have to put an end to this," she said, almost to herself.

"You'll never find anything out. I'll never tell, Claire. You know that. And you'd only be betraying your friends. Your friends who wiped your tears when you thought about your sister."

Claire took her hand away from Phyllis's grasp. Their entrees arrived. She didn't know how she was going to choke any of it down. "I have the ad, Phyllis, and let me say that as an attorney, you're only asking for trouble by placing ads like this in national magazines. You can't run gun-for-hire ads anymore. You remember what happened to *Soldier of Fortune* when they were caught. In fact, I can't even believe you were able to get this ad through."

"No one knows what it means. In that magazine it'll get the message to the right men. You see? We ran it in the personals with a woman's name. Most will think it's a desperate, lovelorn female searching for her cowboy in the white hat and that's what we'll claim our intentions were should we ever get caught—which we won't. Now, trust me, Claire. The authorities will never get wind of this. You'll never tell."

Claire shook her head and gazed at the ceiling in disbelief. "It's brutally obvious what the ad means. Anyone with any sense could read this for what it is. The New York police are probably monitoring the box at Grand Central for responses right now."

"We have more women working on this case for ZOE than they could ever put on police. We've enough resources to check out any respondent and make sure he's not a plant."

"Who are you hiring this one for? Is he the first or the tenth or what? Who's won the lottery this time?"

"Claire. Oh, Claire." Phyllis put down her fork. She seemed to have lost her appetite too. "I wish I could convince you how right this is. I wish you weren't a lawyer. If I could only give you the feeling I feel now knowing that I'm no longer a victim having to stand by and just take it. I don't know if they'll ever catch the bastard who took my leg, but I don't care as much now, knowing that at least I'm finding justice somewhere, for someone."

"Who is the next lottery winner?" Claire didn't care if she sounded angry. She was angry and terrified. She wanted to get to the bottom of this dangerous nonsense, and she wanted to get to it now.

"Claire," Phyllis sighed, her face mirroring her reluctance.

"Who the hell is it? Whose name came up on the lottery?"

Phyllis reached over and grasped her hand once more. Sorrow etched her fine features. "The ZOE victim doesn't ever know her hired assassin, Claire. Only the judge knows that. And the Zoe victim is chosen by lottery, except in special circumstances."

The world froze. Slowly, Claire gasped, "Who's the next lottery winner?"

"The members got together just last week and decided we had to honor our founder. We didn't use the lottery this time. We just picked her."

"Oh, God."

"We picked you, Claire. It's you."

## ❧ 3 ❧

She knows not love that kissed her
She knows not where.
Art thou the ghost, my sister,
White sister there,
Am I the ghost, who knows?
My hand, a fallen rose,
Lies snow-white on white snows, and takes no care.
                                  —*Algernon Charles Swinburne*

Claire tossed her purse on a chair, slipped out of her pumps, and eased herself down onto her couch. The dinner at Café des Artistes had left her in shock. Nothing familiar seemed real anymore, not even her drab, disorganized apartment. It was now past eleven, and she was dead tired, but she knew she wouldn't sleep that night. Her talk with Phyllis had changed everything in her world. She didn't know how she would get back to normal ever again.

Even now she was paralyzed with disbelief. It just couldn't be that this organization that she had created was a Dr. Jekyll and Mr. Hyde. She thought she'd known the people involved, but she didn't anymore. Her confusion left her vulnerable and indecisive just when she needed to *do* something. She should go to the police. She should pick up the phone and dial the nearest precinct and tell them everything. But she would sound as crazy as Phyllis had turned out to be. Even now, in the solitude of her apartment, it sounded nutty that there could be a group of middle-aged women running a lottery to see who next gets to snuff their victimizer. And it would really go over well that she had nothing better to show them than an obscure ad and the name of the woman who was the mastermind of the whole thing, a woman who by all accounts loved nothing better than having lunch and her nails done. The entire notion was weak and pointless. All she had was her theories. They didn't convict people on that, and she knew it better than anyone.

Her gaze turned to the familiar photo on her mantel. It was in an Elsa Peretti sterling frame from Tiffany's that had cost her the sun and moon in the days just after law school. Back then, she had felt like Atlas beneath the weight of those school loans. Columbia Law School wasn't cheap, and it was sure as hell a myth that all Jews had money. Her father had been a schoolteacher in New Orleans and her mother had stayed home. Education was a pay-your-own-way proposition, but she had done it. She had survived, even flourished. Even now she could remember the elation of the day she had passed the bar.

She'd gone out for a walk; it was one of those rare days in Manhattan, crystal blue sky, soft breeze; the old West Side buildings stood in sharp relief in the sun. She'd walked and walked, her happiness like an engine pulling her along; past Lincoln Center, past Columbus Circle. She turned on Central Park South and took one of her favorite jaunts by the New York Athletic Club, grand old Rumpelmayer's at the St. Moritz, and the shabby remnants of the Stork Club. Central Park South all the way to the Plaza was the best part of Manhattan. It was like the skeleton of an old movie set: All the ghosts were David Niven, and Fred and Ginger, and all the moves were elegantly dictated by the likes of Noël Coward and Frank Capra.

She had turned at the Plaza and for a moment watched the tourists photograph the fountain. This place spoke to her. It was Jackie Kennedy buying her pillbox hats from Bergdorf's next door. It was big black Studebakers lined up at the Plaza door, patiently awaiting a starlet in mink to dash into one so that she could be chauffeured to '21'.

The tourists with their disposable Kodaks had depressed her that day. In her mind, out-of-towners had no place milling around in their I heart NEW YORK T-shirts and hideous fanny packs, defacing an institution such as the Plaza. The Plaza stood for an era of class that had passed away. Perhaps it had become extinct by natural selection, but there was still within some people's hearts a small longing for men in fedoras and women who put on nylons and white gloves just for an hour's shopping. Cary Grant and Irene Dunne were dead, but their memories lived on. Claire had always thought there should be a little more respect.

On that fateful day, she had turned down Fifth Avenue. Finally, there it was. The shrine she had unconsciously come to visit.

The deco building was as familiar a sight as the Plaza. Tiffany's. She had never even once dared to go inside. After all, what business did a poor law student have inside a jewelers, and such a famous one?

But that day, Claire Green had become different. She wasn't just some wide-eyed displaced Jewish girl from way down yonder in New Orleans. No, that day she was accomplished and special. It wasn't good enough for her to just press her nose against the windows and wish she were Holly Golightly, a chic, wide-eyed waif eating a danish at dawn in a shockingly expensive black Givenchy. No, this time, she was Claire Green, Attorney-at-Law, and she wouldn't need George Peppard to rescue her from her wayward existence. She had passed the New York bar examination and she had an associate position just waiting for her at Fassbinder Hamilton. She had saved herself on her own.

She had drummed up her nerve and walked inside, sweeping through the revolving doors with the same kind of tourists that were gawking at the Plaza fountain. Diamonds were on the first floor, and though the tourists loved them, she had no interest in them. Once inside, it didn't sit well with her buying herself jewelry. But she knew she wanted to buy something to mark this momentous occasion in her life. Now she could see the sole purpose of her outing that day. There was almost a cosmic force pulling on her, guiding her to this store.

She walked to the back and took the elevator. She got off at silver. Gold and diamonds weren't in her budget, but maybe a small sterling . . . *something*.

That was when she saw it. Perched over cases of sterling pins, bracelets, and writing instruments was a large picture frame. It was in the shape of a heart, but the sculpted edges were so fluid, expressive, alive even, she couldn't take her eyes off it.

It was the purpose of her pilgrimage. She'd bought it that instant, praying her Visa card wouldn't go over her limit. The price choked her—now that she'd graduated, she still had an apartment to rent and furniture to buy—but she had to have it. The sterling piece was destiny. There was poetry to this prize. A picture frame from the legendary Tiffany's was just the thing to frame the reason for her great accomplishments. A thousand-dollar house for a photograph was almost good enough for the reason behind her intense motivation that had kept her going through three grueling years of law school. Three years of hell. Three years of reading until her eyes felt as if they were going to fall out of her head. Of demanding cold, clear-headed logic until she was ready to go insane, three years of memorizing until she knew it all backward and forward, and until she graduated Law Review and *summa cum laude.*

She hadn't done it for herself. Not even for that astounding first year associate's salary from Fassbinder. She'd done it all for Zoe.

Zoe's picture would go in the Elsa Peretti frame.

Claire stared at the picture on her mantel, mesmerized with the memories of the day she'd bought it. Finally, she rose from the couch and retrieved the photo frame. Inside the heart they were both there, two smiling, identical faces. Twins. Two girls the exact same age, with the exact same looks, and with two such totally different personalities, it was hard sometimes to believe they were even from the same family.

She fingered the face in the photograph, unable to believe her father had taken the picture of herself and Zoe only five years before. She had been home for the summer from Barnard, and Zoe was finishing junior college near the lakefront. Claire was undergoing the agonies of picking a major, while Zoe simply dreamed about Mr. Right, the handsome, rich, as-yet-unmaterialized man who was going to sweep her off her feet and carry her into the posh Junior League life with a Mercedes-Benz station wagon and 2.3 kids.

They couldn't have been more different. Claire had always thought her sister a piece of fluff. Zoe's desires seemed trite and outdated to the point of being retroactive. Zoe, on the other hand, referred to Claire as a humorless bookworm with no joie de vivre.

They were both right and both wrong. Claire loved to laugh and no one could make someone laugh like Zoe. And if Zoe had always struck Claire as a bit frivolous, Zoe had certainly managed to change all that when they found her raped and mutilated body in that ditch behind the fire station in Des Allemands, Louisiana.

A splash of something wet and salty hit the picture-frame glass, and Claire realized she was crying. True grief, she'd come to understand, came more in silent, unexpected tears than in huge, dramatic purges. That was the curse of it. The pain never really seemed to be relieved, so it never seemed to go away. Especially when a twin was lost. The memory was only a mirror away.

She put the frame back on the mantel. The idea of coffee suddenly seemed like a good idea, so she went to the kitchen in her stocking feet and ground some espresso beans. She had to think. The organization ZOE was in way over its head, and she had to save it. It wasn't even so much that they might implicate her—that was a given since the group was named after her sister—but she couldn't afford to look the other way when she had a fiduciary duty to them. They were breaking the law.

*A law that hadn't served them.* The thought echoed through her mind like a taunt while she frothed the milk, but she couldn't listen to it. She couldn't allow a victim's resentment and anger to color her duty in this manner. They'd never caught Zoe's murderer. And Claire doubted even this gun for hire they were going to get for her and all the resources of ZOE would catch him. Zoe's murder was a statistical aberration. Most people knew who murdered their loved ones. They might not have the evidence to convict the perpetrator of the crime, but they knew who it was nonetheless. Sometimes it was just a gut feeling that grew: Perhaps they realized the boyfriend told a different alibi to different family members. Or perhaps all the evidence, damning as it was, was thrown out on a technicality and the guy walked. There were several women Claire knew in ZOE who had to see their attacker every day. What they wouldn't give to have a chance at the lottery, the game that was threatening everything she held dear. It was her problem.

And her chance.

Claire sipped her cappuccino and denied the funny thrill that went through her. The very idea of it simultaneously sickened and enlivened her. They would never find the guy anyway. There was barely any evidence to go on. In Zoe's case, it wasn't a family member or friend who'd killed her.

Her murder had all the markings of a serial killing even though the police had never been able to string together any other murders.

She remembered going over again and again all the evidence with the homicide detective. Being the family representative, she'd forced herself to stomach it in order to spare her parents. The authorities had called in the FBI, but there was no other match to any other murder in the country. Claire could still hear the frustration and cynicism in the detective's voice when he told her that Zoe seemed to have been murdered by the only monogamous serial killer known to history.

Now her name had come up in the lottery.

Claire mentally shook herself. She couldn't allow herself to fall into the abyss of vigilantism. It would at best get her disbarred, at worst land her in prison. There had to be some way to make the members of ZOE understand how dangerous their new thinking had become. How wrong it was. The women were her friends, not just anonymous faces in a crowd. She could appeal to them. The ZOE members had held her hand when she'd felt as if she'd scraped the bottom of her soul and would never work her way up again. And she'd held their hands too. Now it was her duty as a lawyer and a friend to make them aware of the consequences, force them to see the error of their ways. Turning down her appointment as a lottery winner would certainly set an example. Too, explaining the futility of finding a criminal the police could not might discourage some of them. Some of them.

But there were still plenty of women who'd been maimed and shot and who'd had loved ones murdered who knew exactly who'd caused them their grief. They wouldn't become disenchanted with the lottery; they wouldn't be affected by Claire Green's appeal for rational thinking. She wondered, if she were in their place, if she would let it go. Revenge was too much of a rarity for modern victims. It would be hard to pass up.

She returned to the couch, depression following her. The coffee was hot, the cinnamon sweet, but it didn't chase away her blues. Nor did the drab yuppie beige of her living room. Zoe would have called her on the decor, Claire knew it. Already she could see her sister insisting upon adding some Mario Buatta chintz to enliven things, because that's what Zoe did. She made things alive. She created laughter and she made her sister want to have lunch with her and hear about her day even though Zoe didn't do anything "important"; she wasn't a CEO of a Fortune 500 corporation, she wasn't a name partner at a big New York law firm. She was just that kind of rare person who made things alive and someone had killed her.

And now there was no justice. None.

Claire frowned and sipped the cappuccino. Perhaps her apartment was a bit bland. She should throw in some chintz just because she knew it would have made her sister happy.

The newspaper still lay flung over the cushions, where she had abandoned it in her morning rush to get out the door. She picked it up and scanned the headlines. Certainly there was nothing optimistic there. More abominations going on in Africa. Somewhere in the former Soviet Union, a small little country with a name so long and complicated she couldn't even pronounce it was practicing ethnic cleansing.

Flipping the page, she scanned the interior, wishing for an article that would take her mind off ZOE. But it was all more of the same. More Turks killed by neo-Nazis in Berlin, more children murdered by children with guns.

Then her eye caught something odd. A shot of ice ran down her spine. She grabbed the paper and read the name again and again. Halbert Washington. She knew a Halbert Washington. A young woman, Earnestine Darby, was in ZOE because her mother had been viciously murdered by her boyfriend while Earnestine and her brother and sister lay sleeping in the next room. Earnestine had been eight years old at the time, her brother and sister four and five. Halbert

Washington, the boyfriend, had been arrested, tried, and convicted of manslaughter. Because they were just children and their testimony considered unreliable, Halbert Washington copped a plea. He served five years for what was claimed as a domestic dispute that had ended in unintentional death.

But Earnestine had known better. She might not have been old enough for the courts, but she'd been old enough to know what had really been done to her mother. And at twelve she got to watch the man who'd done it walk in her neighborhood again. He could look her in the eye without a twinge of conscience because Halbert Washington had paid his debt to society. But where had he paid his debt to Grace's three children, Earnestine would whisper through her tears at the ZOE meeting.

A strange numbness gripped Claire. There were probably several Halbert Washingtons in the New York area, she told herself as she read the small, inconsequential article. It stated that a Halbert Washington had been found hacked to death inside a Dumpster. Perhaps it was mere coincidence that Grace Darby had died from knife wounds too, and perhaps it was just a strange twist of fate that the man in the article had happened to be the same Halbert Washington who had killed Grace Darby. A bad character meeting with an appropriate bad end. Claire wondered why she was even questioning it. Perhaps justice had been served without the hand of ZOE. It was possible. Sure.

Trembling violently, Claire reached for her Filofax. She found the number and dialed, the whole time whispering a prayer. "Earnestine? This is Claire."

"Hey baby, how you doin'?"

"I'm doing well, thank you." Claire curled up on the couch, eager to sound calm. "I just called because I saw the strangest article in the paper and thought I should bring it to your attention. It seems too good to be true. A Halbert Washington was found—"

"Yeah, I know, baby. It was him."

"It was? Hey, that's great. It's over for you, then. I guess he finally got into more trouble than he could handle, huh?"

"That's right."

Earnestine's two little words were like icicles. Claire was almost sickened by their confidence.

"Do you know how it happened? I mean, was he dealing? Did it go sour for him?" Claire could even hear the quaver in her voice.

"Listen, Claire, I don't know nothing about it. I—I just wish that you could feel this way, baby. It is over. I'm free at last, you know what I mean? Free at last."

Claire felt tears suddenly come to her eyes. Her voice sounded like a little girl's. "Tell me, Earnestine, did you win this lottery thing?"

There was a long silence on the end of the phone. Earnestine didn't seem able to hide the choke in her own voice, or the sniffing as she began to cry. "Baby, you've got to understand what I've been through, what I've seen, what I see every day. You've got to feel what I feel now to know how sweet the feeling is. My mama's smilin' this day, girl. She's smilin'."

"Oh, God." A numbness penetrated Claire's body, then reality came crashing down on her like a bucket of antifreeze. She couldn't fathom what was happening to her. The dinner with Phyllis seemed like a dream, and if she could have only woken up, she might just be okay. But now she knew it was no dream. It had happened. ZOE—or, rather, her closest friend Phyllis Zuckermann—had actually contracted Halbert Washington's execution and accomplished it.

"I just have to know the truth. ZOE was named after my sister, Earnestine. My *twin.* I know how you feel. I saw Zoe's body at the morgue. I saw what had been done to her, and at times I've felt it as if it had been done to me. I just want to know what's going on. Just give me that." She swiped at the rivers of tears streaming down her cheeks.

"Nobody understands your pain like me, child."

"I know that. I know. So just tell me. Just give me a straight answer. Did you win the lottery?" Claire sobbed.

"It's hard for you, baby. You're in the middle, and I feel for you, girl. But all I know is my mama's smilin' now."

"Did you win the lottery, Earnestine? And were you the first one, or have there been others? You've got to tell me. You've just got to." There was a spike of desperation in her voice now.

"She's smilin' now, girl. I finally made my poor mama smile."

"You've got to tell me. I've got to know—just tell me— just tell me—did you win the lottery?"

Earnestine hung up the receiver.

## ❧ 4 ❧

Jameson sat at his desk, mentally reciting a memo.

Utah. Idaho. These were the states where racism galloped now. It used to be the South. Mississippi burning, but the fire was going out. The South had come a long way in twenty years. There was probably more racial harmony there than in most East Coast cities, certainly more than in L.A. or the Bronx. It was more likely now that today's white supremicist sat with his survivalist militia arsenal holed up in Tribbley, Idaho, than eating in a diner in Selma, Alabama.

So just as he'd finally come home to Tulsa, they were thinking of transferring him west again. Sure, it was where he was needed; still, he didn't want to go. He'd hated Quantico and D.C. They weren't his kind of people. He was a Tulsa boy. Listening to Chris LeDoux and drinking cheap beer was his idea of a good time.

Hell. Then again, maybe he was redneck enough to belong in Tribbley, Idaho.

He balled up the paper he'd been working on. Aiming for the trash can, he slam-dunked it, only to find McBride standing in his doorway, an irritating grin on his face.

"Love letter for you, farm boy." McBride dangled a rather thick envelope from his fingers. "It's from your girlfriend Zoc. I guess she's decided to send you a 'dear assassin' letter."

Jameson took it. There was a fine sediment of black powder on the edges of the envelope. "No prints?"

"Nope. Not on the envelope or the contents."

Turning the envelope upside down, a letter and an airline ticket fell out of the slit. Jameson sat back in his chair. "Did you check—?"

"Yes. The ticket was paid by cash, small bills. No memory of who bought it. The clerk can't even say whether it was a man or a woman."

Jameson unfolded the letter. It was laser-printed on a piece of white Xerox paper. No handwriting. Just type that said:

*If you would like to be interviewed, be at the perfume counter at Bloomingdale's, the last Saturday of the month, at two P.M.*

ZOE

All at once he started laughing. "Did they read this downstairs in the lab?"

"Yeah. Can't you just see the evil thought process at work here? Let's arrange a date with Charles Manson at the perfume counter at Bloomie's. 'Oooh, Chuckie, I just *love* Giorgio!' "

Jameson howled. He laughed so hard, his sides hurt and tears welled in the corners of his eyes.

A head peeked through the door. Both men looked up and Jameson recognized Agent Wynn. She'd been in his class at Quantico. Now she specialized in undercover work and was known as one of the best agents around. Jameson consulted her a lot, especially when he needed a feminine point of view.

"What are you guys laughing at?" She leaned against the doorjamb and crossed her arms. Jameson always got the feeling around her that she regarded men as nothing more than inebriated fraternity boys.

"Jameson's got a hot lead into a murder-for-hire scheme

going down at the panty parlor at Bloomies," McBride volunteered.

Jameson threw another balled-up memo at him.

McBride snorted.

Wynn turned to Jameson, eyebrows lifted, her expression appropriately disdainful.

He flashed a grin. Hey, maybe they were all just frat boys. "We saw an ad that looked suspicious and I answered it. It seems this woman wants to meet her assassin at a perfume counter." He began to chuckle. The very idea of it was really funny.

"What did the ad say?" she asked.

"A woman wrote asking for . . . what was it? Oh, yeah. A man who could slay dragons." McBride leaned over and tugged on Jameson's ponytail. "Does this guy look like he could kill a dragon, huh?"

"I swear you're a latent, man. Get away from me." Jameson looked at Wynn and rolled his eyes.

"This is just a case of a Little Miss Lonelyhearts looking for her boyfriends in places she shouldn't. This ain't no gun for hire." McBride snaked his arm around Wynn's waist. "You wouldn't be going around calling yourself Zoe, would you, Wynn? Taking out ads? Lookin' for a big, strong man? Are you lonely, Wynn? I mean, all work and no play—"

"Makes a woman recognize a cow patty when she smells it."

McBride grinned. He extracted his arm from Agent Wynn's waist. "I suppose next you'll be crying sexual harassment."

"You haven't got half the authoritative power that I do. Please. If anyone's going to sexually harass anyone, it's going to be me."

"Then, oh, God, Wynn, sexually harass me!" McBride got down on his knees. "I beg of you. Make my life a living hell!"

"Sorry. I'm not ready for a relationship."

Jameson couldn't take it anymore. He walked over to McBride while the man shuffled out of his office on his knees. He was still pleading when Jameson shut the door on him.

"What an asshole." Wynn plopped down on the chair opposite Jameson's desk. "Too bad he's cute."

"Yeah. Too bad."

"Hey, Jameson," Wynn looked at him with large, pretty blue eyes. "Don't let him talk you out of this Zoe thing. I mean, why can't you meet an assassin at a perfume counter? Maybe this woman's trying to knock off her husband?"

"I suppose." Jameson looked at her. Every now and then, when the mood was right, he found himself attracted to Wynn, but not wanting to look like the pup McBride was, he always refrained from showing it. Still, there was no way around the male primal instincts. If given the choice, he'd probably nail her if he could. Even if she was a colleague.

"You have to understand. Women don't think like men. They don't meet at construction sites. They meet at coffee shops and department stores."

*Women don't think like men.* How many times had he heard that? But God, it was true. Mary Elizabeth had had him jumping hoops because he was so bewildered all the time, and the only question he ever thought to ask her was how high to jump, and even then he hadn't been able to please her. He couldn't conform to her expectations worth a damn. He supposed in her mind she had it all mapped out how she shouldn't be blamed for ending up in another man's bed. It was just that good ol' Liam didn't understand her.

But he did blame her. To this day his gut fired with anger every time he just thought about it.

"Okay, so women don't think like men," he said. "So what? Most of them don't kill either. Remember statistics class at Quantico? If something's running at twenty percent or less, it's an impossibility. So it's almost an impossibility for a woman to be the perpetrator of a murder."

"The statistics go up every year."

"Yeah. Every year you gals achieve a little more equality." He looked at her. Wynn seemed almost uncomfortable, as if he were accusing her of something.

"What does Gunnarson say about the letter?" she asked softly.

"I haven't shown it to him."

"You should go, you know. To New York, I mean. Meet this Zoe. If she's just lonely, maybe she's not dangerous."

"This is not my specialty. I'm into hate crimes. They need me in Idaho, or maybe they'll just up and ship me to Berlin now that there's talk of getting rid of the CIA—"

"But you should answer the letter. You're just what they'd expect—"

"Which is?" He lifted on eyebrow.

Wynn turned quiet. Then a wry little grin turned up a corner of her mouth. "Well . . . you *know* . . ."

"You mean someone like yourself with that blunt haircut and that Princeton undergrad degree might come off as too classy for a gun for hire?"

"You have class, Liam. You certainly have much more class than McBride."

"Well, thank you Ms.—with a capital M and a little s— Wynn."

"Now, don't go and get all bent out of shape. It takes all kinds. I mean, after all, not every special agent can be a woman. As much as I think that might improve the world, I at least understand the impracticality of it."

"God, you're brilliant, Wynn. I suppose you've given all this a lot of thought in between rewriting the King James Version of the Bible in gender-neutral language?"

It was her turn to throw a balled-up memo. It landed two feet short of its mark. Wynn threw just like a girl, Liam thought smugly.

"I've got to go. There's a delightful file on my desk two inches thick full of grisly photos that I just can't wait to thumb through." Wynn released a sigh, but she turned to Liam before she left and said, "You should go to New York. Never underestimate a woman, Liam."

Liam watched her. There was a strange kind of feminine mysticism in Wynn's eyes. An inexplicable kind of warning. It seemed to come from that deep place that only women had access to, and that men ended up destroying themselves in the folly of trying to reach it.

"Thank you, Agent Wynn, for that never-before-revealed informational gem."

Wynn just raised her eyebrows. Sarcasm acknowledged, she quietly closed the door.

Against his will, Jameson looked at the airline ticket.

## ❧ 5 ❧

"**D**id you run the ad just for my turn or have there been other advertisements for killers?"

"I'm not going to tell you, Claire. That's how we decided things. I'm the judge, I run the show, I take care of the gruesome details, and everyone else gets a sigh of relief."

"The *High Risk* ad is recent, isn't it?" Claire looked at Phyllis, her gaze unwavering.

"You can see the date of the magazine. Obviously it's recent," Phyllis answered.

The two women were having drinks at the Waldorf's Peacock Alley. The hotel was quiet on a Wednesday night, and it was the perfect location between Phyllis's East Side town house and Fassbinder Hamilton. But Claire wished that instead of them talking about ZOE, their meeting was more like the old times. She wished they were in the sleek deco bar listening to Harry Connick, Jr., at the piano. She wished they were giggling and enjoying their drinks. She longed for the days when the girls went out and had fun.

"Any responses yet?" Claire twirled the cherry in her whiskey sour.

"Now, now. You know I'm not going to tell you."

Claire shut her eyes for a moment. The picture of them casually drinking in the bar seemed almost surreal given the conversation. She moaned and said. "I've talked to Earnestine. I know about Halbert Washington."

"What's there to know? He lived a bad life; he died a bad death."

"No assistance, I'm sure." Claire leaned closer to the edge of the table. Her hands reached out in supplication. "Has anyone ever given any thought to the fact that one of these guys might be innocent? Some of them had fair trials, you know—"

"And they got off on technicalities."

"Some of them. But even so, they still might have been innocent. Look at Audrey's case. It was purely circumstantial. Maybe a serial killer was at large in Rochester ten years ago. Maybe her stepdad really was the one who raped and strangled her like she said, but then again, he was acquitted. So maybe it was Jeffrey Dahmer in the ski mask. Maybe it was a guy we haven't found yet."

"You know most crimes like that aren't committed at random. The victim almost always knows the perpetrator."

Phyllis drummed her perfectly manicured nails on the tablecloth. Their color was Lancome's Vermillion. Claire knew this because Phyllis always used Lancome's Vermillion. She was so close to Phyllis that she even knew the brand and name of her nail polish, but that intimacy hadn't been reciprocated. Claire still couldn't get over the anger and betrayal that so much had gone on at ZOE that Phyllis hadn't told her about. But then, she wondered how she could be angry and betrayed by a person who was certifiable.

"Tell me about the men who've answered the ad." Claire wouldn't let it go. She was going to close this Pandora's box if it took all her strength.

"You're not my attorney, Claire. We share no privilege. I'm not going to tell you anything, darling."

"Whoever answers the ad is probably going to be an undercover cop. I don't know how they allowed that ad to go through after what happened at *Soldier of Fortune.*"

"They take ads from services in the Pacific Rim offering passive Asian wives to all those big, dumb macho-types, so why not an ad from a SWF looking for Mr. Right? What's there to question?" Phyllis picked through one of several glossy Henri Bendel bags on the banquette next to her. Distractedly, she said, "Oh, where is it? I forgot I bought you something while I was out shopping today."

"Have you ever thought that some guy who answers the ad might actually be thinking he's getting a girlfriend instead of being asked to commit a crime? He'll rat on you when you lay the cards on the table."

"He won't."

There was an edge to Phyllis's voice that sent a chill down Claire's spine. She just couldn't see how things had changed. How this warm, loving woman who everyone at Bendel's greeted with a smile had turned into this cold, precise murderer.

"How are you answering the ad? Are you asking to see résumés, or what?" Claire turned silent, then she said, "I don't know why you went looking for him. Even if I wanted to use a guy from this ad, I couldn't. I don't know who killed Zoe. He's useless to me, so get rid of him. Get rid of all of them. Do the right thing."

"And what about the next lottery winner? Do I disappoint her just to suit you?" Phyllis resumed rummaging through the Bendel bags. Distractedly, she added, "We've had a lot of discussions about this in the past few weeks. We really need a relationship with a professional."

"How did you kill Washington without a professional?"

Phyllis gave her a censorious look. "Don't let's talk about Halbert Washington. That was a messy impromptu affair and I don't intend to repeat it. The only thing I'll say about it is that he lived and died like so many men in the ghetto. He dealt drugs; he made one too many enemies."

"Like ZOE?"

"Finally!" Phyllis rummaged through her Hermès handbag and placed a small chocolate-striped bag on the table. "I hope you like it. I couldn't believe it. Bendel has such wonderfully unusual things, don't they?"

Claire looked at the package and felt weak. The whiskey in her drink might have been too much, but it was more likely the nightmare of the situation. *Arsenic and Old Lace* live at the Waldorf-Astoria.

"I don't need a gift from you, Phyllis, I need you to be my friend and I need you to stop this. I want you back. I want us to have fun. I don't want to see my friends hurt or go to jail."

"I know, but, what can I say, I saw this and knew you had to have it."

Claire stared at her. Phyllis's mind was completely gone. She felt as if she were staring at a blank board rather than at Phyllis's familiar, beloved face. They were speaking of murder, and all the woman could focus on was the little surprise she'd tucked into her handbag.

Slowly Claire looked into the brown striped bag. The faint scent of the cosmetics counter wafted up from it. She unrolled the tissue paper. It was a silk scarf in reds, blues, and brown.

"Don't you love it? See? It's a souvenir from the 1940s. This vintage silk scarf is a map of New Orleans."

Claire spread out the scarf on the back of the banquette. Printed on the silk was indeed an outline of the Crescent City.

"It's very unusual." Claire couldn't summon enthusiasm. Phyllis was always a wiz at gift giving, but there was a time and a place, and now was not it.

"I got it at Bendel's. You know how they sometimes go to the estate sales and such and put these things in their boutiques on one? Remember the nineteenth-century valentines they sold in February? Well, they're doing Hollywood now." Phyllis reverently ran her hand across the scarf. "*This* little piece of history once belonged to Janet Gaynor. Adrian gave it to her during a trip to New Orleans. It cost a fortune, but you had to have it, Claire."

Claire gazed blankly at the scarf.

"I know that if a busy lawyer like you has any kind of a hobby at all, it's your love of old black and white movies. Why, the thirties and forties just speak to you, Claire. I swear sometimes you must be a reincarnation of a 1940s starlet."

"Thank you . . . really . . ." Claire continued to stare at the scarf. It was so beside the point of what they had to discuss that she could hardly summon a response. The garish square of silk was a fitting monument to Phyllis's growing insanity. Claire suddenly couldn't help but think how smiles and gifts seemed almost chilling if given at inappropriate times.

"Don't you love the figures? They're just darling." Phyllis ran a red nail down the map. Claire's gaze followed. Drawn in vignettes across the map were cute, almost-cartoonish characters that marked each tourist attraction. There was a drunk standing beneath a lamppost on Bourbon Street, soldiers lined up at Jackson Barracks, a maniacally smiling Esther Williams look-alike clad in bathing cap and a bathing suit paddling along the now-defunct Pontchartrain Beach Amusement Park.

"It was meant for you, Claire dear," Phyllis whispered. "Don't you see it? Don't you see it?" The red nail landed on the map southeast of the city.

An old terror pricked the hairs on Claire's nape. She looked at the scarf map, hardly able to focus on the spot through her fear.

"This is where the man did in Zoe, isn't it?" Phyllis whispered. "He dumped your sister there like a wad of filthy, used-up Kleenex."

A spasm of dread gripped Claire's insides. She gazed at the two children who stood on the map, looking like Hummel figurines with their milk pails and Bavarian outfits. The scarf advertised the little town of Des Allemands, because in the forties, during the days of Jim Crow, whoever designed it probably believed the cherubic white children would lend New Orleans the correct kind of white bread flavor. The two little figures of Des Allemands were certainly in sharp contrast to the caricature drawings of blacks dancing the voodoo bamboula in the French Market.

"This is unbelievable," Claire murmured.

Phyllis placed her hand over Claire's. "That's where she was found, wasn't it? Des Allemands?"

"Yes," Claire whispered, unable to take her eyes off the children.

"I can take it back if you don't like it—"

"No, I want it." Claire looked up at her. She could suddenly see where Phyllis was leading her. Phyllis wanted her to give in. She wanted Claire to feel that old hatred and helplessness and forget what was right and wrong, legal and illegal. Phyllis wanted to inflame her so that Claire would be glad her name was chosen by ZOE. The scarf was a morbid gift, but sometimes morbidity was necessary. Sometimes morbid things gave one strength of purpose. No matter how wrong that purpose was.

"It won't work, Phyllis. It won't work," Claire said, but Phyllis began to prattle about her trip to Bendel's.

Claire turned again to the scarf. She could almost picture Janet Gaynor in a canary-yellow convertible riding down highway 90, her perm neatly tucked into the outrageous scarf à la Thelma and Louise.

"Now, back to the ad." Claire managed to look Phyllis in the eye. "Who has answered it? Anyone?"

"I can't tell you." Phyllis suddenly looked nervous. She glanced at her Hermès purse lying open on the table. Her hand reached out to take it, but before she could, Claire had it in hand.

"Have you been to the post office box today? Are you corresponding with someone?" Without ceremony, Claire began to dig through the handbag. It was strange invading her friend's privacy as she was, but life was getting stranger by the minute. "What's this?" She found a letter postmarked Tulsa. It was in an ordinary white envelope with no return address. "Do you have a pen pal I don't know about, Phyl?"

Phyllis's lips drew into a thin, disapproving line.

Claire looked away. She couldn't think about guilt and privacy and manners. Not when she was trying to save her friend. All her friends. "You know I can't sit by and watch you all go to jail. You guys have meant everything to me. I love you too much."

"No one's going to jail."

"Tell me about him. Who is this guy?" Claire shook the letter at her.

"Eeek, you lawyers are all the same. Probing, probing, probing." Phyllis began to pout. "Fine, then. You can have it, because there isn't much. He answered the ad. This letter is his second 'interview,' if you will. He's from Tulsa, Oklahoma. He's a hick probably with the IQ of a small Dan Quayle 'potatoe', but he has delusional military fantasies; he claims he's worked in Nicaragua, Panama, and the Philippines all during the Reagan-Bush years, and he's paranoid enough to keep his mouth shut. He says he can perform any job in a professional, discreet manner, and he can't spell 'discreet' worth a damn."

"Jeez, what were the rejects like?" Claire said under her breath. She then sobered. "Look, Phyllis, I hope you haven't arranged to meet this guy. I swear, someone from ZOE could be killed by one of these psycho pseudo-military types." She paused and studied Phyllis's expression. Then she shut her eyes. "Oh, God, you haven't arranged a rendezvous, have you?"

Phyllis said nothing.

Claire scrambled to open the letter. It wasn't but a few words. The time and place of the meeting was confirmed, along with the receipt of a plane ticket. Slowly, she lowered it to her lap. "I'm beating my head against the wall," she announced defeatedly. "You know, as your attorney, I must tell you this is foolish and dangerous—"

"You aren't my attorney, Claire, you're my client, and I'm going to fulfill your fondest wish." Phyllis pointed again to the scarf. "I'm going to give a shot at him whether you want it or not."

"So how are you going to set up this on-going relationship? Are you just going to beep him when there's a job to be done, or will this guy be such an animal, you'll have to hold him in a cage somewhere, prepping him for his kills?" Claire downed the last of her drink. "You've got to cease all contact with him. I'm telling you, Phyllis, this'll only lead to trouble."

"It's your turn, Claire. Take it." Phyllis gave her that maternal kind of stare older women possess, then she waved the waiter forward and ordered another martini. "Why not find Zoe's killer and exterminate him?"

Claire shook her head. "Because. Because this way it's wrong. Even if I could overlook the moral, ethical, and legal ramifications of such a choice, how am I supposed to use my turn? The police couldn't find him, remember? So now I'm going to waltz onto the scene years after the murder and *voilà!* discover the identity of the killer just in time for a hired assassin to get him? I don't think so."

"You might be able to find him, Claire. Remember, you played by the rules the last time. The police and the court system have their hands tied. Look at all the slam-dunk murder one with special circumstances cases that walk every day. You're a lawyer, Claire, you know better than anyone that the courts aren't after the truth, they're after justice, not the same thing at all. In the court system, justice gives everybody rights but the victim."

Claire bit back her growing anger. "So what if this time I don't play by the rules? Maybe I go to New Orleans. Then what? How can I find evidence the police missed?"

"When ZOE decided to do this, we knew we could never

promise anyone results, just a chance. I always had the idea that having resources and at least the possibility of retribution might be cathartic." Phyllis leaned forward. Her voice became an urgent whisper. "Take your turn, Claire. Your chance has come up, and I say take it with both hands."

Claire stared at the melting ice in her glass. The waiter returned with a martini and another whiskey sour. She was about to tell him she hadn't ordered another drink, but changed her mind.

"I'll meet this guy." Clare glanced at the letter again.

"What's going through that brilliant mind of yours? You think you're going to meet him and scare him off?"

"You'll have to leave that up to me. After all, it's my turn. I can do with it what I wish."

"You can't stop us, you know. As much as I understand your ambivalence, we're continuing this. With you or without you."

"We'll see. I'm very persuasive. But in the meantime, mother's come home, and I want all those cats to go back in the hat."

"This is bigger than Dr. Seuss, Claire. Besides, those cats won't fit anymore, and even if they did, remember, the Cat in the Hat always comes back."

Claire swirled her drink and stared at it. She felt as if she were caught in a civil war; the cowboys versus the Indians. It was the revisionists' view of Little Bighorn, where everybody had a point of view and only one thing was certain: There were going to be more victims. On both sides. ZOE was going to make sure of it.

The cherry in her drink went around and around, a hypnotic red blur.

It was blood going down the vortex of a drain.

## ❧ 6 ❧

Bloomingdale's was like a Times Square subway platform at rush hour. Those wonderful, dreadful days between Thanksgiving and Christmas had since arrived and everyone in New York—status-seeking yuppies, bored dinks, belligerent grandmas in fur coats, and gawking tourists—seemed to be frothing at the mouth to get into the store. The line waiting for the escalator was roped off and policed by store security. Crowds were thick and subject to tantrums if the tense, disgusted look on the guard's face was any indication. Without the telltale greens and reds decorating the displays, the place would have looked more like an opening to a Spielberg film than a department store.

Perfumes were at the Lexington Avenue entrance. Claire had come early. She rationalized that she could have a croissant and some coffee in the café upstairs, then scope out the area at her leisure, perhaps even surreptitiously spying on the man who'd answered the ad, the man who foolishly thought he could slay dragons.

The one who'd answered the ad placed by women who foolishly thought dragons could be slain.

Phyllis was right, of course. Claire had agreed to meet him only because she was going to scare him off. It was probably more prudent to say nothing to the man and let him go on his way, but she feared he might hook up with ZOE again through the merc ads, and the next time she might not be able to keep them out of trouble. No better cure than prevention, her mother used to say.

The store was an absurd place to meet a gun for hire. A counter clerk wearing too much maroon lip liner hustled at the registers, while managers and androgynous display artists toyed with the Christmas arrangements. She reminded herself to congratulate whoever it was who thought of meeting the man here. It was brilliant; nonthreatening to a woman, easily dismissed by a man.

"May I help you?" The bored voice of a clerk rang out from across the sparkling glass counter.

Claire glanced at the dark-haired young woman, then nervously checked her watch. It was just a few minutes before the hour. If he was going to show, he would be there soon.

"May I help you?" the young woman asked again, a barely masked exasperation in her voice as if Claire, by standing at her counter, was wasting her valuable time.

"Maybe. I mean, well, I guess so." Claire glanced around the floor. There were few men. The only two at the perfume counter were a couple of window dressers arguing about the decorations with one man whining that management was never going to take his suggestion of doing Christmas in teal and fuchsia.

It was safer to be occupied, she told herself, turning back to the clerk. She would blend in that way. It was better she observe and scope him out than he find her first.

"Let me see what you have in Christian Dior, please." She placed her handbag on the counter and rummaged for her American Express card. Phyllis, she was pretty sure, was fond of the fragrance Poison, and with all the end-of-year work at Fassbinder, she hadn't thought of Christmas gifts yet. This way, she could catch up on her shopping and keep people out of jail all at the same time.

The clerk placed several malachite-green boxes on the counter and waited for her to make her choice by impatiently knocking her too-thick acrylic nails against the glass. Claire asked her about the cologne versus the perfume spray, unsure which one Phyllis would prefer. The clerk answered with only the barest minimum of words and zero eye contact. In typical New Yorker style, the woman acted as if she had many more important things to do than wait on the bourgeois pieces of crap that floundered in through the Lexington Avenue.

Jeez, she probably had to get back to FIT and work on that rocket scientist degree, Claire thought a little ungraciously.

"I guess maybe I'll take the spray," Claire mustered, feeling as uninformed as before. She didn't wear perfume and the choices were mind-boggling.

"The cologne comes holiday gift-boxed with soap and travel accessories."

Claire fought the urge to roll her eyes and ask, *Well then, why the hell didn't you say that when I was asking you about it?*

"I guess I'll take the cologne." She handed the young woman her card and off the clerk went to stand in the register line.

Then she saw him.

He leaned against the far gilt and glass counter, looking about as inconspicuous as a spider on a Twinkie. If he fit into any kind of category, he was the type of man no one wanted to meet alone and in the dark. His kind made passing women hug their purses to their chests.

His clothes were filthy, his face was streaked with street grime and sweat. He wore an ancient army surplus knit skullcap and an edgy, steel-hard expression. On the street, it was possible that people might have tossed him a quarter or two, thinking him one of the homeless, but Claire instinctively knew no one ever did this. The fact that at well over six feet in height, the guy literally loomed over most men, would keep all but the most stupid bleeding-heart codependents away. The majority of people would have enough sense of self-preservation not to make themselves so vulnerable as to offer this man charity. This man took, he did not receive. The gleam in his eye confirmed it; when they fixed on a subject, they hinted of the dark intelligence of a predator.

And those eyes were fixed on her now.

The realization made Claire's stomach drop. Quickly, she averted her gaze and turned back to the clerk.

"Thank you very much." The clerk slapped the credit card and receipt in front of her on the counter—all without her eyes even vaguely turning in Claire's direction.

Nervously Claire took up the pen and scrawled her name. She didn't dare turn to look at the man again. Somehow by madness or instinct, she was convinced he knew she was the one from ZOE. The clerk put the receipt into the bag and handed it to her. Claire took it, suddenly paralyzed by the need for fight or flight.

She had agreed to this meeting in order to call this man's bluff. She'd had plans of threatening him with the authorities if he should so much as even look at any more mercenary magazines. All her grand designs to keep ZOE members out of trouble now seemed incredibly naive. This man was way out of her sphere. He was a kind of creature she had no capacity to deal with, nor any desire to develop such a capacity. Just by his appearance, he frightened her; the notion that he might even be a killer made her hand shake on the bag handle. She'd once been told that the relationship of killer and victim was in some ways the most intimate one in nature. By the red hot siren going off in her mind, she prayed she'd never, ever know such intimacy.

She numbly took the shopping bag and began to trace a path through the cosmetic counters toward the Lexington Avenue door. It was almost painful fighting the urge to look behind her. Animal instinct raged. "Never turn your back on the enemy," it said, but she was forced to. She had to leave the store without an encounter, without incident. Then she promised herself she was going home to call Phyllis and tell every member of ZOE who would listen to her that they were out of their minds if they wanted to have dealings with the kind of man she'd seen today.

"Ma'am. Ma'am." The clerk's now-familiar voice scratched like fingernails on the chalkboard of her subconscious.

Automatically, she turned around.

"You forgot your American Express card, ma'am." The clerk dangled Claire's charge card between the talons of her thickly wrapped and polished nails.

"Oh. Thank you." Claire took the card and shoved it back into her purse, not bothering with the wallet. Then, because she was so anxiety-ridden, she lost a moment's control. Her gaze lifted and she glanced over to where the man had stood. He was no longer there.

Maybe he'd never been there. Maybe he was just a figment of her imagination and terror.

She clutched the cosmetic bag and turned for the Lexington exit.

And there he was, this time leaning indolently against the Guerlain counter. The spider was back on the Twinkie.

She knew only one thing when his gaze pinned her. If she turned away, he would know she was afraid. The fear would translate into meaning, and if he'd come as a gun for hire, he'd know she was the one he'd come to meet. So she had two choices: either confront him, or walk past him.

To the left and right, she could see he was attracting attention from security. One guard left the escalator detail and was talking animatedly into a walkie-talkie. In a minute the guy would be surrounded by security and doubtlessly questioned about his desire to shop at Bloomingdale's. Then she'd be home free.

She began to walk toward the revolving brass doors. All the while, she felt the man's stare cut into her like an invisible laser.

It was not in her best interest to look at him. She knew this, but sometimes self-defensive actions went beyond mere will. A stare was like a subconscious tap on the shoulder; one was compelled to look up.

She looked at him. His gaze was like a cosmic force, and once it took, it held. She couldn't look away. Though she was still walking toward the Lexington Avenue exit at Bloomingdale's, the man's eyes seemed to take her to another world entirely. It was a world of darkness and fear. The world that existed inside herself ever since Zoe's body had been found in the ditch in Des Allemands.

She tore her gaze away. Her hand touched the brass rail of the revolving door, and from the corner of her eye she could see him push away from the counter.

She'd caught his attention and, oh, God, he was going to follow her.

Her breath stopped in her chest. The trapped air was like a lead weight bearing down on her rib cage. Fear left the metallic taste of blood in her mouth. She couldn't let him follow her. No one on the streets would help her. He might drag her down into an empty subway stair or he might just try to talk to her until she found her way home. Then he'd know where she lived.

But maybe this wasn't even the guy, she thought wildly. Maybe she was just being hysterical and she'd caught the attention of some homeless wino who was going to hit her up for some spare change. Maybe. Maybe.

She felt a hand on her shoulder. Half groaning, half screaming, she spun around and faced him, all the while backing into the revolving door.

"Can we help you, sir? Have you something particular you're shopping for today, sir?"

She watched in mute relief as two security men flanked the guy, clearly catching him off guard. The man hesitated and that was all Claire needed.

She drew back into the revolving door and nearly fell onto

the busy Lexington Avenue sidewalk. Running for a cab, she refused to look behind her until she was inside the back of the Checker. The cab doors locked, she stared out the back window as the vehicle drove away. Bloomingdale's black art deco marquee grew smaller and smaller as it drowned in the heavy throngs of Lexington Avenue shoppers. Beneath it, the revolving door still spun around and around. Empty.

It was then she saw the small drop of blood on her hand and realized she had bitten her lip.

## ❧ 7 ❧

"**H**e checks out." A guard with the name Robinson on his name tag passed the wallet with ID back to Jameson. Four other Bloomingdale's security guards loomed over the table, staring. Jameson felt like a paramecium on a wet-mount microscope slide.

"But let me warn you and your fellow agents, sir. If the FBI is going to use my store for surveillance, they should notify me first." Robinson gave Jameson a cursory glance, then made a note on his clipboard. "I've got a job to do, you know. You guys can't just set up a sting operation in my territory and think I'm not going to question any of the goings-on."

*Sting operation?* Jameson made no comment. He just nodded to Robinson and chewed on the inside of his cheek. He was still aggravated. So close; he could have almost touched that woman. And then Barney Fife had to show up and take him to the security station.

"I'm making a report, but you can be sure it will be confidential. None of this will leak out of my office . . . still, I have to record every incident." Robinson continued scribbling. Jameson, slouched in a metal folding chair, continued nodding. And the other security guards continued staring.

Hell, this was probably the most excitement these guys had

seen all year, Jameson thought as he shifted in the chair. It was as if these guys had never seen an FBI agent.

Robinson finally put down the clipboard and held out his hand. "You're free to go, Agent Jameson. Like I said, next time give me a little notice. We want to cooperate with the Bureau."

*We want to cooperate with the Bureau.* Jameson almost laughed. As if anyone had a choice.

He stood and shook Robinson's hand. There was no point in unduly pissing off a megalomaniac. He was just glad Robinson ran a security office at a department store instead of a third world country. "The Bureau really appreciates that, Mr. Robinson. Next time there's a *sting operation* in your store, you'll be the first to be notified."

Robinson nodded solemnly.

"I could use some information before I go. Can I see the receipts from the cash register down at the perfume counter?"

Robinson scrutinized him with an intense look. It was as if he were having trouble making up his mind whether to co-operate. Again, as if he had a choice, Jameson thought.

"All right. I suppose I can go along with that. Harold." Robinson turned to a young guard, one that barely had peach fuzz growing on his jaw. The kid had probably not finished his first semester at John Jay. "Take Agent Jameson downstairs and let him see the receipts. Then report back to me."

*Of course,* Jameson thought, swallowing his contempt with a grunt.

Robinson's walkie-talkie blared with static. A voice came over it. "We've got an incident in juniors, Chief. I think the kid's got a scarf shoved in her purse."

"I'll be right there." Robinson spoke into the walkie-talkie with the air of someone who was late to a Geneva summit.

"This won't take me a second, then I'll be out of your

hair," *Chief,* Jameson bit back. He then looked at the kid, Harold, who was to give him escort to the cash register.

But before they could clear out, Robinson stopped him. "One last thing, Agent Jameson." He gazed around at his men with a shifty, censorious glance. "I know the Bureau likes to keep these things under wraps, but can you tell us. Who were you watching downstairs? Was this chick some kind of a drug dealer or a con artist? What?"

Jameson opened his mouth, but he was at a loss how to explain to this jackass that he was on a non-mission. The incident was probably going to amount to nothing, as so much police and FBI work did. All he knew was that the dark-haired woman downstairs caught his attention, but whether it was the furtiveness of her glance or the strange, almost haunted expression in her eyes, he didn't know. She might not have been the one behind the ZOE ad at all. She might just have been a customer whom he nearly scared to death. Too, he knew himself well enough to realize he was enough of a hound dog to unconsciously zero-in on a woman just because he found her attractive. And yeah, he'd found that one downstairs real attractive with her abundant dark hair and that damned expression in her eyes that made him uncomfortable. But it wasn't possible to tell Robinson that without spending the rest of the day in interrogation.

"I guess you've caught us. We believe she's with the Cartagena cartel. Her boyfriend is Anuncio Estaban. Surely you've heard of him."

Robinson nodded. He was always nodding. Either in contemptuous disbelief or feigning some kind of fraternal crime-fighter bond. "A bad character, that one. I hear things on the street, you know. I hope you can bring him down."

"Thanks." Jameson grinned. He couldn't help it. He'd made the whole thing up. Anuncio Estaban was the Tulsa field office janitor. Besides, what the hell would the FBI be doing in Colombia anyway.

"Well, next time, just keep me informed."

"Will do." Jameson followed Harold out of the security office.

The American Express receipt was easy to find. There hadn't been a lot of Amex charges in the past hour and the cash register marked all transactions with the time. Jameson sent Harold back up to the security office to copy the receipt for him. Meanwhile, he hung around the perfume counter and flirted with the salesclerks. Their attitude had changed significantly after Harold opened up the register and announced that he was now working with the FBI. So much for Robinson's pledges of confidentiality.

Harold returned with the copy and Jameson caught the escalator to the store's basement subway platform. He'd thought about taking a cab back to the hotel, but the way he was dressed he figured there was more of a chance Robinson would become CEO of Federated Department Stores, Inc., than a cabbie would stop for him.

All during the subway ride, he stared at the Amex receipt. Claire Green was her name. With the card number, he'd know a lot more about her before the evening. He was probably sniffing up the wrong skirt, but there was always the tantalizing chance that this Claire Green was a lot more interesting than her name foretold.

The modem was already hooked up to his portable computer in his room. He plugged in the credit card number and sent it to the field office. Figuring it would be a while before he got an answer, he took a shower, pulled on a pair of boxer shorts, then rummaged through the little refrigerator neatly camouflaged in the bureau. The prices were astounding. Nonetheless, he took out a Heineken. Between gulps, he said the Pledge of Allegiance. That was the best he could do to pay homage to the host.

The fax machine began to hum and click. It spat out a

credit report from TRW. The Amex number was on it. The name was Claire Green. Her employer was listed as Fassbinder Hamilton. The address was Wall Street.

He'd bet the cost of one of those little-refrigerator Heinekens that she was an attorney. A Manhattan phone book was in the bedside drawer. He flipped it to the attorney section and found Claire Green. The address was the same as on her credit report. Her home number wasn't listed, and when he called directory assistance, they told him that she had an unpublished home phone number.

"Smart girl," he whispered when he hung up the phone.

He studied the credit report. There was nothing unusual on it. A few credit cards all paid up. A couple of black marks from collection agencies over what amounted to a hundred dollars. With a small amount in dispute, she probably was refusing to pay on principle. He was amused to see that both collectors were physicians. Even attorneys got screwed by the health care system.

The phone rang. Outside, the sun was just going down behind the Chrysler Building; below it, his room's window view of the air shaft was dark.

"This is Gunnarson. What did you find out today?"

Jameson cleared his throat. "Not much. No one from ZOE met me."

"Who's Claire Green?"

"Just an attorney shopping for perfume. She looked at me kind of strange while I was waiting. I figured I'd check her out."

Silence at the end of the receiver.

"You know something?" Jameson asked, lowering himself to the edge of the bed. A small muscle jumped in his jaw. He was a teeth grinder anytime something had him worried or intrigued. It drove his dentist crazy.

"The computer spat out something interesting. On a hunch, Wynn ran her name through VICAP—Violent Criminal Apprehension Program—Now that we have the capacity to look for patterns of serial killers, you can get all kinds of interesting connections. Wynn was right on the mark. The name Claire Green came up. It seems the Bureau and her are longtime friends. Her twin sister was murdered in New Orleans. The Bureau ran it, thinking it might match another killing. No tie-in was found though."

Jameson again thought of Claire Green's eyes. Now he knew what he saw in them. It was the same look in his own eyes when he was a kid and had to bury his best friend.

"You there, Jameson?"

"Yes, sir." He leaned over the bed and took out another Heineken.

"There's one other little noteworthy fact about this woman."

"Shoot." Jameson twisted off the top.

"Her twin's name was Zoe."

Jameson paused, then realized the beer was foaming over the bottle. "Shit." He grabbed a bath towel and mopped his wet boxers.

"I think it's clear what's going on, don't you?"

"Yeah. It's some kind of a gun for hire, all right." Jameson rubbed his jaw. The muscles hurt from grinding his teeth. "She must know who killed her sister."

"You need to find out more, Jameson. It doesn't all add up. According to our records, no one could ever find the guy who murdered Zoe Green. I could understand if they had someone and couldn't make it stick. It would be one thing then to go after him. But according to our files, there's nothing. Nothing."

"Maybe she knows more than we do."

"Check it out, Jameson. We'll see you in a few days."

"Yes, sir. If you get anything else, call me."

"Will do." The receiver clicked.

Jameson stared at his empty Heineken bottle. His gut instinct had told him something was different about that woman in Bloomingdale's, that Claire Green was doing more than just shopping for perfume, but it was almost disturbing having it so quickly confirmed. And that expression in her eyes bothered him even more now that he recognized it. It was too close to home.

"Claire Green, what are you up to?" he whispered, staring down at her TRW credit report. He fingered the American Express receipt and said, "I guess you give me no choice but to find out."

## ❧ 8 ❧

The old mahogany bookcases had been built into the mansion to hold his father's medical library, but when Father died, Everard had them converted into showcases. With beveled glass doors and interior spotlights, he was now able to display a lifetime of his personal mementos from his baby cap hand-crocheted for him by his "mammy" to the culmination of his social triumphs, his Rex costume.

He threw on the lights in the cases. The king was there. Rex, a life-size mannequin under glass, wearing his white satin doublet and breeches. The king's cape took the full length of four bookcases; it was a year in the making with gold sequins and rhinestones hand-sewn into thousands of fleurs-de-lis. Everard had even managed to acquire his pages' costumes, and now they were on display also, two little white satin doublets and caps on forms he'd bought from the children's department at Krauss.

Rex, King of Carnival, 1988. His triumph. His pinnacle. Precisely at noon on that exalted Mardi Gras, the Rex float had parked by the 555 Association on Canal Street, where all the parades ran. The mayor of New Orleans waited at the podium for him. Everard was handed the keys to the city, and as Rex he'd waved his golden scepter over the masses and proclaimed his magnificent benevolence on this Shrove Tuesday. Then, after the masked ball, at the magic hour of midnight, he drank with the King of Comus and personally signaled the end of carnival.

Everard pressed closer to the costume displayed in the cases. His father couldn't have done it. Those stodgy old medical books hadn't made Dr. Laborde a king. *Rex*. It had taken his son to do it. The one and only with the limp and the IQ that was too incompetent to get the boy into medical school.

He took a deep, relaxing breath and moved to the next display case. The bookshelves hadn't been removed from this one but lighting had been added. The unit housed a myriad of objects, all seemingly unrelated except for the brass plaque that had been tapped into the edge of the shelf. On the plaques were Roman numerals, one through ten, with room at the lower shelves to add more.

For more than a decade he'd been honored to reside as president of the 555 Association, the venerable old-line lunch club that had long ago snubbed his father. It was another triumph that Everard only wished Dr. Laborde had lived to see. The case housed nine years of mementos at the 555. There were party favors, invitations, elaborate masks. Then, at various numerals, an incongruous object was thrown in—at the brass plaque number two was a diamond wedding ring, at five, a set of janitor's keys, at six, a pair of ladies red Ferragamo flats. Everard was proud that in the five years the shoes had been in the case, their distinctive grosgrain ribbon bows still were dust free.

He looked down at the day's newspaper in his hand. Today, the *Times-Picayune* read in a small article at the bottom: BODY FOUND, TEN-YEAR MURDER UNSOLVED.

He placed the newspaper aside and went to his desk. He removed a large blue velvet jeweler's presentation box. If it were from Harry Winston's, it might have held an emerald necklace, but now Everard used it. And he was as delighted with the contents as if it had held jewels.

Inside were ten artistically painted Press-on Nails, each painted with almost microscopic carnival masks and the Mardi Gras colors of green, gold, and purple. Going on ten years ago, they'd been cleaned of their owner's residue—the brown and rotting cuticle bed where they'd been torn off their wearer—then they'd been affixed to the velvet lining of the case with Krazy Glue.

After that, Everard had put them away. There was no point in displaying them until the girl was found. Things had to be neat and orderly in his cases. Until there was a murder victim, there could be no murder and therefore nothing to display.

Late last night they'd discovered the girl's head—that is, at least her skull that now bore teeth marks from being mauled by alligators. Everard remembered the waitress because she had been the first. Her death had been kind of an intentional accident. He'd read that people like him never meant to hurt anyone, but at some point in time the impulse takes over, the dread deed occurs. Afterward there comes panic—he remembered it well: the frenzied clean-up, the drive out Interstate Ten to the swampy exit at Ruddock. He'd found out later that the place on the interstate where he'd tossed the woman over was referred to by the police as The Dump. Apparently Everard hadn't been the only one to think of the isolated stretch of highway over the Louisiana swamps. Dead people were found there all the time, but his woman, his waitress who had referred to him as "baby" when he sat down at her table, and who had given him an extra helping of red beans, hadn't been found for over nine years.

And now he didn't panic anymore in the aftermath. He planned things.

Like placing the velvet jewelers box with the ten painted nails in his memento case on the date his girl was found.

He added the festively adorned artificial nails to his souvenirs, to the back of the space delineated by the number one plaque. He stood back and surveyed it. Pleased, he eagerly whipped his pinpoint oxford shirt-sleeve over the brass plaque that said number ten.

The place was empty of souvenirs.

But after Mardi Gras it would be full.


Old Fassbinder's office was much like one would expect from a name partner in a prominent Wall Street law firm. It took up nearly the entire penthouse of the Armestead Building; the views across the bay to the Statue of Liberty and Staten Island were legendary. Antique walnut paneling complemented the rich bottle-green leather of the chairs. It was said that Fassbinder's desk was the exact one that Roosevelt used in his law practice before he made the step up to the White House.

Claire had not been called into Fassbinder's office much. Lowly associates didn't mingle with the letterhead partners, so when the request came that Mr. Fassbinder wanted to see her, her blood pressure rose. Life had been stressful enough with ZOE's antics and the ill-fated trip to Bloomingdale's last Saturday. Now all she needed was a criticism of her work by Fassbinder himself to push her over the edge.

The secretary gave her escort; Claire's heart pounded in her chest. The woman opened the door to the magnificent enclave and Fassbinder rose from his seat. He nodded to the chair opposite the famous desk. Claire took it, all the while wondering if when she was a seventy-year-old lawyer, would she possess such a stunning place of work as this office was. There had been a time when she thought so. At least, before this unexpected summons.

"I've heard a lot of things about you, Ms. Green."

Claire tried to smile. She was too nervous to speak. The idea of having job difficulties terrified her. Her whole life was work. She was still a young woman, perhaps she should have had a boyfriend to take her mind off things, but men were difficult for her. Her sister had been raped and murdered. The killer seemed to be Every Man. Even in law school, dating had been a high hurdle for her to manage, and that was when she'd had time. Now Fassbinder Hamilton was her world. There was Fassbinder, and then there was nothing, except memories of Zoe and pain.

The secretary quietly placed an exquisite Limoges cup full of steaming coffee next to Claire on the desk. The woman laid out the cream and sugar, then exited in the discreet manner of a nineteenth-century housemaid.

"Your work on Allegra v. Weddell has been brought to my attention." Fassbinder flipped open a file. His liver-spotted hands shook as he read.

Claire couldn't fathom what this was about. Allegra v. Weddell was, in her opinion, one of her finest pieces of work. The logic and wording of the opinion had been flawless. But maybe it hadn't been.

Fassbinder closed the file. He stared at her from across the desk. He was the typical old lawyer. Spectacles, silver hair, dark suit. But, of course, the suit was custom-made in Bond Street, and it was rumored that his jewelry account at Van Cleef and Arpels went a tad richer than the gifts he gave his wife. Even past seventy, old Fassbinder apparently had a little on the side.

"I was quite pleased with the outcome of Allegra. Has a problem surfaced that I'm not aware of?" Claire wanted to nonchalantly reach for the coffee, but she knew her hands would tremble. If she spilled it on the priceless Oriental, she'd kill herself.

"The work on Allegra was superb. Johnson, Ms. Duncan, and Mr. Klein have all recommended to me that we speed up your partnership track. And I'm inclined to agree with them." Fassbinder smiled.

Claire's drumming heart slowed to a near stop. She hadn't even thought the news would be good, let alone this good. She stared at him, speechless.

"You're a very good attorney, Ms. Green. I want everyone here at Fassbinder Hamilton to know that we appreciate good work, and reward it accordingly. Congratulations."

"Thank you, sir." Lame words if there ever were ones, but she could think of nothing else to say. The thrill of her recognized accomplishment was suddenly choked by the sickening realization of what ZOE's behavior could cost her.

Yet, as devoted as she was to it, her job wasn't everything. There was still her sister and the killer who probably even now roamed free. She wasn't ready to abandon ZOE, as much as the organization threatened her career, because the real Zoe hadn't found her own murderer. Justice hadn't been even a two-bit player in Zoe's death, and the void that it left in its absence was like an abyss in her soul, so deep and black, she wondered if she could ever climb out of it.

She didn't want to abandon ZOE, but the name Halbert Washington circled in her subconscious like a vulture, ready to feast on the carrion of her ruined career.

"I—I think it may be a bad time to mention this, sir—" Claire met Fassbinder's gaze, and she wondered if the guilt showed in her eyes. "You see, I'm afraid to mention it, but I've been having personal problems and—well, if the firm is as pleased with my work as you say it is, I've been batting around the idea of taking a short leave of absence. I believe I need to return home to New Orleans for a while. I've got to put some things to rest down there. I wouldn't even have asked except that if you're that pleased with the outcome of Allegra, then it occurred to me—"

"Of course. After all the hard work you've put in here, what you need, Ms. Green, is a vacation," Fassbinder interjected. "Your monthly billing hours are phenomenal. We don't want you to burn out before you make partner. Take as much time as you need. We'll be here when you return."

Claire could see he was finished with her. She stood and shook his hand. "Thank you, sir. Thank you. I'll make up for lost time when I return. I promise."

"You've already earned the time. Go and take a break. We'll look for your refreshed self back here in a few weeks."

"Thank you, sir. Thank you so much."

Promptly on cue, as if the woman had had the intercom on, the secretary appeared at the door and escorted Claire out of the suite. Claire took the elevator down to fifty and nearly collapsed at her desk. The roller coaster on her nerves was unbearable.

She picked up the phone. The idea of going home had been rather nebulous until now. She didn't know what she would accomplish in New Orleans, but for some reason her instincts were guiding her there. That was where she had to settle things. Before she returned to New York, she had to make up her mind to abandon the organization ZOE and put herself fully into her work. The only way to do that was to make a pilgrimage back home. She could maybe make one last stab in the dark at finding Zoe's killer herself, and if she could just settle the issue within her heart, she knew she could put it behind her. Better yet, she could turn away from the awful temptation of seeking justice by taking her turn on the lottery.

"Mom?" she said when the party on the other line picked up.

"Claire? How are you, darling?"

"Hey, Mom. I'm doing great." Claire kicked off her pumps and put her feet on her desk. "How's Dad?"

"Oh, he's well. You remember that little prostate anxiety we had, but now that everything's all right, he's as mean as a bear being cooped up in the house until the incision heals."

"That's just like him. Give him a hug for me, will you?"

"I will, darling."

Claire paused. She nibbled on her lower lip, unsure how to bring up the next subject. "Mom? You know . . . I was thinking about coming home for the holidays. We could all take in some of the Hanukkah festivities at Touro Synagogue, do some shopping in the Quarter."

"That—would be lovely, honey."

The hesitancy in her mother's voice cut her to the quick, but, of course, it was Claire's fault. Claire had put it there. The three of them had lived with Zoe's pain for five years, but only Claire had lived with the face. Her parents saw Zoe when they saw her. When she couldn't take haunting her parents anymore, Claire left New Orleans for good, exiling Zoe's ghost to an eighty-hour week at Fassbinder and an apartment on 86th Street. She never went home again. There was always an excuse, even on holidays. Zoe's killer was free, but Claire was in prison, jailed by her looks, her fear, her feelings.

"I'm going to stay at a friend's house," Claire fibbed. "They're going out of town and I can take care of the place—"

"Oh, but you've got to stay with us—"

"No, Mom. The firm gave me time off for good behavior, so I might be down there a whole month. I don't want to get in the way. You two are settled in the new place. You don't have room for a boarder. But we'll see lots of each other. Besides, this way I get a whole place to myself. I can come and go as I please without disturbing you and Dad. I'd prefer it this way."

"If you insist, honey."

A tear slipped down Claire's cheek. Her mother's disappointment was barely hidden, and Claire couldn't blame her. It wasn't easy having twins. For the past five years, one daughter was dead and other in permanent self-exile. But now that was going to change. Claire couldn't ever be an imitation of Zoe, and she was sick of thinking of herself as nothing more than a live, walking-around ghost.

"I love you, Mom. I'll call you when the arrangements are finished."

"I love you too, sweetheart."

A silence permeated the phone line. Claire heard her mother sniff.

"You know we do love you. You're our darling little girl and you always will be."

"I know." Claire's own voice began to tremble, but for her mother's sake, she didn't dare let on that she'd been crying too. Things were rough enough.

"You two were so different. Night and day. Both so unique. You're not anything like Zoe . . ." Her mother lost her voice and finally wept in earnest.

Guilt ran through Claire's body like an electric shock. Silent tears streamed down her cheeks, but she forced herself to show a strong front. "Mom, we're going to get over this." She brushed the back of her hand across her face. "It's just going to take time, and now we've got time. I'm coming home. Someday Zoe won't seem so close."

"I know. I know. But it seems like only yesterday I was dressing you both in those darling pink smocked dresses and showing you off at my mah-jongg club. Could that have been twenty years ago? It couldn't have been. It just couldn't have been."

"I love you, Mom. I'll see you in a few days."

"Oh, but you *should* stay with us . . ."

"No, it's okay. Really. I might have work to do and I need my own space to do it." Claire drew her feet off the desk and straightened in her chair. Already she was thinking ahead. She'd have to drum up an apartment in a hurry. Thank God it wasn't Mardi Gras season yet, or she'd be sunk. "I just want you to know that I love you, Mom." She hesitated, unsure how much should remain unspoken. "Sometimes, when I'm half asleep in the morning, I look in the bathroom mirror and . . . and . . . well, there she is."

"Oh, my darling. How awful . . ." Her mother continued to cry.

"I'll see you soon, Mom. Kiss Daddy for me."

"I will." Her mother quietly hung up the phone.

Claire dabbed her eyes with a Kleenex, cursing the pathetic run of mascara. It was definitely the way to tell an office full of people you've been crying. To calm down, she read a couple of memos and wrote a few of her own to notify office workers of her absence. The secretaries started laughing out in their cubicles. They were packing away their pumps and tying on their tennis shoes. It was time to go home.

She put a couple of files into her briefcase. Work had slowed with the holidays. They wouldn't miss her tomorrow. If she could line up an apartment for a short-term lease, she hoped to be in New Orleans in two days.

She sauntered down the hall and out into the reception area. Suzi, the receptionist, was still answering phones. The woman sat amid a polished expanse of *nero marquina* marble flooring. Behind her, the letters spelling Fassbinder, Hamilton, Villere, Roberson, Grimsi, and Smith were blocked out in gold leaf.

"I'm taking a few days off. Just put all my calls through to Pam. She'll man the fort while I'm away."

"Ms. Green, may I speak with you for a second?" Suzi discreetly put her hand over her mouth and eyeballed the seating area behind Claire. "Do you know anything about Mr. Hamilton having an appointment with someone from Babcock and Williams?"

Claire glanced at her message box, shaking her head, "Everyone knows Mr. Hamilton goes to the Caymans this time of year. How could someone at Babcock schedule—"

"Well, that's what I thought. But this gentleman's been waiting for over an hour and he keeps insisting that Mr. Hamilton's going to show up for his appointment." Suzi stole another covert glance behind Claire. The surprise on her face made Claire turn around.

The seating group was empty. In fact the entire reception area was devoid of persons except the receptionist and herself.

"There's nobody in here." Claire looked at Suzi.

Suzi shrugged. "Well, if that isn't the darnedest thing. The man was insistent Mr. Hamilton was coming up to meet him. I thought that was doubtful, seeing the way this guy was dressed. We're not talking Giorgio Armani here, we're talking street chic, hard-core street chic. So I called Mr. Hamilton's secretary and she said he'd just phoned in; he was still in the Caymans. So she called Babcock and Williams and they told me they didn't even have an attorney there by the name of Jameson. Now the guy's just up and left." Suzi threw up her hands. "No explanation, no nothing."

Claire gazed around the reception area. It was definitely empty. From outside the thick glass doors she saw the elevator gauge slowly clock downward.

"Oh, maybe the guy was some kind of Salvation Army–type looking for a handout. Or maybe he was a messenger from Babcock and realized he'd gone to the wrong office. You know how men can be sometimes. They've realized they've made a mistake and it's like hit and run. They don't want to stick around for the embarrassment." Claire waved her fingers. "Bye. I'll call with the number where I'm at as soon as I have it."

"Have a good vacation, Ms. Green." Suzi smiled and punched one of the lit buttons on her switchboard. "Fassbinder Hamilton."

Claire took the elevator down from fifty, the whole time drumming her fingers on her briefcase. She remembered one of her high school chums had a mother who was a real estate agent. Hale was the name. Hale Realty. She'd have to call the woman tonight and see if she could find her a furnished place to rent for a couple of weeks.

Pulling on her black wool melton overcoat, she nearly ran out of the lobby and down into the subway station. Her watch said 5:12. If she were lucky, she could catch the Number 3 express. She dropped the subway token into the slot and trotted down the crowded stairway, looking much like any other working woman in the throng of commuters.

Except for the man with the intense gaze who dropped a token in the slot and sauntered through the turnstyle, his gaze riveted to her back.

It was after seven by the time Claire arrived at the prewar apartment building where she lived. Riverside Park was dark, but beneath the few and scattered lights she saw people still out walking their dogs. The crackheads and prostitutes rarely came out before eleven.

A strange, incautious, almost hopeful feeling overcame her while she had sat on the subway and thought about her return to New Orleans. She was so giddy, she'd decided to get off at 72nd Street and walk to Zabar's. There she bought fresh bagels for breakfast, pasta salad for dinner, and their signature dessert, a huge chocolate cream-filled profiterole. She wasn't going to regret one minute of the feast.

Julio, the superintendent who had some kind of financial arrangement with the building's owner consisting of bottles of Thunderbird per hour, was typically not on his watch in the lobby. Claire let herself through the iron-barred outer door with her key and stepped into the vestibule to check her mail. Behind her, a laughing couple was buzzed into the building. They let several people in; by the bottles in all their hands, the group was making a pilgrimage to an upstairs party.

The mail consisted of nothing but a dusty old ConEd bill. The deflated feeling of looking into an empty mailbox every day was why she rarely checked it, and now she was sorry she did. The near ebullience of her trip Zabar's seemed once again overshadowed by the mundane—by utility bills, by crimes that were never solved because the real-life fact was that lots of crimes were never solved.

She stuffed the bill into her Zabar's bag. Through the vestibule doors leading to the lobby she saw that the noisy group had caught the elevator. The place was deserted again.

If not for the fixture of the forlorn office chair in the corner that missed Julio like a little bench near the hearth missed Tiny Tim, no one would ever know there was supposed to be a night watchman.

At first the idea that she was not really alone was like a feather tickle at her subconscious—disturbing but not overly confrontational. She might have never looked behind her at all if not for the baby-fine hair that inexplicably rose on the back of her neck. If she'd been a dog, her hackles would have been up.

Slowly, the Zabar's bag pathetically clutched in her hands, she turned around to face the iron exterior door. A sound emanated from her throat. It was a primeval kind of groan, the kind of wail animals make when they're cornered by a predator.

"Need help with those bags, ma'am?"

Claire gasped for breath. Unconsciously, she backed against the tarnished brass mailboxes. The man she'd seen in Bloomingdale's was in the vestibule with her, arms crossed while he casually leaned against the barred doors to the street. He'd cleaned up a bit since she'd seen him, but there was still that streetwise, feral edge to his demeanor. Being trapped with him in a vestibule sent a shot of hot adrenaline through her.

"How did you get in here?" she said, her voice trembling.

He raised one dark eyebrow.

She needn't have bothered to ask. He'd clearly come in with the group of revelers. Somehow, he'd followed her to the apartment, and now this crazy psycho gun for hire knew where she lived.

"What do you want?" she demanded, all the while looking behind him through the doors at the pedestrians on the sidewalk. She prayed one of the passersby would either see her distress or be an entering tenant and scare him off.

"We've met before, haven't we?" He pushed himself off the doors and took a step toward her.

If she could have squeezed herself through one of the mailbox doors, she would have. Her pounding heart suffocated her. Fear blinded her. She'd told Phyllis the ad in *High Risk* was only going to lead to trouble, but she'd had no idea she would be the one trapped in an apartment vestibule with the killer.

"Please," she whispered, nearly whimpering. "I have nothing you want. Go away."

He smiled and took another step closer.

She nearly hyperventilated.

But suddenly she heard a sharp *ding*. A man and a woman emerged from the elevator. They walked toward the vestibule intent upon their conversation. They were bickering and they obviously thought no one was around. Their harsh expletives would have been an embarrassment to Claire at any other time, but now the words were like poetry.

She fumbled for the lobby doors and shot out of the vestibule, nearly knocking the couple to the floor. The Zabar's bag had ripped from her wrist, and it now lay at the man's feet, along with her utility bill.

"Excuse me. I'm so sorry," she nearly cried out to the couple. The two must have seen the fear in her eyes, for their gazes turned toward the vestibule.

Through the lobby doors Claire saw the man pick up her Zabar's bag. He rummaged through it, finding the profiterole. His stare locked with hers, she swore he mouthed the words "See you later, Claire" before he took a ferocious bite out of the confection. Without another glance back, he then turned and casually exited onto the street, the barred doors locking behind him.

"Was he bothering you?" the woman asked, any self-consciousness over her fight with her lover forgotten. The woman even clutched at his arm, obviously also unnerved by the stranger in the vestibule of their apartment building.

"I'm all right. He came in with a crowd. I think he's homeless. Maybe he was hungry. I'll be all right. I just need to get home." With a shaking hand Claire punched the elevator button.

"Are you sure you're okay? Do you want Doug to maybe call the police?"

Claire blanched. It hadn't occurred to her that the police would be no help against that man if he should bother her again. But there was no way she could call them. After all, she'd indirectly summoned the man; she'd invited this mess. The police sure as hell wouldn't be able to clean things up without a full confession on her part.

Sickened, she punched the ninth floor and murmured some more vague reassurances and apologies. The doors closed and the couple disappeared. Claire's only comfort was that maybe her crisis had saved a marriage.

Once inside her apartment, she threw as many clothes as she could find into a bag and called Delta. There was a flight to New Orleans through Atlanta at 11:30 P.M. She'd take it. Her nerves peeled raw, she knocked the entire contents of her medicine cabinet into a carry-on case and stuffed in her red raincoat. She'd stay in a hotel in Baton Rouge if necessary, just to get away from town tonight. The creep downstairs now knew where she lived and she'd swear on the stand he uttered her name before he left the building. She had to get away from him, and quick. With any luck, by the time she returned to Manhattan, that guy would be back beneath his rock in Oklahoma.

Only there was one last string to tie up.

She picked up the phone and dialed Phyllis's number. She got her answering machine.

"Phyl, this is Claire. I'm heading down to New Orleans. The creep ZOE summoned showed up in my apartment building and I want to get lost for a while. Going home. Yeah, I guess it'll be good to think. I—I might actually go over my sister's case again, one more time." Hastily she added, "But I'm still not going to take my turn at the lottery, so, no thanks. And listen, Phyl,"—she didn't bother to hide the anger in her voice—"no more ads. This guy is scary. Make him go home and keep ZOE out of trouble. I'll call you when I'm back in New York." She replaced the receiver and grabbed her suitcases.

"Please, please, please, don't be downstairs," she whispered to herself as she threw the two bags out in the hall and shouldered her purse. If she could just hail a cab without a crisis, she'd be on her way.

Sometimes he wondered about himself. Jameson lay on the hotel bed, hands behind his head, while he stared at the white ceiling. The pasta salad container and the bagel bag sat empty next to the humming and beeping fax machine. There was a stack of faxes waiting, and still they were rolling in. Most of them came from the homicide section of the NOPD.

He'd almost enjoyed frightening her. There was a part of him that was really bothered by the thought, but then there was another part of him that had enjoyed the chase. He'd bet she didn't even know he'd waited for her in the law office. She'd breezed through the lobby, her glossy dark curls held at her neck with a large tortoiseshell clip, her fancy Mark Cross briefcase casually gripped in one hand, and she never noticed him sitting there. It was only when the receptionist began whispering to her that he'd decided to become scarce. There was no need for a scene at her place of work. And he knew that seeing him again was going to scare the shit out of her.

He grunted and rubbed the grid of his belly. There was something definitely sexual about playing this game of cat and mouse with a woman he was attracted to, and Claire Green was a damn fine-looking woman. Now he couldn't wait for the moment he got to throw open his badge . . . and really scare the shit out of her.

But she needed it, he thought, needed it bad. That kick in

the pants was just the thing to save her life. His brows came together in a frown. She had no business getting involved with nut cases like she believed him to be. As troubled as he was by his own behavior that evening, he at least was gainfully employed and trying to help out in this crappy world they all lived in. Skinheads that read *W.A.R.* were just the type to answer an ad like she'd put in *High Risk*. If Claire Green was afraid of him, how would she like to chum up to some white Aryan resister whose idea of a good time was frolicking around the Buchenwald memorial, spray-painting swastikas and singing Hitler Youth songs.

Oh, yeah, he thought, rolling over to grab the last piece of bagel. And the fact that Claire Green was Jewish ought to really make her a hit with the militia survivalist Jesus-told-me-to kill-that-guy crowd.

He got up and opened the little refrigerator. The cave of wonders. Every day, it seemed there was something different placed inside. Tonight it held St. Pauli Girl. Not bad. The field office couldn't even complain, because dinner had been free, graciously provided by the suspect.

He opened the beer and began to read the faxes. They were all the newspaper articles about Zoe Green's murder. Wynn also sent along a little note. *I told you so,* it read.

He grinned. Women. You had to love them.

He read for a couple of hours. The articles, the homicide notes, the coroner's report. There was nothing that stuck out in his mind, but that was because he wasn't familiar enough with the case. If he just kept digging, maybe something would start to nag at him. Maybe Wynn would find a red flag.

The phone rang. He pushed the button for the other line.

"Jameson?"

"Yeah, Jameson here." Liam sat up.

"This is Ray Gorgonzo of the NYPD. Remember? I was sent undercover to stake out the chick's apartment?"

"Yeah? Did she leave?"

"Sure did. About an hour ago. I'm calling from the airport. She just took a flight out of JFK to Atlanta. You'll have to track her from there."

"Will do. Hey, thanks a lot."

"Before she left, we also got a good tape of her phone message to a Phyllis Zuckermann. The stenographer's sending it to your computer right now."

"Great. Great."

"All in a night."

Liam hung up the phone. He went to his laptop and E-mailed the Tulsa office. Then he searched for the steno's transcript. He read it and rubbed his jaw. Whatever the hell the word "lottery" meant, he'd take a bet it was more than the blue-collar-Joe-wins-big-and-goes-to-Vegas-where-he-blows-it-in-five-days vein.

He leaned back on the bed. He'd have to notify the NOPD of her arrival. In a matter of five minutes the message from the Tulsa office arrived: Claire Green, American Express number 3756-800009-30019, booked through to New Orleans on Delta Flight 1086.

He unhooked the fax and picked up the phone.

The jet took off on time, a small miracle probably due to the late hour. Claire closed her eyes and leaned her head back against the pillow. The plane's interior was dim. The steward quietly handed out coffee and blankets.

The man who'd answered the ad had been nowhere to be seen when she'd hailed a cab. Her relief was stupendous. She'd gotten out of town in the nick of time. Without her around to bother with, he'd head home.

But still, she kept seeing him as she did that last time. Before he bit into the pastry. *See you later, Claire. Claire. Claire.* He'd said her name, she'd swear it. But it was impossible he'd know who she was. Impossible, she told herself as she snuggled deeper into the pillow. He'd been saying something else, and in her fear she just assumed it was her name.

Her mind dismissed the subject of that terrible man and she put her thoughts to going home. She'd have to hope Mrs. Hale could work a miracle for her in the morning and drum up a place to stay. Meanwhile, she decided to just check in at the Moisant Hilton for the night. The place was right by the airport and it was too late to go looking for a room downtown. The airport town of Kenner, Louisiana, wasn't glamorous, but it was usually pretty safe. And safety was something a woman with a murdered sister thought about a lot.

She let her thoughts spiral down into sleep. A nap would do her good even though true sleep always seemed to be elusive. There had been no real rest for her since Zoe's death.

Her mind drifted. As always, her last conscious thoughts were about *him*. Zoe's killer. He had no face, no body, no presence, but he was in her dreams every night, taunting her in the shadows. Every night before she fell asleep, she wondered who the man was, and where he was, and what he was doing that very second that she had to face her nightmares in another restless sleep.

He was in prison, she assured herself. Killers inevitably got locked up for some petty crime that had nothing to do with the true violence of their natures. He was rotting in a jail cell even as she jetted toward Atlanta. She might never identify him, but she took consolation that somewhere, somehow, the murderer was bad enough that he'd been put into prison for another crime, and they had thrown away the key.

## ❧ 9 ❧

**J.** Everard Laborde was considered a man of culture. He was an expert on both Strausses, Johann *and* Richard, and was proud to call himself the main contributor to the *L'Opéra Nouvelle-Orleans.* Without Everard, some in town said, there would be no opera. Every autumn, upon the opening of *Die Fledermaus,* Laborde was given the balcony overlooking stage left. From there he could view the opera company and patrons as if he were a king overlooking his kingdom.

Indeed, he had been king. He was Rex, 1988, King of Carnival, and in New Orleans, once crowned a king, always a king. Laborde's father, the physician, had he been alive, would have finally found no cause for criticism of his son then.

Thankfully, there were few in town who looked beyond the trappings of selective Mardi Gras krewes and memberships in exclusive white-men-only lunch clubs. Some said old-Knickerbocker-hyphenated New-York went the way of John Jacob Astor upon the sinking of the *Titanic,* but in New Orleans, the nineteenth century was alive and well, and a man like J. Everard Laborde thrived there.

True, if he were scrutinized more closely, some might say he was simply the failed son of a doctor, that he'd accomplished little in his fifty-four years except being able to parlay his father's status into a self-aggrandized lifestyle, that his character was about as solid as a contractor's signature on a guaranteed maximum bid.

The fact was that J. Everard Laborde excelled at pretention and façades, but that was the stuff of society's mountain and the tools of the social mountain climber. In 1988, Laborde conquered the metaphorical Everest when he became Rex. Now he was the sole decision maker on who could join or move up the ranks of the all-male 555 Association, New Orleans's oldest and most exclusive lunch club, because he was its president. In 1986, it was rumored that Herman Steinberg of Steinberg Auction House fame shot himself in the head not because he was disturbed over receipts but because he was disconsolate that he could not join the 555. Steinberg, natives tsked, couldn't seem to grasp that one didn't apply for membership at a lunch club, and most assuredly *not* the 555 Association. A man was invited to join if he was white, Christian, of a certain decent if not lavish income, and with an old New Orleans family name, one preferably tied to one of the rotting, abandoned plantations near the oil refineries out on the River Road—a place with an idyllic name like Rosemere or Reverie, which had usually held true for only one percent of its population.

Steinberg just didn't *get* it, they said. Mardi Gras balls, krewes, lunch clubs, and country clubs weren't about race or religion. They were about the right to associate with your own kind. They were about keeping the old ways alive. They were about upholding tradition. And their tradition was no blacks or Jews allowed, but it even went beyond that. After all, hadn't the 555 rejected some very prominent doctors and attorneys simply because they were not old-line enough? Certainly they had. Until a generation or two went by and the family established connections in New Orleans, there wasn't a prayer of admittance. So the naysayers were quietly told to keep their progressive Yankee opinions to themselves. Even the black mayor looked the other way because the bottom line was that there would be no Mardi Gras without the lunch clubs and the old-line krewes funding the parades. They were what kept the party alive and, most of all, free. So who was going to take it upon himself to be the one to ring the death knell of carnival, the single most important source of income for the city? Damn right, not the mayor. Or he'd never be mayor again.

So J. Everard Laborde lived his life on platitudes. He was virtually unemployed, living instead upon the family money in his father's old mansion on Exposition Boulevard, but that bothered no one, least of all himself. In the complex anthill of life, he was an appreciator, not a producer. He was put on earth to judge, not be judged. Pretentions, façades and lies, those were his talents. But his genius was in the lies.

He knew it every time the police overlooked another one of his "girls."


Claire stepped out into the warm sunshine. Behind her, the Hale Realty sign swung in the breeze. It was not yet Christmas, but the red and pink camellias were in full bloom and even the azalea buds were beginning to swell. The city of New Orleans was going to look like a garden club exhibit by Mardi Gras.

"Well, that should do it. Just remember that the apartment is on the second floor." A regal-looking older woman hanging in the doorway handed her a brass key chain. "Here are the keys. The security code will be your birth date. I've already told the landlord to program it in." She smiled. It was warm and genuine. "It's so nice to see you again, Claire. Now, you have Ellen's number. I know she'd want to see you. Maybe you girls could have lunch at Commander's."

Claire returned the smile. She actually was getting to the age where she enjoyed being called a girl. It had to be in the right context, of course, but being called a lady and a girl was part of being home. She hadn't realized how much she missed the South and home until then. "I'll give Ellen a call as soon as I'm settled. I can't wait to hear about her two boys."

Mary Hale smiled. The slow, gentle smile of a southern belle. "I'll tell her all about our meeting."

Claire waved, then looked down at the brass key ring in her hand. Here it was. Her final chance. She was going to flee the limbo she'd been living in and either find Zoe's killer, or say good-bye to Zoe forever. There was no longer any middle ground.

She tucked herself into a leased BMW convertible and took off for the Garden District. The rental was in an old pre–Civil War mansion that had been converted into upscale condos during the '80s oil boom. Mary said the owners spent every Christmas through Mardi Gras in Vail; she promised Claire would love it.

St. Charles Avenue was swagged in Christmas cheer. Even the old drab green streetcars were adorned with crimson bows. With the sun shining and the sky above a clean crystal blue, Claire couldn't hold back the rush of optimism. Maybe it was fated that she return here. She'd missed it. She'd really missed it.

Turning onto a side street past Prytania, she parked the BMW in front of Lockstein's grocery store, figuring she might as well pick up a few things before moving in. The store was just as she remembered it, nothing more than a glorified mom-and-pop grocery like the ones that were scattered on the Upper West Side, but Lockstein's was still special. In the era of rubber-stamp mammoth supermarkets, Lockstein's carried fresh-from-the-oven French bread, crawfish boiled daily, and the best ice cream in town. The founder's wife, now long dead, had been from Italy, and she introduced New Orleans to *gelato.* Already, Claire was longing for some pistachio and mocha, her favorites as a kid growing up around the corner.

She got her groceries and on the way out, just for the hell

of it, made a point of saying hello to old Mr. Lockstein. Like statuary, he still sat at the front door, eyeballing customers as if they were all stealing from him. Every now and then he'd get upset and start waving his cane and one of the young black bag boys would have to step over to him and calm him down. Mr. Lockstein had never been a very nice man; Claire remembered how she and Zoe and most of the kids were afraid of him. It took her years to understand that he'd originally come from Poland and that the numbers tattooed on his forearm had a lot to do with his suspicious, unfriendly disposition.

She stepped out into the breezy sunshine, not envying the cold and snow in New York. Clutching her two brown paper grocery bags, she peered up the street. All clear. Her parents' house was only two blocks away, and she prayed she didn't run into them. She wasn't really ready for that yet. She wanted to get settled into the apartment, maybe have a couple of nights to formulate her plans before her parents sat her down to a big meal and gave her the third degree about her visit. They would want quick answers and she had none. She didn't know what she was doing, nor had she decided how much she was going to tell them about her true reason for coming home.

She pulled the BMW out of the parking lot. In the rearview mirror she caught a glimpse of an ancient run-down house that sat next to the Gates of Prayer cemetery. The neglected house was decrepit and ready to fall over. The gray, ramshackle weatherboards sported not one flake of paint, and the dogs were still barking. Claire never knew who lived there, but there were always dogs barking. The hermit either loved dogs, or ate them, and the neighborhood kids passed around a lot of stories about him come Halloween.

The cemetery was to her left as she turned onto Prytania. It was strange how it felt to be home; to see the old sights that had held one memory and explanation when she was a child, and find them evolved into another memory and explanation with adulthood. The old Jewish cemetery she was passing was like that. She used to be terrified of it. All the rows of crumbling Stars of David, all the weeds that cracked the mortar, sometimes giving daylight peeks into the inside of the crypt, was usually too much for Claire's childish imagination. She could remember telling her mother that she would go to the grocery with her only if they walked on the other side of Prytania so as not to see the cemetery. On Halloween the neighborhood kids toilet-papered the crepe myrtles that grew around the graveyard's perimeter; in other years she could remember the outrage and fear whenever vandals spray-painted the usual swastikas across the gates. There were so many reasons to be afraid of the cemetery, but Claire was no longer afraid. It was Zoe's home now. Claire wasn't up to a visit yet, but as she passed the Gates of Prayer in her car, she felt a tenderness toward the place she could never have felt as a child. She missed Zoe.

The old mansion was on Seventh Street, an Italianate villa of some ten thousand square feet. Surrounding it was the New Orleans clichéd iron fence, but this one had posts that were cast in the shape of grapevines, giving the property an added richness and uniqueness.

Claire drove through the circular drive and up to the front of the building. She parked the BMW behind the house, where three other cars were parked. Lifting out her bags of groceries, she went around to the front and unlocked the door.

The foyer was spectacular. Painted cherubs floated on the cloud-strewn ceiling, floor-to-ceiling gilt mirrors lined the piers while intricate plasterwork graced the curving mahogany staircase. Through the doors that had once led into the ubiquitous double parlor a brass plate now signified that it was the entrance to Apartment One. She was in Three.

Above, the staircase hinted at further marvels. She climbed the stairs with her grocery bags, acutely reminded of the walkup she'd had in a brownstone on Riverside Drive while she was finishing law school. It was going to take a day or two to get used to it again. Sixteen-foot ceilings required a lot of stairs.

Number Three was at the end of a light, airy passageway near the old servants stair, where she spied an elevator, the kind with the iron gate like she had in her apartment in New York. It just might come in handy, she thought as she heaved the grocery bags to the floor and fumbled for the brass key ring.

She got the door open and dragged the bags inside. The apartment was more than even Mrs. Hale said it was. The main room had fourteen-foot ceilings, plaster medallions, and French doors that led to a veranda shaded by the branches of an enormous live oak. The furnishings, a tasteful mixture of antiques and plush upholstered pieces, looked liked they were right from the pages of *Architectural Digest*. A comfortable master bedroom suite done in gold damask and taupe linen completed the picture. Claire was reminded of the luxury flats she'd seen in Paris during her stay there the summer of her senior year. Those places had always had a balcony, sometimes ones that overlooked the Tuileries or Montmartre, just as this one overlooked the ancient gnarled oak and the brick courtyard. The ultimate Parisian apartment was rich but small, a place big enough for only a couple. A place designed for romance. Just like the apartment Claire was in now.

She put the groceries away in the tiny stainless steel and granite kitchenette, poured herself a diet Coke, and plopped onto the down-filled cushions of the couch. It was time for strategy. All through her plane trip she'd come to the conclusion that she had to begin at the end.

From her briefcase she extracted a scarf-wrapped bundle. She'd given Zoe the Chanel scarf herself. Her first year at Barnard, Claire had moonlighted at Bergdorf Goodman just to have a taste of the good life, and she was able to bring home treasures she might never have been able to afford otherwise.

The silk knot was tight, twisted by tears and time, but Claire managed to loosen it. A burgundy leather volume landed in her lap, pages flapping. It was Zoe's Filofax. Zoe had always been meticulous about recording her schedule as if she were some kind of society matron who had to make sure she could squeeze in one more charity ball.

But her record-keeping efforts hadn't paid off in the end. The police had no luck at all with the information registered there, and, after a year's time, the family had petitioned for the return of Zoe's belongings confiscated as evidence. Claire still remembered the brown, crumpled Schwegmann Supermarket bag that the policeman handed over to her mother. Inside was the Filofax, a Coach briefcase, empty, stiff from laying in a garbage can in the rain for three weeks before someone found it, and a pair of small stud diamond earrings the medical examiner had required removed during the autopsy. That was it. Zoe's clothes were in ruins and kept in evidence. Her shoes were never found. Her grandmother's things had been delivered the same way. Unceremoniously, in a crumpled grocery bag. The family had been leaving the hospital, ready to head to the funeral home, when one of the nurses walked up and handed Claire her grandmother's belongings all balled up in a cast-off brown paper bag. Claire wondered how most people would react if they knew how their real end would come. The idea certainly hadn't done much for her.

She sipped the diet Coke and flipped through the Filofax and the handwritten pages she knew so well. Inside was every trip Zoe took to have her hair cut and dyed blonder than maybe suited her, every visit to her manicurist, her leg waxer. But by late in the year there were notations that began to supersede the recording of parties and teas and lunches with her friends. Around September, Zoe had decided to look for a job.

Work was a rather foreign thing to Zoe, but the oasis of her social aspirations was beginning to run dry. She had had no steady boyfriend that might marry her into the New Orleans circle she so admired, nor was she successful at insinuating herself into it. Her old high school friends were still around, but the social glue of school came apart in the real world. Zoe's girlfriends now spent their days at the Town and Country Club in Old Metairie; no longer did they giggle with Zoe by her locker, or whine to their fathers because the Krewe of Romus wouldn't let Zoe Green be a maid because she was a Jew. Let her join Bacchus or Endymion, they were told, that's where the Jews belonged, with the other rich doctors and lawyers. But Zoe's father was a poor schoolteacher. Bacchus and Endymion were as out of reach for Daniel Hezekiah Green as the Mystick Krewe of Romus was for his daughter.

So while her sister Claire went off to finish at Barnard, Zoe looked for a job.

Claire felt the old sickness crawl through her insides. The pages were filled with notes about outfits Zoe wanted to wear that day, her shopping trips to Canal Place to buy pantyhose or scarves, her exclamations over certain men she found attractive at charity functions in the Garden District.

Then, promptly after March 15, the notes stopped. Zoe was dead. The pages continued, though, and Claire didn't know what hurt the most, seeing the blank pages that should have been filled with all of Zoe's appointments, or seeing the few appointments that had been scribbled in for the future, appointments never kept.

Claire spent five minutes just going through the month of March. Still, she turned again and again to the fifteenth. That was the important day. The day Zoe disappeared. She wasn't found until five days later.

Claire forced herself to go through the routine again. With pad and paper, she wrote and rewrote the notations of Zoe's last day.

> 8:15—Café du Monde with Erica (Rex). DKNY handbag, Raspberry boucle suit (don't eat any beignets!!!)
> 9:45—Royal Street—find gift for Mrs. Ware for hostessing Zoo-to-Do. (Romus)
> 11:30—lunch with mama. (Talk her into new haircut)
> 3:00—interview, admin. assist., 555 Association
> 6:00—cocktails, March of Dimes, Audubon Place (Rex)

Biting back tears, Claire wrote down all the places Zoe had visited that day. Those who knew her said she'd never made the party on Audubon Place; that was certainly unusual. Audubon Place was the one of the most prestigious neighborhoods in the city, and it was rare to be invited to a fundraiser at one of the mansions. Zoe wouldn't have missed it if she hadn't had to. She was so tied into the idea of being one of the in crowd, she'd even remarked in parenthesis who was in what Mardi Gras krewe.

It was all so stupid, Claire thought, the idea of Mardi Gras and krewes and lunch clubs. Who was in and who was out should be the realm of Hollywood and Best Dressed Lists, and didn't belong in the twentieth century. But it still remained in the banana republic of New Orleans. The social heirarchy of the town was nothing but meaningless drivel, no one cared who was who in New Orleans outside New Orleans, but there was no explaining that to an old-line New Orleanian or Zoe. Her sister had caught WASP fever. Now Claire realized that to rub elbows with shallow, inbred southerners and talk about whose daddy was whose must have been one hell of a triumph for a Jewish girl who'd been left out of most of her high school friends' debuts because *her* daddy had been nobody, and a Jewish nobody at that. To Claire, Zoe's aspirations had always seemed rather trite and diminutive, but her own heart hadn't been broken like Zoe's every time the expected invitation hadn't come. To be a social butterfly was a tiny wish, especially for a dead girl, and now Claire burned with rage when she thought about Zoe's dreams that hadn't come true.

She looked down and found herself writing a whole line of fives. The 555 Association was down on Canal Street. It was the oldest lunch club, older than the Boston Club, older than the Pickwick. They were such an exclusive bunch that they used to say if the 555 gave a party, they'd be happy if *nobody* came. Rex, King of Carnival, was crowned every Mardi Gras morning in front of the 555. The grandstands on that part of Canal Street were all Wonder Bread, stuffed to the breaking point with debs, mothers of debs, grandparents of debs. The blacks from Rampart Street and the micropockets of dazed tourists from Iowa were down on the pavement below, desperately trying to catch beads from the krewe floats, but it was useless. The beads all went to the bleachers, because the krewe floats were all manned by brothers of debs, fathers of debs, and prospective grooms of debs.

*55555555555555555*

The interview at the 555 was the last time Zoe had been seen alive. The police interrogated the club's administration. Zoe had been one of five applicants for the job. Answering phones, light typing, dressing well, were the only real qualifications, and her education was more than adequate for that. She had been interviewed first by the president's secretary, and then the president had had a closed-door interview with her. She had left then, the police were told, but she'd been the top prospect. Back at home there was even a message later in the day left by the president's secretary that she had gotten the job.

She would have loved that job too, Claire thought, still

fighting back tears and writing fives. Zoe would have been as close to the perimeter of the illustrious circle as she might have ever gotten, and Claire desperately wished her sister had at least known she'd gotten the job—it would have made her day—but Zoe had never returned to change for the Audubon Place soiree. She was never seen again until the deer hunters had come upon a drainage ditch in Des Allemands and blanched at the sight of what floated in there.

555 . . .

To begin at the end, Claire knew that somehow she would have to start at the lunch club. She only hoped they'd let her in to talk to someone.

## ❧ 10 ❧

It was ladies' night at the 555.

Laborde loved ladies' night. He sat at the president's table, flanked by his vice president and chairman, and watched the dinner guests with all the auspices of the host. Members were always more animated on this night; the fact never failed to amuse him. As the head of the organization, Laborde was often asked how the association justified excluding women—especially the members' wives. The answer was always that the men wanted to be free to release a rousing expletive in the dining room if the notion arose, and how could that be allowed if the men had to restrain themselves in the presence of ladies? The very idea of it!

But, of course, the standard obliging answer was utter hypocrisy, and Everard knew it. It was common during a long Fat Tuesday ride down St. Charles Avenue for the men to drunkenly lay themselves out right in front of members' wives riding on the float and take a piss in an empty bead bag. Somehow the ladies' delicate sensibilities were never a priority then.

The real reason wives were not permitted into the association's halls but once a month had more to do with the private dining rooms upstairs than all the free license needed for impromptu expletives in the main dining room downstairs. The men were allowed to take anyone at all—even females unrelated by marriage—upstairs for a private lunch, but the rooms were a devout secret that was scrupulously kept from the members' wives. Certainly no wives had ever been brought upstairs to dine in one. That was one of the unwritten orders of membership that went back all the way to the founding year of 1832. Traffic was heavy upstairs at the association, and the rooms were regarded like homosexuality in the military: *don't ask, don't tell.* Still, it was fairly common knowledge in the club who was bringing whom upstairs. Sometimes members even brought in common prostitutes from Airline Highway, but sometimes they went into the private lunch rooms with association members themselves. If the family went back, way back to one of those treasured old crumbling monuments along the Mississippi, the trips upstairs even with the other men could be overlooked, rationalized, forgotten, forgiven. Perhaps it was just a business lunch after all.

In some ways, Laborde thought wickedly, the association was quite misunderstood. The 555 was known as one of the last holdouts of free association, but, indeed, with the number of members who took the black waiters upstairs, in truth they were functioning as as liberal an organization as the ACLU.

"I say we do in a contractor for a change this year, Everard. Everybody hates contractors."

Laborde didn't look up from his Bananas Foster, not even to view his board chairman with the usual disgust. "Everybody hates *lawyers,* Abbott, not contractors. Get that straight, you idiot."

"Well, I'm not sure about that, Everard," Hockney Abbott retorted. "Our new house at English Turn is giving me thoughts of murder. The fire was the last straw. You know, all that money and the roof leaks? I'd pay to see that bastard hang."

"Hock, these things happen sometime. You're just like all the rest of my impossible clients. You don't understand the

building process. It's fluid; it's imperfect. It's an art." Fred
LeJaune, the association's vice president and renowned New
Orleans interior designer, took a sip of his brandy. LaJaune,
famed for his clean decors, insipid mannerisms, and the fact
that he was prone to weeping when things weren't going his
way, was a living, breathing stereotype of a homosexual, except for the fact that he wasn't gay. Even now Laborde found
himself amazed, but it was true. Fred was not gay. He'd married a very female portrait painter, and by all auspices lived
happily ever after in a historic creole cottage along Bayou St.
John.

"Screw art, screw imperfections. I didn't pay for imperfect.
Let's ex a contractor this year. It'd be a joy for me, probably
for everyone." Hockney gulped down his scotch. He was the
preppy one, but it was all a façade. Hockney Abbott had been
too dull to get into even a mediocre college, so his parents had
packed him off to an obscure community college in Maine,
imprinting him forever with the uniform of Dock-Sides, blue
pinpoint oxfords, and khakis. When he returned home, he'd
lounged around the house until his thirties, when his father
died and he inherited the family's private boys' school on
Jackson Avenue. He'd been driving that institution into
bankruptcy for years now with his mismanagement and expensive tastes, but the thing hobbled along because the 555
Association still sent their sons there. The old New Orleans
connection was strong, if stupid. Besides the fact that the Abbott school never produced any Harvard grads, even
Laborde thought Hockney Abbott was not the kind of man
to look after a bunch of boys. The rumor was that Hockney
longed for Fred and the private room upstairs. Certainly
Hockney's hints were none too obscure—Laborde and a few
select others who dared to speak of it had picked up on it—
but whether Fred had turned Hockney down and proclaimed
his love for his wife, or, more likely, just never got the sug-
gestions, no one knew. All that was known was that Hockney had lunch in the main dining room with Fred without fail

every Wednesday and that Fred was Hockney's obsession. By Laborde's theory, obsession was either intense hatred or deep sexual love, or, as he knew it terribly, both. Hockney displayed the latter where Fred was concerned.

"Oh, yes, let's kill a contractor. It'll bore us to tears." Fred guffawed.

Hockney reddened. "And what would be better? A decorator?"

Everard looked at them. Hockney and Fred could bicker like an old married couple. If left to their devices, soon one of them would be in tears, and as much as that idea might embarrass any other person, Everard kind of enjoyed it. He loved conflict, no matter how petty. Besides, he knew these two men and their little quirks well. They'd been his chairman and vice president for as long as he'd been in office. His contempt for them ran high—as, truly, most people's did— yet they'd proven to be useful. Eminently useful. First and foremost, because, like the lapdogs they were, they did what they were told.

Fred released a huge sigh. "Working with tasteless people like you, Hockney Abbott, is why my life is such a trial."

"Trial, trial? You're an interior designer, for God's sake. A career for a lobotomy case if there ever was one. Your life is fucking useless!"

"Enough." Laborde took a long, slow sip of his Absolut.

Upon the interjection, the two men gave their rapt attention to Laborde, a vague kind of fear in their expressions that made them look like deer frozen in the headlights.

Laborde turned to Fred. "And let's not linger on the word 'trial,' shall we? We have a murder to discuss tonight, let's not push ahead to the trial."

The two men nervously chuckled.

Fred's eyes shone with unveiled admiration. "You have such a wit, Everard. You really should become a man of letters. An author, I think . . . but here I go again, burdening you with undue verbiage."

Laborde stared at Fred until the man questioningly cocked his head like the dog in the old RCA label. There was a time when Laborde would have ached to explain to Fred what an idiot he was. Sentences like *burdening you with undue verbiage* were constantly spewing from his mouth. Mental vomit was what it was, but the time for such criticism was long past. Besides, it would only make Fred cry.

"We have other things to discuss tonight, gentlemen, so let's get to it." Laborde crumpled his napkin on the table. It was immediately taken away by an ancient black waiter in a white jacket.

"I still think the victim this year should be a contractor."

"The victim is not up for a vote. You know that." Laborde gave Hockney the stare this time, but Hockney at least didn't tilt his head like a dumb animal. He understood the stare all too well from the sudden paleness of his cheeks.

"Of course, Everard," he placated. "You always pick the victim. It's your murder party, after all."

Both men nodded in unison.

"We were just making conversation," Hockney continued to slaver. "No one is trying to usurp you. The 555's Murder Mystery Night is the biggest charitable fund-raiser in all the city, bigger even than the zoo's. No one wants to mess with success. Least of all us."

Laborde nodded. He loved it when Hockney was contrite. Hockney would twitch that preppy gold-gray mustache and looked like he'd give him a hand job if that would make everything nice-nice again.

"You two are the only ones who know all the details ahead of time." Laborde studied them. "You above all understand all the intricate planning that goes into this little mystery party, so let's get on with it. We've usually had this done for months by this time of the year. The kinks are in there, gentlemen, and it's up to you to find them. You both will go along with me and I'll show you the evidence. If, after that, you can pick the killer, then I know the murder we're creating for our guests is too easy to solve. But if you can't, we'll go ahead with the plans." Laborde checked the old Boston clock that towered over the dining room. It was almost ten; time for the ladies to be going home.

He shoved away from the table. The ancient black waiter helped pull back his seat and handed him his signature ebony and silver cane. "Basically, it's murder as usual, gentlemen. This is our tenth year throwing this party for the 555. Do you have any questions before I go to the foyer and dispense with the ladies?"

Hockney and Fred shook their heads in unison.

Laborde carried his Absolut into the foyer and stood vigil at the door. The hall of the Greek Revival town house was superfluously decorated in ruby velvet and sprigs of holly for the Christmas season, but no one really noticed. The only colors its members liked were gold, green, and purple—the colors of Fat Tuesday—and none of that could be brought out until January 6, Twelfth Night, the official beginning of the Mardi Gras season.

If there was one thing Laborde enjoyed about being the 555 president, it was the pomp and circumstance. He found it an inexpressible thrill to be so important as to stand in the revered hall of 555 Canal Street and selectively acknowledge the members. His father wouldn't have complained if he could see his son now, a distinguished, graying man in his fifties, handing out his personal greetings and farewell to the crème de la crème of New Orleans society. Better yet, his father would be proud to see how welcome his son's personal acknowledgment was. A greeting or farewell by the president meant you were Somebody in the association; not every member received such a perk. There was hierarchy even within its own membership.

Now a Laborde had finally mastered the hierarchy. As amazing as it was, it still rankled after all these years that as a child, Everard had been left out of several school chums' birthday parties because, while his father had eventually finagled a membership in the lunch club, the physician didn't rank high enough on the membership roster to merit his son a party invitation. Everard was forced to stay home and play in the yard while his schoolmates were taken to the Yacht Club and entertained by clowns and black-face minstrels.

But the tables had turned. They didn't even hold his mother's tacky makeup and cheap handbags against him anymore. He'd been Rex. He'd earned the title of president.

"Come on, you old tease, give us a hint . . ." Mrs. Sanford, heiress to the huge shipping line, wandered up to Everard and tweaked his cheek. Drunkenly, she wrapped herself in a chinchilla proffered by her husband, and swayed while she wagged her white-gloved finger. "You'll be sorry if you don't help me guess the killer this year. I just might have a murder mystery party at the Junior League and serve up one of you men as the victim. So there!"

"Come along, Heloise . . ." her husband murmured. The two disappeared into the Rolls waiting outside the front door. Mrs. Sanford almost tipped over as her husband with the help of the chauffeur settled her into the backseat.

"I always wondered what it would be like to kowtow to all that money." Fred appeared at Laborde's side, along with Hockney. He made a distasteful purse of his lips—an annoying habit, especially for a supposedly heterosexual, Laborde thought. "Sanford seems less and less tolerant of the old battle-ax."

"He's got the best of everything. Heloise Sanford is usually so sauced, she can't see straight, which is a good thing too, given that Sanford has been seen around town with that wonderful chocolate meringue confection of a newscaster." Hockney eyeballed the two men in the foyer. "Surely, you've seen her, haven't you? She's on Channel 5. Camille Trelangne. Family goes way back. They say her great-great-grandmother ran the creole placage system on Rampart Street before the Civil War."

"You're kidding," Fred gasped, his mouth twitching in shock. "Sanford is a friend of mine. He's never mentioned it."

Laborde ignored them and said good-bye to another member and his wife, who lived in a splendid mansion on Audubon Place. The Bordelon family money was long gone, but they'd managed to make it up again in drug rehab centers. A while back there had been something about a federal investigation and the misuse of Medicaid funds concerning the rehab centers, but it hardly made the news. No one at the 555 ever asked about it.

"We'll see you Mardi Gras, Everard. We wouldn't miss the murder for anything." Mrs. Randolph Bordelon, a twenty-something blonde who was the fifth Mrs. Randolph Bordelon, took her husband's arm and they disappeared into a silver Jaguar.

"You know, Everard, has anyone told you how brilliant you are?" Hockney asked as the Bordelon Jag turned onto St. Charles.

Laborde glanced at him. "What are you talking about?"

"You saved our organization. You saved our way of life, didn't he, Fred?"

Fred nodded. Laborde was reminded of a little dog head on the back of a Latino's Camaro.

"Ten years ago, Everard, if you hadn't come up with the idea of a murder mystery party, and if the party hadn't been so wildly successful, the 555 might have folded." Hockney looked at him in earnest then, as if he were speaking of something reverent and of world importance. "We were losing members back then, remember? It wasn't the thing to belong to the 555. But you revived all of that, and with one stroke of brilliance. By creating an annual mock whodunit benefit, you resuscitated us. And a funny thing, you used women to do it. They've been begging for invitations."

"Women love a good murder. They read all the mysteries, didn't you know that?" Fred piped in.

"Indeed?" Laborde raised one imperious eyebrow.

"Oh, you must have known that, Ev," Hockney sputtered. "How else could you have come up with such a great plan?"

*How else,* Laborde thought, smirking. By all appearances, Murder Mystery Night was planned and calculated in order to make money for the club and make the 555 appear the Good Samaritan as it donated excess funds to the city's children. It had nothing to do with the fact that ten years earlier Everard had invited a waitress to his house à la Hugh Grant. It had nothing to do with the fact that he'd gotten carried away and killed her because she was black and because she wore the same tacky orange color on her lips that his mother had.

It had nothing to do with the fact that now he planned his murders in advance, and worked out all their kinks in the open with Hockney and Fred, all in the name of party planning.

Hockney and Fred had now been the unwitting accessories to murder nine times without one of them even raising a suspicion. Everard always waited for that light to come on. Every year, at some point during the calendar, the murder they fictionalized over the lunch table became a small, unremarkable article in the Metro section of the paper. But Fred and Hockney either never read the paper or just never added things up. The disappearance of the likes of a black waitress never truly captured the attention of a 555 member. And therein lay Everard's power. Satan had his little helpers with Fred and Hockney, but women weren't blameless either. It was the number of women who attended the party that had made it such a financial success. Perhaps it was fitting. Women had to be a part of it all because the night was about them. For eight of the nine years the party had been held, the pretend "victim" of the murder had always been a woman. The only male victim had been a drunken janitor who disappeared from the 555 after watching a man place a body in his car, but after that there had been so many members' comments that dead black males were something they could read about every day in the paper, Laborde, with his keen sense of irony, was only too happy to comply with their wishes. The next year he gave them a real mind teaser involving a young Jewish woman, and it thrilled everyone. So it was only right that the wives and their friends be included in the fun and games.

Mama herself might have even loved the party idea, Laborde thought as he was handed another chilled Absolut and nodded farewell to another society dam. Particularly if the pretend "victim" to the party had been an M.D.

"You never tell us, Ev, how do you come up with all these fantastic ideas for the murder?" Fred pursed his lips again and Laborde wanted to rip them off his face.

"I'm not telling. All I'll say is that you know it takes months for me to plan it and I never have nor ever will put the victim up for a vote."

"Because it must be like a puzzle, isn't it?" Hockney asked. "First, I imagine, you have to develop who the killer is. After all, it's he who chooses the victim and the crime and place, not us, right?"

"Exactly," Laborde said, growing tired of the adulation. Fred and Hockney could really get on his nerves. They were truly the most oblivious twits he'd ever met; cattle prods and ice cubes couldn't wake these two up out of the numb oblivion in which they lived.

But they were his chairman and vice president, and they did everything for him, even to the point of covering his trail. Best of all, they didn't even know it.

He gave them both his most sincere look of affection. He really should make it a practice to be kinder to them. If their finest attribute was their step-and-fetch-it demeanor to the president, their second was their ego massaging, status-seeking tunnel vision wrought from too many years of being a Somebody in a small southern town. They just didn't get the real world. So far, they'd helped plan nine going on ten killings, and not once did they ever want to discuss anything more weighty than who was next in line to be Rex. God forbid, the lightbulbs ever went on! Fred and Hockney might have to see then that their imaginary world didn't exist.

Hockney and Fred returned Laborde's felicitous look and there was a warm and fuzzy moment between the three men. Before Laborde returned to picking and choosing the members to which he would deign to say farewell, Fred's last glance at him appeared worshipful, Hockney's grateful. Equilibrium had returned; all was right with their world.

Laborde wanted to laugh, but he didn't dare. As judged by their mental powers, Hockney Abbott and Fred LeJaune were not God's gift to mankind.

Oh, but to J. Everard Laborde . . .

They were certainly God's gift to him.

## ❧ 11 ❧

Claire bit into her hot beignet. Powdered sugar sprinkled down her front and she cursed the navy silk blouse she wore. It showed everything. Brushing her front, she took a sip of coffee and chicory, and savored it as if it were wine from the gods. All the gourmet coffees in the world couldn't compare with a steaming café au lait on the sidewalk of the centuries-old New Orleans French Market.

A Vietnamese waitress asked her if she wanted another. She shook her head and gave her a generous tip, then Claire sat back beneath the green and white striped awning and just enjoyed the view. Café du Monde bustled on a warm December morning with tourists jamming Decatur in their cookie-cutter uniforms of Gore-Tex jogging suits and fanny packs. Crowds took pictures of Jackson Square while artists and mule-cart drivers hawked their dubious wares. It never failed, Claire thought as she watched a group of tourists crowd around an artist's booth, oohing and aahing over dreary oil paintings of a swamp. The tackier the artwork, the more the tourists loved it. A few black velvet paintings of Elvis among the Spanish moss and they'd probably rush the place.

She stirred an Equal packet into her coffee and made a mental note to do the tourist thing herself. If her memory served her, there was a great booth of Mardi Gras masks right next to the old U.S. Mint. She wanted to bring a feather one back to Pam, her secretary, before they were all snatched up by Fat Tuesday revelers.

Her agenda for the day was already getting filled. She had to do a little shopping and maybe pick up a bottle of champagne for the day she finally summoned the courage to go home for dinner. But before she did any of that, she was going to look up the old homicide detective who'd handled her sister's case. He was probably still at the station on Broad Street. Then she was going to venture down Canal to the 555 Association. They would undoubtedly refuse to talk to her, but she was going to retrace her sister's steps as far as she could.

The throng of tourists parted and she could see all the way to St. Louis Cathedral. Jugglers and pierrots were performing on the steps of the old Catholic church. Through the crowd, a tall, well-built man in his thirties rose from one of the park benches and walked purposefully toward the café.

She was not normally one to gawk at males. Sure, during college she'd done her share of bar hopping, and some of the guys who were still in New York even called now and then; they hadn't turned out to be serial killers. But after her sister's death, her perspective had warped. She'd begun to be a little afraid of men. A pickup now was out of the question. She had to get to know the guy well before she even consented to being alone with him, and such a policy could be stifling to a love life. The few lawyers she'd dated from Fassbinder quickly grew tired of lame dates in clean, well-lighted places. They also grew tired of her questions about their family, their relationships. She was compelled now to screen every candidate, to make sure whoever she was thinking about taking to her bed was the kind of upstanding citizen she wanted them to be. But hotshots didn't like talking about their mothers, and the ones that did liked to talk about Mother too much. Her sex life was almost nonexistent, to say the least, but there seemed no way for her to break loose again. She'd had too hard a lesson about humanity.

So gawking wasn't her style at all, but the man who crossed Decatur was the kind every woman would stare at. He towered over the tourists; his shoulders in the white henley T-shirt he wore were powerfully broad, his hips nicely narrow in faded jeans. Completing his attire was a simple harness-leather belt and scuffed brown cowboy boots. A legal red tie folder was tucked under one arm.

He was too casually dressed to be a lawyer or businessman, but still his appearance was neat and clean-shaven with a slow lank to his step that she found wildly appealing. His hair was dark and slicked back as if he'd just taken a shower, and when he turned sideways to maneuver through the parked cars on Decatur, she suddenly noticed his hair wasn't short at all, but tied into a ponytail.

He was her type all right. She could actually fantasize about a guy like that, she thought.

He crossed the street in front of her, his hips involuntarily drawing her gaze with his confident swagger. As she had once seen put so delicately in a Victorian journal, watching him gave her that *lonely* feeling. An understatement at best. She suddenly longed for a boyfriend. Or at least a sex life.

The man stepped onto the sidewalk of the café. She quickly averted her gaze, embarrassed that he might catch her staring at him. Just because he was good-looking didn't mean he was nice, or even sane, she reminded herself. There was no use in inviting loonies over to her with eye contact. That was the last thing she needed.

The legal folder landed on her table.

At first she thought there was some kind of mistake. But then she looked up.

He really wasn't recognizable without the street grime and the skull cap. Nothing about him had reminded her of the man in Bloomingdale's or the man who'd freaked her out in the lobby vestibule of her apartment, but there he was. The guy she'd just gawked at. It was definitely him, because now, as he stood right over her table, there was no mistaking the eyes. For the first time, she noticed they were not just blue, but intensely blue—electric blue, and with the same dangerous predatory glint that fear had tattooed upon her memory.

She stood up. The plate of beignets crashed to the ground, dusting her navy pumps with sticky white sugar.

"We need to talk, Claire. You've been a very bad little girl." The man reached behind him to his back pocket and retrieved a black wallet. He flipped it open. It didn't take her long to read the initials: FBI.

She could feel the blood drain from her face. Tourists were beginning to stare; it wasn't often that a woman was approached by a man showing off a badge, but she didn't care about appearances. All she was thinking at that point was jail and disbarment.

He replaced the wallet and motioned for the Vietnamese waitress. Ordering coffee, he took the seat opposite Claire and began to untie the folder.

"Sit down, Ms. Green. Let's get acquainted." He looked up from the folder. "That is, unless you want to call your attorney?"

Grimly, she shook her head. She didn't like the fact that he was taunting her, but he had the element of surprise with him. She had nothing.

She lowered herself back down onto the chair. Slowly, the tourists and other café dwellers returned their attention to their own parties.

He tossed several photographs down onto the table. They fanned out over the sticky surface like a child's Colorforms. She didn't want to look at them, but she had to. They were the story of her life the past five years. The first was Zoe's high school photo, the one the police had used in the *Times-Picayune* when she was found missing. Behind that were crime scene photos in Des Allemands, with the body already removed to the morgue, and behind those was the most terrifying surprise of all. An old mug shot of Halbert Washington.

In a quiet voice she said, "How should I address you? Do you prefer mister or special agent?"

He smiled. He had the upper hand and he knew it.

She met his gaze with a cool one of her own, one that hid the torment inside.

"Special Agent Jameson will do for now." He put up his hand in mock objection. "But don't bother to introduce yourself, Claire. As you can see by the photos, I'm already well acquainted with you."

She glanced at the damning photos, then at him. "I'm going to check you, you know, as soon as I get to a phone. You'd better be with the FBI or I'll have you arrested for stalking me."

The waitress came with his coffee. He gave her a five and tossed Claire a quarter from the change. "There's a pay phone by the counter. I'd think less of you if you didn't call, so go ahead. Check me out. Then let's get down to business. We've got a lot to talk about."

She didn't touch the quarter. She didn't need to. She knew he was FBI. It was the only thing that made sense. "What kind of information are you hoping to find by harassing me? I don't appreciate being followed, especially across the country." Her voice lowered and she tried her best to look cold. "I'm a busy woman and this is my vacation. I don't have a desire to spend it with the feds."

"Mmm . . ." He eyed her and dug through the folder again, sifting through a massive number of faxes. He found what he was looking for. He scanned it and said, "You're right, Claire. You are a busy woman. Last year you billed 2,400 hours for Fassbinder. That's an incredible amount. We're talking sixty-hour work weeks at least." He looked up, an infuriating, lazy half-grin planted on his lips. "I know a lot about you. All work and no play, huh, Ms. Wall-Street-Hotshot-Attorney?"

He glanced down at another sheet. "Ah, but here I see you do play after hours. There's a little matter of an ad taken out in *High Risk* magazine using, of all things, the name of your deceased sister. We've also had the phone company give us their records on your calls the past month or so. Let me see . . ." He dug out another sheet of paper from the folder. "Here we are—you made a phone call to a Ms. Earnestine Darby just a few days before you left for New Orleans. Now, that's some damn coincidence, because the New York authorities tell me they've been up Ms. Darby's butt trying to get information on the killing of one Halbert Washington. Did you know her mother was allegedly murdered by Mr. Washington?" He tossed the folder back onto the table. "It's a small damn world, Ms. Green, I'll tell you that."

"I went to Barnard College, *Special Agent* Jameson. I met Earnestine a long time ago up in Morningside Heights. Do I have to account for my friend's alleged actions as well as my own?" She clasped her hands in her lap. Outwardly, she wanted to present an unruffled exterior, but that was hard to do with her hands trembling.

"I know what you're doing."

"I don't know what you're talking about," she said, her gaze leveled at his.

The slow grin returned. "I can't prove it or I wouldn't be sitting here having coffee with you. I'd be having you arrested."

She said nothing. That was one thing she learned in law school. Never run your mouth, especially in the company of the enemy.

He stared at her. His gaze took in everything: the powdered sugar dusting her pumps, the cut of her slim wool skirt, the interlocking gold C's that adorned the Chanel navy hair bow that held her hair neatly to her nape. She could see in his eyes what he thought of her. There was a vague contempt there that said she was nothing but a rich-bitch lawyer.

"Who took the ad, Ms. Green? Yourself or this"—he checked the folder again—"this Phyllis Zuckermann you called just before you came down here?"

They had tapped her phone. Oh, Jesus, they were that close. She tried to shove away the panic. "What ad are you talking about?"

"The ad in *High Risk*. The one calling for a man to slay dragons. The one I answered." His stare burned right through her.

"Is there a law against taking ads out in magazines? If so—"

"What did you mean when you told Zuckermann about 'the creep Zoe summoned'? What did you mean by keeping 'Zoe out of trouble'? Who's Zoe? Your sister's dead."

"I really don't know how to answer."

He leaned across the table. His questions came like bullets. "Why aren't you taking your turn at the lottery—and what is the lottery—and who runs it? Zuckermann? You? Or someone we haven't met yet?"

She leaned back. It took all her effort to keep her nerve. "It's just impossible for me to answer you without a lot more information."

"Your sister's dead." He shoved the stack of photos toward her. "Take a look, Ms. Green. Zoe was found murdered five years ago in a town south of here. She's not involved in these little games you're playing, so why are you using her name? What are you hiding?"

She just stared at him, unable to speak, unable to look down at the photos, unable to do anything but try to freeze the desperation inside her.

The near gentleness of his next words surprised her.

"This is bad stuff you're involved in, Claire Green. You got a lot going for you." He nodded to the folder. "Fassbinder Hamilton. Even me, a redneck from Tulsa, can see they're a big damn deal." He paused as if he knew she wouldn't like what he was going to say next. "Let me tell you, ruining your life won't bring back your sister."

An unforewarned shot of anger ran through her blood. She suddenly had the urge to scream, to hit, to knock things off the table. He had no right to advise her. He didn't know what it was like to love someone who was found dead in a ditch of oily roadside water. He was nothing but a fed who enjoyed tormenting his victims. There were child killers roaming every interstate of the nation, and this glorified cop was being instructed to go after a few lousy women whose victimization finally broke them.

She stood. Now she didn't care if he saw her shaking hands, her trembling mouth. She didn't care at all what he thought. He had no warrant. He had no right to talk to her. He could go to hell.

"I'm sorry, but I've an appointment. This conversation will have to end."

"We're not through."

She snatched her purse from the back of the chair. "Oh, yes, we are. Go back to Washington or Tulsa, or wherever you came from, and tell your chief that there's nothing of interest to the FBI going on down here."

"Halbert Washington never killed Grace Darby."

Claire opened her mouth to retort but bit back the words just in time. She didn't need to reveal any of her own knowledge about the Washington/Darby crime. It wasn't going to help her position, that was for sure.

"Don't you want to know who did it?" He stood and stared her down.

She said nothing.

"Ms. Earnestine Darby took the news badly for a woman who'd finally had the confession of the man who killed her mother. I never heard such wailing and carrying on."

"I really don't know what you're talking about."

"Halbert Washington was innocent all along. Sure, he went to prison for the killing of Grace Darby, but now they know he wasn't guilty. He didn't kill her. He got convicted because he didn't have a big bank account and a set of fancy lawyers; he had a public defender and a lot of heat on him for a confession, so he copped a plea. What else could he do? He and Grace used to argue, sometimes violently, and that's why the kids—and everyone—thought the man screaming at their mother when she was knifed was Washington. But you know what? It wasn't Washington. It was Kareem Darby, her ex-husband and the father of her children. Apparently, he'd come back that night looking for money. He and Grace got into it and he killed her with one of the kitchen knives. He's been sitting in Angola all this time, appealing a death penalty conviction he received shortly after Grace's murder. They did the injection in November, but before he died, he told the pastor that he was the one who murdered Grace Darby. He said he wanted to set the record straight and atone for it. His last words were to 'tell Halbert Washington he was sorry.'" He paused and leaned down toward her to make his point, "But you know, Claire, once the info filtered to the right authorities, there was nobody to apologize to, since Halbert's body was found in a Dumpster."

Claire was suddenly hit by an unexpected nausea. She was sick and frightened and disgusted all at the same time. In her heart she wanted to be out with it. She wanted to unload her soul and tell this man everything she knew about ZOE. Then she wanted to just walk away and abandon her friends to their fates.

But the other part of her didn't know how to betray them. Her friends had gone astray and they needed help. If this man was telling her the truth about Halbert Washington, then the mess of his death might be enough to make them see the error of their ways. Too, if she confessed now what she knew to this FBI agent, they'd all be in trouble, and she had very little doubt she'd be able to walk away clean enough for Fassbinder Hamilton or the New York bar.

Inside she cursed her weakness and vulnerability. If it was true that Darby really did confess to killing Earnestine's mother, then her worst fears had been realized. Not only had

ZOE gone and contracted its first revenge, but now an innocent man was dead; the poor bastard punished twice for a crime he never committed.

"Sit down, Ms. Green. You don't look well. I hope it wasn't anything I said." He mockingly held out a chair.

She backed away. The tourists were watching again, but she didn't care. She felt like a trapped rabbit and all she wanted was out. Her plans for the day were all gone, replaced by the all-consuming need to call Phyllis. If Earnestine knew about Darby's confession, then Phyllis knew, and the only thing Claire wanted at that moment was to hear Phyllis say that ZOE was never ever going to get involved in vigilantism again.

"Where are you going, Claire? We still have so much to discuss." He smiled and took a step toward her.

She avoided him, almost stumbling over an empty chair.

"I'm staying at the Orleans. Give me a call, Claire, when you're ready to talk. Until then, I'll work on that warrant for you if you like."

She turned and nearly ran into the street. Hugging her purse to her chest, she hailed a cab on Decatur.

"All right, then, don't call us, we'll call you," she heard him shout to the departing cab. Then she heard him laugh.

## ❧ 12 ❧

"**P**hyllis," Claire sobbed into the phone. "Pick up, Phyllis."

"Claire?"

"Phyllis, I heard about Darby's confession. I know. Everyone knows, even the feds. They told me."

"Calm down, Claire darling. Where are you calling me from?"

"I'm at a pay phone in the Metairie Mall. They're probably tapping all the phone lines. I didn't dare call from the apartment." She wiped the tears streaming down her cheeks. "Phyllis, Halbert Washington didn't do it. He was punished for nothing. Oh, God, what have you done . . . ?"

"Get ahold of yourself, Claire. Now, who told you all of this?"

Claire hesitated a moment, then confessed. "There's an agent who followed me down here from New York. He won't leave me alone. He's the one who answered the *High Risk* ad, Phyl. He's FBI."

There was a long, deathly pause at the other end of the line, then Phyllis said, "Get away from him, Claire. He's going to get us into trouble."

"Trouble? We're already in trouble!" Claire pressed into the receiver. "Now, you listen to me, Phyllis, as your friend and your lawyer, ZOE has gone over the line. Way over. I won't have to worry about the feds on my tail if you just disband ZOE and never touch this vigilante b.s. again."

"I can't make any promises, doll."

Claire rolled her eyes in despair. "No?" she whispered loudly. "Well, I hear Earnestine isn't taking the news too well."

"We've talked to her. She was pretty low there for a while, but she's feeling better. There was some talk of suicide, but we've dissuaded her of that at the very least."

Claire shook her head as if she were trying to clear it. She swore Phyllis was turning into a schizo. "He was the wrong man, Phyllis. *The wrong man,* do you hear me? Do you know what that means?"

"It's over now. No use in punishing Earnestine any further. We can't bring Washington back."

"Do you even hear yourself? You sound just like them now. You know, the death penalty opponents—the ones that say executing the criminal won't bring back the victim—except here, executing the victim won't bring back the criminal. Oh, God, why didn't you listen to me?"

"Claire, I'm sorry to interrupt, but let me remind you of the big picture. Halbert Washington may have gotten a bum rap, but his record was as long and extensive as Darby's. He was a known crack dealer on 125th Street. Someone would have gotten him eventually."

"I want to know all the details. Who ZOE hired, where it took place, how it was done. You guys are going to need the defense team of the decade."

"Why?"

"To defend yourselves in the trial."

"What trial? There's no trial, nor will there be one. Earnestine's taking it hard, I admit, but she doesn't have any legal worries. She didn't talk. They have no evidence."

"The feds are on to this. They might not have hard evidence, but they're sure going to try to make Earnestine talk." Claire put a shaking hand to the receiver. "Now, listen, Phyllis, too many people know about ZOE. You've got to quit. If there's one major flaw to ZOE's schemes, it's that you can't plan a grand, elaborate revenge and keep an entire group of people quiet about it. It won't work. Quit while you're ahead, I beg of you. You're going to go to jail if you don't."

"ZOE's secrets are fail-safe."

"Yeah? How fail-safe are they? After all, *I* know, and obviously I wasn't supposed to."

"You don't know anything, Claire. I'm the judge, remember? You haven't one scrap of information you can testify about, and you'd do well to remember that if you ever get chummy with the feds."

"Is that a threat, Phyllis?" Claire choked down her rising hysteria. "Do I now get classified as the loose cannon? The unpredictable renegade? Should I be worried? Do you recommend that I watch my back as Halbert, the poor fool, should have done?"

"Please, Claire, don't be like this. You're talking ridiculous. No one in ZOE would ever hurt you. We love you. We're going to help you. You're going to be happy one day, and glad, so glad."

A chill ran down Claire's back. Goose flesh rose on her forearms. Slowly, she said, "Don't you see, Phyllis? This is why it's all wrong. Where does it stop? You can excuse Washington's death, so why not mine? Why not anyone who tries to interfere with your plans for justice?"

"We're not like that, Claire. We're not criminals, we're victims. Remember, we're just like you."

"No, not like me. I couldn't do it. Not what Earnestine did."

"Oh, no? You're down in New Orleans now, my dear. Why don't you see if we can test that hypothesis. Find Zoe's killer. I want you to look him in the face and then say what you're saying now."

"I couldn't do that, Phyllis. I'm not capable of it."

"Go find your killer, Claire. Then we'll see what you're capable of."

The phone clicked; the silence was replaced with the dial tone. Claire hung up the receiver.

Shoppers sauntered by. Weak and shaken, she tried to hide her red eyes with her sunglasses. Wiping her nose with a tissue, she clutched her keys and walked tiredly toward the parking lot where she'd left the convertible.

Phyllis's words stung and echoed and stung again. Claire had wanted reassurances, but she'd gotten none except that somehow Earnestine was going to live with what had happened.

ZOE was still out there, unleashing its vengeance.

She had to stop them. She had every legal, ethical, and moral reason to do it in spite of the costs to herself, and she knew she would do it. She would do the right thing. Confess her knowledge to the feds. But the moment hadn't come yet. She hesitated now because deep down she knew Phyllis was right in some respects. First, she had to look in the mirror and confront the devil within herself. She had to see if she could walk away from her own chance for revenge, because only then could she lead ZOE away from the path it was bent on.

Until she was ready to do that, until her search in New Orleans was through, until she had found any kind of peace with what happened to her twin sister, she had to accept the fact that a big part of her soul was just like theirs. She had the same urges, the same primeval rage. She'd been a victim. Deep inside, no matter how she wanted to deny it, she wanted her revenge. She secretly dreamed of being Pandora. She, too, wanted to FedEx a nice, pink-bowed box to the killer of her sister and watch him open it.

"Hey, Wynn. I got a live one. Let me ask you something." Jameson switched the receiver to the other ear and flipped through some of his notes. "Two-stepping around the entrapment issue, what do you think would lure a woman into talking about her dead sister's killer?"

"Why are you calling me at this hour, Liam?" Wynn slurred into the phone. There was the sound of fumbling and then a curse. "Jeez, it's two o'clock in the morning . . ."

"Sorry. I thought it was only one. I forgot about the time change." Jameson kicked off his cowboy boots and settled into the hotel room's easy chair. "I've been thinking about things. Claire Green, I believe, is down here trying to make one last attempt to seek out her sister's killer. Worst of it is, now that this Zoe has botched Washington's death, we can't say ZOE won't botch another one. Green might be falsely on the trail of some guy who's just some working-stiff blue-collar Joe who's the daddy of four kids. Once she points the finger, he could get taken out."

"Have you figured out who ZOE is?"

Liam scratched his chin. "I've thought a lot about it. I think it's a name she and Zuckermann and probably others are hiding behind. ZOE might even be some kind of network or cabal. I've got someone digging to see if they can identify it."

"Good."

"You still with me, Wynn?"

"Yeah. So you want to make Claire Green talk? Get to know who she's thinking about going after."

"Right."

He heard the covers rustle, then a small squeak, but whether it was the bed springs or Wynn, he wasn't sure.

"Listen, Jameson, can I think about this? It's so late. The only thing you can do is try to maybe befriend her. Give her some information on her sister she doesn't have now. That'll win her trust. Then maybe she'll talk."

"All right, but do you think—?"

"Get off the friggin' phone, man. It's the middle of the night."

"McBride?" Liam sat up.

"Liam?" Wynn was back on the line.

"Was that McBride?"

"Oh, God, now everybody's going to know." Wynn released a moan. "It was that last margarita. I told him I didn't want it."

"You got McBride there with you *now?*" Liam shook his head.

"You couldn't hate me more than I hate myself."

"Don't let her fool you, farmboy, she was beggin' me for it," McBride broke in.

A muffled thunk came from the receiver. Liam wondered if Wynn hit him with it.

"Listen, Jameson, I'll call you when I get in first thing in the morning. And just forget this ever happened. I'll clean up my act, I swear it."

Liam grinned. "I just never would have believed it of you, Wynn. I mean, *McBride?*"

The groan of despair was audible. "I've lost my mind, but I'll get it back in the morning."

"Happy Mardi Gras, farmboy," McBride shouted from afar.

"You guys are starting the party early. Mardi Gras's not for a couple more weeks." Liam chuckled.

Another groan. "I swear this was a fluke."

"Happy Mardi Gras, Wynn. Happy Mardi Gras, McBride. I'll call you tomorrow if I can't figure this out myself."

"Thanks, Liam. Good night."

There was a pause on the line. Liam thought she'd hung up, but instead he heard her mutter, "Jeez, I'll never live this down. You're such a jerk, McBride . . ."

Silence came, then the definitive wet, sucking sound of kissing.

Liam cringed. His shoulders shook as he muffled his laughter. Quietly, he placed the receiver back in the cradle.

He'd have done the same. In some ways, he was almost

jealous. Wynn had always caught his eye, but he could never quite break down the barrier of professionalism that separated them.

Now he was relieved he didn't have the complications of an internal relationship. He was particularly glad, because of late instead of thinking about Wynn's long, shapely legs, he'd been thinking about flyaway brown curls and eyes that mirrored a soul he seemed to already know.

He hadn't stopped thinking about Claire Green since he'd first spied her in Bloomingdale's. Already he was itching to take Wynn's advice.

Thumbing through his massive notes, he searched for the exact tidbit about Zoe that he could use to lure in Claire Green. It would probably take him the entire next day getting to know Zoe Green's case, but it would come to him. The answer always did.

It was the middle of the night and he was exhausted in yet another hotel room in yet another strange city, but he was eager to get to work. Against his better judgment, he found he relished the moment he gained Claire Green's trust. Not only would he be able to avert a potential vigilante scheme, but he'd also be able to stare into those eyes, and maybe for one dark moment see what was still inside himself.

## ❧ 13 ❧

"My family keeps me in touch with who I really am."
　　　　　　　　　　　　—*Orenthal James Simpson*
　　　　　　　　　　　　(interview in *Parents* magazine)

The picture of Zoe stared down at her.

Claire watched it from across the room, awash in the outside floodlight of the courtyard. The Elsa Peretti frame was on the room's 1860's rococo marble mantel. One piece was modern, one piece old, but remarkably the curves were the same. Some things didn't change.

But some things did.

Grimly, she sat up in bed and shoved the pillows behind her back. She couldn't sleep. A breeze wafted in from the French doors, and outside she could hear the yowl of a cat, probably the old gray tom that lived in Number One. She had to get some sleep. She had a lot to do. Tomorrow she was going to 555 Canal, and no one, not even the feds, was going to stop her.

She glanced at the picture. Claire had had her hands on Zoe's shoulders. Their faces were together; they were smiling, but one was the smile of a confident young woman who had the world all figured out, and the other was that of a naive Cinderella who was waiting for her prince to show up at the door.

Some things never changed.

Oh, but some things did.


The pictures of Zoe stared down at him.

Liam had tacked them up to the hotel's outdated grass-clothed wall. Now all the Zoes were lined up in chronological order, ironically, twelve pictures of them. A jury of one. With no criminal to convict.

She looked like her sister. They were identical twins, the same in every way except that Zoe had a bit of a tilt to her mouth he'd not seen in Claire Green's. The expression in the eyes wasn't the same either, but he had no way to quantify it without knowing the women better. Zoe, too, kept her hair Junior League–short and lightened, but not Claire, who unwittingly enticed with a mass of lustrous brown that swung down her back.

He drank lukewarm room-service coffee and stared at the pictures. The last was the hardest. It was like looking at Claire Green, her lips freshly made up in a mango-orange color, her eyes frozen wide with fear, greasy mud splattered across her pretty cheeks.

He'd had to take down the full nude body shots. It was hard enough to look at Zoe's face. Right now he didn't need all the gruesome details in glossy eight-by-tens.

Now all he looked at was a face. Claire Green's face, staring down at him, the law officer, the self-ascribed hero, the man who was paid by the taxpayers to rid the world of the scum that did this to women.

Zoe stared down at him. Silently accusing him of not doing his job.

\* \* \*

Everard Laborde lay in a massive mahogany bed and stared at the ceiling of the Scalamandre-upholstered tester. He'd purchased the bed in an estate sale after he'd made Rex. It was a Prudent Mallard piece *with* provenance. The bed had once belonged to Valsin Monparnasse, the builder of Ascension Alley, whose allee of 350-year-old oak trees was perhaps the most photographed scene in the South.

Monparnasse probably plotted out his empire in just the same manner, Laborde thought as he propped himself up on the pillows, his eyes focused on the silk rosette at the center of the tester. Valsin had made his fortune in sugar. He'd immigrated from Germany in the 1830s with a small family stipend and turned it into a hugely profitable six-hundred-acre plantation. Everard couldn't help but admire the man. Yes, there were cruelties back then, but he didn't blame Monparnasse for the situation. In some ways, life was better back then for everyone. No one, slave or master, was free to starve at Ascension Alley, and if you worked the cane fields, you were fed. And if you refused . . .

Well, they did tell the parable of the young fourteen-year-old houseboy Monparnasse bought in New Orleans. The boy claimed he was too good to work as a field slave, so Monparnasse made him dig a deep grave, and he shot the boy where he stood.

Yet there was an injustice in the tale of Valsin Monparnasse, Everard thought. No one ever spoke of Valsin Monparnasse's contributions to the economy, nor of his deep appreciation of beauty which left behind one of the greatest plantation houses in the United States. No, all everyone ever focused on was that fourteen-year-old houseboy. He'd heard the story was even in the brochure being given out with a tour of the house, and it had angered him, as it did most of the members of the 555. There was no need for such vulgarity, he thought even now, his mouth twitching in distaste. Once upon a time in the South such things were not mentioned.

They were not necessarily denied, but they weren't flung over everyone's head either. Instead, people talked of the greatness of the old South; the heroism of the War Between the States. They talked of beauty and gentility and charm.

In his youth, Everard remembered an author who lived in the Garden District. The woman was nothing but a lame Tennessee Williams-wannabe; she wrote of the oppressiveness of southern social propriety; the alienation of dressing for dinner; the haunting absurdity of formal parlors. The woman author won some award for her work, and now, years later, was a rich, drunken grandmother who'd racked up more years in Barbados than in her home town of New Orleans. The critics still lauded her, but not him. Not J. Everard Laborde. He was a true southerner, and to read Eulaleigh Rockwell was a blasphemy. She had felt the need to apologize, but he didn't. Anyone who apologized for the South didn't understand it. Nor belonged there.

Only southerners understood that a great price was paid for great beauty.

And that after the Cause was lost, sometimes great beauty was forced to pay a great price.

People just didn't get it. The South wasn't all about racial injustice and white supremacy. As most things, it was more complicated than that, but the perceived stereotype was never altered.

Laborde thought of himself. To many, as the age-old president of the 555 Association, he would be called a bigot. It was almost laughable. He was no bigot. The only woman who had ever really loved him was his father's black housekeeper, his "mammy" as he liked to refer to her now. She died of cancer when he was fourteen, and there had never been any love in the world for him ever again.

White or black, he didn't care about skin color. But it had certainly mattered to his father, and that was who Everard had spent a lifetime trying to impress. It would be difficult for outsiders to understand, but J. Everard Laborde's life was not a case of shunning blacks, it was a case of impressing a small, select enclave of whites who had so impressed his father.

Everard's thoughts turned to Fred and Hockney and how five years earlier the two men were on the board to preserve Ascension Alley. The public had become outraged that the plantation house was being threatened by developers. Everyone—particularly Fred—got all up at arms and passionate over the threatened extinction of another palace to bigotry. Finally, through much work and effort, an organization was developed that ultimately raised over two million dollars for Ascension Alley's preservation.

But did the public knit together like that when each of his girls was found missing?

They did not.

Did the masses raise their fists in outrage at the waste of another young woman?

They did not.

There was hardly more than a mournful cry by the family, an obituary in the *Times-Picayune,* and a filing down at the homicide division of NOPD. Then silence. A quiet so deep and profound that even Everard found it difficult not to take it for approval.

He stared up at the magnificent Scalamandre-dressed bed and thought of all the pretty faces in his past. How fickle the public was to value a house over a young woman. How strange and irrational they were. Not southern at all. Further proof that the old South was gone. It now was a relic, like the bed he slept in and cherished. The trappings of the South—the plantation houses, the mahogany beds—could be salvaged, but they were nothing but firewood without the ideas behind them.

And the ideas were gone. Preserved only by those like him, men who took their presidency at the 555 Association seriously.

It was a great honor to preside where he did, Laborde

thought, his insides growing warm over the notion. He and his kind were keeping alive the metaphorical equivalent of the California condor. Only when they were gone would they be missed. It was his job to make sure they were never gone.

The gala Murder Mystery Night had taken them far from fiscal extinction, but it still bothered him how poorly missed his girls were. If beauty paid a great price, then each in her turn was a sacrifice on the altar of the old South. Each was so pretty. He still saw them as he first did, their smiles wary and tremulous, their relief when they realized he was a gentleman. The deep question in their terror-filled eyes when everything had been answered except *why*.

The terrible WHY. Why did Atlanta burn, why did Valsin Monparnasse shoot the fourteen-year-old? Jesus, why did he buy a damned houseboy in the first place?

As if J. Everard Laborde could answer these questions. Attraction was part fate, part hormones, part destiny. He couldn't say why he killed the girls he did, he knew only that when he found them, he wanted them. And after he wanted them, he knew he had to kill them.

The Why. It was the great unanswered maw every man would gape at on his way to the grave. Even now Everard couldn't figure out his father. It astounded him that the man had married his mother. Cummings Laborde was a well-known, respected surgeon who had had no business marrying a showgirl from New York. There were times Everard could almost understand his father's outrage at his mother's inbred lack of class and taste. The cheap makeup, the tawdry outfits, they were enough to make any man cringe. But then, why had he chosen her? And why had he hit her?

Anabel Laborde was what she was. Anyone could see it. Cummings wasn't going to change her, not even with his fist, another irony, because Cummings Laborde was considered and certainly supposed to be a healer. He was a medical doctor, and yet he'd probably inflicted more injury upon Everard's own mother than the man saw in a typical night at the

*Hotel-Dieu* emergency room. Everyone stayed quiet about the abuse, of course. His father was a respected figure. No one would have believed Anabel and her black eyes anyway. Society didn't like her. They politely stayed away as best they could, only further outraging her husband.

The Why was agony, Laborde thought as the memory of his mother clarified in the twilight between sleep and wakefulness. He would always be mystified why his father had hooked up with her, stayed with her, hit her. But to a young boy, more inexplicable than that, was why Anabel took it. And took it. And took it. She'd allowed her son to see her treated like a doormat by her husband, beaten like a stray cur day after day. Yet she'd stayed with the man. Worst of all, she'd produced a boy who had to make sense of it, and probably screwed the whole thing up because he was so goddamned angry that she had stayed, and taken it, and taken it, and taken it.

Laborde had enough personal insight to know what people would say about him if ever he was caught. They would expound upon his cruel, egomaniac, domineering father who had driven him to kill, but it wasn't his father at all. For the most part, Everard believed he understood his father. He was simply ashamed of that to which he was inexplicably attracted, and thus, in his difficulty with the conflict, took it out on his mother's face.

But in the end, what the public would never know, was that it was his mother who created the monster. She was not worthy of the deep feelings her son had for her. She couldn't have been, or she wouldn't have let anyone treat her that way. Her silences said it was okay what was done to her, that she somehow deserved it. He'd had no place expressing outrage at her treatment when that was obviously what she wanted, even deserved.

Everard thought long and hard on what kind of monster he was. He thought of all those pretty faces, and all the silent graves. In his mind, the pictures of his girls appeared before him, clear smiles; trickling blood; surreal photos branded into his mind, but they were good company. He loved them in their own way.

Sometimes a great price was paid for beauty; and sometimes beauty paid a great price.

He remembered the Jewess who'd come to him for a job some five years earlier. He'd found her so terribly attractive; she was downright preppy; a WASP in every detail except one: in the interview, even she had admitted she was Jewish.

Zoe Green was completely wrong for him. In some ways she was just like the trashy waitress with the Mardi Gras–painted nails. She was as wrong for him as Anabel had been for his father. He'd hated Zoe Green then. She'd not been worthy of the feelings that had come to him during their interview.

He shut his eyes to the Scalamandre confection overhead. Slowly, he forced himself to drift into the nirvana of sleep, as a man who had a clear conscience could. He certainly wasn't the cause of all his monstrosities and he didn't need a shrink to tell him that. He mourned alongside the families of his girls whether the families knew it or not. No one despised the destruction of a woman as much as J. Everard Laborde.

His eyes inexplicably opened. Again his vision met with the lush, coffinlike upholstery of the tester. A face seemed to form in the rosette of fabric at the center, a face he saw often and knew well.

Zoe Green had come to haunt him the most, perhaps because he'd been the most attracted to her. She, unlike the rest—even his mother—had been the only one who seemed to be honestly trying to change what she was. The red Ferragamo flats and the St. John knit dress were there to say conservative and preppy. With her dyed hair, Zoe Green wanted to say white Anglo-Saxon Protestant, but the façade didn't quite fit with the Semitic tilt to her brows, the high cheekbones, the dark, ethnic eyes, the mouth that was full and rosy and, in the end, tragically truthful, because it spouted out all kinds of facts that she'd have best kept to herself. The girl might have been a WASP at heart, but the truth was, she was a Christ killer by birth and by confession, and the fact that he'd almost been touched by her still left an acid etch of rage on his guts.

Zoe Green stared at him from where he imagined her face was on the rosette. It was not an accusing stare; it never was. He was no bigot. He was no David Duke, porno-hawking Nazi freak. In the end, if they should ever catch him—which they wouldn't—they would understand what he was.

And they would mourn the fact that Anabel had never once fought back.

# ❧ 14 ❧

A loud pounding woke Claire. She thought it was from the jackhammer they'd been using at the construction site across 86th Street, but then she opened her eyes and became disoriented. She wasn't in New York. Outside a pair of French doors, southern sunlight dappled through magnolia trees. From the balcony, blue jays perched on the railing as they took turns swooping down on something in the courtyard.

They were attacking the tomcat in Number One. She suddenly remembered. Now she knew where she was. She was in New Orleans; she was home.

And there was someone pounding on her door.

"Just a minute." She fumbled for a terry bathrobe and glanced at the clock. An unconscious epithet came out of her mouth when she noticed the time. It was five minutes after six.

Flinging the robe over her silk pajamas, she tripped sleepily to the door. "Yes? What is it?" She peered out from behind the chain.

"Ma'am."

She silently moaned. No need for a geography lesson to recognize that Tulsa drawl; she'd had nightmares about it just last night.

"If you're here to arrest me, I'll need to see your warrant. If not—"

"Arrest? Who said anything about arrest?" He grinned and put his hand on the door jamb.

She fought the urge to slam the door on it. "Agent Jameson, isn't this a little early for a field visit?"

"Hell, no. Why, back home we'd have been up for hours, feeding scratch to the chickens, slopping the hogs, baling the hay . . ." He moved his hand to the door's edge. Now she'd never get the door closed without a tug-of-war, one she'd lose if body size had anything to do with it.

She stared at him, willing herself to be calm. After all, she was an attorney. She knew her rights better than most. He couldn't make her say or do anything she didn't believe prudent. He wouldn't catch her off guard, not even at six A.M.

But he was so damn tall. The ceilings were fourteen feet and he still seemed to loom over her, even with the door and the chain between them.

"What on earth could you possibly need at this hour of the morning?" Her voice was barely over a whisper.

"I need a long talk with you, ma'am. About Zoe." His grip on the door tightened as if he expected her to slam it in his face.

"You're FBI. You can get anything you want on my sister down at the homicide division of the NOPD. As far as anything else, I'm sorry, but—"

"No, don't take the Fifth. I've heard it all before. I didn't come here to talk about *High Risk* or that shadowy little women's group you started. Yeah, I've got my sources and they told me about that victim's rights group you started up at Columbia after your sister died. But right now I don't want to talk about all that. I want to talk about your sister. And who murdered her."

"I don't know who murdered her. No one does. You know that."

He stared at her. Something in his face—or his eyes—seemed to soften, as if he somehow empathized with her, but that was impossible. He had yet to treat her with much regard or respect. The act of showing up at her condo at dawn didn't speak of empathy, it spoke of intimidation.

She tried to close the door, eager to put an end to the conversation, but the hand on the door edge was as tough as she feared it was. The door didn't budge.

She glared at him. "If there's nothing else?"

"Did you ever notice that there was something odd about Zoe when she was found?"

Claire was silent. She thought she knew what he was going to say. Her insistent comments were probably all over the police files even if Homicide had never taken her observations to heart. Finally she said, "Yes."

"The murderer wore gloves, but they were old surgeons' gloves from the fifties. The rubber had worn out and they were cracked. That's why her hair looked so funky in the police photos. Tiny pieces of glove were stuck in her hair."

Claire tried to hide her surprise, but it was difficult. What she'd thought he was going to say he didn't even seem to know about. The glove evidence was brand new to her. The few police reports and photos she'd been allowed to see told nothing of it.

"I guess you never saw the autopsy report." His eyes narrowed. "No, of course you didn't, because the police don't show people those things until they get to trial. They don't even show it to the family, because for all they know, someone in the family did it."

"They told us the cause of death."

"Yeah? But did they mention the hairs found on her? The tip of the rubber glove found in her mouth with one partial fingerprint whorl still imbedded in the rubber?"

The room seemed to tighten in on her. She knew there were things the police withheld—the world of murder wasn't like a weekly TV show where the family worked closely with the police, step by step until the killer was caught. In real life the lack of knowledge was just another agony the family had to deal with. The police told them nothing or very little; the bulk of evidence was held for trial, when and if there was a trial. Zoe had never had her day in court.

"There's more." He smirked. "You want to let me in, or should I just head back up the trail?"

She took a deep breath. "Why are you offering this to me? I can only think this is some kind of setup—"

"No, ma'am. No setup. You'd just get it thrown out of court if it was, slick attorney that you are."

"Then why?" She stared at him. It was stupid for her to be tempted by his information. He was FBI, for God's sake, but she wanted what he could so easily find out. She wanted the information so badly, she felt it like an ache in the back of her throat. "You're not offering this for free, so what's the price?" Her practiced, cool façade returned.

"The price is easy, Ms. Green. The price is cooperation. But we don't have to talk about your end right now. I'm here to tell you about your sister, and we'll do it on credit for the time being." The coaxing Tulsa accent was like warm butter dripping over biscuits. She had a hard time remaining detached.

*Think about this, Claire,* she cautioned herself. *This man is dangerous,* she repeated over and over again in her mind as she stared at him. But the warnings were useless. What he had to offer was too great a temptation. She wanted it too badly. To let him in her condo, to even allow herself a prolonged conversation with him, was beyond idiotic, but she helplessly caved in because she knew that in the end the lure of information would make her do it anyway.

*An attorney who represents himself has a fool for a client,* she thought as she closed the door, released the chain, and let him into the condo.

"Nice place," he said as he made himself at home on the couch. The ubiquitous red tie folder rested on his lap.

"Is the autopsy report in there?" she asked, nodding to the folder.

"Maybe." He glanced at her, his gaze taking in her messy, bed-rumpled appearance with a look that was thorough and insulting. His perusal took maybe a fraction of a second, but it seemed like eons to her. She wasn't used to a good-ol'-boy, hungry male stare. It was the kind of thing a woman got from construction workers on Staten Island, and for that reason she stayed in Manhattan.

But if the glance unsettled her, worse was the aftermath. Jameson had the act down perfectly. He further taunted with the fact that now he seemed so damned smug about what he saw.

She pulled together the lapels of the robe and ran another hand through the thick tangle of her hair. He scared her. Maybe he wasn't the wild-eyed degenerate he appeared to be when she first spied him in Bloomingdale's, but he was capable of being such a man, if only because he could play the part so well.

"I—I need to get dressed. Maybe we should take this discussion out to breakfast. There's a little café down at Prytania and Washington."

She hoped she hid the relief on her face when he nodded. "I'll be only a second."

In horrid fascination she watched as his gaze locked on her bare feet. He seemed to study everything about them, their size-seven length, the natural polish on her nails, the fact that her ankles and the part of her calves that stuck out from beneath the terry robe were smooth and winter-pale.

She backed away and went to the bedroom. Slowly, she closed the door. Softly, she locked it.

It was perhaps the part of her life she hated most now. The fear. Just about any man could do it to her; one overtly sexual look and she locked up like an engine without oil.

But it was worse coming from him. Definitely worse. He was out there on her couch, his presence violating the quietly classical condo like a bear crashing through a museum. He was obviously on the vigilante warpath and right now he was going after her hide. He was tall and strong, and he held all the cards. Legally, she might outmaneuver him, but physically, she would never be able to. He was a big man, and if he chose, there wasn't a whole lot she could keep him from doing to her. She had only her wits to protect her, and the trust that he was the kind of man she thought he was.

But she could be wrong. She could be wrong about any man. Zoe had been wrong. She'd looked for Prince Charming and she was betrayed.

"I'll be right out." Did her voice show her fear? She hoped not. He had information that could be eminently useful. If they could reach a bargain, it would be worth the wear on her nerves. He might put her that much closer to Zoe's killer.

She reached for her underthings and a pair of linen trousers. Buttoning the matching black linen shirt, she splashed some cold water on her face, clipped her hair back, and slipped on a pair of flats.

"Just another minute." She wrung her hands as if that would keep them from trembling. Checking her purse for cash, she flung it over her arm with a silk bomber jacket, then silently unlocked the door.

He stood with his back to her as he looked out the French doors to the courtyard. The blue jays were still mercilessly dive-bombing the tomcat; the magnolia leaves bristled in the wind. On a summer eve the scent of blossoms must perfume the whole condo, she thought.

She studied his back for a moment and wondered if he knew how frightened she was. Being alone with him was a special terror because he was FBI and she had so much to lose, and there was the added danger of finding him physically attractive. That especially worried her. It wasn't possible to be attracted to someone without letting down one's guard. Sexuality required trust and self-abandonment, and she had big trouble with both. It was her curse, this perennial conflict.

His broad, strong back was like a fortress. It seemed invincible. She wondered if he knew she had locked the door while she'd changed.

He turned around. Their gazes met, and she had all her answers. It might have been her imagination, but she swore the strange empathy had returned to his eyes. He took in her appearance, but his gaze was gentle this time. Wary. As one looks at a doe one has surprised in a clearing.

He went to the door and held it open for her, motioning for her to walk under his outstretched arm. She hesitated, then felt foolish. Despising herself, she walked beneath his arm and went down the antebellum staircase. He followed behind her, whistling.

*Who's afraid of the big bad wolf? The big bad wolf, the big, bad wolf . . .*

She turned around and looked at him.

He smiled. "I see from the reports that you have family down here, Ms. Green. Why the fancy rental, when you could stay with them?"

Outside, the old brick sidewalks were bumpy with tree roots. She was glad to give her attention to her feet and not to him. "I might be staying down here awhile. My parents' place is small. I don't want to get in their way."

"Yeah. I see from my background check that you took a long sabbatical from the firm. How will Fassbinder Hamilton get along without their prodigy?" He lifted an eyebrow.

She stared vacantly out across Prytania. "I'm hardly their prodigy, and they have good help. Snooping around, I'm sure you noticed the caliber of my secretary and paralegal. I don't lie awake at night worrying about Fassbinder."

"So what do you lie awake at night worrying about, Ms. Green?"

She didn't answer.

"Dragons?" he whispered just as they got to the door of the café.

She didn't answer that question either. By the look in his eyes as they held hers, she didn't have to.

"So what does the rubber glove signify?" she asked after they were through with their café au lait and pastry. Still nervous, she picked up the stray crumbs from her scone and little blue bits of paper from the sweetener packets and made a point of depositing them in her used coffee cup.

"They have a partial fingerprint," he said. "It might be good enough to nail him."

"To nail whom? Who is this man who murdered my sister?"

He glanced at her, his eyes dark, his face grim. "He's white, under sixty-five, a serial killer. The glove indicated premeditation. Zoe Green's murderer didn't rape and kill her in a one-time deal. The glove proved he'd thought about her murder. He'd done it before."

She continued picking up bits. "The latex in the glove was cracking and disintegrating because it was old, but why did he use an old glove when he could have used a new one? And where did he get the old glove?"

"Don't know. It's a good part of the mystery. You solve it, you might just be able to find this guy so ZOE can off him."

She stiffened. Then her old prudence came back to her. He couldn't lead her down the garden path to damnation if she didn't let him. "Is that your specialty, Agent Jameson?"

"What? Vigilantism?" He leaned forward menacingly, the bulk of his frame ridiculous in the tiny bistro chair. "If you really want to know, it's hate crimes, but vigilantism, survivalism, separatism, cults . . . they're all cut from the same paranoia."

"I was talking about the way you ask leading questions. I'm surprised most of your evidence doesn't get thrown out of court the way you handle an interrogation."

His hand slid over to hers, where she still picked away at

the crumbs on the marble-top table. Their fingertips almost touched. She could feel him next to her like she could feel her heart quicken. And there it was again. The abominable attraction.

"This isn't an interrogation, Claire," he said, staring at her, his voice low and husky. "I'm talking to you now because of your sister. You want to find the guy, don't you, one way or the other? If so, I can help."

His offer seemed so heartfelt, she almost bought it. But then she remembered who he was, and who she was, and she hardened herself. Smiling as though a frown would crack her face, she said, "Let's get one thing straight. All you really want to do is entrap me."

The space between their fingertips shortened. It seemed there was only a molecular layer of air between them holding back skin contact. She swore she could feel him. Feel his heat.

"I've seen other women end up like your sister." A muscle ticked in his jaw. His face seemed to grow leaner, more hard, the expression in his eyes more distant. "You may not believe this, but I'd like to catch the guy. Shit, it's my job—"

"No, your job right now is to catch me, and I'm not a vigilante." She hated the way the emotion in her voice broke through her façade.

"My specialty is many things, Claire."

She glanced down at the table, but there were no more crumbs to pick up, no more bits of blue paper. She would have to leave her hands where they were or pull them back and reveal her fear. "If you're such a Renaissance man, then why did you answer the ad in *High Risk?* And most of all, why are you here now? Why not let the FBI here in New Orleans talk to me?"

He took a deep, slightly exasperated breath. "My section chief is Frederick Gunnarson. Ever heard of him?"

"No."

"Well, he's a big deal in law enforcement. He took down some of the most gruesome inhumanity of our time—Dalton Lee Wayne, Cecil Baron, Les Schnell. He even developed a numbers theory on how to track serial killers that we still use today."

"I still don't get it," she said. "What's a hate-crime specialist doing working beneath a man with Gunnarson's expertise then?"

He smiled. His grin was slow and lopsided. Sexy. She wanted desperately not to look at it, but it captured her.

"Gunnarson has a theory about agents too. He insists on us branching out whenever we can. He'd like us to do everything. Gunnarson holds that crime isn't pure. His conviction rate has been twice most other agents because he attacks the criminal at all angles."

She must have looked confused, because he shifted in his chair and a furrow appeared between his eyes. "Let me explain it to you this way," he said, still not moving his fingers a millimeter closer, nor a millimeter farther away. "If you can't get Al Capone for extortion and murder, you lock him away on tax evasion. If you can't convict a bunch of whites in Mississippi for lynching a guy, then you shift the whole damn thing out of the state court, and you take it into federal court with the idea of convicting those same white folks for violating the poor bastard's civil rights. But you've got to have a wide net, and most feds have tunnel-vision. That's why Gunnarson wants his agents to know everything. Most criminals are screwups in a lot of areas. If we can take in all of it, then we're sure to get the guy, one way or another."

"So all you're really telling me is that in the Tulsa office a hate-crime specialist can go after anybody he wants." She lowered her gaze to their almost-touching fingertips. In an act of defiance, she finally moved hers back and put her hands in her lap.

"I can go after a murderer. Zoe's murderer."

"You won't catch him. There's nothing to learn down

here. Even I have to face the fact that Zoe's killer is probably long gone. Go back to Tulsa, Agent Jameson. Serial killing isn't your field."

"Liam, the name's Liam."

She looked at him. "Liam," she said softly, succinctly.

The corner of his mouth lifted in a half-smile. "Just remember one thing, Claire. I know more about killers than you'd think. Killers come in all ways. Sometimes they're born out of racial hatred, or out of profit and greed; sometimes they're created out of sheer stupidity. I know about all kinds. People who wear white robes and burn crosses are sometimes just good-ol'-boys out for a joy ride. Usually they're dumber than dirt, and when something stupid happens, sometimes somebody gets killed. But I know, too, that other kinds can lurk behind the white robes or the army fatigues and the shotguns. They're not the followers, they're the leaders. They can ramble on about the Constitution and do a snow job the Vail chamber of commerce would pay for on a warm day, but let me tell you something. These kind of guys deep down are serial killers. They're just Jeffrey Dahmer with an agenda. The doctrine they hook up with is their excuse to kill, and it really doesn't matter what the doctrine is. It's secondary. So if one guy's wearing white robes, and another swastikas, and another's spouting Jesus and Armegeddon all the while holed up with a bunch of hostages, they're all the same kind of guy inside. Do you get it now? Sometimes sadomasochists burn crosses on lawns right alongside their nigger-hating friends, but they're apples and oranges. So let me tell you, I know a lot about killers, Claire. My training was thorough."

She looked down at her crossed hands. "This conversation has been very enlightening. I appreciate it, really I do, but you, Agent Liam Jameson, haven't answered the most important question of all: Why would you help me? What's in it for you except the chance to confirm one of your own pet theories that I'm in some kind of vigilante group?"

"Well, aren't you? Isn't that why you named the victims group ZOE? After your sister, whose murderer was never found?"

She didn't answer.

He leaned back in his chair and stretched his legs out in front of him.

Long legs that went on forever.

"Let's put this behind us, Claire. I'm on to you. You may not think you're doing anything wrong with that women's club you have going in New York, but I know otherwise. Halbert Washington's death wasn't necessarily a tragedy, but it wasn't an accident either. That little playgroup of yours is dangerous." He leaned forward, his eyes—those eyes that terrified her with their savageness—became menacing. "Just remember, darling, what you nourished just might turn around and bite you in the ass."

A strange coldness settled in her belly. Last night at the mall, as she cried on the phone to Phyllis, the unthinkable had occurred to her. But she was wrong, and he was too. ZOE wouldn't go after her. They were out for each other, not after each other. Halbert Washington's botched death aside, ZOE wasn't going to waste its time keeping her in her place. Not when it was her organization. Besides, Phyllis was right. They loved her. They were her friends, her sisters-in-victim-hell. It would be against anything any of them ever believed in for them to turn on her.

But she *was* the lawyer. And they *had* tried to keep things from her.

Suddenly she became inexplicably angry. She glared at him and stood. "I've got to get going. I've appointments this morning—"

"Don't you want to see the autopsy report?" He motioned to the folder. The folder lay on the table like a rattlesnake.

She sat back down. She wondered if her face betrayed the sickness she felt in her stomach. "I want to see the autopsy report . . . but that's really all I have time for, so if you'll show it to me . . ."

He shoved the folder toward her. With shaking hands she untied it and removed the sheets of paper.

She braced herself for the contents, but she knew that to flinch would mean to back away, and she couldn't do that. She had to read everything, no matter how painful, for Zoe's sake.

Her eyes focused on the first page. The autopsy was dated five years earlier. Minnefield was the coroner. Everybody knew him. He was an elected official, and had been in office for years. A politician, even one with a medical degree, was certainly her idea of the worst choice to perform an autopsy. Best was a forensic pathologist, but New Orleans didn't have one. Everyone had to rely on Minnefield, and he was only adequate, or so she was told.

The report was literate and complete; the technical language almost a comfort to her. Cold and without bias, Minnefield's words detached her from the object of his scrutiny. What he reported on was just another body, not her twin sister, not her parents' beloved daughter. The autopsy was easier to get through than she had feared.

She flipped through the superficial wounds until she reached the part about Zoe's makeup. It was hardly noted in the report what had been so wrong in the picture Claire had seen of the body. Zoe's makeup was just makeup to the coroner. Nothing unusual there to note, according to Minnefield.

She continued glancing through the sheets of paper. The autopsy went in layers, like the sheets of paper that made up the report. The description of sexual trauma was hardest to get through. Claire forced herself not to dwell on it, but when she finally flipped the page, tears streaked down her cheeks. She hadn't even known she'd been crying.

Finally she put the report aside. She couldn't allow herself to picture her sister on the slab being dissected like a lab rat. It wasn't Zoe Green, it couldn't be. It was just a body that any student of medicine would find interesting given the trauma it had received, and the clues that it wore like battle scars. And that's how she had to start thinking, she chastened herself, or she'd never endure the investigation long enough to do any good.

"You don't look too well, Claire."

She glanced up at him, surprised at the concern in his voice. Wiping her cheeks with her hand, she said only, "She was my sister."

"Tough reading."

"Yes." She looked down at the coroner's seal that marked each page along with the name Zoe Melissa Green that was neatly typed across the top. Overdosed, she shoved the report across the table to him. "Thank you for showing it to me. At least now I know the details of what happened to her."

"There's more in the homicide report." He opened the red tie and dangled a few more papers in front of her. "Some of which you might find very interesting."

She reached for them; he pulled them back.

"Not yet. First, tell me about her. What was she like?"

"Zoe?" She frowned. "She was my sister, my twin."

"Identical?"

"I'm sure you've seen the police photos. What do you think?" She gave him that level gaze, the one she'd practiced during the mock trials at law school.

His mouth twisted into a sardonic resemblance of a smile. "Identical. Except for the lips." His gaze seemed to burn into her facial features. "Zoe's lips were slightly less symmetrical. . . ." His gaze lifted. "And her eyes, well, her eyes . . ."

"Eyes are nothing but expression." She felt the lump of tears in her throat. "Zoe's eyes couldn't possibly have looked like mine in the pictures you saw."

"They didn't. Yours don't hold the terror she must have felt in the end. Yet . . . there's terror in your eyes too."

She lost the standoff again; she blinked.

Nervously, she said, "None of this has anything to do with me. Zoe and I were very different. We looked alike, but we thought in separate worlds."

"What do you mean?"

"I mean—well, what I mean is—that I wanted a J.D. and she wanted an M.R.S., but I really don't know what this has to do with anything—"

"To find a killer, you must first know the victim."

"Are you really going to find her killer?"

He took a long, ponderous sip of coffee. The silence became deafening. "I could try finding new evidence to revitalize the case. I could certainly do that."

"Would you?" She hated the way the words sounded so small and pleading, but she was in New Orleans to look for the man who killed her sister and she didn't even have access to her sister's autopsy report. And he did.

"I'll look into your sister's case." He put down his coffee cup and shifted again in the small café chair. "The deal is, however, I tell you about Zoe, and you tell me about *ZOE*. The first thing I want to know is what's Phyllis Zuckermann's role in this. I see she's a rich widow who got mugged one summer in Central Park. Is she out for vengeance too? What is she? Some kind of ringleader?"

Shock was now tempered by disgust. Claire pulled back, amazed at how she'd let down her guard. He was one smooth operator. "You've got a tap on my phone, so you already know Phyllis Zuckermann's my friend. There's nothing I can add to that."

"We know you both know Earnestine Darby. It's just circumstantial now, but if we get anything more—"

"You won't." She snatched up her purse. Reality, cold and wet, slapped her in the face. He wasn't going to help her with Zoe's killer, not really. He was only going to seduce her into incriminating herself and the others in ZOE. "It's been real fun, Agent Jameson, but I've got to go now. I'll be making all my calls on pay phones from here on in."

"You haven't even called your parents."

"I was going to do that today," she snapped, but then stopped herself. Stunned, she realized she'd answered before she'd even thought about the question. He even knew her Achilles' heel.

She looked at him with rigid eyes and wondered how he could so easily slip under her skin. "Good-bye, Agent Jameson. I think this puts a closure to our relationship. You keep your police files to yourself, and I'll keep to myself."

"You can't do anything without help from the authorities. Are you going to use my help or lean upon the tender mercies of NOPD? They've got the highest murder rate in the country and I know they're real eager to dig up evidence on a five-year-old murder." He smirked. "If you're wise, Ms. Green, you'll take my help."

"And what help is that? A one-way ticket to a jail sentence?" She stood and walked to the café door.

Shocked, she felt him grab her arm.

"Do you want to find this guy?" The gentleness of his touch was in inverse proportion to the anger in his eyes. "Can't you hear me? I want to help you. I want to help your sister."

Contemptuously she looked down at his hand on her forearm. "Your baboon tactics fail to impress."

He dropped his hold. "Her killer should be found, Claire."

"What do you care?"

The lean planes of his face softened. "When I see how a man treats a woman like Zoe was treated, it makes me want to kill somebody." He moved closer. His gaze locked with hers. "And it makes me extra protective of the women around me."

Perhaps it was the huskiness in his voice, the tenderness in his expression; she didn't know, yet his words got through to her. She almost believed him. But even if he was totally sincere, it wouldn't help. She couldn't get involved with him. He was a fed, one she found sexually attractive. Dangerous on two counts. He'd never hand her Zoe's killer; he'd give her nothing but a broken heart.

"I wish that made a difference," she whispered, looking everywhere but at him. "Still, all the police photos in the world don't tell you what it's really like. Losing your twin, it's like cutting off your arm . . ." Her eyes suddenly filled with tears. "I wish you could help me . . . I guess I really wish there were someone to slay this dragon . . . but there isn't. You can't."

She rushed out the door. Dodging the traffic on Prytania, she crossed the street and half ran, half jogged all the way to the mansion. Her instincts told her he didn't follow, but she chanced one look back at the café before she turned the corner. He stood in the doorway and stared after her. The perplexity on his face was no surprise, but the stiffness in his jaw was ominous. She knew if she was nearer him, she'd probably see that glint in his eye. She'd told him to back off, and it was like jerking a Rotweiler away from a steak. Now she had trouble.

## ❧ 15 ❧

Claire stood in front of the building at 555 Canal. Except for the address, it was unmarked. Most of the people on Canal had no idea that the double walnut doors that rose above the curved granite stair was the home of the illustrious 555 Association.

Black men hung against the club's wrought iron fence just watching the throngs of pedestrians. Several older women, probably domestic workers for the big houses on St. Charles Avenue, lined up along the sidewalk, waiting for the bus. The ubiquitous groups of tourists went by, tagged by their cameras and casual attire. Claire ignored them all. Her attention was held by two young white men, both good-looking, in dark tropical-weight worsted suits. Slick and confident, they ignored the blacks who lounged by the wrought iron fence and went right up the granite stairs to the association's door.

Lawyers, she thought as she followed them up those same steps. No doubt these young Turks could afford the 555 because they worked for Daddy, who was a founding partner of some old-line firm. The very idea of it made Claire glad for New York. In the big anonymous city it was easy to get an even break. But nepotism was a killer in New Orleans. And worse than that were those ugly Great Gatsby seersucker suits attorneys sported in the humid southern summer. New York spared her of that too.

"Excuse me," she murmured as the two young men ignored her. "I'd like to speak to one of the managers of the association, if I might, someone who's been here at least five years. Would you know if that's possible?"

The men looked a little surprised to see her standing behind them on the stoop. One of them, a handsome one with black hair and slate-blue eyes, actually smiled. "This is a private club."

"I know that."

They evaluated her. Perhaps it was the black linen pants suit, or the sleek Mark Cross handbag, she didn't know, she just supposed she was presentable enough for them to decide to help her.

"Come on in. You can talk to the secretary." The handsome one held open the door. The other man just gave her that up-and-down look that men often do when they're checking out a prospective female.

She walked into the foyer. The walls at the entrance to the dining room were painted to look like marble and gray silk-satin drapery. A maître d' stood at a mahogany podium. He seemed engrossed in reworking some kind of schedule sheet, probably the day's reservations.

It was odd, but Claire felt a bit let down by the club's tasteful, quiet interior. She'd heard so much about the 555, particularly by the Jews who felt the sting of its rejection, she was expecting a more sinister environment. She remembered one fellow Columbia grad who'd returned to New Orleans to help his father run the family's chain of appliance stores. Jordan had never gotten over the fact that he could not gain admission to the lunch club. His father told him to forget it, but he just couldn't, and he used to bitch to Claire about it. It was absurd to her that she was supposed to drum up sympathy for him because he was a Jew and couldn't get in to a stupid lunch club, when Jordan didn't seem to understand the idea that the 555 wouldn't have her even if she weren't Jewish but because she was a woman. She could never quite get him to quit whining about it, so in the end she could do nothing but rack up Jordan's obliviousness as a good lesson in male self-absorption.

"Mr. Boudreaux, this young lady would like to see the secretary." The handsome one grinned at her again.

She smiled back, feeling like she needed a big pink bow atop her head and a lollipop to match. "Thank you," she murmured, doing her best to sound sincere.

Mr. Boudreaux stepped from behind the podium and nodded to her to follow him. She left the two men behind, an expression of faint gratitude plastered on her face.

"This is the president's office. If you will wait here, I'll get his secretary, Mr. D'Hemecourt."

She made herself comfortable on the love seat positioned in front of the secretary's desk. No dark secrets in this office either: an Apple computer, a Rolodex, and a scratch pad with the association's pelican logo on it. The office looked like any other secretary's, excluding perhaps the beautiful arrangement of pale pink antherium that adorned the credenza.

"So nice to meet you. I'm Gerald D'Hemecourt, Miss . . . ?" A man in his early twenties appeared with Mr. Boudreaux from behind a pair of French doors. He was preppy in gray trousers and a navy blazer. She noticed his silk tie was adorned with the 555 pelican logo.

"I'm Ms. Green. Claire Green." Claire took his extended hand; the young man shook it. His fingers were like cold trout, and she wondered why he bothered with the greeting at all.

"What can we do for you, Miss Green?" The man's mannerisms, such as the way he distastefully pursed his lips when he gave her his attention, made Claire think the man was just a run-of-the-mill pretentious jerk.

Mr. Boudreaux left them alone in the office.

"I don't want to be an inconvenience," she began, "but

I've come for some information about a crime. One committed five years ago." She paused and looked at the man, unsure how to continue. "I can't help but notice your age. I was hoping to speak with an older gentleman. Someone who's been with the association at least five years."

"I've been here five years exactly," D'Hemecourt said in a tone that confirmed he was indeed a pretentious jerk.

Claire edged forward in her seat. "My sister came here five years ago seeking employment. They may still talk about her. Her name was Zoe and this was the last place she was seen before she was murdered."

The pleasant, meet-the-public expression on D'Hemecourt's face didn't change. "I know about her. I wasn't here then, but I know she applied for the job I have now."

She gave him a supplicating look. The guy might be human. "I'm hoping the police will reopen the case. It's been unsolved all these years and I thought if I came down here and found out any little tidbit of information that might have been overlooked, well, I hoped to be able to convince NOPD Homicide to look into the murder again."

"There's nothing I can add to what the police already have. I've only heard about your sister through the grapevine."

"Can you at least tell me about the interview process? I don't have access to the police files. I don't even know who she talked to here."

"I interviewed with Mr. Laborde himself," D'Hemecourt stated, the screw-you tone creeping back into his voice.

"Who's Mr. Laborde?"

D'Hemecourt looked at the pair of French doors that led from his office. "J. Everard Laborde is the president of the 555. He has been for years. I believe the position your sister interviewed for was for his secretary. That's my position now."

"I think my sister spoke with him."

"I'd say that was likely."

"Is it possible for me to speak with Mr. Laborde? I could make an appointment."

He glanced again at the French doors. "I will certainly mention that you stopped by. Mr. Laborde is very busy."

"Let me leave my name and phone number. If he'll speak with me, you can just let me know and I'll be there." She stood and rummaged through her handbag for her pen.

D'Hemecourt handed her a small card with "555" embossed in gold at the top. She scrawled her name, address, and phone number.

"Thank you for your help." She made a point of making eye contact with him. "I know you'll do all you can."

D'Hemecourt walked her to the door. The speaker phone on his desk buzzed and a harsh voice broke the silence.

"Dem, come in here. You didn't clean my desk today."

D'Hemecourt rushed to the phone and punched a button. "Right away, Mr. Laborde."

"I'll see myself out," she said.

D'Hemecourt barely noticed she'd spoken. He scurried over to the mahogany filing cabinets beneath the credenza and madly dug out a bottle of window cleaner. Then he flew to the double doors, straightened his tie, and entered the hallowed sanctuary of the great J. Everard Laborde.

From the open door she got a glimpse of him. Laborde sat at a huge glass desk that D'Hemecourt was probably enslaved to hourly care with the Windex. She barely caught note of an unremarkable profile and graying head before D'Hemecourt closed the door and left her alone in his office.

Maybe it was a blessing Zoe never got the job, she mused. By D'Hemecourt's behavior, Laborde was a tyrant. Zoe, with her free-spirited ways, and lack of talent with any kind of cleaner let alone Windex, would have come to loggerheads with a boss as exacting as this one.

She put her hand on the doorknob, ready to leave. But suddenly, she looked behind her at the bank of filing cabinets behind D'Hemecourt's desk.

It was unlikely any file remained of her sister's interview. As unlikely as this self-important president of the 555 Association was going to give her an appointment.

Quietly she stepped over to the filing cabinets. From behind the French doors she heard Laborde say, "And over there . . . and over there . . . how many times do I have to tell you? First thing in the morning and right after I leave for lunch you're to come in here and clean this . . ."

"Yes, Mr. Laborde. Of course, this looks terrible without maintenance. So sorry . . ." D'Hemecourt's murmurs could be heard through the trigger spraying.

She didn't have much time, but it was worth a shot. In silence, she eased open the *G* file and flipped through it for *Green*. There were none. Big surprise. But there were files on just about every old family name in the city. What she wouldn't give to flip through them, she thought as she pressed the file drawer back into the cabinet.

D'Hemecourt was still cleaning, if Laborde's curses had anything to do with it. She almost laughed out loud when Laborde shouted that his secretary had managed to Windex a pile of personal invitations to Mardi Gras balls.

She knelt by the *Z* file drawer. It held very little. Just old Louisiana family names: Zeringue, Zatarain, Zachary. To the back there was a mysterious file with the initials ZG on it. She peeked inside. Her gaze lit on the name Zoe Green like a heat-seeking missile. She was about to thumb through it, when she suddenly realized Laborde was telling D'Hemecourt to leave his office.

In a panic she grabbed the file. The French doors began to open and she tore out of the office.

In the hallway, her back to the wall, she listened. Any second she was sure D'Hemecourt was going to come after her. He was going to call out and then he was going to have her arrested for stealing.

But there was only silence. When he got on the phone and RSVPed a party invitation for his boss, she knew he hadn't seen her. Relief hit like a brick wall, and she stared at the stolen file in her hands with a mixture of triumph and self-contempt.

She was an attorney, for God's sake. She was supposed to interpret and uphold the law, not break it.

But now she had her sister's file. She had one more thing that she hadn't had just a few hours before.

Folding the slim manila folder into halves, she stuck it inside her purse and sauntered down the hall. Boudreaux met her in the foyer. He escorted her outside and crisply shut the door behind her. Once on the sidewalk, she couldn't wait to get to her car. She was going to dash back to the condo, and there, she promised herself, she was going to go over the 555 file with a microscope.

It made for very light reading. Zoe's application for the secretarial position was in her own distinctive handwriting: circles for dots, long flourishes at the end of words. Zoe wrote that she was right for the position because she had lived in New Orleans all her life, was very familiar with the social calendar, and loved dealing with the public. All true.

There was nothing more remarkable about the contents of the file. Zoe's picture was inside, along with her résumé professionally typed and copied on linen bond to look as impressive as possible given the dearth of credentials. There were also a couple of recommendations from acquaintances of Zoe's, socialites whose husbands belonged to the 555, but none of these were particularly revealing. They said all the usual things. What a dear friend Zoe was, how classy she was, what an asset she would be to the association.

The small purple doodles were the only unexpected piece of information the interviewer had made in the margins of the application. They were neither particularly enlightening or damning. A Star of David was artfully sketched onto the right-hand corner. A number six was scrawled onto the left-hand corner, probably the order in which the interviews were taken, and the initials—or word—RIO was etched along the bottom of the page.

*Rio. River.* What meaning did that have? Zoe wasn't found in a river, but in a ditch. RIO. It was probably initials for some kind of interviewer language. Reject-Interviewee-Occupation, or something like that. It probably meant nothing.

But the letters stayed with her, running through her mind like a tangle. RIO.

She picked up the phone, her gaze still on the file.

"Hello, Mom? Yeah, I just got in." She was glad her mother couldn't see the guilt in her eyes. "Dinner? That'd be great." Her smile died. "What kind of surprise? Well, just tell me. Yeah, yeah, then it wouldn't be a surprise. All right. I'll be over around four. We'll catch up and I'll help you with the cooking. I love you too. Bye."

She hung up and went back to the file. There was Zoe's pretty face smiling at her from the picture, all hopes and dreams and possibilities. Touching the strange purple marks, she outlined the letters. RIO. *Rest in Oblivion, Rest in Occlusion, Rest in Overkill.* She wondered why the file was kept, but it was probably just a clerical oversight. Someone had filed it away and forgot about it. Mostly, though, she wondered whose handwriting made the marks in the margins. And she wondered how to find out.

She had to get Everard Laborde to write to her.

But that wouldn't accomplish much. Even if it were his handwriting in the margins, it didn't mean anything. He'd marked Zoe as a Jew, but that wasn't even proof she was being discriminated against for the job; she got the job, she just never lived long enough to know that she'd been hired. All the Star of David meant was that the interviewer had made the observation and doodled it on the corner of the application. Relevant or not, Zoe's Jewishness had come out in the interview.

Not too surprising for a place like the 555, she thought, finally pushing away the file. Frustrated that there wasn't more to go on, she went to the bathroom and ran the water in the tub. She needed a long, relaxing soak before going home. The day had already been nerve-racking, and now her mother had some kind of surprise for her. She couldn't wait. The last time her mother had said that, she'd bought her daughter a lime-green and fuchsia silk dress, the kind that said "this dress requires a week of shopping to find the right shoes." It was also a walking testament to the fact that the woman who wore such a dress *had* a week to go shopping for a pair of shoes. A Junior Leaguer would have loved it. It was a Zoe dress. Definitely not a Claire dress.

"I hope it's not clothes," she whispered to herself as she sank into the warm bubbles.

## ❧ 16 ❧

Claire stepped onto the front porch of her parents' house and braced herself for that first horrible moment. It was worse in her mind than it would ever be in reality; still, she already cringed at the way her parents would greet her. They'd see her and their smiles would be held in a split-second freeze. The shock that would shadow their expressions would be brief but visible, like the shock of seeing a ghost walking past. But then it would be over. They'd see her again, Claire, and they'd hug and cry and things would be okay for a while. She kept telling herself this.

She pressed the doorbell. A good family dinner was really tempting just then. Between Phyllis, Halbert Washington, and that damned FBI agent, she was ready to crack. Her mother's garlicky fried chicken and a couple of glasses of real southern iced tea was just the prescription she craved.

"Darling! Darling!" Her mother answered the door and immediately threw her arms around her. "Oh, I have missed you!"

Tears welled up in Claire's eyes at the sight of her mother. Rachel Green's neatly shorn hair was grayer than she last remembered, and she was thinner too, but there was an animation to her face Claire hadn't seen before. Maybe the memory of Zoe was finally going to be buried.

"You're home, darling," her mother cooed as she led her into the house.

Claire laughed through her tears. She hadn't seen her mother so alive in years; her lack of grimness was almost a shock. The way Rachel Green hugged her daughter made Claire feel like old times, back when she was an undergrad returning from Columbia. Then, there had been only joy at a homecoming. Never sadness.

"The place looks wonderful. Oh, you got a new couch!" Claire exclaimed as her mother led her into the living room. Taking a deep breath, she said, "And the smell . . . the smell of home . . . it's been too long."

Her mother smiled. "I made your favorite, fried chicken with gravy, collard greens dripping in butter, and for dessert, banana cream pie. Tonight might kill your father—you know his cholesterol is still terrible—but that's the price you pay for living in the South. Every now and then you've just got to have some white-trash cookin'!"

She hugged her mother again, encouraged by how well Rachel looked. Her mother had always been trim and could wear the most fantastically bright colors. In acid-green trousers and a matching hand-knit cotton sweater, she looked positively youthful in spite of her sixty years. Claire only hoped she looked half as good at that age.

"So where's Dad?"

"He's in his study with the surprise."

Claire grinned. "Okay, 'fess up. What's this surprise?"

Her mother's expression was luminous, as if Hezekiah Green were in his library, having just found a cure for cancer. "It happened the other day. We had given up, your father and I, of ever finding out what happened to Zoe. And then, well, a new ray of hope entered our lives."

"The police turned up something?" Claire could hardly believe it. What extraordinary fortune to arrive back home just as some new evidence arose in the case.

Rachel beamed a smile at someone in the hallway behind

Claire. "There's your daddy now. Hezy, your baby's here. I'll let you tell her all the news."

Claire found herself in a bear hug. Her daddy's arms felt so good. The old schoolteacher smelled just as she remembered: of foxing books, pink rubber erasers, and a cheap old lime cologne he'd been wearing since God parted the Red Sea. It was the most wonderful scent in the universe.

"There's my girl!" he exclaimed, obviously reluctant to let her go. "Boy, oh, boy, have we got a surprise for you!"

"You've got to tell me!" She laughed.

But suddenly the laughter choked down in her throat, replaced by an undistinguished gasp.

At the end of the hall stood a man. Suffocated in her father's embrace, she blinked to dispel the vision, but it wouldn't go away. The man was really there. Liam Jameson. He leaned against the wall that held a collage of her and Zoe's school photos, watching the proceedings like an old family friend. One of the Greens' glasses was in his hand— an old etched-by-the-dishwasher one that had Tweety Bird on it. She and Zoe had gotten the glasses at the Burger King when they were six, and her mother still used them—and now this profane man was using one, sipping tea from it as if he were quite at home.

"What—who—?" she choked out.

Her father's arms fell away and Claire felt him take her hand. "This is Special Agent Jameson, Claire." Hezekiah's voice shook with happiness. "He came knocking on the door a day or so ago with some questions about Zoe. Today he just announced to us that the FBI is reopening her case."

Claire stared at Liam, unable to make a decision. If she went along with the introduction, she would need an Academy Award, and yet, if she didn't, she was going to destroy the first bit of happiness her parents had had in years. If she told them the truth, that Jameson was probably in their house to investigate her, she could hardly bear the consequences. No matter how foolish it was to go along with the charade, she didn't think she was capable of killing her parents' hope.

Lamely, she held out her hand.

Grinning, Jameson shook it until her spine turned to rubber.

"Pleased to meet you, ma'am. Your parents have told me a lot about you."

She wanted to rip the smile right off his face.

"Pleased to meet you too," she murmured, her stare pingponging between his arrogant face and the dazzling light of Rachel's and Heze's.

"Agent Jameson's come all the way from Oklahoma," her father said. "It seems his boss is an expert on serial killers."

Claire turned to him. She hadn't noticed how frail her father had become in the time passed. He was still handsome, with salt-and-pepper hair and a quick smile, but he wore vulnerability in the worry lines of his face. He was a father who'd had to endure the ultimate violation; he could not protect his daughter. Suddenly she wanted to wrap her arms around him and cry into his chest. "Daddy," she said gently, "they've never determined whether it was a serial killer, have they?"

"That's one of the things Agent Jameson is going to investigate. You know, they have all these computers now. They can do fantastic comparisons to other cases they couldn't do five years ago." The light in his expression was blinding. It wrenched Claire's gut.

She glared at Jameson. He was despicable. To give these tragic people false hope was the ultimate cruelty. Her stare could have made a worm crawl back into the earth, but he didn't even flinch.

"Let's eat, shall we?" Rachel headed for the dining room, chatting away. "Agent Jameson came here on his day off to tell us the wonderful news, so the least we thought we could do is invite him to the table."

Claire helped herself to the iced tea in the pitcher and wished she had a jigger of vodka to put in it. It was the only thing she could think of that was going to help her get through this meal.

She sat opposite Jameson at the family's old 1950s Duncan Phyfe dining table. It had been one of Rachel and Heze's wedding presents. It was blasphemy to see Jameson at it. He took a long sip of her mother's iced tea out of the cartoon glass and the resentment built inside her like steam. That was her and Zoe's Tweety Bird glass and it belonged in the family to be used for welcomed guests. She didn't care if she was reverting to a six-year-old, she despised the sacrilege of him using their old beloved things.

"Your mother tells me you're a lawyer, Ms. Green," he said nonchalantly, passing the fried chicken after taking three pieces.

*The pig,* she thought, her gaze glued to his piled-high plate. "Yes, Agent Jameson. I'm an attorney. I graduated in the top of my class and I'm very good at comprehending all the nuances of the law." She hoped he got the implied threat. It would be interesting to see what his boss thought of him showing up at the suspect's parents' house for dinner.

"Please call me Liam." His eyes glittered beneath the lowered hood of his lids. She could tell he was enjoying this recent game of cat and mouse.

"Claire, is that what New York has taught you? How to toot your own horn?" her father admonished her.

She looked at him. She hadn't seen her father for five minutes and he was already rebuking her. Thank you, Special Agent Liam Jameson. "I don't know what made me say that," she murmured, passing the collard greens without taking any. Her plate was hardly full, but the big appetite she'd developed in her anticipation of home was gone.

"Tell me, Liam, I know you have to be cautious about giving us information, but is there something that's happened to convince the FBI to reopen the case?" Her father dolloped the mashed potatoes on his plate and quickly filled them with gravy.

"We reopen cases regularly. No law enforcement agency likes an unsolved case." Liam ate his chicken like a starving man.

It wasn't right that he should love her mother's cooking, she fumed. "Well, tell me, Liam," she broke in, "if that's true, then why isn't the NOPD reopening the case? Why the FBI? They were hardly involved with Zoe's case to begin with."

"Darling, you sound downright hostile." Her mother stared at her, perplexed.

"No—ah—it's not that." She glanced at Jameson, appalled to see that he seemed to be enjoying her distress. "It's just I'm curious. Why now?"

"Maybe when they use all those high-tech computers, they randomly pick unsolved cases to reopen. You know," Rachel offered, "something like a lottery."

*Great choice of words, Mom.* Claire couldn't even look at Jameson at that moment.

"You could say it's kind of like a lottery. But in the Zoe Green case there was other impetus to reopen the case." Liam devoured the mashed potatoes.

"Can you tell us?" Heze asked, almost breathless.

"Sorry. I really can't." Liam looked directly at Claire.

Claire stared back, torn between wanting to leap over the table and throttle him, and wanting to slink under the table and never face her parents again. The name Halbert Washington flitted through her subconscious, along with the word *vigilantism,* and great big knife-thrust of guilt. Suddenly the meal she'd been so hungry for seemed to turn her stomach.

"I'm sure Agent Jameson can't talk about the particulars," she mumbled, swishing her fork through her potatoes. "We'll know soon enough if his theories have any substance."

"That's right." A wry smile tipped the corner of his mouth. It was a sexy smile; a dangerous smile; a hidden smile, just for her.

A shot of adrenaline pumped through her veins. Between

a bout of nausea and lightheadedness, she asked for second helpings as she tried to look as relaxed as possible. Her mother heaped another piece of chicken on her plate and remarked that she had hardly touched her first, but Claire didn't comment. She just wanted to look normal. Later she could deal with Jameson; right now she had to think of her parents. She couldn't ever let on what was between Jameson and her. She couldn't give them another daughter to worry about.

"Are you a native of Tulsa, Liam?" Heze asked in the ensuing silence.

Claire found herself unspeakably grateful for the mundane conversation. She didn't want to talk about Zoe and the FBI. Even hearing about this clod's home life was better than that.

"Yep. Born and raised in a little town outside of the city. Taylorville. You ever heard of it?"

Heze leaned back in his chair, clearly satiated. "Funny. The name rings a bell but I can't think how I might have heard of it. Does it have some significance other than being near Tulsa?"

"Yeah," Jameson said quietly, so quietly that even Claire was forced to look at him.

"And what's that?" Heze asked.

Suddenly Liam released a cocky grin. "Well, hell, Mr. Green, that's where *I'm* from. Jameson Avenue goes right in front of the trailer park."

Heze and Rachel laughed.

Claire almost found herself smiling. Still, the undercurrent of something dark seemed etched on Jameson's face, and briefly she wondered if there was more to Taylorville than he let on.

They made some more small talk: Heze remarked how much he'd liked Tulsa when stationed there in the army, Liam recounted the sights he'd taken in during his short stay in New Orleans. Finally dinner was finished and Rachel stood to clear the table. "Let's have dessert on the front porch, shall we?" she said, frowning at Claire's barely touched plate of food.

"I'll get it, Mom," Claire offered, grateful to have a respite from Liam Jameson's scrutinizing gaze.

Once in the kitchen, the two women turned quiet. Claire cut the meringue-topped pie while her mother turned on the percolator.

"I don't know what it is about your cooking, Mom, but if given the chance to eat at the Four Seasons or right here in the kitchen, I'd take right here every time."

Rachel came up to her from behind and hugged her. "It's emotion, darling." She laughed as she watched her daughter lick the spoon. "No one in their right mind would think vanilla wafers, cornstarch pudding, and sliced bananas is anything special."

"Ah, but it's the stuff of childhood. *My* childhood," Claire answered. "It's so good to come home."

"Really? I feel like we're making you tense. You hardly ate. And you definitely seemed testy with Agent Jameson." As if sensing her daughter's need for privacy, Rachel turned to the cupboard and refilled the sugar jar. Casually, she remarked, "He's certainly a good-looking man."

"I hadn't noticed." A lie. All a lie. And she was stupid to think her mother wouldn't see through it.

"Yes, I suppose six foot plus, brilliant blue eyes, and a face that reminds me vaguely of Burt Lancaster—oh, I know, Burt Lancaster is long gone, but in my day, believe me, Burt was the thing—yes, I suppose that kind of combination wouldn't make much of an impression on a young single woman."

"He's probably married with five kids. You know how these redneck types are, Mom, they marry at seventeen."

"He's not a redneck. He might act like one, but he's too smart to really be one. Your father checked on his credentials over at Homicide, did you know that? The department couldn't believe he was getting involved in Zoe's case. Daddy found out that the Tulsa branch is the elite of the FBI. They've been begging the man who runs it to move to Quantico, but he's staying put. Says he has the best of the bureau right there in Oklahoma, and a lot of that has to do with the fact that Liam Jameson's there."

Rachel turned to her and her eyes were shining with hope. "Oh, this must be our lucky day, Claire, to have that kind of man come down here and get involved in Zoe's case. He just might prove to be our hero, huh, darling?"

Claire swallowed. She was sick inside. There was nothing she could say except "I hope so, Mom. You can't know how much I hope so." She only wished she could believe it herself.

An unseasonal thunderstorm struck the city just as Claire said good-bye to her parents. She made a date with her mother to go shopping the following Friday and said she'd call about the time. Jameson said his farewells too, taking great care to extol Rachel's virtues in the kitchen.

Claire thought it all rather much. As façades went, the evening had been one of the most precariously veiled social occasions she'd ever experienced. The anxiety of it left her exhausted. Behind the wheel of the BMW, all she craved was her pajamas and a long night's sleep.

But the night had barely begun.

Lightning crackled across the black sky above the oaks on St. Charles. Drops of hot Gulf of Mexico rain slicked the road. It was a terrible time to be out on a pilgrimage to the French Quarter, but she was headed there. After a perfunctory good-bye to Jameson, she'd gotten into her car with all pretenses of leaving to go home. But she was not going to go home. She was going to Jameson's hotel and tell him in no uncertain terms to back off.

He was giving her parents such a renewed sense of hope that it was killing her to think about it. All so he could stay up her butt and harass her. Convict her.

The rage that she'd suppressed all evening finally surfaced. It made her face flush and her heart ram in her chest. He was a lowlife if there ever was one. And she was going to warn him off her parents even if she had to get a court order to do it.

His hotel—the Orleans, if she correctly remembered him telling her—was one of the less seedy ones off Bienville. It was a guest house really, moderately priced, comfortable, the kind that leased suites in the servants' quarters to the rear of the courtyard. It was certainly the kind one would expect a government official to check into, especially one who expected to be in town awhile.

She parked the BMW alongside the curb as close to the address as possible. The sky was releasing the wrath of the gods, and she'd be soaked before she ever got to the hotel's lobby, but there was no point in waiting in the car. This was New Orleans; the rain could take hours to let up. She couldn't spend the night in the car.

She opened the door and ran through the pouring rain until she found shelter beneath the lacy cast-iron balcony at the front entrance. On either side of her, Bienville disappeared into a rain-shrouded lane; there wasn't another person to be seen. Tonight the crumbling, decaying French Quarter lived up to its creepy reputation.

To the left of the hotel's entrance was a box and a buzzer for after-hours visitors. She pressed the button. A voice boomed out, "Can I help you?"

"I'm looking for Liam Jameson. Could you give me his room number?" she shouted above the din of rain hitting the cast metal balcony overhead.

Behind the locked iron bars of the entrance a door opened and a disheveled young night clerk appeared. He was, by her guess, little more than a Tulane undergrad performing his work-study. He eyeballed her wet hair and dripping shoulders, then scratched his grungy head. "Bad night, man."

"The worst." She wiped the rain from the bridge of her nose. "I'm here to see Liam Jameson. Can you tell me where he's staying?"

The kid unlocked the iron door and she followed him into the guest house. The lobby was nothing more than a small parlor with the ubiquitous antebellum antiques, yet in one corner, as if in homage to the twentieth century, a computer screen beamed a surreal blue haze onto the turn-of-the-century cabbage-rose wallpaper.

He looked down at the computer screen, then picked up the phone.

"Can't you just give me his room number?" she asked almost furtively. She didn't need to be announced. It would take too much of the sting away.

"Sorry. House rules. The owners can't afford to have someone suing. You know how it is, man, we're all at the mercy of the lawyers."

*If only . . .* she thought.

He turned his attention back to the phone. It rang and rang. She stood in front of the desk, her blouse dripping water even down through the cleavage of her bra, and still, the phone rang. Jameson, the bastard, had foiled her again. He hadn't come back to his hotel.

The clerk's face suddenly animated. He said into the receiver, "Mr. Jameson, there's a woman to see you. Name's . . . ?" He looked at her, waiting for her to fill in the blank.

"Green," she said softly, already deflated. Her anger, her indignation, couldn't cloak the obvious futility of the visit. Jameson was now all set to meet her. Forewarned. Forearmed. There was no catching him with his drawers down as he had caught her at her parents'.

"He's in Room 305." The clerk hung up the phone and smiled rather sheepishly. "I hate to tell you this, but 305's at

the back of the building in the old servants' wing. You'll
have to go out in the rain again, because it's through the
courtyard."

"I see." She nodded, realizing how pathetic she must look
with her hair frizzled and wet, her clothes wrinkled and damp.
Boy, she was sure going to show Jameson, she thought wryly.

She left through a pair of French doors to the rear of the
guest house and stood beneath a balcony for a minute. Going
home seemed to be the only rational choice. She wasn't going
to impress upon him the honorable idea of leaving her parents alone. Not while she was soaking wet and angry. If anything, the best she could accomplish would be to give him a
sense that she was no opponent at all.

The fury inside her rose. But going home after she'd already been announced would make her look like a coward.
And she sure as hell would go to the grave before she'd give
him that impression.

She took a deep breath and looked across the courtyard.
Room 305 had to be on the third floor of the detached servants' quarters. A tall, well-built man stepped out of one of
the balcony doors, and even through the blur of pouring rain
she could tell it was Jameson. He leaned against the wooden
railing, surveying the watery courtyard below.

He paused. His body stilled. He was looking at her.

She walked across the courtyard. The rain gushed over
her, but to run seemed humiliating. Besides, it would do no
good. The rain fell in buckets. She was going to get wet no
matter how fast she was.

She climbed the two flights of stairs, and when she reached
the third floor she saw him standing at the other end of the
balcony in the dim glow of the gas lamps from the courtyard.
Behind him, a pencil-thin stream of yellow light spilled from
his door, casting him in silhouette.

She took a step forward, closer to the point where his
shadow drew down the length of the balcony. Long and ominous, it fell over her, but it was her fear that became the bar-

rier. He intimidated her. But still, she wasn't ready to turn and run. Her mind whirred with all the things she was going to tell him and threaten him with. Finally, she forced her legs to move forward. Five feet. Ten feet.

At last she drew close enough to make out the details of his form. His eyes, directed toward her, gleamed in the dim light. To her dismay, she found he was barefoot. His hair was as wet as hers and slicked back. He wore only a white T-shirt and jeans, and he'd slipped the Wranglers on so quickly, he'd forgotten to snap them. He'd probably been in the shower when the night clerk had called.

"I expected you, Claire, but not quite this soon. I'd bet the rain would keep you home tonight. I bet wrong."

"Stay away from my parents." Her words were low and harsh, but much too insubstantial against the drone of falling water. "It's reprehensible of you to use them against me. Can't you see they're still in pain over their murdered daughter?"

"I see it," he answered, his voice velvet compassion. If the words had come from any other man, she might have felt a tingle of warmth run through her, but they were from an FBI agent, and her soaked body shook from the chill.

"If you don't cease contact with them," she said, "I'll be forced to file a TRO. Also, I do believe there must be penalties for fraudulently claiming to reopen a case when all you're trying to do is perform an entrapment."

"We're reopening the case, Claire. It's not bullshit. It's true."

She stared at him in the darkness for what seemed almost a full minute. All the while she was trying desperately to gauge his truthfulness. "I can't believe that. You're down here to go after me, not find my sister's killer."

"Our reevaluating the evidence in Zoe's murder has nothing to do with you. The Zoe Green case was incomplete and should be reopened. Besides, we do it all the time. The field office agreed that while I'm here—"

"But how could you possibly work on two cases at a time? You can't find her killer and dig up evidence on vigilantes in tandem."

"Going after you has been easy, Claire. We know who some of the women are in New York. We know a lot about Phyllis Zuckermann and her tribunal. I hate to say it, but it's just a matter of time before they—or you—pull a wrong move and get nabbed. Sure, compiling the evidence will take a while, it always does, but make no mistake. If you're really into this gun-for-hire bullshit, you will all be caught. You will all be prosecuted."

The words were like a cold wind that passed through her. "I'm a lawyer," she gasped. "Don't be so sure of the outcome."

He walked toward her. His silhouette loomed enormous, until it seemed to swallow her with its darkness. It was a scene right out of an Orson Welles film.

"Why don't you cooperate, Claire?" he whispered. "We could give you immunity. Help us prosecute the ZOE group, and then you'd be free. Free to help us with your sister's case."

"You're innocent before proven guilty, Jameson. Maybe the women you speak of didn't do anything wrong."

"Don't you want us to find out who murdered your sister? If I didn't have to spend so much time playing good cop/bad cop with you, I could spend more time going after him."

"You never even knew Zoe. What makes you her hero?"

His mouth quirked. "Maybe she deserved a trial. Maybe she deserved some justice. It doesn't take a hero to want that."

"Yeah. Sure." Her voice quivered. She paused and collected herself. "But these things happen—cases go unsolved, justice remains elusive—all the time unfortunately. So why pick my sister for added favors? Why?"

"I don't know why. Maybe . . . maybe because she looked so much like you."

He stepped even closer. The rain thundered down. He was so near, she could smell him. The clean cotton smell of his T-shirt, the hotel soap mixed with a male essence that seemed to be all Oklahoma dust and cowboy sweat.

He lifted his hand. His eyes were shadowed; she couldn't quite read their expression. Then his hand brushed her damp cheek.

Her mind screamed to pull back, but for some godforsaken reason, she couldn't move. She stood stock-still and looked up at him, letting his thumb draw fire across the pad of her cheek.

The touch was so gentle. So quiet and tender. It held hardly more pressure than a puff of breath. It was unmistakably the caress of a lover. Of want. What it was was foreplay, and the terror and exhilaration of it reamed her insides like poison.

"I want to help you, Claire."

She closed her eyes. Suddenly she felt the cold of the night and the dampness of her clothes. She shivered. His hands took her trembling arms and he drew her closer to him. His chest was so enticing. Even in a T-shirt it appeared impossibly warm and protective. And that was the damned thing about a man. One could put you in a ditch; another could protect you like armor.

"You're freezing," he whispered. "Come into my room."

The chest drew nearer. The knight clad in Jockeys.

She expelled a deep breath, not realizing she'd been holding it. Numbly, she shook her head. "I can't. You're an agent."

"Forget about that. I don't wear the hat all the time."

"But I'm a suspect."

"Yes—you are—and I'm human." He drew his hand lower and clasped her chin. Haltingly, he bent to her, whispering, "Remember that—remember I'm human."

A half-sob escaped her mouth before he covered it with his own. He kissed her; she let him; she wanted him to. And the rain beat down like a primeval drumbeat, the noise throbbing in her veins as much as the heat from his touch.

It was crazy, a small voice rang out from her hormone-induced haze. His mouth was as sensuous to kiss as it was to watch; hard and yet sensitive, demanding but not forceful, and yet, to be kissing a near stranger after what had happened to her sister was unwise at best, to be kissing an FBI agent when she was one of his investigations was pure lunacy. But her attraction was a weakness that had seeped into her bones. Even now she realized she leaned against him limp and wanting, her hands grasping the thick cotton of his undershirt in a piteous gesture of need. Her attraction to him made her soft, and it was accentuated only by her long-repressed loneliness that now struck her like a thunderbolt.

"Come into my room," he whispered against her hair when they parted.

She closed her eyes and stilled her head against his chest. His heartbeat was strong and sure, and definitely accelerated. He was human, after all, not some kind of steely Dudley Doright. No, he was all too human and *much* too male. She had to stay away from him or she would end up not only in jail but in a cell, nursing her poor broken heart.

"I've got to go home," she sputtered, trying desperately to shock herself out of the fantasy of what had just happened. "Please, I've really got to go. I just wanted to tell you not to play games with my parents. They can't take it. It's too cruel." She glanced up at him. His heated, arrogant gaze embarrassed her. What the hell was she doing anyway, kissing him? She needed a straitjacket.

"I didn't mean to do that. You've got to believe me. It's just that—well—I find you . . ." He lifted his brows. His electric-blue eyes darkened in a way that only a woman could understand. He'd said enough.

She nervously stepped from his reach. "I really have to

go." She backed away, too humiliated to look directly into his eyes. Her hair was drenched, matted to her skull and hanging down her back in thick black hanks. Her feet were like ice in her water-logged flats. With a sudden shiver she crossed her arms over her chest. It killed her to think about it, but he probably could see every bit of café-au-lait lace on her bra through her damp shirt. Worse, maybe he'd been able to see even more than that.

"This sounds like a line, but I want you to know I'm not in the habit of doing that." He didn't walk toward her. He stood completely still, as if he were holding a halter and watching a skittish filly in the paddock.

"I understand," she lied, clutching the banister.

"You didn't stop me."

She paused. She barely breathed.

"Why not?"

His gaze caught her. She gave him one last look and then swore she was not going to look at him again unless they were forced to face each other in a courtroom. He was an attractive man. To her, maybe even wildly attractive. But God, he was dangerous. And she was a fool.

"I thought you'd stop me," he said, his husky voice less than a whisper. "I know Zoe's made you afraid."

She stood like a piece of statuary stuck to the staircase. He was the first man she'd ever met who'd seen through her. It was the nature of his business, of course; he would know all about the phobias of a victim, but it threw her for a loop that her emotions were so transparent to him. Her luck with men had been hampered mostly because they translated her reserve into being cold; one prematurely attempted kiss and she was gone. But it was only because she was afraid. She had every reason to be.

"Sex is not a gentle act," he said, his eyes hooded in shadow. "By its very nature it's violent. We don't judge men enough by how violent."

She wiped a hank of wet hair from her eyes. Her hand

shook. Behind her, the relentless rain fell like a sheet of plastic wrap, ferocious and inhospitable. She ached to be warm and dry. Someplace safe that was far away from this man who terrified her.

"I don't blame you, Claire. I don't blame you at all for this. It was my fault."

"Then leave me alone."

"I'm attracted to you. I can't help but want to be the man who dispels your fears."

"Don't. Don't. Just don't," she burst out. She turned away, hating the vision of his tall, muscular body leaning against the balcony, despising the smell of clean cotton and less-than-squeaky-clean smell of male. He was capable of violence. She knew it because it was there in his gaze, in the manner in which he seemed to view the world, in the things he'd done, and most certainly in the things he'd seen. Maybe because he knew it was there, he somehow had a leash on it. Maybe the more dangerous man was the one who didn't know he had it in him.

But she was too afraid to find out. Sex *was* a violent act, no matter how loving and gentle the intentions. And even though she was a desperately lonely woman, even though she had cravings, and could look at him, smell him, touch him, and understand completely her longings, the precipice was so narrow.

The abyss, so deep.

She took a long look at him. Frustration was etched on his face, and the lines that gave his handsome face so much character deepened. She wanted to believe there was more in him than just the desire to nail a woman he'd found himself attracted to, but she couldn't sway herself to believe otherwise. Men were pigs. Shallow, tunnel-visioned, groin-motivated, and that was all that this was. Jameson was attracted to her; he wanted a conquest. She couldn't let herself think it was anything more than that. Because if she did, she might definitely fall for him.

And the abyss was so deep.

She turned and stepped down onto the staircase. Behind her, she thought she heard him grunt some kind of epithet, but she squeezed it out of her mind. Down the stairs, through the courtyard, she was suddenly glad for the cold, pounding rain. The chill of it took the edge off of any sexual cravings. It washed the heat away. It took her thoughts away from Liam Jameson and sex and the idea of going to his room. The rain was good, she told herself again and again like a mantra. The chill of it took away her breath. The cold wetness became as a baptism. It was confirmation of her celibacy; it was forgiveness, distraction.

A cold, blessed ablution.

## ❧ 17 ❧

The holidays passed with minimal fanfare. New Orleans, humid, happy, and grotesque, geared up for Mardi Gras. Claire had been corralled into spending New Year's Eve in the French Quarter with some old high school buddies, but no matter how hard she laughed, no matter how many times she and her friends paraded down Bourbon Street and shouted in the new year with the drunken crowd, it wasn't the same as in years past. Most of her friends had children, and the baby-sitters were available only until one A.M. For the first time in her life, Claire had found herself home New Year's morning before two o'clock.

The drunken revelry of the Quarter had never bothered her much before; after all, she was a New Orleans girl, partying was in her blood. But in bed in the early morning hours of the first day of the new year, still hearing the occasional boom of a roman candle being fired off the Seventh Street wharf, she found herself inexplicably blue. Her mind returned to midnight, when all the couples were laughing and kissing and hugging like koalas. It had been hard to stand by, alone and unwanted. It had been almost impossible to dig up an optimistic smile for the coming year.

Especially when she thought of Jameson.

He hadn't bothered her in the past few days. She'd surmised he'd gone home to Tulsa for the holidays. Maybe to be with the wife and kids. It was astounding to her that she didn't even know if he had a wife and kids, but she knew how he smelled in a white cotton T-shirt with the rain falling hard and sweet.

That he'd be back on her tail she had no doubt. It was just a matter of when and how. Until then, she decided to go easy on herself. She'd done a little more research on Zoe's murder, reviewed all the old articles in the papers; she'd even promised herself a day trip to Des Allemands, but with the holidays, and her friends looking up the old address, she'd found the time flew by. There was also the newfound ease with her parents to while away the days. She prayed her parents weren't changed just because of the hope that Jameson had dangled in front of them. Instead, she wished that mere time and distance had finally broken the ghost hold Zoe had on them all. But there were moments when that wish seemed weak, especially when her mother's eyes would glaze over and stare into Claire's face with a frightening intensity as if she were seeing someone she wanted resurrected so badly, she'd gladly give up her own life to see it done. It was moments like that that Claire wanted to flee to New York and never let her parents lay eyes on her again.

But it was a brand new year, Claire thought to herself as she finally drifted off to sleep. Anything could happen. Anything was possible. Ghosts could be banished. Dragons could be slain. A whole new start. She looked forward to it with determination. And fear.

Prisoners from the Sheriff's Art Program lined the scaffolds that covered the windowless exterior wall of central lockup. It was that time of year when the men painted Carnival purple, green, and gold over the Christmas scene. The mural was the only sign of cheer in the city block that held the prison, the courthouse, and the main police precinct.

Homicide was located on the third floor of the complex at South Broad. It was a cold Monday after New Year's Day when Jameson finally paid a call.

Huddling in his jacket, he held out his identification and asked the policewoman at the front desk for Detective Williams. The woman pushed extension 1301 on her phone panel, and with a bored expression on her face she let the phone ring while she gazed out the plate glass doors. It was a helluva view, Liam thought. An Arctic wind blew trash by Nguyen's Gas-n-Go across the street; public defenders in trench coats walked by blocks of bail bondsmen's offices to the prison to interview their clients; every now and then, skeevy-looking inmates with their personal belongings clutched in plastic bags trickled out the main prison door, a constant reminder of prison overcrowding and the revolving-door justice system.

"Detective Williams, FBI to see you." The woman motioned for him to hold out his badge again. "Agent Jameson. Tulsa office. All right." She put down the receiver. "Elevators are to the left. He's in 329."

"Thanks." Liam grinned.

The woman smiled back, a spark of interest caught in her eye. Too late for small talk now though. Jameson walked away without another word.

Williams's office was a shabbier rendition of his own. The vinyl chairs were the same, but the detective's were cracked and the stuffing popped out the back of one of them. Duct tape held the rest together. The room was hot and stuffy, fragranced with the scent of mildewed paper. Williams, a black man in his early forties with just a touch of silver in his closely cropped hair, sat behind a desk, a grim what-the-fuck-do-you-want expression on his face.

"I'm here to see the Green files."

"Which Green files? We probably got forty-six of them."

"Zoe Green."

"Oh. That one."

Liam grasped the back of a chair and lifted his eyebrows in a "May I?" expression.

Williams nodded. With a great sigh he punched some letters into the computer beside his desk. "Zoe Green. Yeah, I remember that one. Hey, man, the bitch was found in Des Allemands. Why don't you guys go and bug *them?*"

"I want to see the rest of your files here first. She disappeared from New Orleans, remember?"

The detective picked up the phone. "I'll call the file room. There's not much there, if I recall. Why you botherin' with this one after five years?"

"We're officially reopening the case. We want to see if it's the work of a serial killer."

Derrell Williams locked stares with Jameson. Only when the file room picked up on the other end did he look away. "Bring up the Zoe Green files. Yeah." He hung up. "Why the fuck do you guys think she was pulled down by a serial killer?"

"Pretty fantastic, isn't it?"

"Yeah. Pretty fantastic. Especially after five years."

Jameson smiled. "She didn't have a boyfriend to kill her. Her dad didn't do it. There was no one around her with any kind of motivation at all. So what's left?"

"Is that how you big-swinging-dick FBI agents think? Man, I got to get out of this job and go where the work is easy. What a job of deduction: If A is true and B is true, then it all adds up to Z."

Jameson finally laughed. He slouched down in his chair to get comfortable during the wait for the files and watched Derrell Williams. "Call it a hunch, man. We're just going to go over everything again."

"Why?"

"Because I'm also investigating Zoe Green's sister, that's why."

An officer appeared from the file room with a stack of files. He laid them on Williams's desk and left without a word.

Williams picked up the files. A photo of Zoe slipped out of one. It was a picture of the twins. Williams stared at it for a long time. "They were beautiful, weren't they?" he said.

"Yeah," Jameson answered, this time without the disarming grin.

"We weren't able to do much with the case. The trail was pretty cold."

"I know."

Williams looked up. "I can't help you with this, Jameson, you know that. I got sixteen cases on my back right now, when the national average of caseloads is less than half that."

"I know. Murder Capital of the USA. You got your hands full. That's why I'm taking this one off your desk. I'll be looking into it."

"I don't mess with no serial killers. We haven't had one in years."

"Nothing since Quinlin was arrested here, huh?"

"That's right, and I'd like to keep it that way." Williams's face took on a vaguely nauseated look. "You know, I was the first officer to go into Quinlin's shotgun house where they found all the boys and their parts. I tell you, I screamed like a girl when I found that first torso. I mean I really got in touch with the sister inside me with that one."

There was nothing Jameson could do but keep his eyes on Williams's face and let him talk.

"I don't like serial killers," Williams repeated.

"Nobody does."

"What you guys gonna do if you find one down here?"

"We're going to catch him. Want to help?"

"I'll think about it. I still say the bitch just got hooked up with a drifter or something and things got out of hand."

Jameson shrugged. He rose from the chair and picked up the stack of files. "Most of this just photocopies of Minnefield's files?"

"I could have told you that without getting the file." Williams rubbed his jaw and watched him. "Is that your specialty, Jameson? Serial killers?" He shook his head and almost seemed to shudder. "Man, I don't envy you. I mean, how can you sleep at night? The nightmares must be hell."

"No problem. I sleep like a babe." Jameson headed for the door. "I wake up every two hours screaming."

The first Mardi Gras krewe of the season to parade down Canal Street was in the middle of January. The smaller krewes were forced to take the earliest dates in the calendar to get out of the way of the kingpins: Rex, Bacchus, Endymion. The largest krewes were the newest. The *nouveaux riches* with too few connections to old New Orleans to get into Comus had gone and done the unpardonable: They'd started up their own krewes. Legions of doctors and lawyers now made up the Krewe of Seraphina, all the 555 rejects. But what the new krewes might have lacked in social status they made up for in sheer crowd-pleasing ostentation. The Seraphina parade was almost forty floats long and was perennially kicked off by a big-name movie star. In recent years the krewe had become so large that they rolled the parade, floats and all, into the Louisiana Superdome for their ball.

But biggest wasn't always best. Not according to the 555 and the Uptown bluebloods. Holding on to tradition was more impressive in those ranks. The old-line krewes, like Dante, and the Krewe of Ganymede, still used *flambeaux,* kerosene-lit torches carried by black men hired on at the beginning of the parade. In a throwback to times when the men lit the parade's way, people threw coins into the street for the *flambeaux* carriers. Those in the old krewes looked at the coin-throwing as a tip, a sign of gratitude, while others viewed the practice as Jim Crow. The kerosene torches were dangerous and unnecessary, people complained. More than one man had been burned to death as the kerosene leaked onto his head, perilously close to the torch. Besides, modern fluorescent streetlights easily drowned out the brightness of the *flambeaux*. Preserving a tradition like the *flambeaux* carriers was nothing more than a show of a Samboism, detractors cried out.

Yet it *was* tradition, the old-line krewe members countered. Along with the century-old wooden wagons that had once been pulled by mules and now by tractors, these were the precious reminders of how long Mardi Gras had been a part of the city, and so they should remain.

Those who loathed the *flambeaux* practice longed to abolish it, yet it grew ever more popular with the masses of homeless men who crowded the beginning of parade routes. It was a well-known fact that most would make at least a hundred bucks in change by the end of the evening, and recently the controversy centered around letting whites carry the traditional *flambeaux*. There were now so many white men from the Salvation Army and Ozanam Inn who wanted to carry the torches, interracial fights broke out before the parades. Some of them bloody.

Just another loop in the twisted knot of racism, Laborde thought while shifting through the mail at his desk and finding another letter of discontent from the NAACP. They complained about the *flambeaux* again, but their complaints were ill directed at him. Laborde was Grand Marshal of Dante this year and *he* certainly believed the *flambeaux* could be white or black, just as long as the tradition was upheld. What he couldn't abide was the complete extinction of tradition, and a static, unmalleable death grip on the old ways was the quickest way to watch them die. He did his best to preach a moderate path. Better to change than eradicate, he said, but not everyone agreed with this. Dante was talking of no longer parading after this year. There had been other krewe casualties in recent years. Against Everard's passionate dissuasion, two of the oldest krewes had decided not to parade in defiance of a new city ordinance that required krewes to open up their ranks to all races. The two old krewes believed the public outcry would back up their decision. The krewes of Charis and Ganymede, after all, had been parading in some form since 1872, and surely that fact was more enduring than having blacks, or a few token Jews, in their ranks.

Everard had warned them though. Maybe the public wouldn't care they'd been around for more than a century, he'd told them. It was a revolutionary idea, but there were times his people needed a little intravenous reality injected into their numb minds. The bourgeois masses couldn't be expected to understand even the most obvious nuances of social position, nor could they be expected to care, he'd railed, shocking them all into silence.

In the end the krewes didn't listen to him. They stood by their decision and made good on their threat not to parade, and the case turned out to be a perfect example of "be careful what you wish for because you just might get it." The public outcry never came. In the end, that Ganymede and Charis had paraded since 1872 really didn't impress the average New Orleanian who just wanted to make big tourist bucks during Carnival. Both krewes, when they bowed out, lost their lucrative parade schedules, lost their media at their Mardi Gras ball. Now that they were invisible, they even lost their status as an organization. They were nothing but a secret society of nobodies, with no clout and no outsiders to impress.

Everard at least had the satisfaction of the "I-told-you-so." He'd said the city council wasn't going to shed any tears if they disappeared off the face of the earth, because there were plenty of new krewes—sadly perhaps, without the tradition of the old—that were lined up to get into the season's schedule.

So tradition lost, as it often does, and Everard was disgusted at the outcome. Ganymede and Charis should have compromised. He was going to do his damnedest that Dante did. They couldn't afford another old-line southern tradition to be gone forever, especially when the only mourners were the dead themselves.

"President Laborde, there's someone here to see you."

"Who is it?" Everard snapped, looking up from his desk. If he had to write the NAACP one more time and shovel the b.s., he was going to burn a cross on his own damn yard.

"An FBI agent, sir." D'Hemecourt pressed his palms together as if he were almost enjoying himself.

Everard looked up. The silence was thunderous. "What the hell do they want?" he asked, his voice deceptively soft.

Being the professional kiss-up, Dem did his best to placate. "I really don't know, sir. It is annoying. Couldn't you just murder them?"

Laborde looked down at his desk. He did his best not to show how aggravated he was by Dem. Something was going on with his secretary and had been for a few days now. He would get to the bottom of it, but he couldn't do it now. "Send him in—it is a him, isn't it?"

"Yes, sir." Dem disappeared behind the double doors. Soon he reappeared with a tall man in jeans and a ponytail.

The agent was one of those men who looked like he'd just stepped out from a Steven Seagal movie. In cowboy boots and an old baseball jacket, he was certainly not the natty dresser Laborde considered himself to be. This man was the kind that spat on propriety. His casual dress should have made him less intimidating, but it didn't.

Laborde couldn't quite pin down the reason for the sudden trickle of dread that dripped through his veins. There was nothing remarkable about the man except for his six-foot-plus frame. Still, the agent possessed a certain piercing, "I'm looking at you, dirtbag" kind of stare that made Everard irrationally uncomfortable. He wasn't used to such a stare; more to the point, he had no desire to converse with an urban avenger, particularly one who worked for the FBI.

Everard's instant antipathy came as no surprise, but he convinced himself of the imperative to swallow his hatred for a ten-minute conversation, which was all this was going to be, he would make sure of it.

"Now, how in the world can the 555 help the FBI?" he said with a wide Cheshire-cat smile. He stood up from his desk. He made grand use of his ebony cane as if it somehow labeled him as more innocent than he was. With it, he motioned to a pair of leather bergères. "Please, shall we have a seat?"

The agent nodded. He fished around in his back pocket before seating himself. The badge he dug out was all too real. "Special Agent Jameson. Tulsa office. You're J. Everard Laborde?"

"Yes." The smile got wider and wider until Laborde felt it had detached from his face and now floated above their heads. "How did you know my name, if I may ask?"

The man's facial expression was as implacable as cardboard. "Your name's in gold letters right on the front of the door."

Everard laughed, his sardonic grin the picture of high-class, sophisticated amusement. "How ridiculous. Of course it is. You must forgive me, Agent Jameson. I see it every day. It's like not knowing your own phone number because you never call it." He jerked his head toward his secretary. "Dem, coffee, if you please."

"Yes, sir." Dem took his time.

"Now, how can we help you?" He loved using the royal we. It was one of the perks of being president. By God, it did distance one, and he sure wanted distance now.

The FBI agent smirked. "The only one who can help me is you, sir. We have a murdered woman who was last seen here in this building before she disappeared. According to police records, she interviewed with you, then vanished."

Laborde's heart beat so loudly, he swore the bumpkin from Tulsa could hear it. "If the girl you're referring to was Zoe Green, her murder was five years ago. Why is this being brought up again?"

"We're reopening the case."

"You have new evidence?" Everard kept his hands

placidly in his lap; it was a true physical hurt to refrain from drawing them into angry fists.

"I can't discuss the evidence with you, sir. I'm just here to ask questions and get some answers and that's all." The cowboy boots stretched out in front of the man. He was all ease and relaxation while Everard wanted to kick those insolent boots right out onto the street.

"I guess I'm just perplexed," he said. "The murder was years ago and you said you were from where . . . ? Tulsa? Where does Oklahoma fit in with the girl's murder?"

"How I fit in is really not the point here. It's how you fit in, Mr. Laborde."

If the man were wearing a Stetson, Everard swore the agent would have been looking at him beneath the wide brim, covertly watching his every move and gesture. Like a snake in the grass.

"Of course it is." Laborde took the china cup of coffee Dem handed him and he found himself most disgruntled when the agent refused his. "But I really have nothing more to offer. The girl came here. She interviewed as many others did who were vying for the position. Then she left. We saw nothing more of her, thought nothing more of her. In fact, we didn't even know about her disappearance at all until the police tracked her whereabouts to here."

"Why?"

Laborde stared at the man. He hoped the rube noticed his distaste of the matter and quit soon. "Why what?" he asked imperiously.

"Why did no one notice a missing woman who had just interviewed here at the club?"

"This is not a 'club,' Agent Jameson. This is a fine and honorable organization that has been around since the nineteenth century."

"Yeah. I think I need to know more about this organization while I'm here too."

Laborde took in a deep, frazzled breath. "Now, how could that possibly aid this ancient investigation I'll never know."

"We can solve a murder as old as this club, Mr. Laborde, if we finally get all the pieces to the puzzle. So why didn't anyone notice the missing woman was last seen here? Her disappearance was all over the nightly news, all over the front page."

"No one noticed because no one but myself really saw the girl, and I put her out of my mind immediately. She was inconsequential, only interviewing for a secretarial position, hardly noteworthy." Behind them, Laborde heard Dem rattle the china. Another irritation and Dem was going to pay for it. Everard continued, "Besides, if you will forgive me, Agent Jameson from Tulsa, Oklahoma, I don't always have the time to keep abreast of current events. A Jewess missing in this size city is hardly an atomic bomb going off, now, is it?"

"*Jewess.* I don't think I've ever heard anyone use that term. You've got a damned fine command of English, Mr. Laborde. They haven't used words like that for years. So what made you think she was Jewish?"

Everard did his level best to keep himself from rolling his eyes in exasperation. "Oh, I don't know how. Naturally we never discussed her religious bent, it's just that her name and her looks made me think she was Jewish."

"So you thought her name and her looks remarkable."

"In my mind, she was just the Jewish girl who disappeared after the interview. I can't add much more than that."

"Did she leave the club right after her interview?"

*There was that word again. Club. Like the members of the 555 were all Boy Scouts or something.* "I believe so. You do have to forgive me. You see, it was a long time ago. I hardly remember the interview. Our meeting was so brief and inconsequential, there's not much for me to go on, now, is there?" His mouth thinned in distaste. "So if that's all, Agent

Jameson, I must be excused because of a luncheon appointment."

"Sure. I'll come back this afternoon."

"You mean there are more questions?" Everard did his best to look insulted and harassed.

"I'd like to know about this place. What's it called again?"

Laborde frowned. "The 555 Association."

"Kind of sounds like a satanic cult."

"I beg your pardon?"

"No, I guess that would be the 666 Association." The beast grinned, but he at least stood up, complying for now. "One last thing before I go. Why did you say Zoe Green was inconsequential?"

"Did I say that? I didn't mean to sound insensitive."

"Does the EEOC make you guys advertise all your positions for hire?"

"We like to think of ourselves as always open to new blood. We don't need a federal regulator to oversee us."

"So they can't make you hire a Jew if you don't want to. You can always say they were unqualified, isn't that so?"

"Are you trying to put words into my mouth, Agent Jameson? For your information, Zoe Green was hired. If my memory serves, she was called but not home and a message left to that effect."

This seemed to stump the man. Laborde loved it when he had the upper hand.

"You mean you were going to hire this girl, and yet no one in this organization made note that her disappearance was on the nightly news?" The agent's gaze drilled right into Laborde. "Before you go to lunch, sir, I'd like her file."

"Fine. Again, what that has to do with her disappearance and murder still mystifies me, but I'll get her file for you. I must tell you, however, that the homicide detectives got a copy when the murder was fresh. I do consider this a bit annoying."

"I'd like another copy. I'll bring it back this afternoon. I promise." There was that grin again, that Tom Cruise flash of white. Laborde began to fantasize what that handsome mouth would look like filled with blood. One good twist of the knife and a stomach could fill in no time. He learned that from his father's *Gray's Anatomy,* and he demonstrated it to himself on number five, the only man he'd yet been made to kill. Number five had been a janitor at the association. He'd seen Everard put number four in the trunk of his Mercedes 450SL. So Laborde had been forced into two murders that year, and the following Mardi Gras, when he'd propose the 555 Murder Mystery be that of a janitor, the outcry had been terrible. Not that anyone had noticed the missing janitor. Black males up and disappeared from their jobs and homes all the time if the police's apathy had been any indication. No, the disapproval over the pretend victim had all centered around the victim's sex. The members wanted a female victim.

The following year, Laborde had been pleased to give them one.

"Dem, bring the Zoe Green file in here, please," Laborde announced when Dem appeared with a fresh cup of coffee.

Dem nodded. "How would that be filed?"

"How should I know? I'm not a secretary."

Suitably chastened, Dem retreated into his office. Five minutes passed. The silence ticked by. Laborde was drained of talk. He just wanted this hick FBI agent out of his office and gone.

"I can't seem to find a file containing anything on Zoe Green, sir," Dem said after another five minutes.

"I'm a stickler for record keeping. I keep the résumés on all prospective hirees in case I want to replace someone." Everard gave Dem a meaningful look. "Go find it."

"I'm telling you, sir, we don't have that file any longer. It's just not in there. You may see for yourself."

Laborde gazed down at his lap and found his knuckles had

gone white. "What would have happened to the file, Dem? Have you purged things you've had no permission to destroy?"

"Certainly not, sir. I've never seen the file."

"Well, we had one. I know we did." Laborde gave the agent a covert glance. He didn't want to be accused of destroying information. The agents would be on him like flies on carrion if he looked like he was hiding something. "It's in the files, Dem. I know it. I saw it just last week as I was searching through the cabinet."

"If you did, sir, it's not there now."

Laborde plastered on his smile once again. He turned to Jameson and said, "Clearly there's some confusion here. Why don't I fax you the contents when we find it?"

"Don't bother. I'll get it this afternoon when I return."

"Yes. Of course. I forgot we're going to be honored with another visit." Laborde stood and held out his hand. "Until we meet later, Agent Jameson."

"Later," Jameson repeated. He gave Laborde what Everard was convinced was a suspicious glance, then the agent left, taking his cowboy boots and accusing stare with him.

"So where is that file?" Laborde said, immediately turning on his secretary when the agent was out of the office.

"I really can't tell you. I wasn't familiar with the file and I have no idea how it was filed—"

"It was filed under Z for Zoe Green. The file went by her initials."

If Dem were taken aback by this sudden wellspring of information, he didn't show it. "It doesn't matter how it was filed, I looked under both G and Z, sir, and I found nothing."

Laborde pushed him aside. He went into Dem's office and shoved open the filing credenza. Flipping through the Z file, he began to curse. "I don't see it. It must be misfiled. You are to spend the rest of the day going through every file to see if it's in there."

"I never misfile, Mr. Laborde. Never," Dem said.

Laborde glared. "If it's not misfiled, then it's missing. If it's missing, then someone took it. Who?"

A strange expression suddenly seeped into Dem's face.

"Who took the file?" Laborde's eyes narrowed. "Was someone in here asking for it other than Agent Jameson? Have you done something with it?"

"No, sir. I never knew it existed until now. But I do have to say that your interest in it is rather strange. Your remark to Agent Jameson was odd too. I never knew you to go fishing through the filing cabinet."

Laborde stood frozen. Anger reddened his face, but he did a brilliant job of holding it back. In a benign tone of voice he said, "I never admitted to looking into the file. I only remember seeing it when you weren't around to retrieve a file for me. Is that a crime?"

Dem seemed almost to smile. "No, sir. That is not a crime."

Laborde stared at him. His eyes narrowed. "You find that file, Mr. Secretary. You find it or you'll be walking those penny loafers right out of here and you will never be permitted to return as a member or otherwise. Do you understand?"

"Yes, sir." Dem seemed to grow angry, but he hid it also.

"I've got a luncheon downstairs with the president of Tulane. When we're done, I want to see that file in its entirety on my desk."

"You will, sir. You will." With that, Dem nodded and busied himself at the filing drawer as if he were sure to find the thing misfiled under *K*. Everard left for his appointment, never noticing the strange glances Dem fired at his back, nor Dem picking up a card on his desk, with *555* embossed across the top in gold, the address and phone number of Claire Green on the bottom.

## ❧ 18 ❧

Jameson wished he could just go home and forget about her. The local authorities could track down any new leads. After his meeting with J. Everard Laborde, he was convinced the guy stank. All he had to do was stick a couple of feds on the guy's ass and they'd have all the new evidence they needed.

But there was no way to tell Gunnarson he wanted to bail out. It would look too strange; it would require explanation. Already he cringed at having to face Gunnarson and say, "I need to leave the case because, well, like the old saying goes, 'There's this woman . . .' "

So he had to stick it out and try not to think of Claire Green. Instead, he was going to concentrate on J. Everard Laborde. The guy was definitely full of shit. Liam didn't know why he was that way, and being full of shit didn't make anybody a murderer, but Laborde was worth hovering over. He wasn't telling the truth about his interview with Zoe Green, that much was certain. And the first thing he was going to ask the old bastard when he returned to the apparently exclusive address at 555 Canal was why was he looking into Zoe's file. That little comment really bothered him, and all the pat answers didn't wash out the bad feeling he had. To notice an old file was innocuous enough, but more murder cases were solved by taking the mundane by the throat and not letting go.

"Snap out of the daydreaming, agent. I don't like that look in your eyes. I feel like I'm going to hear about them killers you go after, and you know how I feel about that." Detective Williams eyeballed him.

Liam grinned. Williams was no fool. He'd been a thousand miles away.

"So you went and talked to the guy, huh? Smacked your butt right down in the middle of the 555 Association." The detective opened a long, paper-wrapped object and uncovered an eighteen-inch po'boy sandwich. "I gotta say, it took an outsider to do that. I'd be damned intimidated."

"I hear they don't let your kind in there." Liam watched him.

Williams finally looked up. "I got news for you, Okie, they don't let your kind in there either, smart ass."

Liam chuckled. "So you want to come with me this afternoon? We can ride the guy hard. He might talk. Seemed nervous enough."

"Mr. Laborde just doesn't want anything to soil the association's upstanding reputation." The detective took a bite of the messy sandwich, leaving a string of iceberg lettuce in the corner of his mouth. "You know that place has been around for a long time."

"Yeah. So I was told. And told. And told. That doesn't make them all St. Francis of Assisi." Liam watched Williams take another big bite.

"That doesn't make them all Hannibal the Cannibal either." Derrell wiped a drip of mustard and mayonnaise off his chin with a paper napkin.

"So you want to come?"

Williams took another bite, and then another. He chewed pensively. Liam waited, his gaze glued to the sandwich.

The detective seemed to notice Liam's stare. "You eaten lunch yet, special agent?"

"Naw. I came right here." He leaned forward and pointed. "What's in that thing? That sure is some strange sandwich."

"Fried oysters."

"You've got to be kidding me."

"No, man, it's good. You mean to tell me you never had an oyster po'boy before?"

"Where we gonna get oysters in Tulsa?"

"You gotta try this, then. Shit. And I was hungry too." Williams shoved the paper toward Liam with half the sandwich in it.

Liam picked it up. He took a bite and most of it seemed to fall out the bottom of the French bread. But it was good. Damn good. There was enough cholesterol in it to kill an ox, but he could have eaten the whole thing. Derrell Williams was a bigger man than he was to have shared it. "Where do you get something like this?" he asked with his mouth full.

"Mother's."

"Mother's." Liam would have to remember it. He was going to eat dinner there.

"So you think I should pay a visit to the 555 Association?" Williams scarfed down the rest of the sandwich, patting his mouth with the last paper napkin. "Me, a certified member of the Zulu Social Aid and Pleasure Club going to pay a call at the 555? Hey, I think I like it, man. I think I like it."

"Don't call it a club. I already got that lecture."

"I hear you." The detective stood and strapped his .45 under his arm. He took a gray suit jacket from the back of his chair and slipped into it.

"Nice suit. I got one at home like that." Liam wolfed down the rest of the po'boy. "You could be a fed, Williams."

"Yeah, well, why don't you wear the damned suits? The way you dress, Jameson, you oughta be a homeboy."

Searching for a napkin, Liam gave up and wiped his mouth with the back of his hand. "Can't be a homeboy, detective." He shoved up his sleeves and held out his arms. "Look, ma, no tattoos."

"Great. A smart-ass fed."

"Hey, is that Mother's on the way to the club?"

Williams heaved a sigh. "Yes."

"Oh, man," Liam said. "This is my lucky day."

"I'm here to see Mr. Laborde," Claire said to the man at the front door of the 555.

"Do you have an appointment?"

"Yes," she fibbed. The lie might not have been necessary, but she'd been calling for days, ever since the holidays, and she had the definite suspicion Mr. D'Hemecourt, the president's secretary, wasn't giving the illustrious Mr. Laborde all his messages.

"I'll take you upstairs."

She followed the man along the route she'd taken the last time she'd been there. He knocked on the office entrance, but there was no answer. Putting his head through the door, he saw Mr. D'Hemecourt's desk was empty.

"His secretary must have stepped away for the moment. Why don't you wait in here. Mr. Laborde is downstairs having a meeting with the president of Tulane, but I'm sure he won't be much longer. Mr. D'Hemecourt will make you comfortable as soon as he returns." The man watched while she took a seat on the couch opposite D'Hemecourt's desk, then he left her and went back downstairs.

She never thought she'd be alone in this office twice, but at least having the file back at her condo rid her of the temptation to snoop.

There were several magazines on the spotlessly clean glass-top coffee table, and she flipped through the current New Orleans periodical *Preservation in Print,* halfheartedly skimming the pictures. Before long, she heard someone walking in the hallway outside. She expected to see Mr. D'Heme-court's familiar face; she was surprised.

There was a second when the man didn't see her sitting on the couch, but it was enough time for her to get a good look at him. He wasn't very tall. He was somewhere in his mid-fifties with partly balding gray hair and a paunch, but he hid his defects well behind a dark custom-made suit, and there was a certain aristocratic bearing to the strong cut of his chin and slim Anglo nose that most would say was quite hand-some. Even at his age, Claire knew that women would find him attractive. He walked with the ebony cane with all the comportment of a Shakespearean actor.

"Sir," she blurted out. His gaze met hers and there was al-most a savage expression in his eyes, as if he not only not ex-pected someone to be in the room with him, but that he was not expecting *her*.

"Sir, I'm waiting for Mr. Laborde."

"I'm Everard Laborde." There was caution in his voice, the same kind of caution that movie stars use when accosted on the street by a fan.

"I was hoping to speak with you, Mr. Laborde. It's about my sister."

"Do you have an appointment?"

She cringed at the supercilious tone in his voice. "I've been trying to make one, but your secretary never gets back to me."

"Why do you want to talk to me about your sister? Who is she?"

Claire had the distinct feeling he already knew the an-swers to those questions. "My sister was Zoe Green. She was here five years ago, interviewing for a job. Then she disap-peared. She was murdered."

Laborde stared at her. The seconds passed like minutes while he seemed to note her every feature right down to the make of handbag she carried. It was a distinctly unnerving stare, a critical, analyzing, dismissive stare, and Claire wondered how long she could suffer it before she said something rude.

"May I speak with you, Mr. Laborde?" she asked, growing impatient.

He seemed to contemplate something, but then, as if his attention had suddenly snapped into place, he smiled and gestured toward his office. "Will you come in here, Miss Green?" He stepped aside and motioned for her to precede him.

"I know you're busy. This won't take long," she said rather apologetically as she sank into a plush seat by the infamous glass-topped desk.

He shut the door behind them. She wondered if D'Hemecourt would show up and be fired for letting her get in, but she couldn't worry about the secretary. She had her own problems.

"My sister, perhaps you remember her." Claire placed Zoe's picture—the same one that had been clipped to the resume in the ZG file—on the glass desk.

Laborde picked it up. He studied it. "What was her name again?"

"Zoe. Zoe Green."

"Green. That's a Jewish name, isn't it?"

"Sometimes it is." She gave him a level stare. "You didn't think it was a problem in Zoe's case, did you? I mean, you were going to hire her, remember?"

He smiled. "She was murdered. That gave me little chance to hire her, wouldn't you say? In any case, the 555 is an equal opportunity employer. Religious preference plays no part in our choice of whom to hire, Miss Green. It is Miss Green, isn't it?"

She opened her mouth to correct him, but she didn't want to bicker over her marital status. He could label and humiliate her all he wanted as long as he provided a little bit of information on her sister's last hours. "Miss Green will do. Do you remember my sister, Mr. Laborde? Were you the one to interview her?"

He eyed her up and down. It might have even been a sexual assessment if not for the strange, rather distasteful expression on his face. "I interviewed your sister, and I seem to recall the candidate looked a lot like you, Miss Green."

"As you can see from her picture, we were twins."

"Yes. Identical."

"Identical, but not the same. She was a very trusting person. She really worshipped certain things and certain kinds of people. I think she trusted and worshipped too much." She gave him the courtroom stare. "Did she mention anything in the interview such as where she was going next?"

"No, and I told the police the same thing five years ago."

"Did she mention anyone in particular, maybe someone who had given her a recommendation that she was going to meet for a celebratory drink?"

"Her recommendations were sterling. One came from Welsh Energy Company, another, Gannon Enterprise. The heads of these companies are friends of mine, Miss Green. They are the crème de la crème of the Louisiana business community. By your questions, I almost think you believe these pillars of society had something to do with your sister's disappearance."

"No, I just—"

"You just what, Miss Green?"

He threw her off balance. "I don't mean to imply anything."

He nodded. "These two men are members of this organization, and fine, upstanding members, I might add. They were gracious enough to write your sister recommendations."

"I understand that. I just want to find out what happened to her."

"You cannot find that out here."

It was her turn to stare. She fought off the hopelessness

that threatened to make her capitulate and go home. There was only one last card to play. "I saw her résumé, Mr. Laborde. I was hoping you could tell me what RIO meant."

The smile on his face shocked her. It was such a nice smile. By all rights, it was friendly and helpful. The undercurrent of malice was something maybe only a woman could see. "Have you stolen the file from me, Miss Green?"

"How do you know your secretary didn't give me a copy?"

"He didn't."

"What does RIO mean?"

He leaned forward on his glass desk, his hands gripping the edge, leaving prohibited fingerprints. "It means river, doesn't it? Or the city in Brazil. The city of Carnival and fun and decadence. What does it mean to you, Miss Green?"

A coldness glided down her spine. "It means nothing to me. Should it?"

He didn't answer. In the ensuing silence he stood and held out the door for her. "I think that's all there is to say, Miss Green. I enjoyed meeting you. I wish you luck in your investigation."

She rose from the chair. "Why don't you want to help me?"

He released a laugh that was half chuckle, half smirk. "I want to help you, Miss Green, oh, that I do, it's just that there's nothing I can do for you. You must believe that."

"What does RIO mean, Mr. Laborde?" she repeated, desperate to get just that bit of the mystery solved.

He held the door for her. She had no choice but to pass through it, but when she did, he reached out and put his fingers on her lips as if urging her to be quiet.

The intimacy of his touch shocked her. His fingers were whisper soft, but cold, like the brush of a snowflake. She drew back in revulsion, and for the life of her, she couldn't understand why he'd just done what he'd done. It was a strange gesture by an archaic character, but there was more to it than just eccentricity. It was just too out of the blue. Suddenly she was burning to understand.

He smiled at her bewilderment. "What do you do for a living, Miss Green?"

She waited until his hand was at his side. "I'm a lawyer."

He gave her an indulgent smile. "How appropriate."

"What does RIO mean? Just tell me why you wrote that on her résumé."

"I've told you." He nodded good-bye, then closed the double doors to his office, leaving her alone with D'Hemecourt's still-empty desk.

She left the office and wandered down the hall like a battle-numbed foot soldier. Her mouth tingled; the phantom touch of fingers still remained on them. She was scared, but it was an irrational fear that came from deep inside her subconscious.

"Well, if it isn't the little vigilante. Violated anyone's civil rights lately, Green?"

She looked up and found Jameson being escorted by the man who had answered the door for her. With him was the NOPD homicide detective who'd been in charge of Zoe's case.

"Jameson." She nodded to Williams. "Detective." She met Liam's gaze, but her thoughts were confused and far away, still back at Laborde's office, obsessing.

"You look like you've seen a ghost, darlin'."

She focused on Jameson and found she really wanted to talk to him. Maybe being FBI, he could sort out the strange feeling she had. Her conversation with Everard Laborde was far from revealing; Jameson would probably even laugh at her. Still, she wanted to share her thoughts with someone—someone who would tell her that dragons were only the stuff of fairy tales.

"I've just been to see the president. He was the man who interviewed my sister." She looked at Detective Williams. "I

can't really make sense of our meeting other than to say that
I've just had the strangest feeling—"

Jameson took her by the arm and pulled her out of earshot
of the 555 doorman who stood next to the detective. Whispering, he said, "No sense in telling the world, Claire."

She looked up at him. She wondered if her eyes gave away
her fear and worries. By his expression, they probably did.
"I didn't like him, Liam."

"Laborde? I don't think anyone does but the Aryans that
hang around this club."

"He gave me the strangest feeling."

"Hey, he's a creep. They tell me he runs around town in
an old Bentley and he always turns his headlights on even in
the middle of day like he's perpetually going to somebody's
funeral."

"Could he possibly—?"

He put his own fingers against her mouth. This time the
touch was warm and gentle even if the fingers were hard and
callused. "He's an asshole but not necessarily a murderer.
The thing he lacks is motivation. And he has an airtight alibi.
Two of his cronies vouched for his whereabouts at the ap-
proximate time Zoe was killed."

"But Minnefield couldn't narrow her time of death to anything less than four hours. If he had just a twenty-minute window, he could have—" The fingers were on her lips again,
silencing her. Her shoulders slumped. She pulled his hand
down. "I guess I should have figured he'd have an alibi. He
was the last one to see her alive. Of course he's got an alibi."
She leaned back against the wall. The terror inside her seemed
to die along with the hope. "Maybe I just want to find her
killer so badly, I'll see something nefarious about anyone."

"I'll come by your place later."

She looked at him but could barely meet his gaze. "I'm not
sure that'd be a good idea."

"I want to know what he did to scare you."

"It's just that I knew my sister so well . . . ." She shook her head. She'd be worse than a fool to hand him her intuition here and now. She looked at the 555 doorman who was with Williams, impatiently watching their discussion out of earshot. "I've got to go."

"I'll pick you up at eight for dinner. We'll discuss your conversation then."

"No, really, I shouldn't." She pulled away and glanced at Williams. "I've really got to go. There's a lot I need to sort out here. If anything concrete comes up, I'll call the detective."

She gave Liam one last stare, then she left them, her mind overwhelmed with thoughts of ZOE, and Zoe, and the strange touch that remained on her lips like a phantom limb.

Claire stared at the waxy leaves of the magnolia tree through the French doors. It was overcast and growing colder. She'd changed out of her suit into black stirrup pants and a fluffy turquoise mohair sweater, pulling on a thick pair of gym socks to warm her feet.

She was still numb. What seemed obvious to her subconscious was also unspeakable. And it lacked any hard evidence.

She leaned her head back on the couch and recalled the day they'd found Zoe. She remembered everything. The trip downtown to the morgue. The polished stainless steel room. The cold air. The vague scent of ether and chicken fat.

She'd had to tell herself to take each breath, as if the pain had erased her own abilities to go on living. In Technicolor clarity she remembered Zoe; the body beneath the sheet; the child of parents too broken to come and officially identify their daughter. The image of Zoe's face was burned into her mind like the unerasable image on a negative. The death mask. Claire had not been seeing only her dead sister, but she was also staring at herself dead. Any youthful optimism of immortality was crushed like a fly beneath a boot heel.

The experience had been so terrible that it had been only later when she could find the stamina to call up the detective handling her sister's case and tell him what was wrong with her sister. Williams hadn't listened then. It was just the rantings of a grief-stricken relative. He probably heard things like that all the time. Claire's observations were at best anecdotal, and he told her so just weeks before, when she'd first arrived in town and had again implored him to open the Zoe Green files to her. And he'd refused.

She wondered what Williams would think of her rantings now. Laborde had touched her lips. Her lips, she'd insist.

And the detective would look at her from beneath all his case files, the weight of the dead and the unsolved slung around his civil-servant shoulders, and he'd probably laugh.

The Bentley left the alley before four o'clock. Private parking behind the 555 was just one of the perks of being president. The day had darkened and a fine mist had settled over the streetcar tracks on Canal. The Bentley's headlights were on, casting ghost shadows over the pedestrians at the bus stop.

The car turned onto St. Charles for the excursion home. Built in 1968, the vehicle showed its age in the pea-green exterior paint and burnt-orange leather trim, but still the car took the potholes like a divan on wheels. It had been Everard's father's. Cummings had always turned the headlights on because it made him noticed. Like father, like son.

Laborde's hands were trembling as he drove around Lee Circle. Next to him on the leather seat was the picture of Zoe Green. Her sister had left it on his desk.

It was like killing the same person twice. She was supposed to be gone, exorcised from his soul and this world, but she'd just resurrected herself in her twin.

The damned girl would never know what a shock her face had been to him. She would never know how he was very much captured by her sister. Every few weeks he still found himself rooting through Dem's cabinets, looking for her file, just to take another gander at that face. That face he still saw in his bed at night. Zoe Green was dead. He'd killed her, but she lived in his memories like a loved one. He thought he'd exiled that face to the lifeless, two-dimensional snapshot he kept in his files; now the face was back live in the flesh, accusing him just by the very life that animated it.

She wanted to know what RIO meant. He'd show her if she kept bothering him. And what an experience that would be. To kill the same person twice. He could almost imagine the applause he'd get on mystery night for that idea.

The thought was just a little nugget of desire in his subconscious, but it grew and began to overpower him. Twins. The idea was ingenious. This year's murder had been planned, but he could do Zoe's twice. Next year he could wow the members with double the pleasure. He'd have to test out his thoughts on Hockney and Fred, but he already could see the admiration in their eyes.

He rubbed his jaw. Time to put aside games for now. He'd have to shave for cocktails. Ironically, he was due at a reception at the Welsh mansion, the exact house on Audubon Place that Zoe Green had been going to after her interview. Bernard Welsh owned the biggest oil patch in Louisiana. He'd always been a generous son of a bitch—like giving recommendations to his daughter's Jewish friends—but only because he could afford to be. Others, such as Everard, had had to work too hard to get what social position he had. Everything had been hard fought and hard won. Everard had taken his father's status and quadrupled it. He couldn't let it slip through his fingers because too many people were suddenly tramping through his office asking old questions. So first things first. He had to put his house in order.

He picked up the car phone. Dialing his office number, he waited the four rings before the recording of Dem's voice told him no one was in.

"Dem, I just wanted you to know that I played nursemaid to Agent Jameson and our friend Detective Williams all afternoon without you. We waited and waited for you to show up with the file. You did not. So now, when you come back from whatever errand you're running, I want you to drop the file off at my house. Don't fail me on this. I'll be at Welsh's until ten. I expect to see you at my door at ten tonight precisely."

He replaced the receiver. He was going to fire that little bloodsucking preppy, and he relished the anticipation. But first he was going to get back that file.

He pulled into the alley behind the mansion on Exposition. Hitting the opener, he parked the Bentley in the garage and watched the garage door shut in his rearview mirror.

RIO. He shouldn't have made that notation on her résumé when he gave her her number, but it was just that he'd been thinking it so hard, it came out through his pen like automatic writing. They would never connect it to anything, but strange things happened in this world. Like meeting the twin of a Jew girl you'd left dead in a town named after a bunch of krauts.

He got out of the car. Merino, his houseboy, waited for him at the door.

"I started the sauna at quarter to four just as you asked, señor."

Laborde nodded. Merino Escobel was a wetback from Chihuahua whom Everard had saved from a life of brothels. His sister cleaned rooms at the 555 and had recommended him. Theirs was a perfect match. The young man worked twenty hours a day, and Laborde could afford him because he was an illegal. Who said slavery was dead.

"Merino, go call your sister and see if she wants company this evening. I'm giving you the night off."

Merino looked a bit dumbfounded, as if such an event happened with the frequency of the Second Coming. "Are you sure, señor? I thought you wanted me to clean the guest house tonight?"

"No, take the night off."

"Very good, señor."

Everard smiled. The bus trip to Merino's sister's apartment in Gentilly would take two hours from Uptown. It was perfect because he wanted to be alone when he fired Dem. He didn't want Merino to ever be able to say that he'd heard J. Everard Laborde raise his voice in anger.

Inside the house, he went to the master suite. He tossed his suit jacket over a chair. The old mahogany tester bed crouched in the corner like a gargoyle. He saw his tuxedo had already been laid out on the coverlet.

A sauna was just the thing. His back felt as kinked as his insides. It was stress. He'd spent over two hours with those baboons from the FBI and NOPD. The adrenaline was killing him.

The mansion's bathroom suite had not been changed since his parents had it remodeled in 1952. Chrome fixtures and Jayne Mansfield–pink tiles lined the shower/sauna, but the plumbing was still superb. Like the Bentley, the room was a bit outdated, but the quality was top of the line.

He stripped down to his boxers and sipped the cold martini that had been left near his robe. The party at Audubon was routine; he really didn't look forward to it. His mind was elsewhere, on that girl who had visited him.

He walked over to the double sinks. The vanity held a bank of drawers custom-made from Louisiana cypress. He opened the third one from the bottom and peered inside.

It was all his mother's makeup. Crumbling, rotting, caking. Bottles of half-empty nail polish, dried-out mascaras, and bleary tubes of lipsticks. Cheap drugstore makeup in the strange, rather garish colors that became a redhead. It was still all there. Nothing had been changed since his mother had died. Merino knew never to open the drawer. The houseboy astutely seemed to sense that Everard would not take the violation well.

Laborde took a tube of lipstick out of the drawer. It was

his mother's favorite, a neon-orange color made by Hazel Bishop, the working girl's cosmetic company. His mother never changed her makeup brand even after she left the stage and married his father. Then she could have gone to God-chaux's, New Orleans's premier department store, and bought herself a whole line of Elizabeth Arden, but Anabel stuck to Hazel Bishop. Because, Everard theorized, it was the same dime-store trash that she was.

He twisted the tube and revealed a phallic rod of bright waxy lipstick. The lip brush worked well, so well, in fact, he was on his third one.

From his briefcase he'd placed near the bed, he extracted Zoe Green's photo. There were two gilt mirrors over the sinks; no one knew that there was a button beneath the bottom rail of the mirrors, and when pushed, the mirror released just like a picture mounted over a wall safe. Behind the mirrors were medicine cabinets built into the wall. Everard had long since emptied them of his parent's toiletries and now he used the space as a hidden picture gallery.

With one of the red thumbtacks he kept in Anabel's makeup drawer he tacked the photo of Zoe Green next to the duplicate that had been in the paper. Now there were two Zoe Greens in his medicine cabinet, he thought with strange satisfaction. Two Zoe Greens smiling at him, along with the portraits of all the rest of his girls. He'd gathered the pictures mostly from the newspaper and eventually they'd turned yellow and crumbled. That was why he'd invested in the copier. So now, every year, the faces were replaced with fresh copies. Every year before Mardi Gras, he dolled them up with the lip brush. It was Claire Green's turn.

He dabbed at the tube of lipstick and began painting Zoe Green's pretty lips. They had to match the color on the photo next to her. If he was obsessive-compulsive at all, it was that all his girls' photos had to have Anabel's Hazel Bishop lipstick painted on them. He didn't quite know why he had to do it to them, but somehow it titillated him. "Clown lips" was how his father had mocked Anabel whenever she put on the garish color. Now Everard felt a sense of completeness when he saw his girls in the bright orange. The color drew out their lips and made their other features disappear. Black or white, the girl's individuality faded and he was left with a gallery of clown lips.

Zoe in duplicate looked down at him from his gallery. Clown lips twice. One for the social climber, one for the lawyer.

Everard closed the medicine cabinet. The tube of lipstick was still in his palm. He thought of Claire Green and his shock at seeing her, and his hand shook while he painted lips on the mirror.

He relived Zoe's death. Cold cream. It took away the smears of orange around the mouth. After the struggle, after Zoe was dead, he cleaned her mouth with Pond's and reapplied the lipstick, this time neatly, before he sent her away to Des Allemands.

Two pairs of lips were painted on the mirror. Zoe times two.

Her real name was Claire. He'd have to remember that if he ever saw her again. He pictured her as she sat in Dem's office, her eyes large, her face wary. She was there, asking questions, making trouble.

Zoe was the girl who had stayed with him the longest. It wasn't right that she have a twin to come haunt him.

He stared at the second pair of lips he'd drawn on the mirror. It was easy to pretend they belonged to a warm, struggling mouth. In fact, he did it all the time.

"Claire. I've got to remember that your name is Claire," he whispered before he leaned over the sink and placed his lips on the mirror.

After a moment he drew back. There he was in the mirror again, orange smeared on him just like it had always been smeared on his father while his mother lay bleeding and crying on the floor.

Hastily he grabbed a handful of Kleenex and wiped his mouth. The Pond's took off the rest. He cleaned the mirror also and threw the offending tissue in his wastebasket.

The sauna was delicious. He stepped into it and closed the door, seating himself on a tiled banquette of Jayne Mansfield pink. God, he needed to relax. There were so many pressures, so many details to remember. The gallery was safely hidden in the wall; he didn't lay awake at night worrying someone might discover it, but he'd forgotten to flush the soiled Kleenex again. Merino probably wouldn't make much of it if he'd ever found the telltale orange lipstick smears on the tissue, but it wouldn't do to leave it around. He was a bachelor, living alone, one who rarely, if ever, dated. A woman's lipstick left on a tissue in his personal bathroom might leave one to think he lounged around in kimonos and liked to try on the pantyhose sold at the K and B.

After all, people loved to talk. They were monsters really, these gossips. He was president of the 555 Association, he lived in a mansion on Exposition Boulevard, and had no visible means of support.

They would love to think the worst of him.

## ❦ 19 ❧

The buzzer screeched at the front door. Claire opened her eyes, realizing she'd fallen asleep. She glanced at the clock. It was eight o'clock in the evening. She feared Jameson was making good on his threat of dinner.

She sat up on the couch. Her hair was a mess, she was drowsy. In the mirror, her eyes were puffy and red from lack of rest. He was now banging at her door.

Without even bothering with shoes, she tramped over to the door and swung it open.

"Listen, Jameson—" She stopped dead in her tracks.

"I've come for the file you stole, Ms. Green." D'Hemecourt, Laborde's secretary, stood at the threshold, his mouth twisted in a contemptuous sneer. "I've been trying to reach you all day. You've either not been home or not answering your buzzer. Which is it, Ms. Green?"

"You have no right to be here. Leave," she said angrily.

"Mr. Laborde should have you arrested."

Claire stood speechless while he sauntered into the condo.

"I want the file right now," he demanded.

"You can't just come into my home uninvited. Leave at once."

"You let me in, Ms. Green."

"I thought you were someone else. How did you get past the front door?"

"Your neighbors let me in as they were leaving."

"Great. Just like back in New York." She released a groan of frustration.

He walked over to the desk and began to sort through the piles of papers.

Furious, she held open the door. "I said leave."

"Give me the Zoe Green file or, so help me, you'll pay for it." His trademark pleasant smile turned into a snarl.

She stared at him in shock. "Are you threatening me? Why is the file so important? What's in it?"

"Mr. Laborde had a conniption when he couldn't find it, and now he blames me for letting you grab it from my office. He wants that file bad, so bad, he's just got to have it. So give it up, Ms. Green."

She stood fast by the open door. D'Hemecourt had a rather creepy manner in a calm circumstance—his polite veneer had a lot to do with it—but angry as he was now, he looked like a maniac.

"Leave right now, or I'll call the police," she warned. "And tell that boss of yours that I find his interest in a five-year-old file remarkable. Yes, you tell him that. I find his interest quite noteworthy."

"Yeah. So do I." A strange glint appeared in the young man's eye. She almost wondered if he was here doing his boss's bidding, or if he had another agenda altogether. "So hand it over, bitch. I'm not going to let you keep it." He gave her a nasty look, then walked over to her briefcase. Flipping open the locks, he dumped the contents on the couch.

"Stop it! Stop it at once!" She ran over and pulled on his arm. Zoe's file was snapped into the accordion holder on the lid and hadn't fallen out. He hadn't seen it yet, but she couldn't let him ransack her place until he did. "I'm calling the police." She walked over to the phone. D'Hemecourt watched her, a sour expression on his face.

"Go ahead and call them. I'm sure the 555 wants to bring

charges as well. You took that file, Ms. Green. That's theft. Now, what do you want to do? Do you want to call the police or do you want to give me back the file? Mr. Laborde is going to rip me another asshole when I see him, and I sure as hell am not going to that meeting without the file."

"Fine. You can have the file back." She heaved a disgusted sigh and walked back to her briefcase. She'd copied everything in it anyway. There was no point in coming to blows over something that was useless to her. "Here." She unsnapped the file holder. "Give this to Mr. Laborde with my blessing." She nearly threw it at him. "Then ask him what the Star of David means. And ask him about RIO. That ought to set him off."

D'Hemecourt curled his lip. "Thank you, Ms. Green. I'll do that."

"Just ask him about RIO."

"*Shalom.* If I ever catch you back at the 555, I'm going to throw you out personally." D'Hemecourt waved the file at her, then jogged down the mansion stairs.

Claire closed the door to the condo. She really hated that guy. D'Hemecourt didn't need another asshole because he was a big enough one already. Now she wondered what he really wanted that file for, and she almost hoped he'd use it against his boss. D'Hemecourt had to hate Laborde. The Windex scene was excuse enough.

But she couldn't think about D'Hemecourt now. She had bigger worries than the 555 going after her for theft. When Everard Laborde was told she had stolen a file from him, he could get pretty angry and dangerous. If he was Zoe's killer, that meant things were probably god-awful for her right now.

The buzzer went off again. She nearly jumped to the ceiling. She thought she had her fear in check, but it wasn't. Her imagination didn't help.

"Who is it?" she said into the intercom.

"Who do you think?" came the familiar drawl.

Suddenly inexplicably relieved, she didn't press the gate-release button, but ran down the mansion staircase and threw open the front door.

"Aren't you going to bring a purse?"

"Jameson," she gasped, giving him a tremulous smile.

"I told you I'd pick you up at eight. Hey, what are you, from Mississippi? You don't even have on any shoes."

"I didn't think you'd come."

"I got hung up over at the NOPD. Williams sends his love."

"Yeah?" She sounded like an infatuated schoolgirl, but she couldn't hide her relief. The idea that maybe Laborde had done something to Zoe left her more alone and frightened than she thought.

"What was the funeral director's secretary doing over here?"

It took her a moment to know what he was talking about. "Laborde's secretary? He said I took a file from his office."

"Did you?"

It was her turn to give him a sarcastic look. "Do you think I'd tell a law enforcement officer if I did?"

"What did the file say?"

"I'm taking the Fifth." She smiled and held the door out for him. He followed her, his manner uneasy, as if he found her unusual warmth and friendliness suspect.

"Darlin', did something happen today? You seem real glad to see me." He took her hand.

She turned to him. They were on the staircase and he stood two steps below her. They stared eye to eye. "You're helping me with Zoe. Why shouldn't I be glad to see you?"

"Well, there's that little matter of the *High Risk* ad back in New York and the way we met, and then there's that other night in the rain—"

"I've thought about all of that, Jameson, and, you know, I've just dismissed it from my mind. It's erased. You want to solve Zoe's murder, and so do I. The other stuff is just en-

trapment, and I'm smart enough not to let you entrap me."
She smiled again. She couldn't stop herself. With him around,
even though she knew he'd put her in jail if he could, she suddenly felt safe. It was a sweet, wonderful rush to suddenly be
safe. It was better to be alive even in jail than dead in a ditch.

"Something's definitely changed about you, sweetheart."

She gave him another bright smile. "I just realized it would
be better to work with you on this than against you. So let's
go to dinner and see what we can come up with on the case.
If we put our heads together, maybe we can go somewhere."

"Yeah, but you know and I know I'd rather put something
else together."

Jameson stared at her. His mouth was an enigmatic hard
line, his gaze was shadowed, yet probing.

The man astounded her. She probably should have
laughed, but she couldn't. Sexual innuendo coupled with
brutal honesty was unsettling at best. The fact that what he
said was the truth for both of them made it even worse.

His hands went around her waist. She could hardly
breathe. Her emotions were doubly intense, given the scare
she just had. Now, just like that, he'd brought her again to
that moment they'd had in the rain. She'd dropped her guard
for one small second, and here he was, ready to kiss her.
Here she was, ready to let him.

She put on the brakes. She wanted to have dinner with
him, not sleep with him. The bogeyman hadn't scared her
that badly yet. Besides, she still didn't even know if the fool
was married.

"You know, I've got to tell you, that other night in the
rain"—his smile was almost playful—"well, in Tulsa, being
chased by a girl in a wet shirt is almost a proposal."

"I wasn't chasing you. I went to your hotel room to talk
to you and it happened to be raining that night." The answer
was pure logic. She was proud of herself. The steel magnolia
inside her was coming back.

He grinned just like the lout he was. "Yeah, sure. That's

what they all say. 'Oooh, I just happened to be standing out in the rain, when this cold breeze came by . . . .' "

She pushed him. He stumbled back a few steps, laughing.

She couldn't believe she'd almost let him take her again. The man was just out to get in her jeans and she kept inviting him in. "Let me ask you this, Jameson, are all men troglodytes, or is it just you?"

"Claire." He took her hand and looked deeply into her eyes. "Darlin', I got some bad news for you."

Her heart began to pound again. When he was being charming and funny and boyish, it was easy to forget the maelstrom around them. The feds might have found something incriminating in New York and he could have an arrest warrant for her right in his back pocket. But everything seemed to fade away when he was around: ZOE, Halbert Washington, the noose she wore around her neck that he yanked every now and then. She must be more attracted to him than she thought, because he was constantly getting around her armor.

"What is it?" she asked, once more calmly trying to ward off all the anxieties that ate at her.

"It's true."

"What's true?"

"We are all troglodytes."

She yanked his hands from her waist and jammed them onto the banister. The man should be shot. He was infuriating. Worst of all, he always left her disadvantaged. She was nothing but a slave to the undercurrents of fear and intimidation that went with his badge. There was nothing to be gained by spending time with him, nothing.

"Go back to your hotel room, Liam. I'm sure a dirty magazine and a little mistletoe-for-one ought to cure what ails you. Happy holidays."

"Christmas is over. It's a brand new year and we're going to dinner, Claire, so get your purse."

She eyed him. "Is that an order from the feds? 'Cause it'd have to be for me to—"

"Now, there's the girl I know." He grinned. "Go get your purse, Claire. I want to know about your visit with Laborde."

Unconsciously, she brushed her fingers against her mouth. "I don't know if it has any relevancy."

"Let me be the judge of that."

"He has an alibi, an airtight one. You told me that yourself."

"The way I look at it, the definition of *alibi* is *lie.*" He stared at the hand that still lingered on her mouth. Slowly, he pulled it down to her side. "What's scaring you?"

She looked at him and remembered the fear she felt in Laborde's office, and later, after D'Hemecourt left her condo. Doubts came back to her. A chill traipsed down her spine. Laborde had touched her lips. She might have been caressed by the hand of a murderer.

Suddenly there was this need to put instinct into words. She felt the urge to drag into sunlight all the horrors lurking in her subconscious. Maybe it was time to see them for what they were.

"I'll go to dinner with you. Just give me a minute. I've got to get myself together."

"Don't be long."

She glanced at him. He was always so cocksure, so arrogant. His was the kind of confidence usually attributed to lawyers, but, as she knew from her own personal experience, lawyers weren't confident at all. It was all a sham to mask the peril of their existence. The law was subject to interpretation, and even when the interpretation seemed clear, a judge could come and blow all rational thinking to kingdom come.

"Just let me get my shoes," she told him, a wariness in her eyes. "And I'll need an umbrella. It might rain."

\* \* \*

Dem pounded at the door to the darkened mansion. It was ten o'clock precisely. For this meeting, he didn't want to be late.

But no one was answering. The house was empty.

He stood back from the door and stared at the empty black eyes of the mansion's windows. A wintry wind blew leaves off the live oaks, scattering them in the sky like a colony of bats. He clutched the ZG file to his chest. Thank God he got it. He was sure it was his ticket to promotion and the good life.

Headlights flashed and subsided at the back of the house. He heard the deep rumble of an expensive car engine. The Bentley had returned.

Laborde's garage was at the rear of the house and Dem figured he might as well walk around and meet him there. Trailing the path of headlights, he waited until the Bentley had pulled into the well-lighted garage. Laborde hit the button to close the door. The noise from the overhead chain was deafening. The garage door cranked down. It was obvious Laborde didn't hear his visitor arrive, but Dem could see in the side mirror that Laborde finally noticed him.

"I retrieved the Zoe Green file." Dem walked over to the Bentley.

Laborde lowered his window and took the file as if it were a burger tray at the drive-in. "It's all here but the picture," he said woodenly.

"I—I didn't know there was a picture." Worried, Dem leaned through the window to study the file as if he might find what was missing when Laborde could not. "She told me this was everything."

Laborde pressed the window control before Dem noticed. The window slid up silently. It stopped only when it had Dem's head in a choke hold.

"Hey! Hey!" Dem cursed, trying to pull his head from the door.

Laborde took no notice of his discomfort. Quietly, he stared through the windshield and asked, "Who was *she?*"

Dem couldn't wipe the murderous expression off his face. "Who the hell else? Claire Green. This one's sister. She came into the office to see you. I turned my back and she was gone, obviously with this in hand. Now, open the window."

The request was ignored. "You gave her the file."

"No! I'm telling you, she stole it. Now, open the window. This hurts."

"You let her steal it, then."

"No! No!"

Laborde looked down his nose at the young man. "Don't come back in the morning. You're fired, D'Hemecourt. The 555 wants nothing to do with you."

"The 555 wants nothing to do with me?" Dem laughed. "You killed a girl and they want nothing to do with me?"

"What proof do you have, Dem, that I had anything to do with Zoe Green's disappearance?"

"The board would be mighty interested in the visitors you've had. Besides, I know what you do all day in that office, lurking around on your computer, hoping you can talk to some sicko just like yourself. I've snuck a peek at your screen, Mr. Laborde. It makes me want to vomit just thinking about those bulletin boards I've seen on your computer screen."

"You know no such things about me." Laborde's color was up. He was finally showing some anger.

"Oh, yeah?" Dem cursed. "Well, I sure as hell know what you do while you're on the Internet. I'm your secretary, remember? I clean that fucking glass desk of yours."

The window got tighter. Dem reddened. Another quarter inch and he'd be lucky to breathe. "Look, I didn't come here to threaten you, I came to make a deal."

The window suddenly came down. All the way down. Dem lurched back and Laborde got out of his Bentley.

"What kind of deal, Mr. D'Hemecourt?"

Dem massaged his throat. "I want a promotion and a payoff. My parents dumped me on the 555 and took off for Switzerland. I haven't had any money for five years, and I miss it."

Laborde suddenly smiled. He slapped Dem on the back. "I had no idea you were such a go-getter, Dem. The nerve it took to come here and blackmail me, why, I admire it. Really."

"I didn't mean to threaten you. I just want a deal." Dem started to smile.

"But you did threaten me. If you start complaining to the board, they might not want me to remain president of the 555 any longer. My whole way of life would change."

Dem quit smiling.

Laborde had reached back into the Bentley and pulled open the glove compartment. A full five seconds elapsed before Dem realized the black metal object in Laborde's hand was a gun.

"I really can't forgive you for this, Dem. This is going to be a mess and I'm going to have to clean it up. I always prepare for these things, but I'm unprepared now."

"Unprepared for what?" Dem blathered.

"This." Laborde didn't even flinch when he pulled the trigger.


Blood and skin and cartilage were everywhere. The relentlessly clean garage was now the scarlet-sprayed scene of a massacre. If Everard hadn't been immune to such sights, he might have leaned over the pea-green leather seat of the car and thrown up. At least Dem had had the grace to blow over the garage door and not on the Bentley.

He'd never forgive Dem. Things were a mess and he hated to improvise. The blackmail had come as a shock. He'd been prepared to fire the man, not kill him, but Everard never suspected his secretary was spying on him. Dem's family roots were some of the oldest. They'd had great plans for him at the 555, but then, Everard had figured Dem had better breeding than to lower himself to being a snoop. He could forgive the blackmail, but he wouldn't tolerate someone watching him. Dem had to go.

And now, certainly, as Everard surveyed the carnage, Dem had to go again.

He gingerly stepped out of the Bentley, avoiding dipping his cane into the pools of blood. What luck that he'd given Merino the night off, or else he'd have two dead bodies to deal with.

Inside the house, he changed into some old clothes, pulled on a pair of his father's surgical gloves, and tore the shower curtain liner from the guest bathroom. The phone rang. He went to the answering machine and stood stock-still while his neighbor's voice rang out, leaving a message. The man thought he'd heard something like a gunshot in the alley and was wondering if Everard was home to hear it. Satisfied he was not, the neighbor hung up, obviously becoming more and more convinced that what he'd heard was nothing.

Laborde smiled. Now he had the neighbor to claim he was not home. It might come in handy if they ever found Dem, but with his father's surgical instruments in tow, Everard was determined they would never find Dem. His secretary was going to be alligator-size chunks within hours. Along with a little Spic and Span and the pressure wash for the garage, he'd be in business.

He laid out the shower curtain on the dry side of the Bentley and dragged Dem's body onto it. Studying the mess that had once been his secretary's face, he heartened. The blast had hit Dem in the jaw. There'd be no dental records to identify him. There was nothing left to piece together.

He mentally listed all the things he had to do. He'd put Dem in the Bentley's trunk along with his surgeon's tools, then drive to the dump after he cleaned up the garage. He again assessed the mess, and resentment built inside him.

He'd have to work like a servant the entire night because of an idiot. And then there would only be more messes. The authorities were already asking questions; Everard didn't relish them asking where his secretary ran off to.

But there was no helping it now. It was just like all the other times.

No way to change things.

He fished through Dem's pockets. He had to make sure to wipe him clean of identification. To his surprise, Dem had nothing but his wallet and a small cream-colored card with 555 embossed in gold across the top. Scrawled beneath it was the name *Claire Green,* an address, and phone number.

"Dem, Dem, how could you be such a fool?" Everard clucked, then he smiled and pocketed the card.

## 20

Jameson leaned back in his chair. He held a wineglass loosely in his hand. It was either the Bordeaux, the warm, dimly lit café, or the company, but whatever it was, he hadn't felt this relaxed in some time.

"What was your impression of him?" The question was something he'd ask in any other interview, but this wasn't just any interview. Nor was Claire Green just another victim. His interest in her was getting to be considerably more than that.

"Enchanted and chilled." She ran her finger along the lip of her own wineglass. Her face, cast in shadow, was pensive. "My impression of Everard Laborde is that he's very intelligent. Cultured also, but still a racist, an anti-Semite. But maybe I'm being too analytical. Deep inside I got the feeling he was most motivated by basic instincts: anger, fear, lust." She took her finger off the wineglass. "He's the kind of man women really like, I think. They look at him and believe they can have great sex, then play a game of chess afterward."

"Were you attracted to him?"

She gave him that cool, challenging gaze. He bit back the desire to see it hot, wanton, and satiated.

"Yes," she answered, a bit of color rising on her cheeks. "I was, a little. He was quixotic. I didn't know what to expect next from him."

"Does that kind of thing excite you?"

Her embarrassment seemed to turn to anger. "Is that a strictly clinical question, Agent Jameson?"

"I want to know how women react to him. That could tell me a lot about his victims, if there are any."

She seemed to accept his answer. "I don't usually find myself attracted to older men. Everard Laborde was an exception."

"Yet, you found him menacing."

"Yes. He frightened me." Her brow wrinkled. "But then, maybe I'm no judge. After Zoe . . ."

"Men frighten you."

The cool gaze met his. She visibly seemed to back away. "Some men."

"Me."

It was not a question.

He swirled the wine in his glass. "Still, I'm not a monster." The corner of his mouth lifted in a wry smile. "But maybe he is."

A moment of quiet ensued. She said, "What do you know about Everard Laborde?"

"Daddy was a doctor."

"How does that fit in?"

"The bit of latex in your sister's hair, remember? It was from an old surgical glove."

She looked as if her jaw were going to drop open. He squelched the urge to gloat. "But he still has an alibi. Remember that before you go accusing him of anything."

She took a sip of wine. It was almost too casual, as if she were trying to hide that she was excited. "I never would have even thought to find out what his father did for a living. I suppose you do have a talent for this, Agent Jameson."

"Gunnarson trained me well."

She seemed to want to say something. After a few more sips of the Bordeaux, she said, "Why did you become FBI? What was it? Was your father a fed?"

"Hell, no." He snorted. "My dad worked in a beef processing plant. Shit work if there ever was any."

"Did you like him?"

He glanced at her, unsure where she was going. "I loved him. He was my dad."

"But you didn't want to follow in his footsteps."

"I had no aspirations to come home to the trailer park every evening spattered with blood and smelling like grease and rusty iron."

"Is that what made you join the feds? Rebellion?"

"Why are you asking about it?"

She toyed with the remaining filet on her plate. "It's just that it's a big leap from the trailer park to Quantico, Virginia. Something happened to you to make you expand. What was it?"

He could feel his insides jam up like traffic on the I-244 at rush hour. The openness and comfort of a few minutes before was gone. He didn't want to talk about his father, Sunset Trailer Park, or anything else connected with that part of his life, so how the hell had they gotten onto this subject?

"You know so much about me," she said. "Everything that's important about me and my family is sitting in a file somewhere down at the NOPD, but I know nothing about you. Nothing except that you're from Tulsa."

"Taylorville."

"Yes. Taylorville. That's right outside Tulsa, I think you said. So what happened in Taylorville that made you say 'Hey, I'm a smart guy. Let's book the old man's factory and enroll in the FBI academy'?"

If a man's heart could grow stone cold, Liam's just did. He didn't like talking about Joey. Hell, he spoke with victims of crimes day in and day out, and he knew Claire Green, of all people, would empathize with him. But he wasn't seeking common ground. Joey Ableman's murder was different, maybe because he'd only been a kid, or maybe because Dalton Lee Wayne had taken out his whole family. Or maybe it was the sheer randomness of it—that some dirtball would see a kid's picture in the town paper and decide that was where to go because the boy had no father around to interfere—maybe that was what made Liam go wild inside.

Heroes. Where the hell were they anyway? They were like Joey's dad, who had ditched the kid when he was three. Never the fuck around when you needed them, that's where.

"I could've been like Pa. He was a quiet man. Maybe no great thinker, but steady and honest. I can't find fault with that. Not at all," he said quietly.

Her eyes narrowed. It was almost imperceptible, but he wondered if she was latching on to his discomfort. Her next question confirmed it.

"You wanted to be like him, didn't you? That is, until he disappointed you."

The ice inside began to melt with a hot poker of anger. "Patrick Jameson didn't disappoint me. He led a dog's life, is all, working in that meat factory, slaving for all those kids, watching his wife grow old before her time as she reused the waxed paper from the previous day. But he was steady, like I said. He was around, and that's what counts."

"Counts for what?"

"Counts for being a hero."

Her stare seemed to go right through him. "Is that why you went into the academy? You wanted to be a hero?"

"If I wanted to be a hero, I would have been like my dad. I would have stuck around and seen to it everybody was taken care of. But I didn't. I was always the troublemaker, the one taking chances, the one who wouldn't play it safe. In the end, the FBI came after me."

"The FBI doesn't recruit out of trailer parks, so how'd they come after you?"

"I knew Gunnarson, is why." He could feel his mouth turn into a hard, unyielding line. "He had a job in Taylorville once. It took him almost a year to get out of that place, but in the end he did his work. He tied everything up with a neat little bow and skeedaddled back to the Tulsa office, but only after putting the bug in my ear that that was where I should be too."

"He had a case in Taylorville?"

"Yeah."

"Anyone related to you?"

"Yeah. My other hero." The words burned like acid in his mouth. God, he wanted to change the subject.

She said nothing. She just watched him for a moment, the expression in her eyes hidden in the dim light.

"I asked Williams about you during my last visit to the NOPD." Her gaze lowered to the wineglass in her hand, then rose to lock with his. "He said you were a wild son of a bitch."

"He told you that."

"Yes. He said you were notorious for taking undercover work that most at the field office wouldn't touch. He'd heard your last assignment was to bring in the Kineson militia. We all know about that from CNN. The standoff took what—five days?"

"Six."

"Six." She chewed on her lower lip as if she were wary of saying more. "Williams told me what you did. You were the only one who knew the children of those fanatics were in the bunker with them. He told me how you waited for forty-four hours knowing the feds were going to storm. Williams said you'd had your chance to leave before the bunker was taken, but you didn't go. You held on to your cover and kept at it, because you knew you could keep the kids out of the gunfire if it came. And you did it too. I remember on the news, after the standoff, how shocked everyone was at the number of children that were in the bunker. I remember, too, how relieved we all felt that none of them got hurt. They never mentioned your name."

"They never do."

"I'd call that a hero."

He rubbed his jaw. The aggravation was building inside him like a steam engine. "Look, it was nothing."

"You could have been killed any number of ways, at any given time."

"But I wasn't, okay?"

"Back in Taylorville, someone you looked up to was killed, wasn't he? That's why Gunnarson was working there, and that's why you don't want to be anyone's hero. Sure, it's fine to take crazy chances and go out on a limb, just as long as you're bad enough to counter all the heroism. Williams also told me how easily you convinced the men in the bunker you were one of them. You got annoyed at one guy and you shot him. You just up and shot him and to this day he's still having trouble sitting on his metal bunk in the jail cell. If he ever gets out, he's promised to kill you."

"Yeah, well, he'll never get out."

"To be a hero is to die, isn't it? Slow like your dad, or fast like whoever it was you admired when you were a kid."

The anger inside him boiled over. Almost blinded by it, he stood and threw some bills on the table. "I'm taking you home. It's late." He took her by the hand and nearly dragged her out the door. He'd never realized how tiny she was, how delicate her wrist bone was, how easily he could hurt her.

"Are you afraid of me for a change, Agent Jameson?"

He looked down at her. She leaned against the brick wall of the outside of the restaurant. The café was on Gallatin Street in the back of the Quarter, where it was quiet, isolated from the Carnival frenzy that was building on Bourbon. No one was on the street. They were alone. She was next to him, her back against the wall, and all he could think about was how white-hot his anger was.

"I'm not a man to slay dragons, Claire," he whispered, drawing his hand around her nape and pulling her closer to him. "I'd fuck you on a dime bet, and you're one of my investigations. Some hero."

He stared down at her. Her pretty face seemed to lose some of its color. Her masses of dark hair only accentuated this.

He gave her a cold smile. "Here you are, with those large hazel eyes of yours full of fear because some man killed your sister, and now you see that ugliness inside every man, that urge to procreate gone awry, metamorphosed into the need to punish, degredate, dominate—" He paused; his breath came hard and raspy then. "Now who's afraid, Claire?"

"You were going to take me home. Unlock the car, please." Her voice was tremulous, her gaze searched for his rental, where they left it on the street.

"Why don't you start it, Claire?" he said roughly, leaning against her, pushing her farther into the wall. "Why don't you just pull my head down and give me a long, hot French one? You know it's going to happen sometime. It almost happened that night in the rain. I say it's long overdue."

"I don't know what you're talking about—"

"C'mon. You begin this, Claire. You do it. Then, when Gunnarson gives me my dismissal and asks why I fucked my investigation, I can say you started it—"

"Stop. Stop this now—"

He pulled her head toward his. Her nape was warm and baby-soft on his hand nestled beneath the thick masses of hair. He leaned down, his lips almost brushing her, then he paused. The unspoken question of permission hung in the silence. He waited. But she said nothing. She didn't push him away. She made no protest. So he kissed her. His mouth pressed to hers, and her soft, full lips grew pliant. She seemed to release a moan that was more in her chest than her throat, but then she began a reluctant participation, slowly twisting her mouth over his, hesitantly letting his tongue push between her teeth.

The kiss was as hot, sweet, and long as he'd imagined it would be, and when a couple of drunken revelers walked by, hooting and whistling, he hardly noticed. All he wanted was her. All he could think of was her taste, her smell, the give of her chest, of her hands, as they crushed against him.

He kept telling himself that it was only carnal need that drove him. After all, Claire Green had everything: nice tits, a nice ass, slim legs, a pretty face. What man wouldn't want her? But when his mouth found hers, he knew he wanted beyond the physical. He was one hell of a sap because the hurt inside her touched him. It was too much like his hurt. He hadn't been able to put her out of his mind ever since he'd first seen her at Bloomingdale's. Now, with this last kiss, he'd never be able to do it.

Another group of partiers wandered by on their trek to Decatur Street. Another set of hoots and whistles, only this time he heard them.

Breaking off, he put his mouth to her hair and whispered, "Let's go back to your place. Now when anyone asks, you can say in good conscience that I started it."

He took her by the hand and unlocked the car door. She got into it. The lack of conversation should have been a relief—he hated chatty women anyway—but he began to pray for conversation. Anything was better than watching her touch her kiss-swollen lips. Anything was better than to glance at her in the darkness and see her staring at him with Zoe's eyes.

*She was going to sleep with him.* It was the only really coherent thought Claire had during the entire ride back from the restaurant. She was going to sleep with him because she was lonely and wildly attracted to him, and because something had happened in Taylorville that made this big, strong, ponytailed heathen a little kid who believed in the bogeyman like she did.

He parked the car in front of the mansion on Prytania and kissed her. It was only a quick, needful peck on the lips, but it held reassurance. And she desperately needed it.

He helped her out of the car. In silence they walked toward the front door. There wasn't much to say. No point in analyzing what was sure to be inevitable damage. She put the key in the lock and turned it.

They didn't even turn on the lights. She stepped into the room and immediately he took her in his arms. She thought about offering coffee, maybe a chat on the couch, but it all seemed absurd. When he kissed her in the dark, she knew that was the only thing he could do. Fate was rocketing them to this union. She didn't see the point in hesitating when he took her hand and led her to the bedroom.

There his kiss grew more ferocious, more needful. If a tongue could lick fire, his did every time he pushed it deeper into her mouth. He demanded and she gave, and made ever-increasing demands of her own. Finally, she pulled him down on top of her on the bed. His body completely covered hers, making her conscious of how much bigger he was than her and how achingly gentle a man of his size could be.

He pulled up her turquoise sweater and kissed the swells of flesh that peeked from the top of her bra. In the light from the courtyard, she could see the contrast of his hard-planed face against the lush paleness of her chest. His mouth trailed down through the valley between her breasts, teasing her with the feel of his unshaven jaw, and he bit at her nipple through the satin and lace brassiere cup, mercilessly building her desire. Unwilling to fight the urge any longer, she took his face in her hands and pulled him to her lips. He kissed her; she kissed him, the touch of their two mouths like lightning.

They parted and she lay beneath him, her breath coming hot and fast. He nuzzled her ear, her nape, the sensitive hollow at the base of her neck, and all the while she held him close, the feel of his hard, broad chest against hers wonderfully safe. He pulled at the sweater. It went over her head and landed at the foot of the bed, a tempting pile of abandoned mohair.

He took her hand and put it to his belt buckle. She fumbled and finally removed it. It was some kind of cowboy belt. The silver caught the light from outside, and she could see it had a bronc rider embossed on it and the initials PRCA. It was some kind of rodeo trophy.

"Is there nothing you don't do, Agent Jameson?" she asked almost playfully as she dropped the belt to the floor.

"I got that when I was twenty." He smirked. "Killing yourself on a bull's one way not to be a hero."

"I suppose bedroom rodeoing's the only kind you do now?" She lifted one eyebrow.

"Yes, ma'am. You wouldn't know it, but I'm not twenty anymore." The corner of his mouth lifted in a slow, sexy smile. His hand moved up and cupped her breast. She arched back, luxuriating in the feel of it.

If someone had read her fortune and told her that the Barnard grad, summa cum laude from Columbia Law, would one day be in the sack with a former rodeo-riding federal agent who was out to throw her and her friends in jail, she'd have never believed it.

But truth *was* stranger than fiction.

He tugged on the black stirrup pants; she slung off her flats. Soon she was down to her panties. He shrugged out of his shirt and she snaked her hand down between her and his Wranglers. The top snap was still fastened. She made quick work of it.

He kissed her and put his hand on hers. He guided her toward his zipper; she complied and soon she found him.

He heaved a sigh. She ran her other hand through the dark mat of hair covering his chest. He kissed her and his tongue moved so hard and fast through her mouth, she writhed from the heat that was building between her legs.

"Are you ready for this?" he whispered, his breath coming at a pant.

"It's soon," she answered, her own breath shallow and quick. "I see you trogs aren't game for a lot of foreplay."

"Not tonight. Not with you." He stared down at her. His

expression was etched with want. She touched his cheek. He turned his head and kissed her fingers.

He slipped out of his jeans. Her need for him surged like a building tide. She let him anxiously back into her arms. He unfastened her bra and just stared down at her body. She lay beneath him naked, the volume of her messed hair blessedly hiding some skin, but not enough. He took her nipple in his mouth and she moaned, flinging her head back against the pillows, all thoughts, all rational caution, thrown from her mind.

He grabbed the front of her white satin panties. She supposed he'd meant to slide them off her, but he'd misjudged his strength. The fragile bit of lace ripped and a thunderbolt of memory hit her.

She went rigid. Fear and panic came through her in a jolt. She felt his naked body press down on her, and every corded bulge of muscle was a threat.

"No, wait," she panted, ice now flowing through her veins where before there had been lava.

His hand slid between her damp thighs.

"Wait," she nearly whimpered.

He stared at her. His erection moved against her, a sword to protect and to kill.

"I'm afraid . . ." she whispered.

The expression in his eyes changed. Lust had darkened them, now they became even darker, filled with some unnamed emotion that was part frustration, part anger, and yet, part mercy.

But the hand didn't move from between her thighs.

It was on the tip of her tongue to tell him to get off. If she pummeled him and screamed at him, she thought he'd probably get up. Probably. But the uncertainty froze her, and the need for long-awaited fulfillment made her weak.

Slowly he kissed her, easing her back into the never-never land that fueled her sexual response. He tugged her thighs apart and moved where his hand had been.

She didn't evict him. His knuckles brushed the hair from her eyes and her smell clung to his fingers. He brushed them across her lips and then he kissed her again, her own taste erotically mingling with his.

There was no sweet invitation and no grand request of permission. He thrust into her and she relinquished. Her fear, her desire, her self-control, her body, all gave way to the primal instinct to mate. He pushed into her with the same kind of frenzied need that she grabbed at him, and the meeting built and built until everything spiraled down into one essential moment.

"Liam," she moaned darkly as she came.

He shut his eyes and pounded into her, the rhythm of his hips as sure and wild as any bronc rider. He said nothing. He merely took his time with his pleasure, and then with one whispered curse he fell against her, spent.

## ❧ 21 ❧

**W**ith silence came peace. The idea was like a haiku flitting through Claire's thoughts as she lay in Liam's arms. Both their bodies were slicked with sweat. The bedding lay balled up on the floor, but she wasn't cold. He was enough warmth for her, and if they didn't talk, she knew they could lie there entwined forever, and the world would never intercede.

But she hadn't counted on the screech of her door buzzer. The noise shattered the night. It blared and blared again, sending shock waves through her.

"Don't answer it. It's the middle of the damn night." Liam pulled her down again, but she fumbled in the dark for her robe.

"It could be my parents. I never checked the answering machine. Maybe something's wrong."

She left the nest of their bed reluctantly. Almost like a psychic, she just knew they would never return to it.

She turned on the intercom and asked who was there. Only silence answered her, but this was an ominous silence. A threatening one.

"Who's there?" she demanded, pulling the terry belt tight on her robe.

Jameson came up behind her. He'd pulled on his Wranglers and was running his hand through the tangle of his hair. She saw him only in silhouette. They still hadn't turned on the lights.

"Maybe the intercom's not working. Let me take a peek at the front door." She left the condo and went down the mansion's staircase. Through the beveled glass of the front door she could see no one.

"Someone's pulling away. Do you hear the car?" Jameson was still behind her, still her watchdog.

"Let me see who it was. Maybe I'll recognize the car. Hey, maybe they were just pushing the wrong buzzer." She opened the door. But as far as she could see, there was no one. Even Prytania was quiet. All the tourists were down in the French Quarter this time of year.

"What's that?" Jameson said.

She hadn't noticed the black and red Saks Fifth Avenue bag at her feet until he spoke.

"Who the hell is dropping things off to you at this hour?" he mumbled.

She picked up the bag that had her name clearly marked in white letters. "Maybe my mother stopped by. She's always trying to buy me things." The excuse was weak. It was not like her mother to go shopping at Saks or to drop things off at midnight. The wife of a high school teacher was strictly MacFrugal's.

"You look worried."

Her gaze met his. "It's just that I guess I really don't know who left this. I'll just have to open it and see—"

He put his hands over hers and took the package. "I'll open it. Let's go upstairs and turn on some lights."

She followed him, her body shaking as if she'd caught a sudden chill. A sense of foreboding enveloped her like a dark, suffocating blanket.

Once back in the condo with all the lights on for comfort, she watched him take a clean dish towel and withdraw the glossy red box from the Saks bag. He gingerly put it on her dining room table and checked all the seams for wires. Finding nothing suspicious, he slowly pulled off the top, being careful not to let his fingers touch the glossy red lid. Inside was a mass of white tissue paper. He removed it.

"Jesus Christ." He rubbed his jaw the way he did when he was aggravated.

"What—what is it?" she said, trying to look over his shoulder.

He replaced the lid. "Don't." He glanced around the condo as if he were trying to think. "I'm going to call Williams and have him send a car."

"What is it?" she repeated, hysteria building within her. She numbly felt his arm go around her waist. "Is my family okay? Oh, God. Oh. God. Wait. I need to call my mother—" She dashed to the phone and immediately dialed the house.

"Hello?" Her mother's sleepy voice answered the phone.

"Mom?"

"Claire—why are you calling at this hour?"

"I just wanted—is Dad there?"

"Of course. It's almost one in the morning. Is anything wrong?"

Claire looked at Liam. She released her breath. "No. I just got in. For some reason I got the crazy urge to tell you and Dad good night. Good night. I love you guys," she whispered before putting down the receiver.

Without another word she walked over to the package and stared at it.

"You don't have to look at it. I'll tell you what it is," he said.

Her gaze met his. "I want to know what it is and who sent it."

"We'll find out."

Using the same dish towel, she lifted the lid. Tucked inside was what appeared to be a piece of dough cookie-cuttered into a Star of David. A large smear of blood had turned the nest of tissue the same color as the box.

Her voice seemed disembodied from the terror inside her. "Why is it so white?"

"Skin does that when there's no more blood supply." He looked at her, his gaze worried.

"Where is it from? From what part of the body?"

"No telling. We'll need the lab to analyze it."

She stared down at the package still in her hands with the dish towel. As if it were fine crystal, she placed the box on the foyer table. "I suppose I've gotten fingerprints on the bag. I've destroyed evidence."

"He didn't leave fingerprints."

"It was Everard Laborde who did this, wasn't it?"

"Him or his secretary." He ran his thumb over her cheek. "Sit down. You look like you've lost a little blood too. Let me get you a drink."

Again she felt that strong, sure arm go around her waist. He led her to the couch and poured her some armagnac from a decanter near the French doors.

"Drink this. I'll get a patrol car here."

She lifted the glass to her lips, every now and then her eyes turning to the red Saks box on the foyer table.

"He killed Zoe." The words were quiet and much more calm than she felt.

"If he did, we'll find it out."

She gazed at him, but her eyes never really focused. "You'll never prove it. Everard Laborde's gotten away with this for five years, he'll get away with it forever."

"It's not time to call Phyllis yet."

She couldn't miss the warning in his voice. "I've given the police the chance to take care of this. I look into it for a few weeks and see?" She waved to the glossy red box. "I've already hit a nerve. Why should I wait around and give this guy another try?"

"Because you haven't given me a try."

Suddenly the terror and confusion that was dammed up

inside her broke free. Tears filled her eyes. "But you don't want to be anybody's hero, isn't that right, Jameson? You don't want to be a hero and I don't even believe in heroes, so we're one helluva pair." She rose from the couch and quickly wiped her face with the back of her hand. Desperately trying to gather herself once again, she stared out the French doors at the magnolia lit by the floodlights of the garden. She hugged herself and said, "I think I finally understand Phyllis."

"I'll see your ass in jail, girl, if you mess with this."

"Screw you, Jameson. What's that car going to do that you want to call in? It'll bring a bunch of uniforms in here, they're going to take it all down, and then they're going to file it away, never to be seen again. They're the greatest damned secretaries in the world, but what I need is someone who isn't bound and gagged by the Constitution."

"You don't know what this is about yet, so take off your vigilante hat and calm down."

The hands, warm and gentle, pressed on her shoulders. She pulled them off. "That's how it's going to be, isn't it? 'We don't know,' 'We can't be sure.' You guys'll dance around the obvious because all the evidence isn't as concrete as the D.A. would like, so Laborde will go to his club every day and put his headlights on while he drives around town and Zoe will rot another day in her tomb."

"You're talking crazy. Crazy and—and—"

"Hurt," she whispered, her eyes finally focused on him. "Oh, God, it hurts. And I'm so scared."

His face looked devastated, as if by that one small word she'd somehow opened a gaping wound in himself.

She turned back to the French doors and the magnolia lit by the floodlights. Seconds ticked by; a silent stream of tears coursed her cheeks. Then she felt the arms go around her.

He'd come up from behind, his arms crossing her chest in a bear hug. She wasn't really shocked by his actions. She was a woman who was frightened and upset. There were many men who would hug a woman in the same circumstances, but he wasn't just any man. He was Liam Jameson, and there was a mountain of emotional garbage in both of them.

She looked up at him, he looked down at her, and for a split second their gazes met. But the engagement proved too raw for both of them. He stepped back from her and she gladly stumbled away. There couldn't have been a colder, more awkward disentanglement.

"I need to call Williams," he said curtly.

She nodded. She was barely able to look at him.

He picked up the phone and dialed Williams's direct number. The conversation was kept to a minimum. Finally he hung up and went into the bedroom for the rest of his clothes.

The siren in the background was the perfect music for the situation, she thought as she finally pulled back on the mohair sweater. Two people trying to avoid each other in a small bedroom, their emotions as frozen and crippled as their hearts.

The buzzer jarred them both. She pressed the release button and two uniformed police officers appeared at the condo door. Jameson showed his ID and told them to check the grounds. Soon Williams buzzed. When he arrived upstairs, he looked rumpled as if he, too, had just gotten out of bed.

"What you got?" He yawned and flipped open his little black notebook.

"A present. For Ms. Green here. Somebody wanted to let her know she was Jewish." Jameson handed over the red Saks box using the dish towel. Williams glanced into it. Smacking his lips in distaste, he gave the box to one of the uniformed officers and told him to get it downtown.

"It probably came from a thigh or buttock. There's a layer of fat there that gives something like this substance," Liam offered.

"Thank you, Dr. Jameson. Would you like to join the team in the lab?" Williams looked up from his notebook.

Jameson grinned and shrugged. "Forensics was my minor at Quantico."

"Ms. Green, why do you think you were sent this?" Williams finally turned to Claire.

She glanced from the detective to Jameson and back again. Somehow everything seemed a bit surreal. Jameson had just made love to her and now he looked as cool as a cucumber, just shooting the bull with the detective. She, on the other hand, was on the verge of a nervous breakdown. She was rattled and afraid, and in desperate need of a shower to make her forget the ill-fated moment when she'd decided it wouldn't be foolish to let Federal Agent Jameson into her bed.

"Everard Laborde's secretary and I got into a scuffle this evening. He was angry because he believed I stole a file from the 555 Association," she said.

"Did you?"

Claire didn't answer, but she refused to look at Jameson.

"You forget she's a lawyer, Williams." Jameson stared at her, or at least she believed he stared at her, from the prickle of anxiety that raised the hair on her nape.

Williams scribbled in his notebook. "Okay, so you think the secretary sent this?"

"No." She shook her head. "I think Everard Laborde did this. I think—I think he wants to kill me just like he killed my sister."

Williams glanced at Jameson. "What leads you to that conclusion, Ms. Green?"

"He drew a Star of David on Zoe's résumé. He makes a big point of the Jewish thing."

"You know better than I what his lawyers are going to make of that."

She nodded, her heart heavy. "Yeah, I know. 'Hearsay. It's just a stab in the dark.' But I don't care. Laborde did this, I know it."

"I can still check him out, harass him a little."

She tried to smile, but it was useless. "Thank you, detective, but he's not going to slip up and tell you anything, and in the meantime there isn't much to go on."

"Do you have any disgruntled clients, Ms. Green?"

"None that I know of." She sat down on the couch. She could hardly bear looking in Jameson's direction. "Can I get you some coffee, detective? I have a feeling this is going to be a long and unproductive night."

"No, thank you. Just keeps me up."

Claire dropped her head back against the cushions and stared at the ceiling. She herself was exhausted, but after all that had happened to her that night, she couldn't imagine sleeping.

"Can you get me a list of your clients, Ms. Green?" Williams asked.

"I'll call Fassbinder in the morning and have them fax you a list."

"Good."

"Whose skin is it anyway?" She lifted her head, and for the first time was able to look at Jameson. The thing in the Saks box was so disgusting and unnerving that she hadn't given the source much thought until then.

"The guy either killed someone, or he works in the morgue, where there's lots of available skin," Jameson answered.

"But he doesn't work in the morgue," she said.

Jameson gave her a grim smile, his expression haunted by all the ghosts of the victims he'd ever seen. "Well then, there you go."

It was four in the morning by the time Williams and the uniforms left the condo. Claire was exhausted, but it was the kind of running, sleepless exhaustion that made her feel if she stopped, she'd drop off a cliff.

By now the awkwardness between her and Jameson had

been warded off by a silent dread. Claire imagined herself in the center of a hurricane, her emotions whipped every which way. In just a matter of hours she'd gone from tenderness and full-bloomed desire, all the way to horror and complete, black hopelessness.

When the last officer had left, Liam made no move to go and she made no gesture to make him go. The quiet between them was better than the quiet alone. Alone, she'd think of Everard Laborde and Zoe. She'd think of that piece of skin, and whom it might belong to. And how it might be her next. No, she'd come to the conclusion that being with Jameson was far better than being by herself.

Dawn was just breaking through the magnolia branches. Jameson made some comment about making coffee and disappeared into the kitchen while she leaned her head back on the couch. Afraid of the vulnerability, almost against her will she closed her eyes.

It might have been her imagination, but at some point she felt warm, strong arms around her. They were like a steel protective cage that no killer could penetrate.

She felt herself being carried into the bedroom and laid on the mattress. She wanted to awaken, but exhaustion won. She knew those arms were just luring her into a false sense of security, but nonetheless she fell into a deep, restful sleep. And all night long she dreamed of St. George slaying the dragon.

## ❧ 22 ❧

Claire woke to find herself in her bed. Her black stirrup pants and the mohair sweater had been removed and she was burrowed beneath the down comforter in just her bra and panties.

Jameson was gone. There was no note, no bouquet of roses, not even a freshly brewed pot of coffee to mark his acknowledgment of the night before. Sore and shamelessly satiated, she rolled from the bed and turned on the shower.

The water eased the tightness in her shoulders and cleared her mind. Her thoughts seemed like they were working in a fog; she didn't know if it was the wine and armagnac she'd drunk the night before or if it was instead the emotional riptide she was riding.

She let the water run down her face and turned it even hotter. What she needed to do was return to New York. She would be safer there—from everyone. Laborde might just forget about her seeing that file—she was certainly in denial there—but in the city she'd put Jameson out of her mind. There it was. Denial again.

With a long sigh she lowered her head and let the shower pound her scalp. She could come perilously close to falling in love with Liam Jameson, she concluded, and she needed that just about as much as another visit from D'Hemecourt. Liam could protect her from lunatics, but he was still an agent, he would still do his job no matter what that was, and she could hardly imagine the betrayal she'd feel if he should decide to pursue her role in ZOE now.

She turned off the shower and rubbed herself with a thick peach-colored towel. Wrapping her hair, she slipped on her robe and went to make coffee. A quick glance out the French doors reassured her. The two uniformed officers whom Williams had left behind were in their car, still on surveillance. She didn't know how long the detective could keep up the service, but even if the cops were all just glorified secretaries, with Jameson gone from the condo she felt much better seeing those blue uniforms on the job.

The phone rang. For a second she hesitated, a feeling of menace prickling the back of her neck. Admonishing herself, she picked up the receiver.

"Claire? It's me, Phyllis."

"Phyl," Claire said, uneasy. She hadn't wanted to think about ZOE today. After the glossy, red Saks box had arrived, she had her own problems.

"Doll! You've fallen off the face of the earth! And you haven't been answering my messages." Phyllis's raspy voice filled the earpiece.

"I've been busy. Real busy."

"Have you seen your mother and father? How are they?"

"Fine, just fine."

"Wonderful. Listen, darling, I need to talk to you. I got a visit from the FBI this morning, and when I called Fassbinder to see if they had your number, they told me agents were all over that place."

Claire could feel the blood drain from her cheeks. Great. This had just made her life. "Fassbinder? Did they say what the feds wanted?"

"Well, they didn't tell me, but I would guess you and I are under the microscope, Claire."

She groaned. They were probably having a coronary over

at the law firm. A wild, hot rage suddenly engulfed her. Jameson was making it with her at the same time he was sending his minions down Wall Street to ruin her career.

"Listen, doll, we need to talk. Needless to say, this is a little upsetting. I'm doing all right, but the others . . ."

"Maybe I should fly to New York—"

"No, it's not that bad."

Claire wrapped the lapels of her robe closer to her. Suddenly she was cold. "Well, we can't talk now, Phyl. We're not the only ones on the line."

Dead silence. Then, "Yes, that's another thing that has people rather upset. Are you sure the lines are bugged?"

"I'm sure, Phyl. Every time I pause, five people bump into my rear end."

"I'll come to you. I've never seen New Orleans. Maybe I'll stay until Mardi Gras. When we're together, then I can tell you what's really going on."

"Oh?" Claire suddenly felt sick. "Well, what is going on?"

"I've taken care of everything."

"How so?"

"Claire, I'll be on the first plane from LaGuardia. Will you pick me up?"

"I don't know, Phyl," she answered numbly.

"Listen, darling, don't worry. I'm not worried. This is still going to be a wonderful thing for you. You'll see."

"I met an agent down here, Phyllis. He says he wants to help me look into Zoe's death." She didn't get into the fact that Jameson was the man who answered the ad. For some reason, she didn't want to give Phyllis any more information than she had to.

Another long pause, then the woman admonished her, "He's just saying that, Claire, to get to you. You know that, don't you?"

"No. Oh, hell, I don't know." Claire suddenly felt a lump in her throat.

"Are you all right, darling? I wish you hadn't gone down there. I don't think the visit's been good for you. You need looking after."

"No, I don't need looking after, especially from you and ZOE." The stress and worry suddenly came to a head. Claire sniffed and gave it away to Phyllis that she was crying.

"Have you found out who the man is who did that terrible crime to your sister?" Phyllis asked.

"I've had some things open up maybe." Claire calmed down.

"Do you have a name yet?"

"How could I tell you that? How?" Claire's insides were being ripped apart. If it was true that Laborde killed Zoe, she wanted him dead, wanted it to the point that she might even ask ZOE to do it. But she wasn't one hundred percent sure yet, and until she was, she didn't want to face the temptation of ZOE's services.

"Just tell me his name."

"Phyllis, if I do that, the next thing I know you'll—"

"Watch what you say, doll."

Claire closed her mouth.

"I'll take the next flight down."

"How's Washington?" Claire didn't want to bring the incident up, but she wanted Phyllis to be reminded of it. Halbert Washington might keep the vigilante streak subdued.

Phyllis laughed. "Fine. Everything's fine down in Washington. Not a peep from there. And our friend's doing much better."

Claire felt some relief. She supposed the feds didn't have enough evidence to do anything about Washington anyway. For once the justice system messed up in their favor.

"I'm packing my bags, darling. I'll call you from La-Guardia and let you know the flight number."

"I just don't know, Phyllis. I don't think that's a good idea. I don't want to talk about ZOE." Claire couldn't quit frowning. She wanted the temptations Phyllis offered to go away. She was too vulnerable and stressed right now. In the heat of anger, Claire feared she herself might to do something stupid that she'd regret.

"I can't wait to see you. I'll call you with the flight number, doll. Bye-bye."

Claire couldn't get her back and reason with her. Phyllis had hung up. So she replaced the receiver and put her head in her hands.

"We'd like to speak to your secretary, Mr. Laborde," Williams said. He sat in the leather chair opposite Laborde's glass desk. Jameson sat next to him.

"My secretary has been let go, gentlemen."

"Why?" Williams asked, jotting in the ubiquitous notebook.

"Inappropriate conduct. Now, if there's nothing more, I've got to interview some candidates to fill the new position—"

"What did he do that got him fired, Mr. Laborde?" Jameson interrupted.

Laborde paused. He looked up from the papers he'd been reading and pushed the specs down the bridge of his nose to stare at Jameson without the shield. "He was caught doing filthy things on the Internet. Now, if that is all, gentlemen, I really must ask you to leave. As you know, it's Mardi Gras season. I'm heading up a parade tonight and I don't have much time. Besides, my attorney has instructed me to refrain from speaking about Mr. D'Hemecourt."

"Why?" Williams asked again, the detective's favorite question.

Laborde glanced at him. "Obviously because to speak of a fired employee is to invite a libel suit. Therefore, gentlemen, I ask that we conclude this meeting."

"Where does D'Hemecourt live?" Williams said.

Laborde jotted down an address on a cream-colored 555

card. "Here you go. Please don't take this badly, gentlemen, but now I hope this is the last I see of you."

Williams stood and took the card.

Jameson didn't move. He slouched farther into his chair and said, "Could you explain to me, Mr. Laborde, why it is on my first visit here you said you'd just looked into the Zoe Green file? To refresh your memory, your now-missing secretary said there was no such file, but you insisted that was because you'd seen it 'last week,' I believe you said. Why were you looking into the Zoe Green file?"

"Did I say all that? I don't recall. Besides, I wasn't looking into the file, I just remember seeing it. But it's been purged somehow and it's missing, so I can't help you, gentlemen. Now, really, if you will excuse me. The Krewe of Dante rolls at five this evening and I'm the grand marshal." Laborde paused, clearly expecting them to leave.

Jameson got up from his chair. He glanced at Williams and the two men left the office.

"Fuck this shit," Williams said as they walked down the hall. He got on his flip phone and called headquarters. "Yeah," he said into the receiver. "Get a car over to . . . ?" He looked at the card Laborde had given him. "It's 13324 Versailles, Apartment B. Yeah, that's it. Tell them we'll be right over." He closed up the phone.

"A real problem," Jameson said as they left the association and got into Williams's car. "If D'Hemecourt's not in his BVDs watching the soaps when we get to Versailles, I'm telling you it was a piece of his ass sent over to Claire."

"Oh. *Claire,* is it? Why the hell is it Ms. Green to the rest of us? Explain that one, special agent."

The two men exchanged glances. Williams rolled his eyes. He put the Oldsmobile into drive and they sped up Canal Street toward Mid-City.

\* \* \*

Phyllis's plane was due to land in an hour. Claire locked the condo and slipped into her silk jacket. Already she felt like a new person. After Phyllis's phone call, she'd had a minute or two of self-reckoning. Granted, her life was in shambles: the partners of Fassbinder Hamilton were probably in a meeting right at that moment determining how to persuade her to leave the firm, people were sending her body parts, and last night she'd let herself be nailed by the FBI agent who'd been sent to tail her because of her ZOE activities. But there was something to be said for going through the motions, something to be said for creating an appearance. After her momentary breakdown, she'd picked herself up, made herself a big breakfast, drank almost a pot of coffee. Now, with her hair freshly washed and her makeup applied, she was determined not to show the strain. If she convinced herself she could handle things, then maybe she could. In fact, she might even be able to tackle some of the bigger obstacles in her way, such as getting rid of that FBI agent and convincing Phyllis that ZOE was way off base in their pursuits, and maybe even catching J. Everard Laborde before he caught her.

She walked from the mansion's front door to the parked BMW. She was so absorbed in her thoughts, she didn't see the uniformed officer until he was almost next to her.

"Claire Green?" he asked.

She nodded. The Beemer keys jangled in her hand.

"I'm sorry, but we've been given orders that for your personal safety you're not to leave your condominium, Ms. Green."

She looked at the police officer as if he'd just grown scales. "You must be mistaken. I have to leave. I've got a friend to pick up at the airport. Who would give an order like that?"

"Agent Jameson, ma'am. He said you were to stay put. But he just radioed the car. He's coming over right now."

Two thoughts crossed her mind. She was either in grave

personal danger, or Jameson had found something incriminating and he was coming to arrest her.

"Did he say what this was about?" she asked, dropping the Beemer keys into her purse.

"He didn't say, ma'am. He just gave explicit orders for you to remain where you were." The man's gaze lifted to a point behind her. She turned and saw Jameson's rental pulling into the mansion's parking lot.

Jameson got out of the car. He looked her way and the memories of the previous night washed over her like a bucket of ice. Suddenly she wondered if she could take much more. Pretending things were okay didn't make them okay.

She went to the mansion door, let herself in and walked up to her condo.

He was right behind her.

He called her name but she didn't listen. If she could have locked him out, she would have, but he came inside and closed the door.

"Where's that cool, calm attorney who used to live here?" he grunted when she tried to shove him away.

"I guess she left, Jameson. You know, you have a lot of nerve and absolutely no legal right to tell that uniform downstairs that I can't leave my own home." She glared at him.

"Is that all?" he asked.

She walked away, giving him nothing but a view of her back. "This damn well better be good. Or I just might bring charges."

"A little testy today, aren't we? Is it just the orders I gave the uniforms, or is it the fact that last night we—"

She whipped around. The expression on her face stopped him cold. "Last night was a mistake. A stupid, stupid mistake."

"No."

All he said was one word and she melted. The hurt and fear resurfaced, and she could do nothing but shake her head. "I don't even know if you're married. Are you, Liam? Have you got seven kids back there in Tulsa to make me feel even worse?"

"No. No kids. No wife."

She took a deep breath. One catastrophe diverted. Now, if she could just forget what he smelled like, what he felt like, what his voice sounded like when he whispered against her hair, then she would be all right. Maybe. "Jameson, I need to leave. You know I need to leave because you're tapping my phone lines. Phyllis is arriving at Moisant and I have to meet her. Why are you holding me here?"

"D'Hemecourt's missing. We went to his apartment, but he wasn't there. Hey, maybe the guy just took off, but we can't do anything about it until someone formally reports him missing or we've got a body."

"What about a search warrant for his apartment?"

"We haven't got enough for that yet."

"Of course not." She wanted to wipe off the cynicism on her face, but there was no way to do it. She'd heard all the lame Constitutional b.s. before with Zoe's case. Now she rubbed her arms as if she were cold. "Even if you could determine the guy missing and search his apartment, you'd have nothing more than coincidence to go on. So D'Hemecourt's boss was the last one to see him alive—just like Zoe— what jury would send a guy to the chair for that?"

"If we can get a warrant to search D'Hemecourt's apartment we might get some hairs on his comb or somewhere else that still has the follicle on them. We could do a DNA match with the skin from last night."

"So even if you could do that, you've no proof Laborde sent the skin to me. The DNA match could be weak too— Laborde's lawyer will just say the hairs on D'Hemecourt's brush could have been someone else's and they'll parade every person through the courtroom who so much as even stopped by D'Hemecourt's apartment."

"I know all that," he snapped. "But there's also the résumé you stole from Laborde's files. It doesn't match the one he gave the police five years ago. He wrote the six on it, along with RIO and the Star of David after your sister was missing."

"Yeah?" she said bitterly. "Well, a judge'd throw my copy of Zoe's résumé out of the courtroom so quickly a bird couldn't catch it. I took it without their permission, remember? That's first-year law school stuff."

Exasperated, he walked up to her and put his hands on her arms. "We don't have much right now, but that doesn't mean J. Everard Laborde isn't one helluva serial killer. And it damn well makes an impression on me when I think he's now focused on you."

She stepped from the circle of his arms. She couldn't let her guard down enough to let him hold her. Not with ZOE pressing down on her with every ticking minute of Phyllis's flight. "Look, I can't worry about Laborde. Not even if he is sending me presents." The statement was mostly bravado, but not all. She wasn't going to run from her sister's killer. She was going to put him away if she did nothing else in her life. "You see, I'm the one who's going to do the chasing here," she added. "Besides, aren't these guys all obsessive-compulsive? He's probably got his victims lined up for a decade, he won't deviate and go after me."

"No, maybe he won't, that's true," he said grimly, "but it should make your skin crawl that he's probably sitting at his desk right now, thinking about you. It doesn't take that long to change plans."

She touched her lips. It was Laborde. Fear like a hatchet drove through her. She might be next. She might end up like Zoe, but she had to stop him. The *legal* way. And yet her hell was trying to prove the case. "I understand I need to be more careful."

"Williams can't keep the uniforms here much longer. Mardi Gras is coming. Every uniform and detective is going to be downtown, managing the crowds. It'd be the perfect time to kill someone."

Terror gripped her, but she fought it. "I understand." She looked down at her watch. Phyllis was due to arrive in twenty minutes. "I've got to go to the airport now, so if you'll excuse me—"

"Haven't you heard what I've been telling you?" His anger was genuine if the spark that flared in his eye was any indication. "You cannot be alone, Claire. Not even for a ride to the airport. He could follow you and take you out to St. Rose, and you'd end up just like your damned sister."

She became irritated herself. "What are you saying? Are you going to take me to the airport to pick up Phyllis?"

"I'm saying I'm giving you two choices: You can get rid of this condo and go and live with your parents until we catch Laborde, or you can just tolerate whomever I can get to cover you at the moment, including myself."

She stared at him. "You've got to be joking. I can't have someone with me all the time. You may never be able to pin anything on Laborde, and then what? Do I hire a bodyguard when I return to New York?"

He rubbed his jaw, clearly aggravated. "I've seen the pictures of your sister. I've seen everything: the murder site, the autopsy, everything. I know it's someone other than you, but when I close my eyes, the pictures flash in my mind, and for a second I think it is you. You're not going to end up like that, Claire. Not you."

"You almost sound as if you care for me, Agent Jameson." She could hardly bear to look at him.

The hands gripped her arms again, but this time they weren't gentle. They were hard and angry. She could almost feel her flesh bruising.

"Let me tell you something, Claire. I've got to do my job. If you and this woman you're picking up from the airport knock off Laborde, I'm gonna put you in jail."

"I know that," she said with more sarcasm than was prudent. "Always and foremost the fed, huh, Jameson? I suppose the unprofessionalism in the bedroom is just something I should forget."

"I thought about sleeping with you, but I guess I didn't think it would really happen. Even *I* thought I had more control than that."

"Right. Sure," she spat out at him. "You probably nail every vulnerable female in your path." She broke free of his hold. "I've got to go to the airport."

"Fine. Go on. I got a fax this morning. It seems your friend Phyllis had a meeting with a bunch of women last night at some hoity-toity restaurant in New York. The feds think the women are all in this group ZOE that you started. The group's going underground, I've heard tell. There's talk, too, that ZOE's hired another hit man, or didn't you know? The bodies are just gonna pile up in Manhattan."

She looked at him. Her heartbeat quickened. Suddenly she felt vaguely nauseated, but from all her courtroom experience, it was almost instinctual to put on a calm façade. "I don't know what you're talking about."

He reached over and caressed her cheek. "Ah, there she is. The cold-hearted attorney. I knew she'd come back if prodded enough."

"I've really got to go to the airport."

He smiled, but it was completely devoid of mirth. "Fine. Then let's go pick up Phyllis. I'd love to give Zuckermann the third degree personally." He picked the BMW keys from her purse and held out the door. "You know, from what I know about her, I'm damn eager to meet her."

## ❧ 23 ❧

Laborde allowed the man to slide open the warehouse door. The huge storage facility was located across the river next to the Mississippi levee. Stuck in the middle of grain elevators and the occasional decaying plantation house, the warehouse was just about the most famous landmark in Harvey.

Inside the dark cavern, Laborde could make out the garish features of a ten-foot harlequin. Bosomy, topless mermaids sat atop another Mardi Gras float. The city council met to hear the public demands that they put bras on the sea nymphs, but, as papier mâché artist Blaise Dufossat had rationally explained, well, mermaids didn't wear bras. Since there was no NEA grant for Mardi Gras, art won. The girls were set to go that night, bare breasts and all.

"Which float do you want to see?" the foreman asked, wiping his fingers on an oily rag.

"I'm riding on this one." Laborde walked around the mammoth piece. It was the King of Dante float. The character that rode on the front of it was Satan.

He definitely approved. The figure was breathtaking. Done in wire and papier mâché, the devil mechanically raised and lowered a nasty-looking pitchfork and paper flames spilled from his mouth while he appeared to dance on cloven hooves. Dante's theme that year was Dreams and Nightmares. At the krewe meeting the previous March, a member had mentioned the idea and Everard had loved it. The King was it. After all, the Krewe of Dante was delighted that J. Everard Laborde had consented to even be their grand marshal. He'd once been Rex—the king of kings—but since one could be Rex only once in a lifetime, he'd now had to move on to lesser conquests. Like being grand marshal of the old line *flambeaux*-lit Krewe of Dante.

"Show me how this works," Laborde demanded of the foreman.

"Well, you ride here." The black man opened a small doorway to the front of the float and they went up a narrow set of stairs hidden by papier mâché flames to the top of the float. Directly behind Satan was a throne dressed in red and gold. "The king rides there, his dukes in the back."

Laborde nodded, smiling. "How many on this float?"

"Not too many. I think maybe you have only five: the grand marshal, three dukes, and the employee who's got to operate the pitchfork."

"Where does he go?"

The man led him back down the small steps to a hatch behind the stairs. There was a cubby back there with just enough room for a person to sit and pull the lever on the pitchfork.

Laborde stuck his head into it. To the rear was a plywood panel loosely nailed to the floor. He tilted it to the side and found a long, dark hollow, the underbelly of the float where the axles and wheels were.

If someone threw a body in there while the vehicle was moving, there was no telling when the thing would fall onto the asphalt below. It would get trampled by the wheels and everyone would think the person inadvertently got caught beneath the float. Drunks and floats didn't always mix well; someone got run over just about every Carnival season.

"How do you like it?" the foreman asked, obviously proud of his work.

"Wonderful," Laborde answered, pulling his head from the cubby. A big smile covered his face.

Fred and Hockney sat in the empty dining room of the 555. The preliminary invitations and mystery clues had come in from the printer. The graphic artist had outdone herself this year. Clues were to be handed out to the ladies in glossy black cardboard coffins. The invitations were engraved with purple, gold, and green Mardi Gras beads bordered in funereal black. One hundred yards of polyester crepe had been ordered to swag the old cornices of the 555 in the manner of a wake.

"It's delicious, isn't it?" Fred commented as he surveyed the mound of invitations.

"Everard was brilliant, as usual," Hockney reiterated, taking a gin and tonic from the white-coated waiter.

"To kill a majorette right in the middle of a Mardi Gras parade—where does he get these ideas?" Fred took his drink from the old black waiter.

"Well, he can't be too mundane. The point is that guests *not* solve the crime. If we get a winner, we have to pay, remember?"

Fred nodded. "But still, Mystery Night has filled the coffers once again. Once more we've triumphed. It's the most popular social event in the city."

"It's the prize this year. It was one thing to hand out trinkets, it's another to hand over the most important piece of rental real estate in the city during the peak of the Mardi Gras season like we're offering. I still say it was too rich."

"Remember the seventies!" Fred squealed like a cavalry officer.

Hockney smirked. "Yes, I know Everard said keep the stakes high so we don't get down on our luck again, but MTV tried to get that suite on Bourbon Street. They offered to pay three times the going rate. Do you know what the Sonesta is going to milk out of us if we have to put a winner in that suite come Mardi Gras?"

"We'll never have to do it," Fred gushed smugly as he reread the invitations. "Everard's so clever in his plotting, so wickedly witty, the members will never guess who committed this year's murder."

Hockney put down his gin and tonic. "He told you?"

Fred gave him an all-knowing smile.

"I thought I was the only one he trusted with that information." It was Hockney's turn to whine.

"But it is clever. The members are going to go crazy when Everard announces the killer. They'll never guess it, never!"

"You've got to tell me, Fred. I thought we had honesty and integrity between us. You know I won't breathe a word."

Fred leaned over and whispered in Hockney's ear. Hock came away grinning.

They looked at each other, then burst out laughing. "Everard!" they both chimed, and began laughing all over again.

Concourse D was packed with tourists and returning relatives. Five black musicians with trumpets and trombones were playing "When the Saints Come Marching In" while a planeload of conventioneers were handed corporate-logoed umbrellas so that they could second-line down to baggage claim.

Man, New Orleans was tacky, Claire thought as she tried to worm her way through the thick, half-drunk crowd. If she took the entire concourse and transplanted it to Bourbon Street, no one had to change at all.

*"Gate 9B from LaGuardia. Arrival Gate 9B from La-Guardia,"* the smooth voice on the loudspeaker announced.

People were already streaming out the ramp door that led to the parked 727.

"What does she look like?" Jameson asked, stuffing his hands into his jeans.

"You mean the section chief hasn't sent photos?" she asked incredulously.

"I'm not doing the Manhattan work anymore, remember? I was sent down here."

"Ah, yes. I remember it now." Claire leaned against the boarding pass counter and stared at the disembarking passengers. "She's about sixty. She has strawberry-blond hair, not natural, needless to say. You can't miss her. She limps and walks with a cane. Some asshole took a shotgun to her leg when he robbed her in the park. Shattered it."

Jameson's lean expression turned leaner, but she didn't know whether he was angry that men took shotguns to nice old women, or if he'd gotten the subtle note of accusation in her voice. She didn't want him around. She wanted him to let her deal with ZOE.

"I don't see her." He eyed the bulk of the crowd that worked its way down the concourse toward baggage. "Are you sure she took this flight?"

"You guys know what flight better than I—or is the tap not working as well as you'd like?"

He glanced at the band of airline attendants exiting the door. They were talking and laughing as employees do when they're finally off. After they moved down the concourse, the pilots came through the door. She tapped one on the sleeve.

"Excuse me, but are there any passengers left on that plane?" she asked.

The pilot grinned. "No, ma'am. We're always the last ones off." He jumped out of the way of the cleaning crew that ramrodded its way down the ramp toward the plane.

She stood and watched the pilots wheel their overnighters toward the X-ray machines at the start of the concourse. Phyllis was definitely not on the plane.

"So where is she?" Jameson asked.

She glanced up at him. The concourse had emptied with

phenomenal speed. Before, there had been throngs of loud-talking people. Now she and Jameson were the only ones for miles, it seemed.

"I don't know. I'll have to call."

He folded his arms across his chest. "Don't bother. She skipped."

"She didn't," she answered, annoyed. "Why would she?"

"Because she probably knew the feds were burning up behind her."

"Were they?" she asked, unbelieving and scared.

"I told you. There was talk that she hired another hit man. The guy who shot her was taken out last Wednesday."

"What else haven't you told me, Jameson?"

He tapped her on the jaw. "The only confessions I make are in the bedroom. C'mon." He grabbed her by the hand. There was a bank of pay phones near gate security. He picked up the receiver and punched in the numbers.

"Yep. Yep," he said after he identified himself and explained the situation. After a minute of silence while he held the receiver, he hung up and dragged her down the concourse.

"Now where are we going?" she asked, half-worried, half-angry.

"We're going to Mother's."

"My mother's?" she asked incredulously.

"No. The restaurant. Aren't you hungry? We didn't have dinner."

"You're crazy, Liam. Did you know that? Just plain crazy." She had to jog to keep up with him. "So what happened to Phyllis?"

"Skipped," he chanted as they rode the escalator to parking. "Hey, but look at it this way, Claire. You'll see her eventually. Because when we find her, she's going to need a good attorney."

"You're crazy, Jameson," she said, but with much less confidence than before.

## ❧ 24 ❧

**D**inner at Mother's was about as romantic as making love on the freeway. It was hot, crowded, the servers barked orders like honking horns, and the line moved slowly, like L.A. at rush hour. Claire and Liam got a tray of food and took a greasy little table at the back next to the kitchen. It was actually the quietest spot in the restaurant.

Liam ate as if he hadn't had a meal in months. She resented his clear conscience. She, on the other hand, picked at her food, her appetite cut from all the stress.

"I bet your arteries are clogging as we speak, Jameson," she said as he slurped down the last of his turtle soup.

"Yeah, you oughta tell Phyllis to bring all her targets here. Think how easy it'd be to off 'em." He grinned and moved on to his fried oysters. She wanted to hit him.

"Tell me why you think Phyllis skipped out."

"She'd had someone break into her files in the precinct. A black male by the name of Louie Russel was doing muggings in the park the night she was robbed. They had some notes that it was probably him who took the sawed-off shotgun to her leg."

"She never knew anything about the guy who hurt her," she said.

"Police don't like to say; you know that. They give all their info to the D.A., and until there's a conviction, what's the point?"

"She was obsessed trying to find out who he was. I guess it was only a matter of time before she got a name."

"She got a theory, Claire, not a name. No one proved Louie Russell was anywhere near her when she was assaulted."

"He never confessed?"

"No, and now he sure as hell can't."

She picked at her jambalaya. The sick feeling returned to her stomach. "How did he die?"

"Shot through the head at close range. A total professional job. He was found behind a liquor store in Newark."

"Anyone could have done it."

"That's the lawyer talking, Claire. You know deep inside that Phyllis did it. She gets her file from the Four Three Precinct and twenty-four hours later the guy's found shot. Man, he wasn't even rolled—he had two hundred in cash in his pockets. Yeah. Sure. Anyone did it."

It didn't seem real to her. Phyllis had talked about an eye for an eye, but in this case the balance was way off. One dead man for a crippled leg; the punishment didn't fit the crime. If Phyllis had hired a hit man, the woman had been wrong and completely unjustifiable.

"What're you thinking about? You're a thousand miles away," Jameson said.

"I was thinking how Phyllis was always my rock. She was the voice of reason. She couldn't have done it. I know it." She paused for a moment and stared at her untouched food. "But maybe you reach a certain age, a certain saturation point, and maybe you go crazy."

"This is crazy, all right. Another dead black guy and no confession. They haven't seen this since Mississippi 1965."

"It's not a black/white thing, Jameson," she said, irritated. "Earnestine Darby was black, remember?"

"Then what kind of a thing is it, Claire?"

"It's a man/woman thing, a victim/predator thing. The skin color doesn't figure."

He crunched on another fried oyster and eyeballed her. "So all that you women feel is left to you is vigilantism, is that it?"

She looked at him, caution wiping clean her expression. "If you're looking for evidence, I'm not going to be the one to give you any." She stared at him, her gaze holding his own. "Did they ever get your dragon, Jameson? The one in Taylorville?"

He abruptly stopped chewing. Swallowing, he said slowly, "Gunnarson put him in the chair."

"Well, hooray for him." She leaned back, still holding his gaze. "That's how it works on TV and in the movies. The dragon is slain, the case is tied up in nice little ribbons and put on the shelf. But that's not how it usually works. No, in the real world it's messy and inexact and unjust. The victim fumbles around in this fog created by the police and the lawyers and the judge. Policy and politics screw things up further. Sometimes I think the only lucky one is the victim—she doesn't have to put up with all the bullshit."

"It *is* bullshit, Claire," he said almost meanly, "but it keeps people from blowing your head off if you just look at them wrong. Without the law you'd have anarchy, and I can tell you, you women wouldn't stand a chance in anarchy. Not one fucking chance. Physically, you're too damn small and too damn weak."

"You're forgetting about one thing that's stronger than all the muscle." She tapped her head. "This," she said ominously. "It's toppled empires."

He began eating his oysters again, but this time whatever camaraderie they'd had was gone. "Finish up. I didn't sleep much last night. I want to get to bed."

"You go on." She took a twenty from her purse. "Here. In fact, take a cab on me."

"Put it away, sweetheart. We're taking that nice expensive BMW back to your place."

She couldn't believe her ears. "And how will you get back to your hotel?" she asked hesitantly.

"I'm not going back to my hotel."

She studied him as if he, too, had taken a contract out on someone's life. "I don't get it. I know the feds are still an old-boy network, but you guys have more women in your ranks. You can't tell me this is sanctioned by headquarters."

There was definitely a dare in his eyes. "Headquarters doesn't know about it, but feel free to contact them. They'd love to sit you down and have a chat about so many things."

"Why are you doing this, Jameson? You're not the sexual-harassment type. I'd think a guy like you'd get all the tail he could want without forcing the issue."

"Maybe I'm shy."

"Maybe you're full of it."

"All I know is that when they find your friend Phyllis, she's going to prison. I like you well enough, Claire, that I'm going to keep you out of the cow pie she's stepped in even if I have to stay on your tail night and day."

"What do you call this, Jameson? Sleeping with the alibi?" Derision was all over her face.

"I can sleep on the couch, but the door keys sleep with me."

"That's all that's going to sleep with you."

He smirked and helped her to her feet. "Why don't we decide that when we get home."


Shakita Jourdan was small for her seventeen years, but she was good in math, pretty, and likable. She was also the best drum majorette at McDonogh 35 High School. That alone wasn't going to get her out of the Desire Project and into Cornell; she had a composite SAT of 1450 to do that for her. So all in all life just burst at the seams. It was one great adventure that waited out there, and she wanted to grab it as tightly as the baton with which she was so proficient.

Warming up at the beginning of the parade route on Napoleon and Tchoupitoulas, she wasn't really thinking about Cornell at that moment. The *flambeaux* carriers were lined up on the neutral ground and one, a young guy who looked like he was about twenty was eyeing her. Like most seventeen-year-old girls, boys were on her mind a lot. She felt an embarrassed flattery when the young man looked at her in her tight, pink-sequined majorette costume. She liked the way he smiled in her direction when she glanced at him, and she wondered if he would try to speak to her at the end of the parade. She hoped so.

Dante was set to roll at precisely eight o'clock.

Claire picked up her mail and sullenly let Liam into the condo. During the ride home she realized there was no point in arguing with him. The uniforms couldn't stay with her around the clock indefinitely; in fact, the squad car was gone when they arrived at the mansion, probably summoned to do duty at a parade.

He could sleep on the couch. It would be like having a bodyguard. There were worse things. Like having a serial killer after you.

She glanced down at the mail in her hands. An uneasy feeling came to her when she realized one handwritten envelope was from Pauline Zeiss. The postmark was Washington, D.C. Trouble was, she didn't know any Pauline Zeiss in D.C. and she certainly couldn't understand how Pauline Zeiss got her address in New Orleans when her permanent address was New York.

There was a desk next to the couch where she did her bills. She placed the mail on the desk and glanced furtively into the kitchen. Jameson was rummaging in the refrigerator, looking for a beer. Already they were like an old married couple.

The letter opener was in the top drawer next to her checkbook. Careful not to smudge any potential fingerprints, she cut the flap of the envelope and read:

*Doll,*
*I knew you'd understand. They were tapping the lines.*
*Several of the women have been brought in for question-*
*ing and I don't think they'll hold out forever. There was*
*no better way to get everyone off me than to just disap-*
*pear.*

*I'll try and find you in New Orleans. Until I do, don't*
*worry about me. My money's in the Caymans. I can work*
*ZOE long distance as well as from New York.*

*All my love,*
*Phyllis.*

She slid the letter between the pages of a junk catalogue that had come addressed to Resident.

"Where's the opener?" Liam asked, holding a cold Dixie longneck in his hand.

"Third drawer to the right of the sink."

He disappeared. She stared after him, unsure what to do. She didn't want to tell him about the letter, but not to do so was wrong. She was withholding evidence on a suspected criminal.

The phone rang. It startled her.

Jameson picked it up in the kitchen.

"Great. Get their records. See what he's been accessing." He hung up.

"What was that all about?"

He eased himself down on the couch, stretched his legs out in front of him, and took a sip of the beer. "Our friend likes to use the electronic superhighway."

She groaned. "I hate that term."

"So does everybody."

"What's he up to?"

"Laborde's been up late at night at the 555's computer, surfing the Internet. Let's see what he's doing. You'd be surprised how revealing it is to document someone's taste in E-mail."

"We've got access to the Internet at Fassbinder, but I confess I've never used it."

"It's getting real big with hate groups. Particularly in Germany, where it's illegal to be a member of the Nazi Party. Computers have changed all that. You click in, have a global meeting of sociopaths, then click out. The cops can't really trace you without a helluva lot of effort, especially if you're just lurking and not posting any messages of your own."

"But you're able to trace Laborde."

"I thought he was going through an anonymous site, but we've discovered he's going through the University of Helsinki. That's typical of someone who wants to hide their net tastes—they get into it through a big user, like a university system—then they surf to find the groups they like. Once they're off, the records are damn hard to find. You have to know who you're looking for, and you have to search through the university's entire system."

"Is he in a hate group? Was that the reason for the Star of David?" Her insides knotted. She began to pace. Being a Jew, it was almost instinctive to recoil at the thought of a Nazi. All she knew is that having met him, J. Everard Laborde would make a good one.

"I don't think so. As I said before, there are hate groups with an agenda, and then there are the followers that make the agenda their excuse. He's probably more the latter kind." Liam shrugged. "But if he's the sociopath I think he is, I theorize that maybe he has some kind of phobia for Jews and blacks. I hear they're pretty much on the outs at the 555 Association, and I'll bet maybe he likes the forbidden."

"So why is he on the Internet?" She finally sat down next to him. The pacing was making her only more uneasy.

"To meet others like himself. To brag. To hear about their fantasies. Sometimes these guys need to read about killings to tide them over between their own murders. There are groups out there to satisfy anyone: sadomasochists, dominatrix round tables, child pornographers. And just think, to be an anonymous member, all you have to have is a generic computer and a phone line."

"You think his computer's going to lead us to him?"

"I think it's going to show us how exotic his tastes are." Liam took her chin in his hand and rubbed his thumb across her cheek. "Be prepared to be shocked."

"Nothing shocks me anymore."

"Nothing?" He put a lazy knuckle beneath her chin and tilted up her face. Slowly, he moved to kiss her.

She pulled away. Getting to her feet, she said lightly, "I hate to admonish you, Agent Jameson, but this is hardly the way to protect someone. Remind me never to go into the Federal Witness Protection Program."

He watched her.

She began to pace again.

"It's the talk, isn't it? The idea that he's out there, wallowing in his perversions. That really sets you on edge, don't it, girl?"

She looked away. She didn't need him analyzing her. "It doesn't put me at ease that he's out there on the Internet in some kind of orgiastic feeding frenzy."

"If they find a board he likes to put his own messages on, they might get a confession out of him."

Even she had to admit that surprised her. "Would he name names? I can't believe he'd be so foolish."

"If you think no one knows who you are or where you are, it's not such a risk. These guys really like to talk about what they've done. Rehashing it titillates them, let's them live it all over again."

"I think I heard about this stuff before. People v. Schnell, right? They discovered all the body parts in his office because he was posting messages, didn't they?"

"Yeah."

"Can I see the message if Laborde posts one? I might recognize something he says or does."

"I'll get a printout."

She finally gave him a slow, wan smile. "I guess I should say thanks, then, but somehow it doesn't seem appropriate."

"No, it's not appropriate." He took her hand and pulled her down onto the couch with him. With both hands he brushed back the hair from her temples and said, "I told you I'd help you find your sister's killer, and I'm doing all I can. But now you need to reciprocate and defang that organization of yours."

"It's not up to me, Liam."

"Look, Gunnarson's really putting the heat on. The New York authorities aren't fooling around either. I can't just look the other way while you and your cronies go about your business."

"I understand, but *you* have to understand that I'm not running things there." She sighed and stared through the amber glass of his beer bottle to see if he was ready for another one. He wasn't. She placed it back down on the table. "It's the *Sorcerer's Apprentice,* Liam. It kind of frightens me, but I don't think I can do anything about it anymore."

A repressed anger seemed to rise to the surface. He said, "This is not the kind of thing women should be involved in. Murder is an ugly business. Real ugly."

Her own ire raised, she shot back. "You make it sound like men can do it but not women, Jameson. What? Murder's a little more palatable when the perpetrator has a penis?"

"It's never palatable, but women are the life-givers, not the life-takers. It's just not the kind of thing a man likes to think a woman is capable of."

"Murder's within anyone, Liam, if you're pushed to the point of it."

"Within you?"

She didn't look at him. "There are moments when I think about Laborde. I think about him gone, and I wish—well, I wish he were gone."

"But you don't want to soil your hands to do it, like the rest of the women in ZOE, so you take an ad and hire a man to do your dirty work—like you tried to hire me. Hey, listen, I've seen the record of the guy they think took out Phyllis Zuckermann's perp. He's a killer, all right. He's snuffed 'em from Angola to Zimbabwe. So what right do you women have to say who lives and who dies, when you won't even participate in it? How responsible are you women at killing? Not very, I'd say."

"What are we arguing about here, Jameson? I'm not going to defend their actions, I'm just not going to say the women are weak either."

"Look, you need to decide a few things before you get into the vigilante business. You tried to hire me, remember? Do you want a man to slay your dragon, or can you slay it yourself? I say, if you have to hire out, you shouldn't be doing it in the first place."

"This conversation is absurd."

He touched her face.

She turned to look at him.

"Slay your own dragon, or get out of the business."

She drew away, rubbing her hands on her upper arms as if she were cold. He was right, but he angered her nonetheless. His philosophy cast women as the perennial victims. They either needed a man to do their dark deeds, or they had to do them themselves, and, therefore, risk harsher reprimand because they were supposed to be soft and supportive and passive.

"You know, Jameson, I think you're right. I need to slay my own dragon," she said softly.

"The real dragon is ZOE, Claire. You need to disband this group. The victims are becoming worse than the killers. You and Phyllis Zuckermann and the rest of that coven need to repent."

*Coven. Witches. Burned at the stake. Men always fear women with power.* "How do you suppose I slay my own dragon?"

"Through the justice system."

She smiled. "You answered the question perfectly, Jameson. Why, this could be on *Dragnet*. Thank you for the lecture on moral turpitude."

"I'm not kidding, Claire. I've got a lot of heat on me, especially since Phyllis Zuckermann's guy was found dead. I can't cut you much slack even if we are—"

He didn't say it. Thank God, he didn't say it, she thought. Somehow, she still couldn't believe the other night. It seemed more and more surreal with every passing hour. She and Jameson? Making love? It didn't happen. It couldn't have. "Not anymore, Agent Jameson." She walked to the hall closet and grabbed an armful of bed linens and a blanket. Throwing them on the couch, she casually saluted him, then went to her bedroom, alone. She would think about how to get rid of him tomorrow.


At eleven P.M. the crowds were lined up twenty thick on the St. Charles Avenue streetcar tracks. On the other side of the street, yuppies hung off the balconies of nineteenth-century mansions, swilling beer in plastic Carnival cups. A fraternity of young black men from Xavier University were throwing a party in a ground floor apartment of the St. Charles House, while little kids hustled for beads they could sell to next year's krewes. It was the best example of organized chaos there was. The cops made sure all the ladder chairs holding young children were out of the parade path. They mediated the few scuffles and generally gave everyone the evil eye, lending weight to the theory that it was indeed difficult being around a bunch of drunks stone-cold sober.

The parade was almost a mile away. Faraway rhythms of a steel drum resonated through the live oaks as the navy band played a crude version of "Easy Skanking." Dante was a big parade with thirty-four floats. Typically, the grand marshal's float moved in stops and starts while it waited for the rest of the parade to catch up to it. Way down the avenue, the streetlights picked up the first glimpse of Satan raising his fearsome pitchfork.

The crowds were thickest around Lee Circle. Laborde knew the floats would all bottleneck there in order to pay homage to the dignitaries in the grandstands. He benevolently waved to the crowds and rehearsed his crime in his mind.

In front of the float, the McDonogh 35 band pumped out a hot Janet Jackson number. The majorettes, with their spangles and white gloves, were a particularly fetching lot this year, but there was one who stood out of the crowd. She was a petite girl, all pert little breasts and big, innocent smile.

Laborde watched her through his white reveler's mask, his eyes not missing a sequin. He crouched on his throne like a puma staring down a wild rabbit. He could barely wait.

The parade rounded Lee Circle. City council men and women sat in the first viewing stand, and Laborde, old hand that he was, nodded and gestured in a kingly manner while they drank toasts to his health. It was all pretend, but not pretend. Dante wasn't real, but that didn't stop even the politician from playing make-believe during Mardi Gras season.

The grand marshal's float lurched through the circle, then sat on Howard Avenue while the rear floats caught up, and each in their turn stopped at the grandstands. The short jog onto Howard was notorious because it was the longest wait and the most pressured. The crowds were a mixture of French Quarter tourists and project types who had walked from the Florida housing development. They were all driven to catch throws. At this turn in the road, the choice was to throw the terrible writhing masses beads or risk appearing stingy and take your life in your hands. What most parade riders did during this part of the route was hide down below in the bowels of the float, take a trip to the Jiffy John that was camouflaged there, and drink a beer. The crowds didn't attack a float if they saw no idling white guys. An empty float for some inexplicable reason didn't piss them off.

Laborde had the whole thing planned out. He watched his dukes climb down the hatch, one by one, as they disappeared to avoid the anxious mob. Now it was execution time.

"You wanna beer?" he called down to the guy in the cubby behind the stairs who pulled the pitchfork.

The man widened his eyes. "Sure, but I'm not supposed to leave. Dufossat'll lynch me." He was an employee of the float builder and not one of the krewe.

"Don't worry about it. Take a break. I'll pull the fork. Just come back when we're ready to move again." Laborde watched the man rise out of the cubby behind the stairs. The guy went on top, then descended the rear set of stairs to get into the belly with the resting krewe members.

Everard barely fit into the snug space. It was made for a thinner man. He pulled the lever a couple of times to get the hang of it. According to his experience, they'd be stalled on Howard Avenue, waiting for the rear floats, for forty minutes. That was the usual. He had more than enough time, especially if Blaise Dufossat's employee liked to bend his elbow.

The majorettes were milling around the front of the float as bored and restless as the crowd. A few members of the Mc-Donogh 35 band continued to play, but most looked weary; the parade was just past the halfway mark and they still had to deal with the crowds downtown. Thick walls of people milled around, every now and then surging toward the float as one of Laborde's dukes came on top and decided to toss some Dante-imprinted cups or a gross of plastic beads. Everard knew he had to take his chance when the crowds surged. There were probably ten thousand people on the one block around the float. If those numbers couldn't hide a crime, nothing could.

"Throw me somethin', mister!" A drunken tourist who'd probably been briefed on Mardi Gras by Fodor's wildly waved his hands. George St. Amant, one of Dante's old krewe members, rose over the edge of the float. Beer in hand, white reveler's mask hiding his identity from all save the float riders, he titillated the crowd with a pink-feathered spear.

The people on the street, bored with a parade that had come to a dead halt, suddenly came alive with the teasing spear. The crowd came forward like a wave on the beach, no one paying any attention to anything except the drunken, masked reveler atop the float who taunted the pedestrians with the made-in-the-Philippines rubber spear.

Laborde crawled from the cubby. The majorettes were jammed against the front of the float even as the chaperons in marked fluorescent vests barked at the crowd to move back. But attempting control was useless. Pandemonium ensued and all the happy inebriates raised their hands and jumped for the toy spear.

This was what Mardi Gras was all about, Laborde mused as he reached around the edge of the flame-camouflage stairs and grabbed the collar of one of the majorettes.

*Catching things,* he thought as his other hand clamped over the black girl's mouth, and he pulled her with him down into the cubby.

## ❧ 26 ❧

"**T**wo weeks to Mardi Gras day and they've already got a casualty," Claire commented as she glanced at the front page of the *Times-Picayune,* scanning the article about the majorette who was killed beneath a float. "As a lawyer, I find it hard to believe they still have Carnival. The city must really get stung with liability."

"Mmm," Jameson answered, his eyes half closed with sleep.

She surreptitiously looked at him from above the newspaper. He lay on his back on the couch; last night he hadn't bothered with sheets, and the blanket was now a crumpled ball at his feet. His chest was bare, his jeans barely on. At six foot plus and without an ounce of spare fat, he looked just like the bull rider he said he'd been. A hair-sprinkled torso, the rock-hard grid of a stomach; she had a difficult time not thinking about her satiation the other night. Looking at him now, she didn't need to ask herself why she was attracted to him.

"I have to go to the post office and run some other errands, so get up if you're going to play bodyguard." She threw her slipper at him. It hit him square in the middle of the chest.

"I've got to see Williams. You'll have to take me. The feds sent me a computer whiz."

"You mean the Internet stuff?"

"Yeah," he grunted.

They really were Neanderthals. Especially in the morning. "I'm leaving in five minutes. If you're not up, I'm going alone." She walked into the foyer to check her handbag. It was a bluff. She wasn't going to go without him—or some-one—she was just too scared.

"I'm leaving," she called out. To her relief, he showed up in the foyer door, jeans snapped, shirt on if still unbuttoned. He hopped pulling on the second cowboy boot.

"I'll drop you off at the Café du Monde," he said, going out the door with her. "It's a better wait there than at police headquarters. It's a public place. You'll be okay there while I have my meeting. Let me check in with Williams, then I'll pick you up again and we can run your errands."

"Spoken just like a baby-sitter," she said, but she was still grateful. Until she had a finger on Laborde, she didn't ever see herself safe again.

"Let's go," he said belligerently, his eyes bloodshot from lack of sleep.

"Fine," she answered, then followed him out the door.


Jameson dropped her off at the Café du Monde. Claire was sipping café au lait before Jameson even returned to the wheel of the Beemer.

He drove away, promising to return in twenty minutes. She relaxed and let the ceiling fans run a breeze through her hair.

"Darling?" A familiar voice made her sit up. She looked at the woman standing over her table and blinked. It was Phyllis. She hadn't skipped after all. She had found her.

"What are you doing here, Phyllis? Where are you stay-ing?" she asked as she helped the older woman to her seat.

"The Windsor Court. Isn't that where all the rich people fleeing the country stay?" Phyllis smiled.

"I—I can't believe you're here. The authorities are looking for you, Phyl." Claire just stared at her. At any previous time she might have hugged the woman and told her how glad she was to see her, but the weeks had passed like years. She didn't really know Phyllis anymore. "I thought you left the country."

"I'm going to after our chat, Claire. I don't want to leave the country, but worse is the thought of spending my twilight years doing a legal dance with the court system."

"I heard about your mugger, Phyllis. Did you have him killed?" Claire was being blunt, but she saw no reason not to be. The feds might have evidence against Phyllis, and the punishment in her case no way fit the crime.

Phyllis shrugged and placed a Chanel backpack on the seat beside her. A Vietnamese waitress took her coffee order. "I'll tell you, Claire, this organization of yours has been a godsend. You can't imagine the feeling of freedom—" She suddenly eyed her younger companion. "Tell me how you knew about my man."

Claire took a deep breath. "That FBI agent I met in Bloomingdale's is still hovering over me. He told me what they have on you and how your guy was found dead, shot. They say they have a lot on you."

"Me? How lovely. I had nothing to do with it, really. Not when our new knight is working out so well. Doll, you must meet him."

"I don't want to, thank you. The last knight is still causing me trouble."

Phyllis laughed but Claire couldn't.

She continued. "I don't want you to call my organization ZOE anymore either, Phyl. I'm disowning it. You're way out of line, and I can't let myself get messed up with you."

"We're not going to make any more mistakes." Phyllis smiled at the waitress and tipped her a five. She bit into a hot beignet and rolled her eyes as if to say, "Heavenly."

"In the first place," Phyllis said, "our mistake was to advertise. We should have known that ad in *High Risk* would only put the authorities on our tail. We should have listened to your warnings, Claire. I'm sorry." She took another bite. "In the second place, especially with Halbert Washington, we should have never gone on Earnestine's memory. We should have checked things out ourselves, checked, and double-checked, and checked it blind. We're doing that now, Claire. We've a member in the police department who can access all the computer systems in every precinct in the country. You'd be surprised how automated we've become and how much we know. That J. Everard Laborde fellow, for example. He did kill your sister, you know. It's much too coincidental to believe. The police are just one small piece of evidence away from being able to get a warrant for him. I hope they can find that evidence soon, before it's too late."

Claire felt as if she'd just been hit on the jaw by a fistful of iron. Her head turned fuzzy, her breath caught in her throat. "Wait a minute. Let me catch up. You know about Laborde?"

"Detective Derrell Williams keeps excellent files. He's notated all your theories. You think he's ignoring you, Claire, but he's not. The coincidences are shocking."

"How do you know all this? How could you possibly?" Claire babbled, unable to believe it.

"I told you, darling, ZOE is all automated now. It's gone into the twenty-first century. We've grown fivefold from the last time you saw me. Everyone wants in. The word is that we offer results along with compassion. We've got unimaginable resources now. There are so many victims who want to offer their help. We've struck a chord, Claire."

Claire stared dumbly out across Decatur to the statue of Andrew Jackson. "You know what it's taken me weeks to find out, all with the click of a mouse. I suppose I should never have come down here. What good has it done me?"

"You've found him. You've looked him in the eye. He's your sister's killer, and you know it."

"I don't know. I *think* I know. That's all."

"He did it, doll. Trust me on this one. He's no gentleman. I have a whole printout on him. The coincidences are like a connect-the-dots game. And the picture they make isn't pretty."

"Still, there's nothing conclusive."

"What do you want, Claire? A Perry Mason confession? Let me tell you, you won't get it, so take some advice from me: Just put the thing behind you. Go back to New York and live your life to the fullest. Do it for me and for your sister Zoe, okay?"

"I want to, it's just—" Suddenly an awful thought came to her. With the blood leaving her cheeks, she said, "You're checking on him, aren't you, Phyl? You're following me around, you even knew I was here. What are you going to do, Phyllis?"

"It's your turn, Claire. You deserve it. ZOE wants to do this for you."

"But only you're ZOE. Nobody else hires the killers, just you. You told me so yourself. I don't want a hired killer down here, Phyllis. Listen to me, I don't want that."

"Calm yourself."

Claire almost leapt out of her seat. "Are you kidding me, Phyllis? I can't just let you ride off to the Caymans and let you take care of Laborde."

"And why not? Think how easy that would be. Think how clean."

"It's not clean at all. It stinks." Claire's voice rose to near hysteria. "Tell me what you've done, Phyl. Tell me so I can stop it."

"It can't be stopped."

Her heart was beating so fast, Claire was sure she was going to have a coronary. "What have you gone and done, Phyl? Have you got this hit man down here? Does he have Laborde's address? Are you going to make me protect that bastard when he probably killed Zoe? Say it isn't so, Phyllis. Deny it!"

"Claire, Laborde will never confess. You'll never be more sure than you are now."

"But I want a jury to convict him!"

"Based on what? Even if he were processed by the system and given a lethal injection, if he never confesses, you still wouldn't be one hundred percent sure. You'd feel as guilty as you feel now."

"Say this isn't happening . . ." She dropped her head in her hands. "Now what do I have to do to get this monkey off my back? How do I call the hit man off?"

"You can't, darling. It's done."

"No, it's not done. What's the guy's name? How do I reach him?" she demanded desperately.

"You can't. It's done. I'm all automated now. I've learned not to mess with the cogs. The hit man's been paid, given pictures, everything. The only thing you can hope is that the time runs out."

"There's a clock on this thing?" Claire felt like she was in a nightmare, one from which she couldn't wake up.

"Two weeks." Phyllis took out a leather-bound calendar from the Chanel backpack. "Why, that would be Mardi Gras. How fitting. Wasn't he some kind of head of Mardi Gras one year?"

"He was Rex," Claire said numbly.

"Rex, that's king, isn't it?"

"Yes."

Phyllis lifted her cup of coffee. With a sympathetic smile on her face, she said, "I've got to be going, Claire. This visit was imprudent of me, but I wanted to see you one last time. Be happy, Claire, and know that I love you. Remember the gift I gave you." She raised her cup higher and toasted, " 'The king is dead. Long live the king.' "

In the end, J. Everard Laborde was going to be slain, whether he was Zoe's dragon or not.

Claire still couldn't shake the thought, or the numb desperation, the horror that gripped her ever since she watched Phyllis leave in the cab. She didn't want to protect Laborde, and yet she couldn't stand by and watch him be assassinated.

Worse, she still couldn't go to Jameson with her fears. Whom would he go after then, she asked herself. He would go after her, even though she didn't know the women in ZOE anymore. Even though she didn't know the hit man or his instructions. Even though she really had no role in the scheme.

Her conclusion was that she would just have to hope that two weeks would pass without a murder. She had to hold her breath and hope the hit man wouldn't be able to perform his duty in the confusion and congestion of New Orleans during Mardi Gras.

But now that Phyllis had left and she was alone in the café once again, Claire realized she was guilty. She'd allowed Phyllis to depart. She also knew she wasn't going to go to the police with the information Phyllis had given her. She was just going to do nothing, and that alone would make her take part in the murder.

She finally saw the devil in the mirror. And it was herself. She rose from the café table and took a short stroll down

Decatur. There were lots of tourists around. She'd be safe, besides, Jameson was due back any minute. She'd see him better from the sidewalk than the café.

The Quarter was damp from an early morning rain. She walked, her thoughts overwhelmed with the dilemma. She had a moral obligation to tell Laborde something, but she didn't know what, and the whole idea of another meeting with him left an acid taste in her mouth. Just the thought of him lurking on the Internet, getting off on messages from perverts, was enough for her to never want to see the guy again. She didn't want to look again into eyes that might have seen Zoe take her last breath.

The siren in the background went almost unnoticed. She heard it as if it were going off on the edge of her subconscious. Two weeks before Mardi Gras, tourists were second-lining, Shriners were revving up their motorcycles. The siren escorts were obligatory this time of year.

It came as quite a shock to her when the squad car roared down Decatur, came to a dead stop at the light, and two men shot out of the car only, to run toward her.

"Jameson, you damn well have given me a heart attack," she cursed when she recognized him as one of the men.

"Where is she, Claire? We just got a tip she's been following you. Tell me where Phyllis is, or so help me, I'll arrest you for withholding information." His face was taut and grim. When she offered no explanation, he flashed his badge. Several people began to gawk and mill around them.

"You're under arrest. You have the right to remain silent . . ."

She watched his lips move with the familiar words as if they were moving in slow motion. The uniform who was with him led her to the squad car while Liam continued the Miranda. A crowd gathered at the curb as the uniform put his hand on her head and sat her in the back seat of the car.

She looked to Liam, her eyes wide and desperate. All she knew when the car pulled from the curb was that she was being arrested, but she had nothing to say except that Phyllis was gone now and she didn't think she'd ever return.

"Attorney-client privilege," she repeated across the table from Jameson.

"You saw her. You talked to her. You know exactly what happened to her little friend in New York. Now, tell me about your conversation."

"You're speculating, Jameson. You don't have enough to keep me here, and you know it. You're just angry that Phyllis found me and you missed your opportunity. Now you're concocting all these nefarious conversations because you have nothing else to go on." Claire took a sip of the water she poured from the pitcher that sat between them. Jameson certainly looked angry, and whenever she thought of Laborde, she had a nauseous, sinking feeling in her stomach.

"Look, Liam, I know my rights. You have to give me a reason for my arrest, or you have to let me go. It's that simple. So why are you holding me? On what charges?"

Jameson nodded to Williams, who sat near the door. As if on command, he left them alone.

When the door shut, Liam stared at her. His eyes were stone cold. She wondered if she'd been given a peek into his heart.

"Claire. You're in deep. You met with Phyllis Zuckermann. The feds traced her to here, and we just found the cab that took her away from the café."

"Where did she go after the cab?"

"She had a car parked on St. Charles. She'll be winging out of the country by this evening, probably from Houston or Birmingham, whichever city she decides to drive to. But you know where she's gone. She told you, so tell us."

"I don't know where she went. I met with Phyllis because she just appeared at the café. You were the one who decided to drop me there. I didn't plan the meeting. It just happened."

"I warned you. I've done everything I can—"

"My association with Phyllis Zuckermann is still not enough to send in the squad cars, guns blazing, like you just did." She met his gaze and gave him a wry little smile. She hoped she hid the hurt inside her. "You know, I almost thought you really wanted to play bodyguard. I kind of thought you were using it as an excuse to stay with me. I guess I didn't want to believe that all the questions and concern was just another sham."

His expression seemed to only grow harder. "Someone sent you that chunk of Laborde's secretary for a reason, girl. You could end up like your sister. The possibility of personal harm doesn't diminish because you're committing crimes of your own."

"That occurred to me when the cop was pushing me into the back seat of that squad car, but I didn't think people got arrested because they're not obeying their bodyguard." She met his gaze.

He went back into the mantra of interrogation. "We've finally got a warrant for Phyllis Zuckermann's arrest. Conspiracy to murder. It sounds pretty bad. You met with her. What did you talk about?"

"I told you, Jameson. Attorney-client privilege."

"You aren't her attorney. She's left the country."

"As her attorney, I would have advised her not to leave the country if the authorities needed to speak with her."

"Did you?"

"When I spoke with her, I didn't know she'd been charged."

"She's going to drag you right down with her, Claire. You're going to end up in the pen. Don't do it, girl. Don't."

The softness of his words must have gotten to her. She stared at him, unable to hide the rawness inside her. "I can't help you, Liam. I can't even help myself right now."

He stood and walked around the table. Touching her face,

he said, "I beg of you, you've got to extricate yourself, and the way to do it is to confess. What did Phyllis tell you?"

Claire parted her mouth, but the words wouldn't come. How did she tell an FBI agent that the man she most wanted dead in the world was about to be killed and she was the only one who knew about it.

"Do you think Laborde killed my sister?" she whispered.

"We're working on it. I told you that. Why can't you just let me do my job?"

The frustration within her suddenly boiled over. Fear and anger made her lash out. "Maybe I'm not letting you do your job because I want to slay my own dragon. Maybe the ad was just a lie. *Wanted: A Man to Slay Dragons*," she recited bitterly. "Maybe I've realized I don't need the man."

He lifted her chin and stared at her, anger sparking in his own eyes. "You need this man."

She pulled away. "I've got to be left alone. You only mess things up, Jameson."

"I have the right to hold you for forty-eight hours without charging you. I think I'll do it. Just to give you a foretaste of the jail to come."

He walked away. She wanted to call him back. To make him let her go, but she couldn't think how to do it. She was trapped. Hopelessly trapped.

"I'm going to talk to Williams, then I'll be back. In the meantime, maybe an hour alone in here will change your mind." He gave her another icy look.

She put her arms around herself and shivered. She couldn't believe she had let the man make love to her. She didn't seem to know him at all.

Pacing was the only thing she could bring herself to do. She'd pace for five minutes, then sit at the table and scratch at the pad of paper Jameson had left. Someone had left the day's newspaper on one of the chairs, but she hadn't the peace of mind to read it.

The hour moved with the speed of a glacier. Finally she heard footsteps.

She knew she probably looked scared and anxious, and that was the last way she wanted to appear in front of Jameson. Before he opened the door, she slid into a seat, picked up the newspaper, and nonchalantly pretended to read it. It was the Living section. Social-column fluff. The kind of stuff Zoe had liked.

*Dreams and Nightmares, Theme of Dante's Infernal Ball.*

Jameson entered the room.

She kept her gaze riveted to the paper.

"Not ready to break?" He kicked out another chair from the table and sat next to her.

"The boredom might get to me after a while," she said, a nice frost to her words.

"Yeah, well, I might get to you after a while. Gimme the chance," he murmured.

*The king rode a devilish float down St. Charles Avenue to the Krewe of the Dante ball held at the Hyatt grand ballroom.*

Her eyes stayed focused on the social column. "You haven't got one thing you can hold me on Jameson. You're just setting yourself up for legal action."

He tweaked one of her curls. "Are you going to sue me for false arrest, Ms. Lawyer? Or are you going to take on the whole goddamned FBI?"

*J. Everard Laborde, prominent socializer and president of the venerated 555 Association, was king of the Dante revelers, leading the procession into the Hyatt.*

She froze.

Something clicked into place in her mind like a piece of a jigsaw. In a rush of desperation, she began shuffling through the stack of newspapers.

"What the hell's gotten into you?" Liam frowned.

"Where's the front page? Where is it?" she cried out.

He gave her a strange look, then shuffled through the sections himself. "Here it is," he said.

She grabbed it. There was the headline. *Majorette Killed by Dante Float.* She read the article, her heartbeat coming fast and terrible.

*The body of a young majorette with the McDonogh 35 Senior High School band was found on Canal and St. Charles at one A.M., after the Dante parade had passed. Her wounds indicated she was sucked underneath one of the floats and dragged to her death. The coroner said this is the city's first such accident involving a parader. Annually a person is crushed beneath one of the floats in the massive crowds of Carnival season, but this death was rare also in that it did not involve alcohol.*

*Shakita Jourdan, 17, was known for talents other than baton twirling. She was honored by the mayor just last fall when she won a full scholarship to Cornell, an Ivy League university in New York State . . .*

Claire looked up at Liam. He watched her as if she'd gone mad. She wondered if she hadn't.

"I need to see her body," she said, her voice taut with repressed hysteria.

"This girl's body? Why?" His brows knitted together in a frown as he read the article.

"Laborde was king of Dante. He killed her—he murdered her just like he killed Zoe, and I can prove it. You've just got to let me see the body."

He looked at her as if he didn't quite know what to think. Their gazes met. He must have seen the terror in her eyes, because for the first time she could recall, the distrust left his expression.

"You want to see the body, you got it, but just remember"—he paused—"you're not used to seeing such things. She's gonna be a mess."

"Just take me to her. I just need to see her face." She began to tremble. Her hands flew to her lips as if to still them.

"I don't know what's going on here, but let's go see the girl. Then I expect a full explanation." He put out his hand. She took it and together they left the room.

## ❧ 28 ❧

The coroner's office was at 2700 Tulane Avenue. Derrell Williams took them in his car. They were brought up to the fourth floor, where the deputy coroner met them.

"Are you sure you want to do this?" Liam asked her, pulling her aside in the hallway.

Claire stared at him, noting the hard line of his mouth, the desolate gleam in his eye. He was a man of experience. He'd seen this thing before. But the idea of viewing a mangled dead body was not nearly as terrifying as what she suspected she would find. "I need to see only her face. Just for a second."

The deputy coroner brought them through a stainless steel room where autopsies were performed, then into a hospital-green-tiled room. The guy chatted constantly.

"Hey, we haven't really gotten to this one yet. You know how it is, we hit a warm spell and the bodies pile up. We're a little behind." The d.c. paused at one of the numerous steel doors. Williams nodded, and he slid out a sheet-covered body.

The girl's legs stuck out at the bottom. She was still in her clothes. Her tights had ripped, and where her foot came through the hosiery, the coroner had placed a tag on her big toe. The tights were flesh-colored, but not her flesh color.

Against her dark skin, they were the mocking color of a Band-Aid.

"Just pull back the sheet on her face," Claire whispered, her nails digging into her palm.

Liam looked to the d.c. "How bad is she?"

He shrugged. "Not too bad. Her torso got the worst of it. Just some scrapes and contusions on the face."

"Okay," Liam said. "Let's see her."

Claire didn't even flinch when the sheet was lifted from the face. She wanted to see the worst of it. She wanted to know that she was right.

She *was* right.

She stared down at the young girl's face and her heart filled with rage. Shakita Jourdan was only seventeen. The puffy, empty-eyed face had no more life in it, no more joy, no more smiles. A strand of fuchsia sequins had come unsewn from her majorette outfit and had wrapped around her throat, ridiculing her with their gaiety. There was nothing here. Just a young, wasted girl, her tights an insult, her sequins tarnished with her own blood, her lips smeared with the same vibrant orange lipstick Zoe had on the day she died.

"That's enough," Claire said, her throat bottled with tears. She shuffled over to the bench on the opposite wall.

"She was just run over—" the d.c. said.

"Get a semen sample," Liam ordered.

"Why bother? There wasn't any found in Zoe." Claire wiped tears off her cheeks.

Williams gave Claire a probing look, then he nodded to the d.c. "Get Minnefield. I want a complete autopsy."

The d.c. went to a phone.

"Let's go get some coffee," Williams said. "I want to know what this is about."

"So do I," Liam said, staring at Claire.

She looked up at both men. The very horror of her discovery was still like a dream, numbing her. "We need to exhume Zoe. The lipstick, you see. The lipstick will match."

"How do you know that?" Williams demanded.

"Because," she said, her voice sounding far away, even to her. "You don't wear orange lipstick with pink sequins. *He* put it on her. It's his trademark. It's his way of branding her." She suddenly began to sob. "Oh, God, this young girl . . . he's going to do it again—"

"Wait," Liam murmured, dragging her to her feet and into his arms. "How do you know all this? How do you know it?"

She tried to gather her thoughts, tried to sound coherent. But it was difficult when her mind was screaming in terror. "I saw he was king of Dante. Dante was the parade this girl was marching in. It's the lipstick, you see? I told the police that five years ago. It's *his* lipstick. Zoe never would have worn that color. Go ahead and exhume her. She'll be the one to tell you. The lipstick will match this girl's color."

"Check the lipstick. Get an exhumation order," Liam said to Williams.

"The family has to okay it," Williams interjected. "I don't have enough for a judge to order one."

"I'm the family," Claire offered. "I okay it."

Williams jotted a couple of notes down in his black notebook. He flipped down the cover and stuck it in the inside pocket of his suit jacket. "I'll get to work on it."

"Let's go get some of that coffee," Liam murmured.

Claire felt his arm go around her waist. He led her from the hospital-green-tiled room, the one she remembered from five years past. The one visited often in her nightmares.

"He's going to kill another girl if I don't stop him," she said.

"That's not your job. It's mine," Liam chided.

"No," she countered, her mind expanding with the realization of her duties. She had to stop him. It was an obligation that went beyond the law, beyond even moral outrage. She had to stop him because she now knew without a doubt he had killed Zoe and this girl, and that he would continue.

She had to stop him simply because she could stop him, and because it was so terribly necessary. Now she had to choose which path to take: She could be passive and wait, or she could embrace the law, the road of frustration and incompetence and difficulties. Her epiphany came like a wind through her soul. She nearly gasped.

Tears still stained her face when she left the coroner's office, but her thoughts were no longer on Shakita Jourdan. They were on the killer who'd been sent down from ZOE.

He was out there, waiting to do his job.

And by God, she just might let him.


The Gates of Prayer Cemetery stood frozen, a crumbling city block of granite, of carved Stars of David and old New Orleans Jewish names such as Hermann and Aron. A fine layer of frost covered Zoe's underground crypt. It was the coldest winter day they'd had all year. Mardi Gras was only ten days away.

Claire watched them take her sister's coffin from the concrete vault. The crane whined and sputtered in the cold. Her parents stood motionless beside her, as if they were unable to believe what they were seeing. A burial in reverse.

"Let's go home, Mom. You look frozen," she said as she took her mother's gloved hand.

"Where are they taking her?"

"The detectives will take her. They'll let us know when they're finished so we can put her back again," she reassured.

"That's right, Rachel," her father said. "They told us it wouldn't take long." .

Claire couldn't stand to see what the stress was doing to her mother. The slim salt-and-pepper-haired woman in the bright sweater she'd seen only a few weeks ago was now being replaced by a wraith. Rachel's face was sickly pale, and though the woman was small, her petite figure was quickly becoming gaunt.

"Did—did that man kill my daughter?" Rachel whispered as she watched the coffin being loaded into the coroner's wagon.

"Come on, Mom. Let's get you warm," Claire said softly.

Rachel nodded, but she couldn't seem to quit asking the question. "Did he kill Zoe? Did he kill my daughter?"

"Let's go home." Claire looked at her father, worry in her eyes. Her mother seemed almost over the edge. She wondered if it had been a mistake to tell her parents, but there was no way to hide it. They lived just around the block. The neighbors would have told them Zoe had been disinterred.

Jameson and Detective Williams stood to the side of the vault as if trying to respect the family's privacy. Heze took one of Rachel's arms and Claire took the other, and they led her past the men. It seemed to be more than Rachel could bear. She stared at the detective in charge of the case for these many years, and something inside her seemed to snap.

"Did that man kill my daughter? Did he? Did he?" Rachel screamed at Williams.

Williams's face remained expressionless, as if he were trying to remain respectful, as if he'd encountered such grief-filled rage before. "We're doing everything we can, Mrs. Green."

"He's sitting there on Canal Street having *lunch* while my baby freezes in her cold grave!" Rachel yelled.

Claire and her father did their best to calm her down, but it was no use. Years of repressed anger seemed to have finally reached the surface.

"I won't go home!" Rachel sobbed. "I want to know if that man killed my daughter and I want to know what you're going to do about it, detective."

"We're going to collect evidence, ma'am, and we're going to do our damnedest to put him in jail."

"That's right, Mother," Claire cajoled, "so let Detective Williams do his job and let's go home. You really look like you need some rest."

"I can never rest," Rachel wept, burying her head in Heze's chest, "not now. Not yet."

"Let's go home, Mom," Claire whispered.

"I can't. I can't." Rachel stared at her through reddened eyes. The pain in her expression was raw and naked. She stared at her daughter's face, but she saw Zoe. Only Zoe.

Claire turned away. She shoved aside the thought, but it came back and flailed her. Her mother's look was why she had moved to New York. That terrible look. That silent erasure of Claire. It left her with only guilt and doubt. She would wonder forever if her mother would have seen her face in Zoe had she been the one killed.

"I think I'd better get her home," her father said.

Claire nodded, fighting back a wellspring of tears. She took it the best she could with the audience of detectives and men from the coroner's office. Zoe had died and now a part of herself had gone with her because hers was the face she feared her parents could no longer look at.

"Go on back to your place, sweetheart, and I'll call you when she's better," Heze said, his face pained and apologetic.

Claire nodded obediently. Her parents staggered away along Joseph Street as Heze did his best to support his hysterically weeping wife.

The coroner's wagon pulled out of the cemetery and Williams had walked back to his car. There was only Jameson left.

She glanced at him, not wanting him to see her wounded expression.

"It must be hell, girl." The word hung in the cold air.

The tears began to thaw. "I'll live," she whispered, fishing out her car keys from her coat pocket.

"Let me drive you home. You don't look much better than your mother right now." He gently took the keys from her gloved hand.

She got into the BMW and let him shift into gear. Soon they were on Prytania.

They didn't speak much. She was almost used to the silences by now, but this one was different. It was hopelessness. An entrenched blackness. It was the feeling that with her twin gone, nothing would ever be right again.

He pulled into the mansion's parking lot. She got out of the car. All she wanted was a bath, a drink, and time alone, where she could sort out what needed to be done next.

He took her hand.

She turned around on the path and looked at him.

"They should see you as I do," he said.

"And what do you see, Jameson, other than a confused, bewildered victim."

He pulled her closer to him. "I see a woman of determination and courage. I see a woman who wants to save the world."

". . . And might not even be able to save herself." She pulled away. Tears burned her eyes. There was too much to think about, too much to sort out. Between Zoe, ZOE, Shakita, and Laborde, she felt as if her universe had exploded.

"You can save yourself, Claire. Just do what I tell you."

She laughed through her tears. "Do you hear yourself?"

"It's no longer a man-woman thing, Claire. You're not trained to handle this. You're a lawyer, not a policeman."

She thought about Laborde lurking on the Internet; she thought of the hit man lurking in the city, waiting for his chance to off his victim. "Did you see her big toe?" she asked him. "She had one of those tags on it like you see on TV shows. Zoe had one of those tags, just looped right onto her big toe, as if she were something for sale at Wal-Mart." She began to cry again, this time in earnest. "What was that girl, sixteen? Seventeen? She didn't have a chance. Someone should have warned her. Now she's lying in that locker, ticket on her toe, all signed, sealed, and just needing to be delivered to her grieving family." It became too much for her. She half walked, half ran to the mansion and entered the front door. She ran up the stairs, but he caught her.

"It's not your fault Shakita Jourdan's dead. And it's not your fault that you look like Zoe."

She wept. "What do you know, Jameson? What do you know about anything?"

He took her in his arms and crushed her against his chest. She sobbed violently, her words coming out in short gasps. "This shouldn't—have happened. I—I can do something. I can—I can—"

"It's my job, sweetheart. It's mine. You've got to let me do it."

"I—can do something."

"I know. But don't." He took her face in his large hands and he studied it for a moment, as if willing an agreement from her. Then he bent and kissed her, and the taste of him was like food to her affection-starved soul. She opened up her mouth and begged him to give her more. Then she felt him pause as if he were surprised by her hunger.

"Don't leave me now," she whispered against his chest. With his hard, warm body against hers, the idea of being alone with her thoughts was suddenly terrifying. The best path to take had eluded her so far and probably would forever. It was so much more appealing to shove aside the decision making, to shrug off the terrible weight of responsibility and just give in to her natural-born instincts. Sex would be the balm for all her wounds. She'd been imprisoned for too long, her natural longings stifled by Zoe's crime, by her fear of men, by her worries for the future. But now she was going to break free, like Phyllis had broken free by going underground.

She pulled him by the belt buckle into the condo. They stumbled about in the foyer, kissing and pawing and kissing again. She pressed her tongue deep into his mouth, and he pressed back, but more and more hesitantly, as if he'd been struck by an attack of conscience, as if he weren't sure about her emotional state.

He was a smart one, she thought as she lifted his hand to her shirt and playfully teased him to unbutton it. Her emotional state wasn't too good just then, but she wasn't ready to whack out altogether. She would at least wait until Laborde was taken care of.

"Let's go," she said, looking down at the large male hands she clutched against her breasts.

"You just might regret this one, girl," he said cautiously.

"No. I'm not going to regret anything after this," she answered, a welter of betraying tears coursing down her cheeks. "I'm just going to live my life and do my duty and screw everything else." A dark smile touched her lips and she kissed him again before leading him to the bedroom.

They had sex and they made love.

The sex part was delicious. His touch was like steel and velvet thundering between her thighs. And when he came, he grabbed her hips in his meaty forearm and pressed her to him until she came violently too.

But the making-love part was the part she liked best. As he was taking off her bra, he cupped her breasts in both hands and lifted them to his face. Breathing deeply, he'd groaned, "That smell. God, how I love your smell. No perfume, no nothing, but sweet, honest woman."

"Not honest," she'd said, a distinct bitterness in her voice. Then she'd kissed him and asked, "But would you make conjugal visits in jail, Agent Jameson?"

"No, because you're not going to jail," he'd stated rigidly before he laid her back on the bed, placed himself in her hand, and teased her until she begged for mercy.

## ❧ 29 ❧

They had never found all his bodies; he'd planned it that way. Refraining from leaving behind a trail of bodies was how to not look like a serial killer. But the bodies they had found, he'd planted with a secret irony that only he could understand and be amused by. Like where to dump a Jew—on the German coast, of course. Des Allemands. And where to dump a poor black girl? On St. Charles Avenue, where poor black women cleaned the houses but certainly didn't live in them.

Now the unexpected had happened. For the first time in his history, one of J. Everard Laborde's bodies had finally been disinterred, and he was not pleased.

Laborde put down the copy of the *Times-Picayune* with the headline: *Majorette Murdered. Police Pursue Evidence of Serial Killer.* He scowled at Fred and Hockney who sat across from his desk at the 555.

"This is most distressing," Fred stated, his hand shaking as he sipped his tea from a china cup. "Most distressing. The coincidence is going to kill us. I really think we're going to have to change the victim of the party."

"I love it," said Hockney, the gray-gold mustache twitching. "The publicity's going to bring us a fortune. In fact, I want a raise right now. I might actually be able to fire my latest crook of a contractor and hire another one."

"Latest?" Fred asked.

Laborde frowned. "Gentlemen, this has got to be settled. It is indeed—*ironic* that this girl might have been murdered and that she was actually a majorette like our pretend victim—oh, if only she'd been just run over by the float, why, she'd be forgotten by now and we could have gone ahead with our plans—but such is not the case. So what do we do?"

"I say we stay with it, Everard," Hockney interjected. "Is it our fault the girl got killed? Why should we be inconvenienced?"

"This is about responsibility," Laborde answered. "We can't look like callous fools."

"Yes, that would be bad," Fred chimed in.

"So what should we do?" Laborde demanded.

"We'll have to change it. Reinvent the whole thing," Fred said.

Hockney rolled his eyes. "Oh, when will we find the time?"

Laborde stared at both of them. He'd always taken sexual pleasure in the urge to kill, but he could see just plain old satisfaction in snuffing these two. "I think we'll have to change it. It would be in bad taste to go forward as planned, so call the actors, Hockney, and tell them we're changing the victim's composite for the party Monday night. You give them whatever details you want to to change the girl from a majorette to a whatever—just change her."

"But things might get messed up if we change her composite. The mystery might not fit so tightly," Fred said. "You know how it is when you change things, you can paint yourself into a corner."

"Just change her." Laborde stood.

It was their cue to leave. Fred and Hockney left the office, obviously unhappy with the outcome.

But Laborde didn't care. He was the unhappiest of all. He stared down at the headlines. They were getting close. He'd heard the police had even exhumed a body in the old Jewish graveyard.

Now, who could *that* be? he thought to himself with mirthless irony. It would take them but a few days and they'd see the comparisons. He didn't know how long he had left.

He twisted the front section of the paper in his hands. It was his duty to the 555 Association to avoid capture. Even if the police discovered similarities between the two women, they still would have only circumstantial evidence, no more.

But it didn't feel right. Things were closing in around him. For the first time since they'd played this social game of Clue, Murder Mystery Night was being held without poetry. The victim wouldn't be real, she would be just some cardboard figure Fred and Hockney cut out with their limited imaginations. The finesse was gone. The symmetry, the beauty of it, was dead.

He hated loose ties, and this situation was full of them. He'd changed the pretend victim, so he'd have to change the murderer too. Otherwise, it just wasn't going to look so good.

The idea came to him like a wondrous line from an old Confederate poem. "Furl the banner," it said. What he needed to do was clear his accounts and leave town. But before he did that, he couldn't overlook a unique opportunity. He might be able to make poetry of this after all. If they couldn't do the new murder he'd planned, then maybe they needed to rerun an old one. Redux, that's what the club wanted. A replay. No one ever guessed the obvious, and if the same murder was performed twice, well then . . .

He buzzed his new secretary. The pink-faced young man who looked like he was fresh from Andover rushed to Laborde's desk.

"Can I help you with something, sir?"

"Yes. I want you to send this out. Never mind putting it in the mail, I want you to take it there personally." Everard scrawled something on one of the association's cream-colored cards. He enclosed the note in a matching envelope lined with indigo hand-marbled paper and addressed it by memory.

"Get this out now. I mean it."

The secretary blanched. He took the envelope and nodded, backing out of the office like a plebe.


"They got it. A match with the lipstick. They haven't identified it yet though." Jameson left the phone and sat down on the couch next to Claire. He rubbed her thigh, she stared at him catlike from behind her large mug of hot chocolate.

"So what's next?"

"We'll identify it. The brand will tell us something."

"I hope so."

The buzzer rang long and loud. She looked at the clock. It was four in the afternoon. "Mail's here." She slipped on an old pair of red hightop sneakers and went down to get it.

Jameson watched her go.

After they'd made love, he'd held her for a long time, back to chest, his hand stroking her hair, his voice sleepy. There was a moment when he thought he might never be able to let her go, but the afterglow quickly frosted over. The phone had rung; he'd answered it; the next time he looked, she'd dressed and left the bedroom.

Now she seemed unreachable and maybe it was his fault. Maybe he had that effect on women. They got all hot and bothered, and then, when they were through, they turned back to the cold bitches he first thought they were.

He kicked aside an ottoman. Hell, it was his fault. He was nailing an investigation, nailing her when he was all too aware of his need for professional distance. She was involved with an organization of female victims that had so far taken out two men, and for all he knew, he could be the third. How deep and how far her relationship went with these women he didn't know. Nobody did yet. All he knew was that the organization was named after her sister. So she was damn well into it up to her neck.

His defenses started mounting. One day he might turn

around and find a knife in his back. He was a fool. Yep. She dangled the scent and he went baying after it like an un-neutered bloodhound. What hc should do was leave her to her own devices, but somehow he couldn't tear away. One glance from those hazel eyes and he was off and running again.

Yeah, he was all kinds of a fool.

He looked up when she entered the condo. A part of him wanted to freeze her out the same way she was chilling him, but he saw her face and he knew suddenly why she had such a hold on him. She needed him and she hated it.

"Look," she whispered; her trembling fingers held out a piece of the mail.

He walked to her. Their gazes locked and he felt the thrill of the hunt come over him. And he needed her. The power was like a drug and she was his source.

"Why did he send it?" she asked in a small, frightened voice.

He looked down at the card. It was cream vellum with triple fives embossed in gold on the top. It had only one word written on it.

*Lunch?*

## ❧ 30 ❧

"Tell me about the 555, Dad," Claire asked. She'd called her father and suggested they meet at Audubon Park. There they fed the ducks crusts from their sandwiches. She noticed her father didn't seem to have much appetite either.

"I was never in the 555, I know very little about it." As her father spoke, little white puffs of breath escaped his mouth. It was cold for noon. Even Claire had a hard time believing Mardi Gras was only a week away. Usually the daffodils and azaleas were blooming by now. The sudden frost had killed all the tender flower buds.

"You know more about it than I do, Dad. Who makes up the membership? What do they do there?"

"It's mostly businessmen. They gather there to have a meal and network. I suppose also that the old retired men hang out with their cronies, that sort of thing."

"Any Jews in there?"

He winked at his daughter. "None that would come right out and tell you if they were."

She smiled. It was good to see her father, to know that he could manage to overcome the pain if just for lunch. "So the Jews are in the closet, but not the blacks. They can't hide."

"There are some creoles in the 555, naturally, but somehow I don't think they count. A lot of these lines get blurred over time, you know."

She nodded. "Have you ever had lunch there?"

"Not a chance, but I do know Harry Weil went there once. He said it was like everybody rushing in, trying to get reservations to eat first-class airline food."

"Sure sounds like something I'd want to do."

"And the worst was, you couldn't just make a reservation. And this is a member of the association I'm talking about. There was a hierarchy even inside the association. If you made a reservation, even if you were a member, someone higher up could bump you. Most members low on the totem pole could eat in the dining room only on standby."

"You've got to be kidding? I mean, what is the point of belonging to a club that won't take your own reservation?"

He patted her hand. "You're too much like your dad, Claire. You see the whole world in your view, not just this small southern town. But your mother and Zoe . . . they saw only what's around them, and I don't think either approach is healthy. You and I, sweetheart, get to be too oblivious of our surroundings, and your mother and Zoe get too caught up in the unimportant details."

"Details such as who's in or out of the 555."

Heze nodded.

"I've been invited to have lunch there."

Her father visibly stiffened. "At the 555? But *he's* there."

"He invited me."

His lunch bag dropped to the ground unnoticed. "You're not going to meet him. I won't have it. It's too dangerous."

"I'll be wearing a wire."

"It's too dangerous." Heze's hand began to shake. Claire never noticed how small he looked when he was frightened. "You're my only girl. You can't do this, Claire."

"I'll have five FBI agents monitoring everything. Besides, it's going to be disappointingly innocuous. He knows the authorities suspect him. He won't do anything to incriminate himself in front of the twin of one of his victims."

"I don't like it."

"I knew you wouldn't. I probably shouldn't have told you. But I have to go, Dad. I know very little about this man J. Everard Laborde. I must find out what he has to say to me." She hugged him and returned to feeding the ducks the bread crumbs from her sandwich. "Now tell me more about the hierarchy of that place."

"Harry used to say that careers could be made or broken on whether the president greeted you with either a handshake or a nod."

"You mean Laborde now?"

"Yes. He's the current president. I suppose it still holds true."

"This is hard to believe. I feel like we're talking about another century."

"New Orleans still lives in another century. At least parts of it."

She threw the rest of her bread into the lagoon. The ducks bit one another to get the last crumb. "I suppose I should go. Jameson wants to brief me on a few things. The lunch is tomorrow."

"I don't like it, darling. I don't like him getting familiar with you. It scares me." His voice was thin and unsure.

She looked at him and kissed his cheek good-bye. She hated making him worry, but there was nothing she could do about it. She was meeting Laborde and that was it.

"What are you thinking, girl?"

Claire felt the words almost more than she heard them. Liam nuzzled the downy hair of her neck and whispered them again. It was midnight. Rain was falling. The unusual cold had been swept away by a tropical warm front.

She didn't know why she had fallen into bed with him again. Time and again she told herself to keep him at arm's length, but then something snapped inside her and the want drove her back into his embrace.

Maybe she just sought protection. Maybe her fling with him was nothing more than some kind of liberating self-validation of her femininity. Her sexuality. Maybe she was just trying to be Phyllis and break free of the past.

Or maybe she was really falling in love with him.

Couldn't be. She never imagined herself with his kind. He was country, she was city. He was strong and sure and, shudder, probably even a Republican, while she was petite and cautious and a true-blue Democrat if there ever was one.

But the superficial differences aside, there was still one fundamental flaw to their relationship that neither of them seemed to have found a way around: This was a working holiday for him. He was an agent, and by her side only because his job paid him to put her in jail.

She rolled over and faced him. He seemed less enormous in the dark. Lying by her side, holding her, he made her forget the heavy-muscled arms that could pick her up like a rag doll. Pressed against the warm, placable steel of his chest, she found it easy to overlook that his height towered over her by more than a foot. And when he kissed her long, hard, and tender, he made it easy to put aside the notion that he was like any other man. Capable of violence.

"So quiet," he said. His voice rumbled in his chest, enticing her hand to press it against his torso.

"This is wrong. Sometimes it's all I can think about."

His own hand found her. His thumb caressed her nipple, back and forth in a pensive, half-subconscious motion. In the throes of lovemaking, such a touch would have excited her, but in the calm after the storm, it lulled her into a sense of security. Maybe a false sense.

"You don't show such reluctance beforehand." His words were rough. He hadn't bothered to hide his displeasure.

She placed her cheek against his chest and listened to his

heartbeat. The sound was instinctively reassuring. "I wonder about this case. When it's over, where will we be? Are you just luring me into the bedroom in order to get a confession about ZOE, or do you really care for me? It's going to take some time for me to discover which."

"I care for you."

She looked at him, but in the dark she couldn't read his eyes. "You could be lying."

"Yes, I could be. I myself never take much stock in words."

She placed her cheek back on his chest. "What do you take stock in?"

"Actions."

"Lovemaking is an action."

"Yes."

"But it can be just as meaningless. Men taken women to bed with them all the time that they don't care about."

He said nothing.

She snuggled even closer, as if suddenly chilled. "Why must women be at the mercy of men?"

"Are they?" He grunted a laugh. "I thought it was the other way around."

"No. A woman will allow a man who is twice her weight to press her against the sheets and enter her, and it's all a conscious decision. It's all a matter of trust. We're not dumb animals mating in the forest, we're thinking beings, calculating and recalculating each liaison."

"How does that make women at the mercy of men?"

"Women want love . . . sometimes all they get is violence." She looked up at him in the dark. "I'm frightened, Liam. Frightened about us, frightened about lunch tomorrow. Laborde, I don't understand him. I'm not sure I'm much of a match for him. I don't know if I can pull the whole thing off."

He leaned over and gave her a reassuring peck on the

nose. "You'll do it. If only for Zoe, you'll do it." He wrapped an arm over her buttocks and pulled her on top of him, capturing her. Enigmatically, he added, "Men want love too. Don't lose sight of that. It's the source of all power." Then he was silent, as if he'd said too much.

## ➤ 31 ➤

The wire pack seemed heavy and obvious even though they'd been able to sew it into the collar of her suit jacket. Claire glanced at herself in the large gilt pier mirror in the foyer of the 555 and found that she looked pale and scared, nothing more than a wide-eyed waif staring out from a mass of dark hair. Little Miss Lost. She would never manage. J. Everard Laborde was never going to admit to anything. This was unproductive pain at best.

"Ms. Green? The president is waiting for you." The maître d' nodded for her to follow. She walked through the crowded dining room, conspicuous in the sea of men. Her stomach turned to lead. She still didn't know why he'd asked her there, and the question mark pressed down on her. Terror was ripe in her veins, heightening all her senses.

Laborde sat at the back of the dining room in a secluded alcove that overlooked the lush palms of the courtyard. He stared at her from across the dining room and his gaze was as tangible a force as a tap on the shoulder. She couldn't ignore it.

She walked toward him. He loomed larger with every step. He waited for her at the table draped in crisp white and he was like a king sitting on his throne.

*Off with her head.*

"So good of you to join me, Ms. Green," he said as he

stood up. He watched the maître d' help her into a chair, then he resumed his seat.

"I was surprised to get your note," she said evenly. "I couldn't imagine why you'd want to have lunch with me. I still can't."

"You can't?" He nodded to the sommelier to open the wine. The man made a flourish with the silver-plated corkscrew, handed the cork to Laborde, and when the bottle was approved, poured out two glasses of Merlot, ladies first.

Laborde raised his glass in a pleasant toast. "They just exhumed your sister and you haven't a clue why I would call you here." He smiled and gestured to her glass. "You must try this, Ms. Green. It's from the Zubre Vineyards just across Lake Pontchartrain. They're a minuscule operation and the bottles are hard to come by. Their motto is: For the discriminating New Orleanian." He raised his glass higher and glanced around the dining room, his eyes lit with humor. "And I guess that would be us."

She stared at him, not touching her wine. "Come now, Mr. Laborde, I've heard even Jews have managed to get by in this place."

He chuckled. "As long as they were well connected and proclaimed to be Gentile, I don't doubt you're right."

"Did you murder my sister, Mr. Laborde?"

The question seemed to lay right there on the pristine white tablecloth, soiling it. She half expected Laborde to wet the corner of his napkin and dab at it.

He continued to smile. In his expensive Bond Street custom suit, he looked polished and handsome, and not even the most vulgar question seemed able to ruffle him. "Ms. Green," he said, a strange admiring gleam in his eye, "we haven't even eaten yet."

"I'm really not hungry."

"But you must try our crawfish etouffé. It's the best in the city. And I hope you don't mind, but I ordered for you. Old customs die hard."

"This is nothing but a charade—"

"Is it?" he asked.

"I came to find out about Zoe."

"I can't tell you anything about that." He smiled again. "What do you take me for? An idiot? The police and the FBI have been here questioning me so much, we've decided to give them their own water fountain. I'm sure you agreed to join me only because they recruited you. Where's the wire, by the way? They're doing marvelous things with microelectronics, aren't they?"

She sat in front of him, stunned, already imagining she heard the agents on the other end of the microphone unplug their headphones in despair.

"Ah, here we are," he said when the salad came.

"I guess I can go now. If you don't want to talk, then this is pointless." She ignored her salad and placed her napkin on the table next to it.

"Don't leave, Claire. Just because I know all about you doesn't mean I can't enjoy your company for an hour or two, now, does it?"

"You didn't ask me here to enjoy my company. It's not possible, so what do you want?" Her frustrated voice must have been too loud even for the semiprivate alcove, because several men in the dining room turned their heads to look at her.

"What do I want?" he answered coldly. "I want you to display some manners. If I may remind you, I'm president of this noble organization. I must require that you use some diplomacy."

She gazed over the room crowded with white men in business suits. "How are you going to break the news to this noble organization when they take you away to Angola and fry you, Mr. Laborde?"

"Everard, please."

That Twilight Zone feeling came over her. She was talking to a probable serial killer, and he was treating her like she was Carole Lombard and they'd just sat down for a bite at "21". "Everard," she repeated, the name strange on her lips. "You asked me here for a reason. What is it? I confess, I want to know."

"I told the other Ms. Green to call me Everard—although, if I remember correctly, your sister was not averse to the title *Miss* Green."

"She admired you and your kind, Mr.—*Everard*. I don't think I'll ever understand why."

"Zoe was very pretty, wasn't she? With that thick hair and those gold/brown eyes. As pretty as you." He tapped his knuckles against his cheek as if he were pondering the universe. "Do you date a lot, Claire? I'll bet you have men just swarming around you."

"No," she answered softly, her gut filling with hate. "I'm not very comfortable with most men, and I haven't been ever since Zoe died."

"But you're not afraid of me. Why, you couldn't be. You came here to lunch."

"The worst kind of fear is the fear of the unknown. No, I'm not afraid of you, Everard. I *know* what you are."

"*Touché,* Ms. Green."

"Are there other bodies the police haven't found?"

He looked up from his salad. A speck of blue-cheese dressing dotted his Hermès tie. Two hundred dollars down the drain, she thought. He was being messy and she bet that was very unlike him. Maybe she was getting to him after all.

"You must be a brilliant trial attorney. You certainly like keeping people off balance with your questions."

"So where are the others? In the swamp? In the batture? Buried in the crawl space of your house?"

"You didn't ask about the furnace"—he put down his fork—"or does your kind not like to talk about furnaces anymore?"

A red, boiling anger overtook her. She stared at him and couldn't believe that all night she'd lain awake wondering if at some point during the lunch she should disconnect the wire and warn him about the hit man ZOE had sent. Now it wasn't a possibility. She wasn't going to save this bastard. No way. "You killed my sister, Mr. Laborde. You know it and I know it. And I won't go to my grave until I see you brought to justice."

"Let's see . . ." He put his index finger out as if he were counting. "Angola for me, and the Gates of Prayer for you. I put my money on the Gates of Prayer."

Her cheeks grew hot. The syrup of adrenaline thrummed through her. "Is that a threat, Mr. Laborde?"

He looked at her, surprised. "Good heavens, no. You think I want to go to jail on a threat? You think I want federal agents swarming in here, throwing judicial orders in my face? I utterly deny it was a threat."

She stood unable to take any more. The eyes in the dining room seemed to all turn in unison to them in the alcove. "When you want to make a confession, I'll be glad to return, but until then, you're just using this lunch to toy with me—"

"But you can't leave. You haven't tasted your Zubre yet."

She tamped down the urge to toss the glass of wine in his face. "You know, you really should confess. There are things you don't control, Mr. President of the 555 Association. You might be looking at your own ditch in Des Allemands."

"Are you now threatening me, Claire?"

"I want you to tell the truth." She leaned over the table and stared at him. "You're not the only one with power, Everard."

She grabbed her purse from the table and headed through the dining room.

Laborde stared after her.

\*   \*   \*

"We've defnitely got a match," Williams said as he sipped a paper cup filled with steaming coffee. "The lipstick residues on Zoe Green and Shakita Jourdan were the same formula. Now we're just trying to drum up a manufacturer."

Claire gazed at the lab results. The police were finally showing her things now, but there wasn't much to go on except a list of ingredients that comprised a lipstick formula. On the list were lots of words that started with "para" and "methyl." The chemical analysis had proven the lipsticks were equivalent formulas. The only damning evidence was that the victims wore it five years apart.

"What's he doing on the Internet?" Jameson asked, his cowboy boots crossed over each other as he stretched his legs across Williams's desk.

"Nothing too incriminating. Nazis. Nazis. Nazis. Aparently he loves that shit, but so do a billion other people, or the public television stations in this country would go under."

"My sister was a Jew. Maybe her killing was a hate crime. Right up your alley, Agent Jameson," Claire interjected.

He shook his head. "Not so fast, woman. What turns him on and what he spends his time hating might be one and the same. I don't see evidence of a hate crime. I see a sociopath."

She put aside the lab report. "I suppose it doesn't make any difference, as long as they catch him."

"No, it makes all the difference." Jameson stared at her beneath heavy eyelids. "It's the why that's going to trip him up. If he hates Jews, then a good Jew is a dead Jew, and any Jew will accomplish that for him." He sat up and looked her straight in the eye. "But on the tape of you and him at lunch, he didn't sound like you were just any old Jew to him. No, he was completely focused on you. You were special. You've caught his interest. He's thinking about you and only you."

"Jesus, I hate this serial-killer shit. It just freaks me out." Williams crumpled his cup and threw it in the overflowing waste can.

"So why has he killed a Jew and a black? He sure as hell doesn't socialize with that set." It sure freaked her out too.

"Because maybe blacks and Jews are forbidden to him. He probably had some kind of anal-retentive father who was part Robert Young and part Himmler. His mother, say that she was passive-aggressive. You have a classic recipe for a real psycho."

"We still haven't got anything that ties him to both murders except slim circumstantial stuff. The wire was of no real use," she said.

"If we wait, he'll come after you. We can't wait."

She stared at Jameson.

Even Williams shook his head in disbelief. "How do you know this shit, Jameson? You're even scaring me."

Liam returned Claire's stare. "Because she challenged him. And because I think he had a big thing for her sister. A real big thing. How many of us turn down second chances?"

"So what are you saying, man?" Williams interjected. "Everard Laborde wants to forget the divorce and he'll behave better this time? Is he going to change for Claire and just ask her out for a date and forget the murder shit?"

Even Claire wanted to laugh. "What is it you're trying to say, Liam? It's all sounding pretty strange to me too."

"I'm saying," he enunciated every syllable, "that if you want to know what he did to Zoe and why, we need to understand who he is. He wants to do you just like your sister."

In the back of her subconscious, she supposed she already knew it was true. She lifted her hand to her lips and touched them, her finger following every curve. Fear froze her insides. "I still can't believe he'd risk it. It would be so obvious."

"People love to overlook the obvious," he said. "My first case was a bank robbery, and you know what one of the witnesses said during his interview? He said, 'I saw the man come out of the bank and get into his car, and then I asked myself, *Gee, why is that man wearing a mask?'* Honest to God's truth. I couldn't make it up. He said that in all seriousness."

"Okay, so it's true. Maybe he is focused on me. Then we should use his attention to trap him. What will I need to do?" she asked quietly.

Williams rubbed his jaw. "You know, if you're right, Jameson, it would be foolish not to try to use her."

"Out of the question. I'm not baiting him. I've seen that go wrong before. I want her to stay as far away from him as she can."

Even she saw the flaw in his argument. "You let me have lunch with him."

"That was a public place and you were wired. You can't live like that on the chance that you might keep seeing him."

"But if what you're saying is accurate, Liam, it's more dangerous to leave him out there when we know he's focused on me." Claire looked at him.

Liam clenched his jaw. "Forget it, Claire. I'm the man with the experience, remember? It's my job to make judgment calls like this one, and I say it's too dangerous. You don't tempt creatures like Laborde, and one reason is that it's too hard to catch these guys and pin the evidence on them—it's only after the bodies pile up that you even have a chance at it, and I don't want you in the pile." He took his feet off Williams's desk. "End of discussion. Now let's go get some dinner."

"I need to be a part of this. It was my sister who was killed."

"Forget it, girl. Just put it out of your mind. A lunch with him is one thing, baiting him, drawing him out into the open, is a whole lot riskier, and you're not going to be the one to do it."

"I either need to help capture him, or—or I might just see to it you don't need to capture him."

Both Jameson and Williams looked at her.

"What's she mean by that?" Williams asked.

Liam's mouth twisted in a sardonic grin. His gaze locked with hers in understanding. "I think I sure as hell know."

"Maybe we should discuss my role in capturing Laborde at dinner. You know, Liam, I've discovered you've got quite a temper when you're hungry." She smiled.

Disapproval darkened his eyes. "Fine. Let's you and me have dinner and a long chat."

She glanced at Williams, then back to Jameson. "I really want to participate in this. It's important to me to do something about Laborde."

"One way or the other, eh?" Jameson leaned over and said, "At dinner I want you to tell me what's going on and I want it all."

Williams looked hopelessly confused. "I think I'll just leave you two to decode your own conversations. In the meantime, I've got to get down to the lab and see if they've identified the make of that lipstick yet."

The detective left. Jameson just gave Claire that good-ol'-boy, heavy-lidded perusal. "Let's go to dinner. We've got a lot to talk about."

She thought about the man that Phyllis said was out there, lying in wait for Laborde, and wondered if her judgment had been too colored by cynicism. Her lack of action in the matter might be decisive; she might have already crossed over the line, because she knew nothing about when and where the hit man might act. The doubts all came back.

But now, for the first time, she actually found some hope. She would be involved in getting Laborde. She could help Jameson. She could *do* something. And it would be legal.

Her spirits lifted. "I think I might have some ideas on how to trap him. We could play up the Jewish thing, you know, fan his interests—"

"His interests are sadism and death. How do you propose fanning that without getting into a bit of a jam?"

She paused. It might be fun playing Nancy Drew, but she had to remember who the villain was. This was not fiction.

"I'll manage," she said.

After all, she had Zoe to remind her.


The Super Bowl Motor Court was a skeevy little dive on Airline Highway that hadn't seen a decent motorist drive through its arch since 1967. Prostitutes were the main customer now, with a little garbage from the Greyhound station mixed in.

Lenny Magda was staring at such garbage now. The guy who stood in front of the registration desk had enough crude, homemade prison tattoos to win a *Cape Fear* contest. But he sure lacked Robert De Niro's looks. His lank, colorless hair was bound into a ponytail. He sported a motorcycle-gang beer belly and greasy Levis. Lenny had seen a lot of creatures in the time he filled in for his father-in-law running the motor court, but this guy was one of the worst. He had a bad case of acne that was still erupting over a cratered face, and the guy's front teeth were missing. Best of all, the man had a trick of wiggling his tongue through the gap in his teeth at every girl in the parking lot who passed by the smeared plate glass window of the office.

He wrote in the registry in large letters: HELL MAN. Then he asked for a room.

"Twenty-four dollars in advance—if you're going to stay the whole night. Otherwise it's fifteen an hour." Lenny felt the back of his neck prickle when the guy stared at him.

"I'll be here tonight and maybe the next and maybe the next after that."

"You can pay as you go." Lenny handed him a key.

"How do I get downtown?"

"You going to the Quarter?"

"No. I'm here doing business for a lawyer." Hell Man

smiled. Lenny waited for him to wiggle his tongue and he was damn relieved when he didn't.

"You can catch the bus right outside. It'll take you to Canal Street."

"Good. That's exactly where I'm headed. I got a job to do, man. A job."

Hell Man picked up his grungy knapsack, turned, and walked away. There was a bulge in the back waistband of Hell Man's jeans, just slightly visible beneath the black leather jacket. He was carrying.

Lenny didn't want to know.

## ❧ 32 ❧

Selling a hit to Gerry Velmun was like selling rebellion to teenagers. He took his work seriously. He stood in front of 555 Canal Street and ticked off in his mind the things he had to do:

Identify Victim

Learn Victim's Schedule

Erase Victim

It was easy. So what if he had less than two weeks to do it in. So what if he didn't make the hit and couldn't collect the other half of the money.

Wait a minute. He was going to collect the whole thing. All he needed was a body, preferably the body he'd come to get, but any body would do. As long as the bitch who hired him was happy, any body would do.

And if the bitch wasn't happy about her hit? He'd just shut the old bag up good, is what. Just her scratchy old voice on the phone told him she was a complainer. He wasn't going to risk it on a bitch who complained about him taking out the wrong man.

He looked down at a grimy piece of paper in his hand: *555 Canal* was written on one side with the name J. Everard Laborde.

On the other side was the name and address of the woman

he talked to on the phone. The woman who hired him. Claire Green. Maison Robert. Prytania Street.

Message board on the Internet:

HUNGRY. WILL KILL FOR FOOD.

REX

Detective Williams perused the computer screen with Johnnie Robbins, the FBI agent sent in from Quantico. The agent was frantically clicking the mouse.

"You're the computer nerd. So where is he? The phone company says he's hooked up to Denmark as we speak."

"We think he likes to post messages on this board." Johnnie, a grungy, generation-X type, clicked the mouse. "See this one? Pretty bad, huh? We're calling it the Cybersadism Club. The messages are really hairy. Body parts. That kind of thing."

Williams swallowed. "Okay. Denmark?"

"We have a line on him going to the University of Copenhagen, and at the university we have proof that someone there is going to this message board. We just need to clamp a name on him."

"What name do you go by on these things?" Williams stared at the screen.

"You can go by any name. There's little if any accountability. The point is to hook up with him and get him playing so that he reveals himself."

Williams rolled his eyes. "This is a needle in a haystack. Do you have any idea who he might be?"

Johnnie looked down at a stack of papers next to the computer. "I have all the material we could get on the guy. What he likes, what he does. The names usually tie in with something. I had a girlfriend once who really liked to bash men.

On the bulletin board she used to sign her name *The Black Dahlia.* If you think about it, it kind of fits."

"All right. I don't know if this is going to amount to much, but keep at it. We'll let you know whenever he calls Denmark."

Johnnie Robbins nodded.


Liam watched her walk across the room. She wore nothing but a long, oversized cotton sweater and socks. He supposed if she were his daughter, he'd find her cute.

But she was not his daughter. She was a woman pushing thirty who was driving him crazy. The baggy socks didn't hide the shapeliness of her calf muscle, and the ribs of the thick sweater molded over her breasts, making unexpected curves and light and shadow on the flat landscape. He found he could stare at that loose sweater on her all day. She was causing havoc to his hormones.

And she was driving him crazy. She still had this notion she was going to bait Laborde, and he didn't know how to explain it any better that she was not going to do it. It was dangerous. She might be killed. He couldn't even think about it. He was even beginning to wonder how he was going to go back to Tulsa without her.

"Coffee?" She held out a steaming mug. He took it and stared after her, that loose, impossible sweater causing his hands to itch.

"I was thinking. We need to go over a list of the 555 members." She curled up next to him and sipped her coffee, the expression in her eyes different from before. There was a light in her face he'd never seen. It was hope. She thought she was really going to help this time, but he wasn't going to let her. No way. He preferred guilt over grief.

"We already have a list of the members."

"You do?" Her eyes widened. "Let me see it. I probably know some of them. We can ask them if they've noticed anything strange about Laborde."

He snorted. "How do you do that with a group of men all stuck together with the same glue? It's like interviewing all the Klan members to see if they'll narc on the one who's bought the most white sheets."

Her gaze fixed on him. "Why do I get the feeling you don't think much of my ideas?"

"I think a lot of your ideas, Claire. For someone who's totally untrained in collecting criminal evidence, you're fuckin' brilliant. It's just that I want you to stay out of this." He set the coffee mug on his stomach and leaned back on the couch.

The sex was great. It was by far the best he'd ever had. They argued all night and then made love until dawn. Five hours on a bronc would be nothing compared with eight seconds in the sack with her. Truly, he felt great. Relaxed and content. He would have reached a state of nirvana by now if not for the annoying fly that was buzzing around his head, wanting to horn in on his case.

"Maybe I should show you some pictures. Maybe that would take away some of this infernal enthusiasm. You want to see sawed-off legs and half-eaten skulls and—"

She held up her hand. "I want to help. I've *got* to help."

He took her hand and laid it against his chest. He even leaned over and kissed it. "Sweetheart. I know you feel that somehow this perfect circle of justice will emerge if you're the one to help catch Everard Laborde, but it isn't going to happen that way. I'm not going to send you out there just to find out you've disappeared."

"I've got to do something." The eyes that so captured him seemed to be covered by a cloud. "One way or the other."

"Sometimes you just have to live with the frustration."

"What do you know of it, Jameson? If you don't solve a case, what's it to you? It wasn't your sister or daughter who died."

"I know about the guilt. I've lived with it. There are faces out there that I can still see when I close my eyes." He did his best to control his anger. "But what can be done about it? I'm not God."

"It's almost shocking how happily you shrug off this mantle of heroism, Liam. Sometimes I think you're almost as cold-blooded as—well, as some of *them.*"

His anger blew. Through a clenched jaw he said, "You don't know what the hell you're saying, girl. You think because I know my limitations I'm some kind of villain?"

"Heroes don't let their limitations stop them." Her expression held reproof.

"Great. And then heroes who do what I do end up dead." He glared at her. "Or worse, they get other people killed."

"It wouldn't be your fault if something happened to me. It would be mine. I make this decision fully aware of the dangers."

"How can you read the future? How can you know what he's going to do? He's out there, you know, drifting, waiting. He's a creature of opportunity. You don't give a beast like that opportunity."

"It wouldn't be your fault," she repeated.

"It would be my fault," he snapped. "Just like it was my fault with Joey. It was me who called the paper, you know. I told them about Joey. It was me who found the spotlight for him, it was me who made him a hero. I called the paper, dammit. *I* called them."

She met his gaze. She clearly knew he was saying something, finally revealing something. He wanted to shove the words right back in his mouth.

Her voice was barely above a whisper. "Was he the kid in Taylorville, Liam?"

He just stared at her. They'd spent so much time together and they were getting so close that he thought he'd already told her about Joey. But he hadn't. Now he didn't want to begin.

"All I'm saying is that in my professional opinion, to go out there baiting this man is crazy. You've got to let me do my job."

"I'm afraid of your job, Liam." Her face looked as sad and beaten as he'd ever seen it. "Let the police handle things and everything gets complicated and bureaucratic. The justice gets thrown out with the bathwater."

"What do you want? A miracle? Do you want me to breathe life back into your sister? I'm an FBI agent. I'm all you've got, Claire. You've got to believe in me."

"I don't believe in heroes." She got up from the couch.

He watched her. "What's going through that head of yours?" he asked softly, ominously.

She didn't look at him. "I don't need ZOE and I don't need you. I'm going to slay this one on my own."

"You don't know how to begin."

"I've got his attention. That's a beginning."

He stood and put his arms around her. She was so small, so feisty, so smart. The thought of losing her sickened him. The world needed Claire Green in it. He needed Claire Green in it. "I'm not going to be a nice guy about this, girl. Nice guys finish last. You should have seen my father. I'll throw you in jail to keep you out of this and then you can just hate my guts."

She wouldn't look at him. "I don't need a man to slay dragons. Just remember I said that when we get to the court-room."


Message board on the Internet:

SHE WAS A CHILD AND I WAS A CHILD IN
THIS KINGDOM BY THE SEA.

REX

Johnnie Robbins stared at the message, then shuffled through the papers on the desk. He perused them, searching for something. In the back of his mind there was something clicking, and it was driving him nuts trying to find out what it was.

He found it. It was an old résumé from the files of the 555 Association. J. Everard Laborde's sole qualification for running the place seemed hinged on one accomplishment.

He had been Rex.

Johnnie's fingers flew across the keyboard. He typed his message, then sat back in his chair and waited. Maybe it was a blind alley, but it was the best he'd done all day. He stared at his words and kept his fingers crossed.

Message board on the Internet:

WILL KILL—WHAT MAKES YOU KING?
YOUR EVER-FAITHFUL SUBJECT

## ❧ 33 ❧

"**D**ad, where's that old handgun? You know, the one inherited from Uncle Jimmy? I'm kind of thinking about taking shooting lessons." Claire looked up from her salad. Her father sat across the table from her, not really eating either.

"Why are you going to take shooting lessons? Why should you have to protect yourself, when we pay taxes? What's that policeman doing for us anyway?"

"He's FBI, Dad. He's not a policeman."

"Policeman, FBI, they're all the same—none of them doing their jobs. They dug up Zoe and that man is still walking around—"

"He'll be taken care of, Dad, I promise you." She picked at a piece of bread. Even her old reliable dad seemed to be losing it under the strain. "Do you think maybe when I drop you home you could bring out the gun? I don't want to disturb Mom."

"Guns? What's this world coming to that my daughter needs a gun."

"I don't need a gun, but I thought it might do me more good than you. It's just sitting in a drawer anyway, isn't it?"

Heze sighed. "Yes, just sitting in a drawer, like your sister. Why haven't they gotten back to us on the exhumation? What are they hiding?"

She leaned over and put her hand on his. "Dad, now,

don't get paranoid. They're not hiding anything. The bureaucracy moves slowly."

"I need Zoe at rest."

"Zoe doesn't need rest anymore. But you and me, well, we're still human, and you look like you could use some. Has Mom been difficult?"

"Oh, your mother. This has destroyed your mother."

Claire was numb as she listened to her father. Maybe it was the resentment, the hurt; she didn't know, but somehow she wanted everyone to snap out of it. They had to try to be a family again. And she was going to make them. Maybe all it would take was getting rid of J. Everard Laborde.

"Dad, I'm going to have to ask you not to speak of this." She looked across the crowded restaurant. Jameson had just excused himself from their table and was now on the pay phone. He'd been beeped five minutes before and he was still hanging on the receiver. "Look, Dad," she said nervously as she watched him hang up the phone and walk back to the table, "when we drop you off, get the gun and put it in a shopping bag. It wouldn't do for the neighbors to see you out front of the house with a .357 Magnum, okay?" And then Jameson won't know what it is either, she thought.

"Fine. Take the blasted thing."

"They think they've cornered him on the Internet. He's saying some pretty weird things. I doubt it'll fry him, but it should bolster our case." Jameson resumed his seat at the table.

Heze and Claire were silent.

"We ready to go?" he asked.

Claire nodded. "We just need to drop Dad off. He's got to get something from the house."

"What is that computer business going to tell you?" Heze asked Jameson, bitterness in his voice. "You need a confession. How I'd like to go down to that club and get one."

Jameson glanced at Claire. "Look, Mr. Green, as I've told your daughter, we're doing all we can, but we have to be let alone to do our jobs. You wring a confession out of him under duress, and the charges, no matter how heinous they are, will never stick."

Heze stood and pointed to Claire. "Maybe. But this is killing her mother. I hope you understand that."

"Yes, sir. I do. It's killing your daughter too."

Liam looked at her. Claire felt her throat lump up with tears.

*Everything* was killing her, she decided.

Message board on the Internet:

THE MAN WHO WOULD BE KING, IS KING.

Johnnie typed fast:

OEDIPUS REX?

The answer came in seconds.

I SAY TO YOU, FUCK YOU, NOT MY MOTHER.

Claire paced the cramped bathroom of the condo and truly wondered if she had lost her mind. She couldn't fathom what she was going to do with a gun. It was stupid to even have the thing around. Guns went off by accident all the time and killed the person they were supposed to protect. This one was a brute too. It weighed a ton.

She looked at the .357 in her hand. It had a long bore and was about as inconspicuous as a car. The idea of her using it was laughable. Really, she didn't know why she'd gotten it from her father, but once she'd thought of it sitting in the drawer, dusty and unused, she wanted it. She felt safer with it somehow. It might come in handy, but she prayed not.

But now the question was how to hide it from Jameson.

She peered underneath the sink into a stack of peach-colored towels. Too obvious. The medicine cabinet. No, it'd probably fall out when she went to get the toothpaste and accidentally kill her.

The laundry hamper. That was better. He'd never look there. And if she put a stack of towels down on top of it, the gun wouldn't get jostled.

"Are you all right? You've been in there a long time. What is it, little woman, that time of the month? The curse?" From outside the door, she could hear him knock.

"Jameson, my, my, how you test my patience. You think I could use PMS as a defense?" She stuffed the gun down the hamper.

"You could damn well try."

"Your sexism is showing, Liam." She flushed and turned on the water, pretending to wash her hands.

"Barefoot and pregnant, yeah, now, that's how I like 'em."

She opened the bathroom door. "I didn't tell you?"

He gave her a double take. She swore he blanched.

"Very funny, Green. Very funny."


Message board on the Internet:
Johnnie typed,

> NOT OEDIPUS REX?
> YOS (YOUR OBEDIENT SERVANT)

The answer came immediately.

> NOT OEDIPUS REX, FOOL.
> TYRANNOSAURUS REX.


The 555 was all decked out for a party. Mardi Gras was only three nights away and the city was in a frenzy of parades and balls and drunkenness. Even the lawyers couldn't get to their offices downtown.

Lundi Gras, the date of the 555 Murder Mystery Night, was the day before Mardi Gras. No one knew how to prolong a good time like the Catholics. Laborde almost wished he were a better one so that he could sin a little more for all the time he spent in penance.

But then, maybe he'd sinned enough.

He strolled past a mountain of small black cardboard coffins. Clues were packed inside them and they were to be handed out at the door, an amusing little token for the female guests. The coffins were tied with chic French ribbon printed with gold Stars of David. Obviously, the victim was going to be a Jew.

"Everard, things are certainly going well, aren't they?" Hockney put his hands in his chinos. The gold-gray mustache twitched.

"Yes, I do believe this will be the best mystery we've put on yet. And who would have thought it, knowing that we had to change plans so last-minute."

"The actors who reenact the murder for the partygoers are getting restless. They want to know who kills her. The guests can't guess the murderer if even the actors don't know. You know how it is, they need motivation and all that stuff."

"That will definitely not come out until the party itself, so you can just tell the actors to improvise."

"Do you even know who you're going to pick to murder the Jewess?"

"I've an idea," Everard said. His mouth turned in an ironic smile.

Hockney surveyed the pile of little black coffins. "This one's your triumph, Everard, isn't it?"

"Indeed."

"Your triumph," Hockney repeated as two young men stacked another row of the glossy black party favors.

## ❧ 34 ❧

"God, I wish I had."
—*Edmund Kemper*
(*his comment after he murdered his mother when she ridiculed him by saying, "I suppose now you'll want to stay up all night and talk."*)

"**Z**OE's gone underground. The group's going to be damn hard to infiltrate now. I need you to get names. You've got to get names." Gunnarson paused on the phone. Liam could hear someone talk to him in the background.

"Did you hear that?" Gunnarson asked. "That was Wynn. She said they've tied Phyllis Zuckermann to a hit man. An assassin. I've got the details here. I'll send them right down."

"Good."

"Where are the names of the women in this group, Jameson? We've got to talk to them. Darby won't say a word and Zuckermann's gone."

Jameson frowned. "I'm working on it." In a voice that was almost a growl he said, "I'll get them."

"I've put Wynn on the case full-time now. She's a woman; I'm hoping she might put some feelers out and find where this group's gone."

"It's not the KKK, you know. They might not want any new recruits."

"If anyone can do it, Wynn can."

"True."

"Get me those names, Jameson." Another pause. "Hey, and listen, I hate to tell you this, but we've traced the hit man to New Orleans. He's down there with you folks."

Liam didn't know what to say. He clenched his jaw so hard, he thought it might crack. "Great."

"Be careful."

"Yeah." He hung up the receiver.

"What was that about? Who doesn't want any new recruits?" Claire asked, looking up from her briefcase.

He rubbed his jaw. An evasive maneuver. His gut was twisted like wet laundry. "We need to talk."

"About what?" she asked warily.

"About the same old thing." He walked over to her and placed her face in his hands. Her skin was chinalike, pale and translucent. Her delicate face made the perfect form for heartbreak-beautiful eyes. "We've come to the end of the rope."

She pressed her cheek against his hand. "Is it ZOE?"

"You've gotten a hit man down here, haven't you?"

Her face seemed to lose all color. She stared at him as if she were desperate for him to believe her. "No. I didn't. Really. It was out of my control. Phyllis sent him down here. She told me I was taken care of and then she left the country. I had no way to call off the attack dog." She hesitated, gave him a furtive look, and said, "Is Laborde dead, then?"

He sat down slowly, as if he were a very old man. "No. But if the guy takes out Laborde, it's murder one for you. Without being able to trace this group ZOE or tie the assassin to Phyllis Zuckermann, you've got the only motivation."

"He hasn't found Laborde yet. He might never be able to do it."

His anger mounted. "You think we can just sit around here and put our heads in the sand and hope he doesn't try anything?" He kicked the chair next to her. The legs screeched on the old wooden floor. "Shit. I'm going out to find this guy and make him give it up." He paced the room, a wild anger in his eyes. "Can you just fuckin' believe the position you've put me in? Why the hell didn't you tell me about this. Now it's like trying to stop Oswald from taking out Bundy."

"You don't have to do it. You don't have to," she implored. Her voice fell to a whisper. "I'm not asking you to do it."

"I have to do it." The words were gravel in his throat.

"Why?" She locked stares with him.

"Because I'm not going to have them take you away. Not now. I've got too much invested in this. I've already risked too much." He pulled her to her feet. She seemed hesitant to touch him, as if he were some kind of bomb ready to explode.

"I've got it figured out, Liam. I'm going to get a confession out of Laborde. I think I can do it."

He ran his hands through her hair. It was knotted, just hanks of thick, lustrous brown.

He tipped her head back. She looked at him. Her pale face. Her large eyes. That glimmer of fear because he was bigger. Because he was a man and his anger made her vulnerable.

"You know what you need, girl?" he whispered, his hands luxuriating in her hair.

She shook her head. Her lips trembled.

"You need to trust someone. You need to trust *me*. Do you trust me?"

"I want to," she whispered.

"That's not a yes." He bent closer. Scrutinizing.

"I want to," she repeated before he kissed her.

\* \* \*

Message board on the Internet:

REX, HOW MANY HAVE YOU DONE?

Answer:

ELEVEN.
BY TOMORROW.

"Do you know what a trophy is?" Liam lay in the dark with Claire. The ugliness was back. No matter how hard he worked to get away from it, it was like surf on the beach, just coming and coming and coming. He could even make love and lose himself in the soft pleasure of her, but in the aftermath the stuff came back. The previous cases. The terrible pictures in his mind.

"What's a trophy?" Her voice was sleepy but not relaxed. Neither of them sounded as if they were. There was too much pain.

"These guys, they like to take a trophy from their kill. That's why Dahmer had all those parts in his place. He could have gotten rid of them. A lot he did get rid of, but he kept what he kept because that was his trophy. His memento of what he'd done."

"Why do we have to talk about this?"

"Because"—his arm tightened around her—"you can bet he has a trophy room. Laborde lives in that big mansion and he's got one all right. And he goes in there and views his collection and masturbates all over it."

"God."

He heard her breathing. He wondered if she was thinking of her sister and remembering what they didn't find in the body.

"I don't want to see anything of yours in his trophy room,

Claire. I want you to promise me that you'll let me take you to your parents while I'm gone. I've got to put a tail on the guy Gunnarson told me about, and I can't do it from here on the phone."

"I'll be fine. Please don't worry about me. Go ahead and find this guy." Her own voice was desperate. "You've got to believe me, Liam, I never ordered the hit. I never crossed over that line. I swear I didn't."

"I don't know what to believe, and I don't even care anymore. All I know is that I'm not willing to lose you."

She was quiet for a long time. "Do your job. It's important."

"It's going to be a bitch to find him. The revelers are packed downtown. Williams said they could hardly get into the Quarter except with an ambulance."

"Tomorrow's Monday," she said softly, holding on to him tightly. "Lundi Gras."

"You've got to promise me, girl. You'll stay put at your parents until this thing has either resolved itself or I can get back to you."

"What if it never resolves itself? What then? Will you hold me prisoner here forever?"

"I don't know. I can't think about the future. Not when everything is blowing up in my face." He rolled her on top of him. "I don't know how this has happened, maybe it's all my fault, but I can't just let you be taken from me. You stay on my mind, Claire. You're inside my head until you drive me crazy. Call it hormones, call it primeval instinct, I don't care. All I know is that I wish I could stay like this with you, protect you forever, but I can't, because the whole fuckin' world has gone nuts."

Her hands balled into fists. She seemed to be defiant and yet hiding herself in the warmth of his chest all at the same time. "This *must* be resolved. This must be," she repeated.

Then she fell silent as if the weight of her thoughts had made her mute.


Message board on the Internet:

> PARTS?
> I LIKE PREFER THEM WHOLE.
> NAMES?
> CLAIRE. CLAIRE. EVERYWHERE.

## ❧ 35 ❧

Velmun watched the parade move along Canal Street. There were grandstands erected all down Canal, but the most elaborate was the one in front of the 555. He'd already made himself at home across the street at 556.

A drunken jester bumped into him, but he didn't notice anything until a man dressed in drag-queen glitter rubbed up against him. She was swinging herself around the lamppost just like in the postcards of Bourbon Street, but she sure as shit was no woman. It was the gobs of navy eye shadow. He'd never met a real woman, not even a whore, who wore navy eye shadow.

"Get outta here, you faggot," he yelled to her in the thick crowds. Taking his hands from his pockets, he pretended he held an AK-47 and shot it right at her head. "The next time you get near me, it'll be real."

The queen slunk through the crowds, the only thing wounded was her expression.

A unified cry ran through the crowd. The floats had stopped in front of the 555 as tradition dictated, and the men and women in the grandstand were being pelted with beads. Pedestrians on the sidewalk were having to make do with the leavings.

The krewe was named Odessa. Its king stopped at the 555

grandstand and toasted someone. Maybe the mayor, Velmun thought.

"Nice tattoo." A mounted police officer on a bay horse paused at the corner where Velmun stood. "I haven't seen art like that since I did duty at Angola."

Velmun glanced up at the black police officer. He was looking down at his forearm. The words Hell Man were tattooed there in fiery blood-red ink.

"You from around here?"

"Why you asking me all these questions?" Velmun wanted to add the word "nigger" to his sentence, but then thought better of it. He wasn't stupid.

"Just being friendly." The police officer saw another mounted cop in the crowd. He nodded to him, then turned his eyes back to Velmun.

But Velmun was gone, lost in the wall-to-wall crowd. Never to return.


"The guy was spotted about an hour ago on the corner of Canal and Bourbon. He had the tattoo that was sent in the fax. He wasn't doing anything but watching the parade, but he was just opposite Laborde's grandstand," Williams said as he shoved the printout toward Jameson.

Jameson scanned it. "He could be anywhere now. Have they got the warrant to search his hotel room?"

"It's coming in now." Williams looked up. A uniformed officer stood in the doorway. "You got it?"

"Got it," the uniform confirmed.

"Let's go." Williams grabbed his suit jacket.

Liam took his feet off the desk.

The trip to Airline Highway was jammed with parades. The city was wild about them. Krewe floats were in every neighborhood, either running or being lined up to run. They played parade-dodge all the way out to Metairie.

"It's not even Mardi Gras yet," Liam said, shaking his head in disbelief.

Williams put the police light out for the fourth time that trip. "Man, I should have taken the marked car."

They waited until an entire band crossed the street in front of them, then slowly they moved through the jammed traffic.

The Super Bowl Motor Court, in contrast, was a ghost town. No parades ran by it; all the guests had taken up to partying elsewhere. In one lone room a woman was laughing hysterically. Man, Liam thought as he stepped inside the registration booth, she was really trying hard to please. It must be lean times out on Airline Highway.

Williams flashed the warrant to the desk clerk. "We've traced a Gerry Velmun to this place. He left the Greyhound station two nights ago and was last seen here. Is he on the register?"

"You can look at it. Hey, we don't want any trouble." Lenny Magda nervously took out the register. "You know, nobody uses their real names. I'd probably drop dead if anybody did."

"Let's have a look at it anyway." Liam placed a set of descriptions and drawings on the table. "Has this guy been here?"

Lenny glanced at the drawings, particularly the one of the tattoo. "If the guy were here, I'd tell you. You know we don't want any trouble."

"You already said that."

"These kind can be pretty mean, you know. You get under their skin and they come back for a visit."

Liam grinned. "He's here. Scares the shit out of you, don't he?"

"Look, I don't—"

"Yeah, yeah. What room?"

"Thirty-four," Williams interrupted. "Look. The idiot

signed the register after all." He showed him the *Hell Man* scrawled across one line.

Liam nodded to Lenny. "Open up the room. We want a peek inside."

"He's got a mini-arsenal in his motel room. They're waiting for him to return, but he paid through the weekend and if he finds a pickup, he just might stay in the Quarter." Liam paused on the phone receiver. "How are things there? Quiet?"

Claire looked out the window. She could just barely see the corner of Lockstein's Grocery from her parents' front window. Things were quieter than normal in the neighborhood. Everyone was up on St. Charles, taking in the parades. "Everything's fine here. Like a tomb, no pun intended." She stared into the receiver. "Hey, I'm sorry about this. I really am."

"I know. We'll get him."

"But who's going to get Laborde." It was more a statement than a question.

"Get some rest. I'm going to be gone all night on this. I can see it already."

"Sure. Be careful."

"Claire?" He paused. "Maybe you should believe in heroes. Maybe we all should."

"Be careful," she whispered again, her heart heavy.

She hung up the phone and stared out the window. Now she had to either face the moral dilemma or run away from it. She either had to back away from the monster or face him.

She paused. Maybe what she needed to do was take the middle ground. Find the back way in.

"Hey, Dad, do you think old Harry Weil would talk to me about the 555?" Her father sat behind her on the couch, reading the *Picayune*. Rachel was already in bed for the evening. To Claire's bitter amazement, she'd found that her mother was now in the habit of taking sleeping pills to get through the night.

Her dad looked up from the paper. "What's all this about?"

"Maybe I could find out something about the club that would help the police." She bit her lower lip. "You think he's home now if I paid him a visit?"

"Probably. He's past ninety. He sure isn't down in the French Quarter drinking a whiskey."

Claire smiled. "I'll be right back. Just a visit."

"I hate to leave your mother after she's taken one of her pills. Why don't you wait until tomorrow, when I can go with you?"

"I've got to do something. I've just got to. Let me go to Harry Weil's. I'll come right back."

"Claire?" Her father's voice was so sad, he didn't sound like himself at all.

"Yes, Dad?" Claire looked at him.

"Take the gun. Do it for me, will you?"

"Sure, Dad. I love you."


Harry Weil lived on Fontainbleau Drive in a villa built in the twenties. He had an old black housekeeper who looked to be as old as Harry. The gray-haired woman led Claire into the parlor, then went to help Harry with his walker.

"Good to see you, Claire. How's your father?" Harry said when he was seated next to her.

"Iced tea?" The old woman poured some iced tea from the tray she brought.

"Thanks," Claire said when she took the glass. She turned to Harry and said, "Dad's fine—I, ah—well, I'm sorry for the unannounced visit. I hope I haven't inconvenienced you this evening, it's just that Dad thought you might help me with my research. I'm looking into the 555 Association."

"Lawyers. They never leave the office at five." The old man rolled his eyes, but there was a twinkle in them. "So you're either snooping into things that are none of your business, or you're writing a book. Which is it?"

She smiled. "Neither, I'm afraid."

"What do you want to know?"

Taking a deep breath, she said, "I guess I want to know what they think of Jews. You're a Jew. How did you get in?"

Harry Weil looked a little perturbed. "That was way back when, my dear. Good old Jim Crow killed it for us, just killed it."

"What do you mean?"

"There were Jews all along in the 555—and a few not-too-white creoles too—you know, of course, there are a lot of old Jewish families in New Orleans. All through the nineteenth century they were very prominent, very accepted. But the Jim Crow era made it acceptable to cast out the blacks, and with them went the Jews. That's when they started weeding them out of the 555. My father was an old-time member and he got me in, but it was clear by the fifties that we weren't wanted. My father died and I quit going. Good riddance, I say."

"So you're no longer a member." She frowned. This wasn't going to be much help.

"I'm still a member. That's one of the good things about the 555. Once a member, always a member."

She studied the old man. His palsied hand barely grasped the metal tubing of his walker, but he seemed as sharp as always. She went ahead and took her chances. "Do you know anything about the current president?"

"Laborde? I know Everard. Can't say I like him though. He's strange."

"How is he strange? Has he ever made anything of the fact that you're a Jew?"

"Not really. My thoughts on him are that he's a team player. If the association says expel the Jews, he expels the

Jews. If they say love them, he loves them—the hypocrite. But he's still not as bad as his father."

"What was his father like?"

Harry shook his head as if not relishing the memory. "His father was a very prominent surgeon. He *liked* to cut on people, they said. And he was a real racist. He petitioned to have my father thrown out because Weil Furniture sold mostly to black folks. It was okay for Cummings Laborde to be up to his elbows all day in black people's blood and sputum, but let some decent Jew sell them much-needed furniture, and we were getting too close. Come to think of it, maybe Everard's not so bad. Hypocrisy can be a blessed thing."

"J. Everard Laborde likes to appear politically correct. At least initially," she said.

"Beat his wife too."

"I didn't think he was married—"

"Not the son. The father."

"I didn't think society people let those ugly things out."

"How can you hide a bruised face?" Harry shook his head. "She was some kind of a chanteuse, from Las Vegas, I think. Anabel Laborde liked to dress a little bit cheap and she wore way too much makeup, but we always thought that was to hide the bashings. They say he beat her up bad the night Everard was born. The baby came out with a broken leg. That's why he uses a cane, you know."

Claire felt as if she had been punched. The very idea turned her stomach. "How awful," she said in a hush.

"But true. Anabel was stoic. She said she either tripped or fell, but we all believed he was hitting her. You just didn't talk about such things back then, so it was hard to get to the bottom of it."

"He must be a little bit mad with a beginning like that," she murmured.

"Yes, I think that's why I never cottoned to him. He shunned me, but that was always okay with me. There are just some people you get a feeling about, and avoiding them makes sense. But I suppose I never liked the murders either. All in bad taste, in my opinion."

She looked at him as if he'd just grown two heads. Her heart pounding in her chest, she said, "What murders?"

Harry gave her an apologetic grimace. "I shouldn't have even mentioned the word. Sorry, my dear. I think of Zoe often."

"What murders?" she pressed.

He shrugged. "Oh, about ten years ago Everard had the idea of having a murder mystery played out at the fund-raiser. The association had fallen on hard times; they really needed a cash cow, and that was it. He decided it would be fun for people to get all dressed up in black tie and play an elaborately acted out game of Clue. He was right. Apparently the moneys just flowed in. It's the hottest party in town—they always have it on Lundi Gras—but I still think it's in bad taste. I would never participate. That was the death knell, if you pardon the pun, for my membership."

She grew numb. A terrible thought had occurred to her, so terrible she couldn't even put it to words. "Who were the victims? Jews?" she whispered.

He stared at her, his eyes rheumy with old age. "Not Jews that I can recall, but I never participated, you see. However, I think the first pretend victim was black. I think she was a waitress, but maybe that's just my old mind making assumptions—"

"Can you get a profile on all the previous pretend victims?"

He seemed to sense her urgency. "I suppose I could call Jayce O'Reilly. He's still an active member."

"Would you mind? Could you call him now?"

Disturbed, Harry rose to his feet. "His number's in my study. I'll be happy to do it now."

Her nerves stretched to the snapping point, she watched him shuffle into his office. He got on the phone and she was relieved to hear him in the midst of a long conversation. That meant he was getting information. Within minutes her god-awful theory was either going to be laughably wrong or devastatingly right.

"Okay. Here we are." Harry returned, his maid at his side with a fresh pitcher of iced tea. "Here's the list. Ready?"

"Ready," she said, trying to smile.

"The first victim was indeed a waitress. Can you believe I still had that right after all these years?" he said, obviously trying to inject some levity into the moment.

"The next one?" she asked, her eyes not leaving his face.

"Number two was another black woman, but this time she was someone's housekeeper—oh—sorry, Mildred." He gave the old woman a grin as she walked by.

"Number three?"

"A Chinese exchange student from Newcomb."

"Four?"

"A black prostitute."

"Five?" Claire could hardly breathe. The next one. If her calculations were right, it was the next one.

"Five was a man. A black janitor."

"Who was number six?" Her voice was low and desperate.

"A white girl. A—a Jew."

"Oh, God. Oh, God." Claire heard the crash of her iced-tea glass on the wooden floor, but she couldn't even react to it. Mildred came running with a towel. She and Harry just stared at her.

Claire shook so badly, she could barely speak. "He killed Zoe on a whim. So that he could have a party and amuse himself with the details of her murder. Oh, God. He did do it. And now I know why he did it." She put her trembling hands to her face. "Des Allemands. Get it? That's the joke. She was Jewish." She began to cry. "He probably did all those people on that list."

Harry grabbed her hand and encased it in his. "Get her something stronger than tea, Mildred."

"No." Claire stood and walked almost blindly to the door. "I've got to go. I've got do something about this."

"Let me call your father. You shouldn't drive. You're much too upset. Maybe this isn't really true."

She looked at him. Her face must have been as pale as a ghost's, because he seemed to cringe.

"It is true," she said. "The idea even occurred to you at that moment. Do you know, it's been almost ten years since they began that list? That means there are maybe ten murders. Or more."

"No, Claire, no." He grew visibly upset. He looked at the list, and bewilderment cut into his aged features. "Maybe I should have kept up with what was going on over there. Maybe I would have seen the connection. You know, I just loved Zoe. She was such a pistol."

"It's not your fault," she wept, fumbling at the front door handle. "It's nobody's fault but the man who killed her. I've got to go."

The night seemed brutal. Everything outside glared underneath the streetlights: the paint peeling on Harry's front door, the damp grime of the curb, the dust on her BMW. Everything hurt to look at because she viewed it all in a different context. Her whole life was changed because she finally knew without a doubt that Laborde had killed Zoe.

She got behind the wheel of the BMW and started it up. She had to go somewhere—back to the condo, over to Detective Williams's, maybe she could even catch up to Jameson. Her man to slay dragons.

She merged onto Napoleon Avenue, and as if being willed from a force beyond the grave, her hand opened the glove compartment.

There it was, the .357 Magnum. Fate. Destiny. Epiphany.

Her fingers ran along the cold steel. She drove. Going nowhere. Going somewhere. She would know only when she got there.

## ❧ 36 ❧

It was growing dark. Jameson sat out in front of a room at the Super Bowl Motor Court and drank a fake beer. A woman sat next to him. She was tipped back in her rickety lawn chair and dozed as if she were drunk. It was not bad acting for a routine patrol policewoman called at the last minute to fill in.

They were really shorthanded. Any other time, Jameson would have requested a full backup. Now there was just him and her and the room. Williams was taking Lenny's place at the registration desk.

He'd have bet money Velmun wouldn't show. It was the night before Mardi Gras. Dusk had settled early on the city and nighttime was party time in the Big Easy. Even most of the motel's prostitutes had gone for the big bucks downtown. The only people left at the place were a couple of pros with their customers, and a young black woman who was slowly working her way through the rooms, changing all the scummy sheets.

And here he was, hanging out again in the sleaze, just as comfortable as a pig in shit. He looked again at the young maid who was going back and forth from her cleaning cart. She made him think of the Sunset Trailer Park. It was the same here. There were a few people trying to make it, trying to do their jobs, trying to have a little dignity, but most were just dirtbags, like the men and women who used those sheets two to an hour. He was sick of all of them. He didn't want to relate to it anymore. The urge to settle down was growing stronger; he thought it was time to get a desk job. It had finally suited Gunnarson. Hell, he could see settling down, even having a couple of kids.

He looked over to the registration booth and signaled to Williams by putting his hand over his ear as if he were holding a phone. The detective nodded. Williams picked up the phone and dialed, waited several seconds, then looked again across the motor court to Liam and shook his head.

"Damn," Liam whispered under his breath.

"She still hasn't come back?" the policewoman asked.

He clenched his jaw. "Nope." He didn't know what to do. When Claire's dad called the precinct to tell them Claire hadn't come right back from visiting a friend, he was caught. The three of them at the motel were all the law enforcement the city could provide, given it was the night before Carnival.

Now it was either go on a wild-goose chase through New Orleans at the height of Mardi Gras season looking for a girl in a BMW convertible, or stay right where he was and at least try to solve the Velmun problem.

"She can't get into too much trouble. Laborde's head of the 555. That makes him one of the busiest people in New Orleans come Mardi Gras." Officer Kerr gave him an encouraging look, then she glanced down Airline Highway. It was dead empty. The entire world was in downtown New Orleans, drinking and watching a parade. And holding their breath till Tuesday.

"Shit." He stood and shook his head at Williams. The detective left the registration booth.

"What you gonna do, man?" Williams asked.

"I'm leaving. Velmun's either drunk and lying in some gutter on Bourbon Street, or he's scoping out the 555. He ain't here." Liam held out his hand. "Give me your keys, man. I'm going back to the condo. See if she shows there."

The detective fished them out of his jeans pocket. "What should we do? Just wait here?"

"Yeah. Keep up the front. Why not. If he shows, arrest him. I'll think of the charges later."

Williams rolled his eyes.

The policewoman laughed.

Velmun could already see he wasn't going to get his hit. The target was just too insulated. Laborde went from his mansion to his Bentley to his club all without ever being exposed to the street.

He needed a bomb, he thought sarcastically as he kept his eyes on the front door of the 555, ignoring the groups of revelers who were disbanding after the last parade.

If the bitch complained that her target wasn't done, he wouldn't get the rest of the money.

He couldn't shake the anger of it. Already he could hear Claire Green's gravelly voice giving him all his instructions. Ranting on the phone with that ugly New York accent. Threatening him.

He wasn't going to let her get sour and put the finger on him. No, sirree.

If the bag had a car accident he might get a little some thing from the inside of her house and be able to walk away even.

He took one last look at the 555 door, then decided to head to Maison Robert. Claire Green. Yeah, her he could find.

Claire drove along Prytania. She'd passed the condo twice, her mind not focused on where she was going.

She still couldn't fathom the waste. It had been nothing but a game to him. He'd thrown a party and all and sundry had come to it and no one had ever put together the fact that the murder victim was always based on a real person who'd been slain sometime the previous year. No one had ever connected all those dots, but she had, and the picture was horrifying.

Gruesome questions flitted through her thoughts like moths. Had he killed the victim before or after the invitations went out? Harry Weil told her the thing was always held on Lundi Gras. It wouldn't be the bodies that had been found before the party that would condemn him, it would be the ones found after. Zoe's body had been discovered March 15. The Ides of March. She'd never forget the date. It was tattooed on her very soul. And if she remembered correctly, Mardi Gras had come early that year too. Laborde had probably devised the game of killing a Jewish girl, and then thought the heavens were opening up to him when Zoe walked in for her interview.

And he'd dumped her body in Des Allemands. Ever since they'd found Zoe there, she'd never been able to hear the name without shuddering. Now it had a whole new dimension of horror to the sound. It held deliberateness. A grand plan. A final solution.

She pulled into the driveway of the mansion. Every window was dark. All the owners were out having a good time.

Not her, she thought, streaks of face powder on her cheeks where her tears had dried.


He was an eighteenth-century man trapped in a modern world. That was how he always thought of himself. It was the excuse. He didn't belong. The grotesque vulgarities of everyday life were an abomination to his very soul. He didn't appreciate telephones and modern medicine. He'd always thought his destiny was the solitude of a grand plantation house, the civility of face-to-face meetings, the living, breathing cycle of life and death that had now been sanitized to hospitals and before-need funeral plans. His acts should have been accomplished in the gentleness of candlelight. They were only an obscenity because electric lighting was such.

Laborde morosely sat in his office at the 555, clicking his mouse. The Apple sat on his credenza. He hated it. But he needed it.

He didn't want to be alone with his acts. He wanted to share them. It was necessary. Even creatures such as himself needed a group in which they could be themselves.

But they should have held their meetings in secret back rooms of grand southern mansions where the slaves would talk in whispers of what really went on in the master's secluded chambers. He and his kind should have shared their terrifying pleasures face-to-face, using strong words. Instead, they had been reduced to tag lines. To sound bites. They'd become the dark, secluded rest stops on the information highway.

He clicked off, then swung around in his leather chair. Downstairs he could hear strains of chamber music as the quartet began to play in the dining room.

The actors had rehearsed just as he told them to. Murder Mystery Night would go off without a hitch. He'd even left the name of the murderer calligraphed in his own hand on the 555 vellum card stock. The envelope sat on a silver tray downstairs in the foyer. Unopened until midnight, it was one of the exhibits to the murder.

The name inside was elegantly penned. *J. Everard Laborde*. They would ask what his motivation was. Why him, he could almost hear them say. The answer was simple. He'd even written the motivation below the name as was the custom.

*Because he'd done her sister*, he'd wrote. *Because he was an obsessed sociopath.*

They'd love it. One of their own. How amusing. They'd

have never guessed. Then, after the ceremonial opening of the envelope, after they'd read the name and digested the official explanation of motivation, the guests would wander back into the dining room, have another glass of Perrier-Jouët, and mingle with the actors.

It would take a while for them to understand. His risk was that they'd catch on after he did Claire. He had to stay away from her, or his way of life as he knew it would be gone.

But he already knew he wasn't going to stay away. He was at the crossroads, and his compulsion was now the sole driver. His life was art. He was an artist. An artist of death. And she was his masterpiece.

Van Gogh did not shield his gaze from the irises.

The beauty, the symmetry of life, was ragged without her. He had to do it. It was a force that seemed outside his skin, propelling him. He was going to have her even if it was the final peg in his own elegant, satin-lined coffin.

He slid his car keys inside the pocket of his tuxedo trousers. He would greet the guests, then go home. The end of the party had no purpose for him yet. The reading of the envelope had no bite as long as he knew Claire Green was still alive.

Besides, he wanted to be alone. He wanted to sip sherry in his library and think. Maybe he would call her. He wanted to hear her voice almost as badly as he wanted to see her face. One day, he vowed to himself, he would smear himself with her life, and he would wallow in her tight, ever-chilling flesh.

One day soon.

Nobody but crazies and muggers walked in Audubon Park at night. She was one of the crazies, Claire told herself as she pulled the BMW into the empty parking lot and turned off the lights.

She'd tried calling Jameson five times, but it was New Orleans, the night before Mardi Gras. She couldn't even get through to the NOPD on 911. Now she wondered if maybe everything being jammed up wasn't for the best. Inside, she was still unresolved. She hadn't crossed the line. But the park lay before her, and beyond it, Laborde's mansion.

If she crossed the park, she might cross the line.

She hadn't been able to go home. She'd pulled the car into the turnaround drive, then pulled right out again. After that she'd driven to the lakefront. She'd called Jameson, then screamed to herself on the edge of Lake Pontchartrain: why. Why had God allowed a man like Laborde to eat and breathe right along with the rest of them?

She searched not for answers but for serenity. Zoe was dead. She would never be brought back to life, but there had to be meaning to her death. She couldn't have been snuffed out just to throw a party, there had to be something more to it than that.

But the only one who knew was Laborde.

And now she was at the park. Thinking of crossing the line. In the stand of trees beyond, the lights of the mansions along Exposition Boulevard winked through the limbs; the Laborde mansion stood in the midst of them.

She got out of the car. Jameson should have been with her, but maybe it was just as well. Laborde probably wasn't even home. Hey, he had parties to go to.

If he was home, though, she knew he wouldn't talk if Liam was around. She and Laborde already had a special relationship. Zoe bound them inextricably together. She wanted to hear the why right from his lips.

She stared at the mansion in the darkness. The .357 Magnum bulked out the pocket of her jacket. Her fantasy was to ring the front doorbell, point the gun in his face, and watch him beg for mercy. Revenge was not a feminine trait, but neither was rage and aggression, all of which burned in the female heart. The Victorian sentiment of the slavish, dependent woman was something even big-time Jewish lawyers from New York got caught up in, but she wasn't caught in it now.

Now she didn't even need ZOE to extract her revenge. All she needed was the gun and her own hatred.

She walked across the park and through the allée of oaks. Every clack of magnolia leaves blowing in the wind was a mugger, a psycho, someone who might stop her from getting to the mansion. But no one did. The park was empty.

She arrived. In front of her were the marble steps up to the Laborde front door. Only one light burned in the entire mansion.

The walnut and beveled-glass front door had a giant bronze knocker. Like in a dream, she lifted it. The sound echoed like dark laughter. It took a while, but finally she heard someone in the foyer.

She raised the gun.

The locks unfastened; the door opened.

"Good evening, Claire," he whispered like a lover.

She stared him right in the eye. At last, at last, she had him.

## ❧ 37 ❧

Liam pulled Williams's car into the condo's driveway. The place looked deserted. Even Prytania Street was quiet. All the traffic was in gridlock downtown.

Where was she? He cursed and fumbled for the police radio.

"What's the status?" he said.

"No word from a Claire Green, but we're backlogged here. We've had more calls than we can handle," came the staticked reply of the radio operator.

"Shit." He turned off the radio. She panicked him, and confounded him. It was the worst time of year to put out an APB, and even if he could do one, they had a better chance of pulling in Velmun.

Man, he shouldn't have left her alone. It was his fault. He just wanted her to stay where he told her to stay, and he wanted to keep her safe.

He got out of the car and stared at the light traffic on Prytania. He hated thinking about her out there. He'd never felt so helpless in his life. Not even when they'd found Joey. At least then there'd been no warning. Not like now. Doom was coming at him like a freight train, and he couldn't make a move.

A shadow crossed the lawn. From the corner of his eye, he swore he saw a figure steal behind one of the magnolias.

The hair stood out on the back of his neck. He reached behind him and unlocked the safety of his gun. In the shadows of the darkened mansion he crept around to the other side, hoping to surprise whoever was hiding behind the tree.

"Move and I'll kill you," he said, pointing his automatic at the man.

The guy backed into the trunk of the tree. Slowly he raised his hands.

"Who are you? What are you doing here?"

"Hey, I'm just looking for my girlfriend, man. You don't have to point a gun at me."

"What's her name?"

"Claire Green."

Liam stared at the man. His finger ached to release the trigger. "Move over to the streetlight. And move *slowly.*"

The guy slunk over toward the Prytania side of the property. Liam shoved him against a telephone pole, holding him by the scruff of the neck. "Let me see your arms," he rasped.

"Fuck you, man."

"Roll up your sleeves or I'm going to put a hole in your face."

"What are you, a cop?"

"FBI. Roll up your sleeves."

The man shoved up the sleeves of his leather jacket. The words Hell Man caught the streetlight.

"Gerald Velmun, you're under arrest for attempted murder."

"What? Did the bitch confess?"

"You have the right—"

"Shut up, man. I haven't even seen Claire Green. She can't pin nothing on me."

Liam stared at Velmun. If he took Velmun in, Claire would be going with him. He was down there to perform her hit. Even if she denied it, it looked bad. Real bad.

Painfully, he recited the words. "Gerald Velmun, you're

under arrest for attempted murder. You have the right to remain—"

Velmun lunged. He charged Liam's midsection and together both men fell to the ground.

"Don't do this, Velmun. You can't know how much I want to blow your face off," Liam said between gritted teeth.

"I'll blow *your* face off, you fucking cop," Velmun growled, and he tried to twist Liam's arm.

Liam kneed him in the gut. Velmun grunted. He rolled off him.

Panting, Liam got to his feet and trained the automatic at Velmun's head. "You'd better cooperate, or I swear you're gonna be maggot food."

Velmun held his gut and rose to his knees. "Fuck you, cop. Fuck you."

"Get up. I'm taking you in."

"Like hell."

Velmun clasped his fist and swung it right into Liam's groin. Liam hunched over, more shocked by his vulnerability than pain. He couldn't believe he hadn't seen it coming. If he hadn't been so caught up in Claire, his reflexes might have been better.

"Stay back," he growled, still hunched over.

"I'm gonna snuff you, cop. Right alongside that complaining bitch if I ever get my hands on her." Velmun leapt for the gun.

"Stay back!" Liam shouted in pain.

But Velmun kept coming.

"You're dead, you hear me? You're dead!" Liam raised the gun. Velmun lunged for it.

He fired.

"I told you to stay back," Liam whispered when Velmun fell to the ground in a pool of blood.

*    *    *

The red police lights were the only signs of life at the Prytania Street mansion. The coroner's minivan had come and gone, taking Velmun away in a little black bag. Williams arrived and spent most of his time on the police radio.

Numbly, Liam sat on the steps of the mansion and stared at the yellow police tapes that sectioned off the scene of the killing.

"Still no word from her. Her parents are frantic." Williams handed him a cup of coffee.

Liam accepted it absentmindedly. "Has he been on the Internet tonight?"

"Yeah. Earlier. Only one message."

"What was it?"

"Johnnie asked him about his next victim."

"And?"

Williams hesitated. "And Rex replied, 'Hath not a Jew eyes?' "

Liam switched on the light of his hotel room. Velmun's blood had spattered his shirt and jeans. He needed a shower, but all he wanted was Claire. He wanted Claire and where the hell was she?

Williams promised he'd be the first to call if she was found. Liam had wanted to send a squad car to Laborde's house, but with every hour, the city hyped up more downtown. Even Officer Kerr had been taken away to patrol the Quarter. There was nobody to spare for a hunch. It was one of the little-known facts of Mardi Gras. If you wanted to rob a bank, do it in New Orleans during Carnival.

He groaned beneath the scalding water of the shower. He thought of going to the 555, but she wouldn't go there. She wouldn't seek him out, he told himself again and again. Laborde was busy with his social schedule, and Claire Green was leaving him alone. She was no idiot. To go and pay a visit to that one was like asking Ted Bundy to carry your books home from school. She knew she needed to stay away. For two reasons. That she'd be killed, or that she'd kill.

When he got his hands on her, she'd better be thinking straight, because if Laborde hadn't killed her, he just might. He couldn't ever remember being so pissed off.

He grabbed a towel and wrapped it around his hips. His balls still hurt and he was shaky. Velmun had come within a millimeter of making him a eunuch.

Limping over to his wallet, he took out the grimy piece of paper. His battle with being a hero was finally over, and it took a woman to decide it for him. He still didn't know if he'd won or lost. The hero thing still confused him. But the little piece of paper didn't.

He'd gone through Velmun's clothing just to make sure he was unarmed and found the paper. It had Laborde's name and address, and Claire's. It was the link they were looking for to nail ZOE.

To nail Claire.

Man, he must be falling hard, he thought as he walked to the bathroom. Damn hard, he cursed as he ripped the paper into little bits and flushed them down the toilet.

The evidence went like toilet paper. Solemnly he watched it go like a man hearing taps. Staring down at the toilet bowl, he thought long and hard about Claire and his life and his honor. He seemed to have lost his way for a long, long time, but now he saw he'd just been running in circles, chasing his tail. He couldn't have all three—life, honor, and Claire. He had to pick. And he chose Claire. Above all, he wanted Claire.

Even as a child he'd been right. The hero stuff was complicated. Sometimes you did the right thing and nobody noticed. And sometimes you did the wrong thing and saved the world.

*A man to slay dragons.*

He released a grim laugh. He'd slain the dragon all right, and the dragon was himself.

## ❦ 38 ❦

They just stared at each other. Predator to prey. A long pause filled with malice and understanding.

"Claire," he said softly, not moving from the doorway. "I must always remember your name is Claire."

"You can't mistake me for Zoe. I'm not Zoe."

He smiled at her as she stood in the dim light of the walkway. "I see that," he murmured, and she believed him.

It was then she noticed he wore a tuxedo. He looked handsome, even stately. The latest murder party at the 555 must have just begun when he left for home. "I'm surprised to find you here," she said. "I thought I'd have to wait. After all, it's Lundi Gras, isn't it?"

"Yes."

"I came for a confession."

He looked down at the gun in her hand. "How so?"

"I know about your party over at the 555. You planned the mystery, then committed the murder, or vice versa. I suppose it doesn't really matter what the order was, all that does matter is that there will be a real murder victim for every party the 555 has given. And you are the common link in all of it."

"Will you step into the parlor?"

*Said the spider to the fly.*

She cocked the gun. "I'm okay with this. I've thought a

lot about it. Maybe the cost of jail might just be worth the sweet feeling of pulling this trigger on you, Mr. Laborde."

"Everard. Please. After all, we're going to be intimate."

His veneer was really something. She could see how a woman would fall for it. He was an attractive older man, and when he looked at a woman, she felt like the only woman in the world. His attention was special because it was utterly rapt. Men just didn't hand out that kind of focus anymore in the era of remote control.

"My sister would have made a good secretary to you, Everard. She would have devoted herself totally to you."

"She interviewed very well, Claire. You may take solace in that."

"It was because she was Jewish, wasn't it?" She suddenly felt herself crying, but the emotion seemed outside herself. The world continued to revolve, but the center of her universe was the gun she held in her hand.

"I confess to reading *Mein Kampf.*" He smiled again. "Now, even you have to admit, Claire, Hitler certainly was . . . *sincere,* wasn't he?" He captured her gaze again. "It wasn't because she was a Jew, it was because she was so terribly beautiful, as you are beautiful."

"You killed her, then. Just admit to me that you killed her."

His gaze flickered down to the gun. "At gunpoint, I'd say this isn't much of a confession. Who wouldn't agree with a trembling woman holding a cocked gun?"

"I am not trembling, you asshole . . ." she hissed.

"Ah, my dear, such language. There goes any chance you'd have of being admitted to the Atlanteans."

"I want to hear from your mouth why you did it. It's over for you, Everard. Williams is going to be in front of a judge by Wednesday, getting your arrest papers. But I want to hear it before they take you to jail, before your lawyers shut you up. For my own personal satisfaction, I want to hear why you killed Zoe and—and—" She grimaced. Biting back tears, she uttered, "And I want to hear about her final moments."

"You torture yourself," he answered.

"Why," she whispered through tears. "Why did you have to do it? What kind of monster are you?"

"Will you come in?" He looked behind her into the darkness of the park. "Don't tell me you came alone, Claire? Why, this is a classic. A dumb-blond maneuver if there ever was one, and yet"—he looked at her and carefully monitored the amount of dismay in his voice—"and yet they tell me you're a Jew."

"I am a Jew."

"Come in, Claire. You look cold. My instincts as a host can't abide conversations out on the stoop." He stepped back and held open the door.

She had the gun, but, then, he had the chamber of horrors. Maybe it was an even match.

She mounted the steps and walked through the elaborately carved front door. It was stupid to enter his house, but only because of the temptation in her hand. If it came down to him or her, he would die and she would kill him. That much she knew.

She held the gun toward his chest. "This is not a game, you know. I will use this . . ."

" ' . . . If I have to ' Isn't that how the line goes?"

She shook her head. "No. I've searched my soul on this one and I've come to the conclusion that I think I can kill you. Maybe I'm just another kind of monster, but I think I can do it, and I don't need anyone to do it for me."

"Sherry?" He walked into the room off the foyer that burned the sole light in the house. It was then she noticed his cane, his slight limp. He was Phyllis, only in reverse, and yet what little pity she could have ever given him had now been exterminated.

She realized they were in the living room. A fire crackled in the hearth. The leather volumes that lined the walls glinted with gold-embossed titles. She hated to think such a creature as he would take mental nourishment in such a splendid place.

He poured himself a glass from one of the decanters next to the pair of oxblood leather chairs. It was an archetypal tableau: the refined gentleman pouring himself a sherry by his fire. She only wished the ugliness didn't show in the corners.

"I see you're an admirer of books." His gaze followed hers as she continued to look at the bookcases. "These books were my father's. I had them moved here. These tomes are just bursting with photos of mutilated, surgically altered, and wounded body parts. He also had a great acquisition of nineteenth-century sadistic pornography. Shall I read you some aloud?"

She wanted to vomit. Holding the gun steady, she said, "I came here for a confession. The authorities need a confession and I'm going to give it to them."

"And who might these authorities be? That tall, strapping Agent Jameson?" He studied her. "Ah, that one. He's quite a man, isn't he? But I don't suppose you've noticed in all your fury to lynch me."

"This isn't a lynching. This is an attempt to seek the truth."

"I thought that's what courts were for." He sipped his sherry. "But of course, my dear, I forget you're a lawyer."

"Why don't you begin. Just tell me and then I'll call in Jameson. He'll arrest you, and that can be your cue to phone your attorney and let the evasion begin. Right now, all I need is the truth, then maybe I can put down the gun and let other people take care of scum like you."

"Would you like to see my bedroom?"

Her heart stopped cold in her chest. "Your bedroom?"

"That's where she died, you know. I didn't put her in that ditch alive."

"How did she get here from the interview?" Her voice was hardly a whisper.

"I stopped her in the foyer of the 555. No one was about,

so I asked her if she'd like to go for a drink. And we had one. Right here in my library. It wasn't until I invited her to my bedroom that she even began to suspect things weren't what they seemed."

"They said you had an alibi for the time she was killed."

"I do. My dear colleagues vouched for me."

"They know about you?"

"Hockney and Fred? Good heavens, no. That would be a bit over the top, don't you think?"

She didn't know what to think. This entire meeting seemed right out of her nightmares. "I'll see the bedroom," she said uneasily.

"Shall I spin a tale with you pointing a gun to my head the entire time? What if I take it?"

"Then I kill you." She stiffened. "All I'll need to say is that you were trying to kill me. Self-defense works real well in serial murder cases."

"Spoken like an intelligent woman. Come"—he put down the sherry—"see where your sister spent her last minutes."

She followed him out a side door of the library. They were in some kind of suite. A French parlor set that was right out of the fifties filled the room.

"This was my mother's," he said, noticing her attention. "She had it upholstered in the blue satin. A terrible chore to remove bloodstains. My father hit her right on that settee, and I remember how her nose bled. Your sister's nose bled too."

Claire was trembling now. Her first hesitation overwhelmed her. She was too close. It was too painful to know Zoe this way. Maybe not knowing was best.

"You look ill, Claire."

She stared at him, not seeing the man anymore, but only a murderer. "How could you have done it? Maybe I shouldn't have come here after all. All your explanations still won't make me understand."

"It's perfectly clear. Pardon the vulgarities, but I get my

rocks off killing young women. Particularly those of whom my father would not have approved. Is that too hard to understand?"

"And the lipstick?" she burst out, wondering if she could take much more.

"Ah, yes, the lipstick. Come, let me show you."

He walked through the suite into a bedroom. A massive full tester bed common to the old South sat against one wall. She'd seen beds like that in museums, but never in a private home.

She entered a pink-tiled bathroom. It must have been fantastic in its day. It was one of those rare bathrooms you could fall down in and never hit your head on anything but the floor.

He rummaged through a drawer of the vanity. Finally he found the thing he sought. He handed her an old tube of lipstick.

"It was my mother's. A cheap drugstore brand from the forties. Hazel Bishop No. 46. Look at the color, Claire. You asked what RIO meant. It's something festive, don't you see? They have Carnival down there too."

She held the tube of lipstick tightly in her hand. Her rational mind seemed drugged by rage. "You're just a cliché, then, is that it? You have some kind of Oedipal thing for your mother and so you go out and kill women."

"No. I felt for your sister very strongly. Her pathetic social aspirations moved me. It's just that I will not feel that way about a dirty Jew. I used the lipstick to make her look cheap. I like them to look cheap. It's my thrill."

If there was a moment she could kill, the moment had come. He wasn't crazy, at least by legal standards. His thoughts went from A to B to C quite cleanly. The only problem was that A was a young minority girl, B was a tube of lipstick, and C was the fact that this guy had developed a sexual appetite for death. Her emotions wound into a tight ball of horror, and suddenly she longed to get out of there. The place was making her claustrophobic. She wanted to go back into the world with her mind still innocent of the intimate details of Zoe's last minutes.

"I overestimate my ability to stomach the truth," she said, glaring at him. "I'm going to summon the police now."

"Fine. Fine. I relish not having that gun pointed to my head." He smiled.

She stood her ground. "In this case, gentlemen first." She motioned to the door.

He nodded. She stepped back and let him pass. In the back of her mind, she supposed, she rationalized that even if he tried to attack her, she had the gun. Bullets moved faster than people. She was even thinking about the gun when he lunged for her and clamped his hand on her neck. She would have screamed, she would have fired the gun, but the most astonishing thing happened.

He wasn't even choking her, yet, to her amazement, everything went black.

"He's not at the 555 and he's not answering his doorbell." Williams slammed down the receiver. They were in the middle of police headquarters on South Broad. It was way past midnight and the place was so packed with people being booked, it looked like Macy's on a half-price day.

"I'm going in there," Jameson said, kicking out the chair from underneath him. "Get a warrant if you can, but I'm going regardless."

"That'll look bad on your record."

"Fuck the record. Where the hell is she?" Liam ran a hand through his hair. He looked like a madman.

Williams shook his head. "What a night. I never thought I'd live to see the day we'd raid a party at the 555 Association. At least we now know what's been going on. If that Harry Weil hadn't called the police, we might never have pieced it together."

"But they were going to do a Jew. He'd planned for a Jew and she's missing." Liam grabbed his jacket.

"Whoa. What are you doing? Are you really going to break into the man's house? What if he's not there? He'll get you for breaking and entering if you don't have a warrant." Williams stared at him. "She's really got you, hasn't she, man? Well, hey, listen, she's been under some stress. She'll probably turn up at any moment and say she was driving around. It happens all the time."

"No." Liam rubbed his jaw, trying to ease the bunched muscles. "Not here. She's got an agenda and her thing was the truth. She's in there. Jesus. I'm going."

"You've got to wait for that warrant."

"You can fuck the warrant. I'm going there even if just to make the motherfucker crawl out of bed and answer the door I just crashed." Jameson slammed out of the office.

Williams got right on the phone. "Where the fuck is that warrant, man?"


The lipstick brush was whisper soft. Dabbing, stroking. Outlining in Carnival vermilion orange. RIO. It was her first wakeful thought when she opened her eyes.

"Now, let me tell you, Claire, as I told your sister. I've soundproofed the bedroom suite. I find the servants sleep better at night not hearing anything from here." He looked down at her and surveyed his artwork. A little more lipstick, he must have thought, for the lip brush went back to the tube.

She tried to crawl away, but he'd hobbled her. There was actually a chain around her leg and it was attached to the bedpost. When it wasn't in use, she supposed all the expensive bed dressing hid it.

"You know, I've done two women this way. That's two mattresses I've had to put out for the trash men, and can you believe it—they look at it, marvel at the stains, then they just put it in their trash truck and they drive away without a word.

"What did you do to me?" Her thoughts fuzzy, she assessed herself. Her clothes were still on, but she couldn't shake the notion he'd probably groped the hell out of her.

He ran a finger down the side of her neck. "My father was a doctor. He thought it rather manly to be able to take his son to an autopsy and force him not to look away. The carotid arteries are quite sensitive. They feed all the blood to your brain, and if you block one of them with a tight thumb hold, you can overtake a person in a fraction of a second." He smiled down at her, the same elegant smile. His calmness was the stuff of legends. "The root of the word 'carotid' is *karos*—it means stupor."

She pushed him away. She touched her lips and tried to wipe off the lipstick. Suddenly she was punched. A knuckle caught her temple. She was down again.

"You've messed yourself." He gazed down at her face once more, clearly angered by the ruined state of her lips. "I'm going to have to do it all over again."

"No," she groaned, desperately clawing for the gun. A small whimper left her mouth when she noticed the .357 Magnum was sitting on his bureau across the room.

He glanced at the gun too. "And here you were, all set to kill me. Why, I've just taken the charm out of the day."

Her blood pumped wildly from rage and terror. "I *will* kill you."

"Oh, that's what all the girls say. Remember, my dear, you are the weaker sex. My mother certainly proved it."

He wiped her mouth with a tissue. She stared blankly into the canopy of the bed. Again she felt the dabbing and stroking of the lip brush.

"I see you're admiring my treasure," he said pleasantly. "This bed is a Prudent Mallard dating from 1854."

"Your treasure, and yet you kill in it." She wondered if she should be crying at this point, maybe even begging for her life. It crossed her mind that Zoe probably had done such things, and the humanity of it sliced into her heart.

"You don't own a bed like this in which to just close your eyes and sleep. No, this piece is a work of art, a precious antiquity of times past, of an era of beauty that will never return. Think about it. This bed is going on its second century. People were born in this bed, and they died in it." He touched her face, one hand pinning down her own. "This bed is not the triumph it is because of its stature or because of the elegance of the wood, it's a triumph for what has been created and destroyed within its posts." He kissed her gently on the lips. She was frozen. She couldn't move. He pulled away and his mouth was smeared with orange. "Oh, what price beauty."

"Please—"

He ignored her. He rose from the edge of the bed and stared at himself in the bureau mirror. His mouth fascinated him. The color was erotic to him. She shuddered.

He turned back to her, the old amused glint in his eye. "The things I've done in this bed."

She stared at him, her gaze imploring. "But the game is up, Everard. Even if you kill me, it's over for you. Jameson will get you. I figured out the murder mystery thing, and he will too eventually. So there's no point in killing me now. It won't change the outcome. I'll just become another stepping-stone to a lethal injection."

"Are you appealing to my mind, Claire, or to my emotions?"

"Can you really kill someone like this?" She cursed herself at the amazement in her voice. "Can you really murder a woman you call by her first name? I thought creatures like you needed the anonymity. The faceless victim. But I have a face. Look at it, Everard. Look at it."

" 'Hath not a Jew eyes?' " he said, touching her swollen temple. "Is that what you're trying to say?" He laughed. "But hath not an Anglo-Saxon a penis? Dear God, we could go on all night."

"Don't do this," she said, moving away from him on the mattress, dragging the chain around her ankle with her.

"But it's because you do have a face, and you do have a name. Claire. It's beautiful. It has meaning to me that will linger as Zoe's name has lingered."

"They will catch you, Everard. Don't add another count against you by killing me."

He kneeled on the mattress and cupped his hands over her face. He was going to kiss her, and a new wave of horror wracked her body. She hit at him, clawed at him, but he easily twisted her arms behind her. Panting, she stared up into the upholstered canopy and felt herself succumbing to hysteria. He was bigger than her, stronger than her, and she was going to lose the physical battle.

But then she recalled what she had told Jameson. She still had her mind. If she could just remove the terror, if she could just put aside the fear for a moment and think, she might be able to survive.

His fingers crept to her blouse. His face was engorged with lust. The shine of a knife suddenly appeared in one hand.

He was going to cut her. He was going to do obscene things to her breasts, breasts that were hers with which to pleasure her lovers and nurse her babies.

She fought to get away. In the struggle, she made it to the other end of the bed. He grabbed the chain on her ankle and dragged her back to the middle. Where he was. There. Waiting.

If only she could think.

If only she could take away the terror and think.

"I've got a wire, Laborde. They're going to hear you kill me. They'll probably be here before you can." Her body trembled so hard, she could hardly still herself enough to focus on him.

His expression changed. It went from utter confidence to nagging doubt. "But where is it? I looked."

"It's in my panties. They told me it was the place you'd

get to last. They were right too." She shivered. The anticipation was a killer.

He looked down toward her hips. She had only this one chance. She had to make it good.

She lifted the chained ankle. Making an arc, she roped the chain up and over his head that had bent toward her crotch. She then pulled her knee to her chest, taking the ankle chain with her. Laborde's neck was now caught between the links.

The hand with the knife stabbed out at her, but she took it in the knee, in the shin, in the arm. She still didn't let go of the chain. With all her might she pulled it tighter and tighter until she knew it was working. Slowly, he began to thrust the knife in and out of the mattress. He groped for air and pulled up only tufts of polyester batting.

"I may be the weaker sex . . ." she gasped as he tried one last time to jerk away the chain. The pain on her ankle was intense. She could feel her soft tissue rip with the strain, but even the knife stabs hadn't held her back. She was going to win this. She kept pulling back on the chain; she didn't dare let up, not even when his face went from red to neon scarlet. Not even when he slumped over the bed, his tongue protruding stiffly from his mouth.

". . . but the difference between you and me has nothing to do with gonads," she panted, looking down at his lifeless body. "You see, Everard, I don't want to kill you. I don't *want* to kill you, and that's the difference."

In throes of agony, she crawled back against the headboard. Her leg felt like Jell-O. Her ankle was broken. J. Everard Laborde lay quiet at the foot of the bed. Silent and unmoving, he was now as inextricably bound to his victim as he had thought his victims were to him.

For minutes she just stared at the man who had killed Zoe. Her dragon slain lay in a tuxedoed mound, his ebony cane braced up against one post of the bed. It was then, when she saw the cane, she started to cry. And that was how Jameson found her.

# Epilogue

Her swordplay moved the world.
Those who beheld her, numerous as the hills,
    lost themselves in wonder.
Heaven and Earth swayed in resonance . . .
Swift as the Archer shooting the nine suns,
She was exquisite, like a sky-god
    behind a team of dragons, soaring.

—Tu Fu (712–770)
From "On Seeing a Pupil of Lady Kung-sun
Dance with the Sword"

"Velmun's rap sheet could cover the Washington Monument. He's the only true link we had to ZOE. We know Phyllis Zuckermann called him. We know he came down here on a job." Gunnarson looked at Jameson. "After that, now that he's dead, we come to a brick wall."

"I didn't want to kill him, sir." Liam looked straight ahead.

Gunnarson studied him. "Of course, no charges will be brought against Claire Green. We've gone through the evidence and her account of that last night. It's clearly self-defense." He released a tired sigh. "Look, I'm going to do you a favor, Jameson. I'm going to keep you here in New Orleans as head of the Special Task Force. J. Everard Laborde committed at least ten murders according to the evidence. We've got only eight bodies so far."

The corner of Liam's mouth tipped in a sarcastic smile. "Thanks for the special treatment, sir. I can't wait." He sat in a chair in Williams's office, which had promptly been commandeered upon Gunnarson's arrival.

"Now, what about ZOE?"

Liam took a deep breath. "We haven't got anything. It's way underground. I confess that I don't know if we'll ever get a grasp on it."

"After Phyllis Zuckermann left the country, the group seemed to close in on itself. We don't know where it is now." Gunnarson paused. He stared at Liam.

Liam shifted in his chair.

"Agent Jameson, if you come upon any evidence that can lead us back up that path, I know you'll bring it to Wynn's attention immediately."

"Is she still a suspect?"

Gunnarson frowned. "I heard a tale out of school that Claire Green is carrying your child, Agent Jameson."

"We've been married a month. What do you want from me?"

"I want you to name it Vilhelmer Gunnarson if it's a boy."

"Vilhelmer?"

"That was my father's name."

"Yes, sir."

"We're going to have to close the files on ZOE, Jameson." He gave him a warning look. "Let's hope nothing occurs to make me open them again."

"Yes, sir." Jameson stood. He took a bulky manila envelope off the desk and shook the chief's hand. He then walked out into the hall.

Claire greeted him with a smile. She was already wearing a maternity dress. He'd never seen her so beautiful.

"Dare I ask? Is it finally over with?" she said in a half-whisper.

"It's all tied up with a neat little bow, as you like to say, but I'm stuck down here, heading up the task force."

"I just called Fassbinder. This is going to be a long-distance marriage, at least for a while. They want me back."

He put his hand on her belly and stared deep into her eyes. "This is going to be a long marriage."

She kissed him. "You know, before you found me, I just lay in his bed, thinking about what I said to you."

"What was that?"

"How you needed to be a hero and I needed to believe in them."

"And?"

"And all I could think about was how gentle your touch was and how much I wanted to feel it again."

He kissed her, then handed her the manila envelope. "I forgot to give you this. It was in the trophy room. Since we're closing that part of the case and there will be no trial, I convinced them to let me have it."

She opened the metal clasp on the envelope. Her eyes were dark with sorrow. "Oh, my God. Her shoes."

"They found them in a bookcase in the library. They matched the description of her shoes the day she disappeared."

Claire looked at them, marveling how pristine they appeared. "Red Ferragamo flats, hopelessly preppy. They were kind of like her trademark. Dad used to call her Dorothy whenever she wore them."

"They're yours now."

"I think I'll give them to Mom and Dad. They can put them in her room and know she's finally gone. I *never* wear red flats." She smiled sadly.

"They're closing the case on ZOE too." He gave her a sharp look. "But only temporarily. You know, I saw the postcard you received the other day. The one from Paris. I meant to ask you, who is Patty Zimmerman?"

She glanced up at him. Her eyes got that faraway look he understood only too well. "Why, she's just an old friend, Liam." The clouds in her expression turned dark. "You can just call her my personal Frankenstein."

He bent down and kissed her. Staring at her as if he could never look away for fear she'd be gone, he whispered, "I can't tell you about right and wrong anymore. You've turned everything I ever knew upside down." His hand found her belly. "I know only that I love you." Slowly, gently, tenderly, he brushed his mouth along her temple, the one Laborde had left bruises on. "Just promise me this, will you?"

"What?"

"Just promise me that you'll let me slay the dragon next time. Will you, girl?"

She smiled and wrapped her arms around him. "I love you, hero." She looked at him and touched her lips to his, the ones Laborde had painted. "You've finally put Zoe to rest."